P9-EKY-851

GUESTS ON EARTH

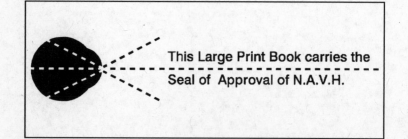

This Large Print Book carries the
Seal of Approval of N.A.V.H.

GUESTS ON EARTH

LEE SMITH

WHEELER PUBLISHING
A part of Gale, Cengage Learning

GALE
CENGAGE Learning·

Detroit • New York • San Francisco • New Haven, Conn • Waterville, Maine • London

GALE
CENGAGE Learning

Photo on pg 9 courtesy of D. H. Ramsey Library Special Collections, University of North Carolina, Asheville, 28804.
Wheeler Publishing, a part of Gale, Cengage Learning.

Wheeler Publishing Large Print Hardcover.
The text of this Large Print edition is unabridged.
Other aspects of the book may vary from the original edition.
Set in 16 pt. Plantin.

LIBRARY OF CONGRESS CATALOGING-IN-PUBLICATION DATA

Smith, Lee, 1944–
  Guests on Earth / by Lee Smith. — Large print edition.
    pages ; cm (Wheeler publishing large print hardcover)
    ISBN 978-1-4104-6603-7 (hardcover) — ISBN 1-4104-6603-5 (hardcover)
  1. Orphans—Fiction. 2. Teenage girls—Fiction. 3. Pianists—Fiction.
  4. Psychiatric hospitals—Fiction. 5. Psychological fiction. 6. Large type books.
  I. Title.
PS3569.M5376G84 2014
813'.54—dc23   2013041209

Published in 2014 by arrangement with Algonquin Books, of Chapel Hill, a division of Workman Publishing

Printed in the United States of America
1 2 3 4 5 6 7 18 17 16 15 14

FOR PAGE

The insane are always mere guests on earth, eternal strangers carrying around broken decalogues that they cannot read.

— F. SCOTT FITZGERALD,
in a letter to his daughter, Scottie,
c. December 15, 1940

O body swayed to music, O brightening glance, how can we know the dancer from the dance?

— WILLIAM BUTLER YEATS,
"Among School Children"

HIGHLAND HOSPITAL
(ASHEVILLE, NORTH CAROLINA)

ASHEVILLE, N.C., MARCH 11, 1948 (AP) —
Fire roared through a mental hospital here
early today and snuffed out the lives of nine
women patients. They died as 20 others,
some screaming, some calm, were led to
safety. Flames quickly engulfed the four-
story central building of the Highland
Hospital for nervous diseases. Wailing of
some of the 29 women echoed over the spacious grounds. Firemen, police, nurses, doctors and townspeople rushed to the rescue.
But seven women were trapped on the up-
per floors. Two others removed by firemen
died in a short while.

Chief Fitzgerald said he believed today's

fire started in the kitchen of the hospital's central building. But that had not been officially determined. Dr. B. T. Bennett, hospital medical director, estimated the fire loss at $300,000. Miss Betty Uboenga of Lincoln, Ill., assistant supervisor, described how she and Supervisor Frances Render of Scarboro, W. Va., first went after the helpless patients. "We felt that the others were awake and would help themselves," she said. "As soon as we got the helpless ones out and safely put away elsewhere, we rushed back to help others. By then we knew some had been trapped. Some of them were awake, we know, and were rousing the others. It seemed no time at all until the entire building was like a furnace."

CHAPTER 1

Canst thou not minister to a mind
diseased,
Pluck from the memory a rooted sorrow,
Raze out the written troubles of the brain,
Cleanse the stuff'd bosom of that
perilous stuff
Which weighs upon the heart?
— WILLIAM SHAKESPEARE, *Macbeth*

"An Institution Employing All Rational
Methods in the Treatment of Nervous,
Habit, and Mental Cases: Especially
Emphasizing the Natural Curative
Agents — Rest, Climate, Water, Diet,
Work, and Play"
— From the manual of Highland Hospital,
Asheville, N.C., founded in 1904

For years I have intended to write my own
impressions of Mrs. Zelda Fitzgerald, from
the time I first encountered her when I was

11

but a child myself at Highland Hospital in Asheville, North Carolina, in 1937, and then a decade later during the several months leading up to the mysterious tragedy of 1948. I bring a certain insight and new information to this horrific event that changed all our lives forever, those of us living there upon that mountain at that time. This is not my story, then, in the sense that Mr. Fitzgerald's *The Great Gatsby* was not Nick Carraway's story, either — yet Nick Carraway *is* the narrator, is he not? Is any story not always the narrator's story, in the end?

Therefore I shall now introduce myself, as humbly and yet as fully as necessary, so that you may know who is telling you this tale, and why it has haunted me all my life. We must strike up an acquaintance, you and I, if not a friendship, as perhaps the circumstances of my early life are dark and bizarre enough to put you well off that.

"Enough!" as Mrs. Carroll used to say, rapping on my fingers with that pencil, above the ivory keys.

We begin, then.

My name is Evalina Toussaint, a romantic name, is it not? A courtesan's name — which, under the circumstances, was fitting, though not — never! — for me, myself, a slight ratty sort of child with flyaway hair and enormous pale eyes that made everyone uncomfortable, then as now. I am at present a thin, bookish sort of person whom you would never notice if you passed me in the street, which you will not. Yet I was always my mother's child, through and through. My mother's beloved child, her only child, her helpful "little right hand," as she called me.

My mother, Louise Toussaint, was beautiful, and kind, and I loved her with all my heart. My early childhood was spent in our tiny apartment upstairs over the Bijou on the rue Dauphine, in New Orleans' French Quarter. I remember the shimmering curtains that swelled in the breeze and billowed to pools on the floor, and the enormous mahogany and red velvet divan that floated like a boat above the old Persian rug. I could see myself, that funny little girl perched upon this great ship, in the huge gilt mirror that covered the wall across from it. My first actual memory is of holding myself up in my bed by the fancy grille work at the open window, looking out at the flashing red neon lights across the way: GIRLS GIRLS GIRLS. I fell asleep every evening in their rosy glow, to the shouts and laughter of the streets below, and even in the deepest night, to the rich, round notes of saxophone or trumpet floating out on the air and the clip-clop-clop of a horse down the cobbled stones and, sometimes, a woman's high-pitched laughter. Often I woke to find that Mamma had dropped into bed with me, still fully dressed and exhausted when she came in toward dawn to kiss me goodnight.

On Sundays I was dressed in white organdy and given a dime for the beggar before we walked the little streets through the Quarter and crossed the cobbled square to the grand cathedral. Everyone we passed knew Mamma and tipped their hats or bowed or said hello, greetings that she returned as graciously as a queen. I gave my dime to the legless man on the wide stone steps at the corner of Pirates Alley just before we entered the cavernous chill of St. Louis, where I loved the candles burning redly in their shrines along the sides, the continual chant and murmur of the prayers, the smell of incense burning and the constant movement throughout — the shuffle of feet, the rise and fall as people knelt to pray and rose again, the high, thin sacred songs. I loved the scary Christ-crucified pictures and the sweet, fat baby Jesus pictures and all the sad virgins and the statues of the saints, which often looked

14

like my mother, for she had a ripeness and a paleness and a stillness about her, too, though she was puffier and softer, like the cotton candy sold outside in Jackson Square or one of the angels floating high overhead in the dome.

She *was* an angel, Mamma, filled with love, always laughing in those early days in the apartment on the rue Dauphine. But everyone loved her, not only me. Flowers and billets-doux were always arriving, brought up the tiny back stair by the hunch-back Georges from the Bijou, for no one was to know where we lived. Georges's wife Anna stayed with me at night until I fell asleep, and I went to school with the nuns in the daytime. I was being very carefully raised, so carefully that I was not even allowed to go to the Mardi Gras parade at carnival time, though Mamma rode atop one of the floats.

"It is good she is plain, this little one," I remember Mamma saying of me to her girlfriends from the Bijou, "so she will not fall into bad company or bad ways. Perhaps she will make a teacher. Or a *nun!*" Much laughter. I wore a white blouse and a green plaid skirt and a sort of bowtie to school. I loved this outfit.

After school I did my homework and

played downstairs in the Bijou bar while Mamma slept; often I helped take care of the other, smaller children. It was here that I first learned to play the piano from Mojo, a Negro boy not much older than myself, who would later become famous. I sat on a stool beside him and did exactly what he did, in octaves, and soon I was playing by ear. This amused even Charlie, who was the boss of everything, and Anna and Georges and all those others who were so kind to me.

Gentlemen did not come to our apartment when I was present, though once I found a hundred-dollar bill in the sugar bowl as I was carefully fixing my mamma her customary cup of tea in the late afternoon and, another time, I found a gentleman's diamond stud on the carpet. I threw it out the window, and never told. It was only the two of us, Mamma and myself, and our cats Fleur and Madame, with an occasional visit from the woman out in the parish, whereupon Mamma would run to the drawer where the money was hid before she went out into the hall, closing the door behind her.

I did not then, and do not now, know what that was about. As far as I knew, Mamma had no family and no past, truly like an angel, for angels have no memories either, *n'est-ce pas?* Mamma often added these words onto the end of her sentences — *n'est-ce pas?* A graceful phrase which always made me feel a part of things. "Such a good time, *n'est-ce pas?*" she might say, tousling my hair, after we had been out with the girls from the Bijou, or, "Delicious, *n'est-ce pas?*" when we bit into our sugary beignets at the Café du Monde.

So it went until, as she put it, "Arthur Graves fell in love with us" — and she with him.

Suddenly there were carriage rides and pleasure-boat trips and new dresses for me and diamonds and shoes for Mamma, who was so happy then that she gave off light like the sun. I am not exaggerating. She *glowed* during the courtship of Arthur Graves. I liked him, too. Though he was a rich and powerful man, a cotton broker with a grand house in the Garden District and offices that took up an entire building on the river, he seemed truly kind, bending down from his great height to ask me how the nuns were, and what I had done in school that day. He brought me a pink glass necklace and a tiny leather book named *Poems for Children* that included "Jabberwocky," my favorite.

Mr. Graves was not present, however, on the day the big truck came with the men who packed up all our things while Mamma stood down on the sidewalk looking suddenly small and hugging the girls and Anna and Georges and me, and then we got into the waiting taxi, which took us to our very own house out in Metairie, near the canal. It was a long, hot ride in the taxi; by the end of it, I felt that we had indeed come to a different country. The yellow-painted frame house had a nice little grassy yard enclosed by a flowering hedge and a picket fence. A sidewalk ran down the shaded street past other, similar houses. It was quiet, so quiet, and the spaces between the houses seemed huge to me. The sky seemed huge, too, hugely blue and distant. I felt loose in the world, no longer cradled by the close Quarter. Our beautiful things from the apartment were carried inside the yellow house, where they looked tatty and odd and out of place. Pictures of people we didn't know, with fat faces, hung on the walls.

Mamma and I spent that entire first afternoon trying to find our orange cat,

Madame, who had run out the door of the yellow house as the men carried the divan inside. We scoured the leafy streets, but we never saw Madame again. At dusk, people came out to sit in their little yards, and finally Mr. Arthur Graves arrived in his long black car, bringing Matilda Bloom, who would take care of us and the new baby.

This was the first I had heard of the new baby.

Mamma ran out the little stone walk to greet them at the gate. "Oh Arthur," she said, clinging to him, "this is just *perfect*!" Then she burst into tears, as all the neighbors looked on with interest.

"Come on, honey," Matilda said, putting her heavy arm around my shoulders. "Now you must show Matilda *everything.*"

I came to love Matilda, who loved me, I believe, though she did not love Mamma after a time. After Michael was born, so small and blue. He could not breathe properly, and Mamma wept all the time, and quarreled with Mr. Graves.

Mamma took the baby from doctor to doctor to doctor; she wore a dark blue suit, and a little round hat, and did not look or act anything at all like herself. I considered Michael to be my own little doll, and spent as much time as possible holding him. I was

19

as good as Matilda at swabbing the mucus from his nose and throat. As time passed, he did grow, a bit; he smiled, and sat up, but his breathing was horrible, the breathing of an old man. His eyes were a pale but bright blue, opaque, like robins' eggs, filled with kindness and goodwill. I adored him. But Mamma was weepy, and spent her time playing solitaire or visiting with her girlfriends, who came out bringing cigarettes and gin and scandal sheets, trying to make her smile. Then there was an argument with Mr. Graves, and the girls did not come anymore. Mr. Graves sent Mamma, Anna, and Michael away on a train to Birmingham, Alabama, to see a famous specialist, who could do nothing. I missed them terribly. I was so happy when at last they came back, and once again Michael's breathing filled our tiny house.

Mamma wept or stared into space or played solitaire while Matilda bustled around taking care of us all. "You gots to buck up now," she told Mamma. "You gots to put on your pretty face for him now," which Mamma could not do. Mr. Graves came to visit less often, though Charlie, from the Bijou, began to appear frequently, bringing Mamma the opium that she required by then, and I knew it, and said

20

nothing, and neither did Matilda. "Honey, honey," Matilda said to me, walking me to school where, as always, I did extremely well.

Then one day I came home to find that Michael was gone, just gone, along with his cradle and all his tiny clothes.

Next I remember standing by myself in the vast cemetery to watch a man place his little blue coffin in a concrete tomb above the ground in that veritable city of the dead, beneath a steady drizzle. Mr. Graves and Matilda were holding Mamma up, one on either side of her; she wore the suit she had worn to Birmingham. They half-carried her back to the car. I stopped to pluck a white flower from a wreath on one of the adjoining graves, then kissed it and put it down on the rounded top of Michael's small tomb. I turned back to see with alarm that Mr. Graves's black car was already pulling out, its red back lights visible in the rain. They had forgotten me. I had to run after the car and pound on the door to be admitted.

For me, the gray drizzle of that terrible morning was to continue without letup, darkening and obscuring what was to follow, as if it all took place behind one of those filmy curtains that used to billow in our windows on the rue Dauphine. Mr. Graves did not come to our house. Charlie came and went. Mamma lay upon the divan eating opium. She would scarcely eat food, not even the little corncakes that were Matilda's specialty, nor the beignets that some of the girls brought from the Café du Monde. I gobbled them up instead, their taste bringing back, in an instant, our old sweet life.

One day I came walking home from school and was surprised to see Mr. Graves's car parked outside our gate, black and ominous against the scarlet flowering hedge. Just as I touched the latch, the front door burst open and Charlie came tearing out, stumbling down the steps, mouth agape, wearing no jacket and no tie, white shirttails flapping behind him as he ran straight down the quiet lane toward the streetcar stop, knees pumping high. I had never seen any sign of such activity in Charlie, normally an indolent, slow-moving sort of man. I watched him out of sight.

Coming up the front walk, I glanced in the front window and saw Mr. Graves slap Mamma hard across the face, causing her to fall over and cut her chin on the marble-top table. Blood poured down her silky white blouse. I rushed into the house and leapt upon Mr. Graves from behind like the little monkey that used to ride on the organ-grinder's back in the park at Jackson Square. Mr. Graves swore a terrible oath and flung me to the floor where Matilda, coming in the door with her net bag of groceries, sank to comfort me. "Now, now, now baby," she crooned.

Then — perhaps most terrifying of all — the great Mr. Graves stood completely still in the middle of that small room looking utterly lost, bereft, his hands hanging open and useless at his sides, for there was nothing he could do here, even with all his wealth and power. He raised his face to the ceiling and began to sob, hoarse, wracking sobs from deep within.

Matilda patted my shoulder and stood up slowly, with difficulty, groaning and brushing off the front of her skirt. "I reckon you better go on home now," she said right to Mr. Graves's face, "for you have sure done made one hell of a mess here, Mr. Graves, and all that crying and carrying on ain't going to do you one bit of good. This is Matilda talking, you listen to me. You was one fine little boy that made a fine man, and now it's time to get back to it. You have done been hoodooed, in my opinion. You have got to get this girl on back to where she come from, so that some peoples can come and take care of this here child."

With a start, I realized that she was referring to me. Michael was dead, and I was still a child. I looked at Mamma who lay bleeding on the divan, in a listless state.

Matilda slapped her thighs. "You go on and call Willie right now on the telephone, and get some mens over here, and as for you and me, we is going on home. Right now."

All these things happened, that very day.

But what about *me*? I wondered and wondered. Didn't Matilda love me, as I had thought? How could she leave me, to go away with mean old Mr. Graves?

Yet I could not ask Mamma, who was beyond such conversation then, and later seemed not to care, as if our episode in Metairie had never happened at all. Even when I mentioned Michael, there was not a flicker of interest in her eyes.

Some things are irrevocable; I know that now. Mamma and I were never to be the same again, though we did move back to the Quarter, this time to a ground-floor apartment with a courtyard just off Bourbon, paid for with the allowance provided by Mr. Graves. In my view now, his generosity (or guilt, or whatever it was) was unfortunate, for Mamma did not have to work, and she never worked again. Perhaps she was not able to, dependent upon the drugs.

I went to the nuns as before, but now there were bad people in and out of our apartment, people we had not known before, and when I came home from school, I had to do everything, even wash Mamma off sometimes, and clean up certain messes. I never told the nuns any of this; at school, my marks were exemplary.

On January 20, 1937, I came home from school to find that Mamma had slit her wrists with the silver penknife that had the fleur-de-lis handle, which she had used to open billets-doux. Blood was everywhere, soaking her legs and the pretty afghan. It had a certain smell, like copper pennies, I will never forget it. I put down my books and took off my coat and climbed up beside her on the great divan and curled into her back the way we used to sleep sometimes, two girls together, and made believe that we were on a ship indeed, sailing down the narrow streets of the Quarter out into the great Mississippi River and far, far away.

What happened next is perhaps the strangest and most implausible chapter of my life.

I had been placed at the Catholic orphanage on the rue Ursulines but had spent only a few days there when a great commotion commenced out in the courtyard where stood the famous statue of the Virgin Mary with her welcoming arms outstretched. Upon my arrival, I had found her comforting. For I had always liked the nuns, as I have told you, and I felt that I might grow to like the shy little red-haired girl from Mandeville with whom I shared my room. But no. Into the quiet courtyard came Mr. Graves like a conquering army. Apparently he had undergone some sort of religious conversion accompanied by grand remorse and a change of heart.

He had come for *me;* he would take me now. He would give me every advantage: an education, a home, a family. "What family?" asked the nuns. Why, his, of course. *His?* I had never met any of his family, not one. In fact, he had never mentioned them. I remembered the pink mansion with the high wall around it. The house took up an entire block of the Garden District. It even had a name: "Bellefleur." Mamma and I had ridden past it once in a carriage, just to look. I did not want to go there. I wanted to stay right here with the nuns, yet I could not seem to speak. Mr. Graves was so huge, bigger than the statue of the Virgin Mary, he filled up the whole courtyard. The nuns began twittering about rules and state regulations. Mr. Graves smiled; he was charming. Had he really hit my mother across the face? A charitable donation was made.

Thus I found myself inside that mansion within an hour's time, meeting Mrs. Graves, a tall, thin woman drawn tight as the string of a bow, and a row of children, three round-eyed boys and a girl who looked like her mother — two older boys were already away at college. This was to be my "new family." They glared at me, and dispersed.

The house itself was ancient, its vast public rooms on the scale of a government building, filled with sculpture and tapestries and silver. Marble columns stood everywhere. I was shown to a fancy little blue bedroom on the third floor, with a puffy bed filled with embroidered pillows and a curvy painted desk in the corner — all my life, I had wanted my own desk. I had dreamed of it. A young Negro maid came into the room to "help me put away my things," which somebody had tied up in an old sheet, as I had no suitcase.

Immediately I lay down upon the pretty bed and fell into a profound sleep that lasted until dinnertime, when the Graveses' daughter, Alicia, was sent to bring me down. She knocked on the door; I opened it.

"It's time for supper," she said in a high, thin voice.

"Thank you," I said.

"You are welcome," she said.

We were like the doll girls I had seen in the windows of the antique stores in the rue Royal.

"How old are you?" I asked as we walked down the forever stairs of the three-story spiral staircase. "And where do you go to school?" for I had been visited suddenly by *manners,* perching like a bird on my shoulder. I had read, of course, any number of English children's books.

"You don't need to know," Alicia said, rounding the first great turn at the landing.

"I beg your pardon?" I stopped and looked down at her.

"We don't have to get to know each other," she explained. "My father has had a nervous breakdown, that's all. Everyone says so. He has made some rash decisions and you are one of them. You won't last."

"I see," I said, though I doubt she heard me, as I disappeared down the stairs.

I took my pencil out of my pocket and held it at a right angle to the exquisitely carved white banister posts, so that the lead made an unsightly black mark on each one as I ran down the rest of the way, taking sometimes two or three steps at a time. Mr. and Mrs. Graves stood waiting for me at the bottom, watching me do this. Her mouth was as thin as a razor's edge, while he blinked back his copious tears — would this man *never* stop crying?

"Evalina, Evalina," he said. He picked me up and crushed me to his chest, the first time he had ever done such a thing in all the three years we had known him. He smelled like something baking — cinnamon or cloves. "I hope that you will forgive me, as God has forgiven me," he said.

I lost all respect for God in that very moment. Mrs. Graves rolled her eyes.

Mysteriously, I was unable to eat a single bite at that immense table, though I was served many choices of wonderful food, which I pushed around on my plate with the heavy silverware and my new, perfect manners. I answered the questions asked me, mostly questions about school, and recited "The Spider and the Fly" in its entirety. Mrs. Graves rolled her eyes again at this, while Miss Ella, the maiden aunt, seated to my right, patted my hand kindly. She wore a ring on every fleshy finger, and lived at Bellefleur, too. After dinner we all went into the music room where I played the "Maple Leaf Rag" on the grand piano.

Later, rice pudding was brought to my room, but I could not eat that either. I ate scarcely a bite the entire time I stayed in that house. I am still not quite sure why this was so, though Dr. Carroll and I were to have some interesting discussions about this phenomenon once I reached Highland Hospital. As I was already a child with no fat to spare, my condition soon became serious. I grew light-headed, and very tired.

Matilda, who had been mostly avoiding me since my arrival at Bellefleur, I believe, appeared in my room with a bowl of gumbo, and sat on the side of my bed. "Here, now." She propped my head up on the pillows. "You stop all this silly behavior right now, Evalina, and eat yourself some of this nice soup. I know you, honey. I know you are a smart girl, and you have got to realize, this is the chance of a lifetime here. Your mamma would want you to take it. She would want you to grab that brass ring that she never got ahold of herself. Why, the Graves will send you off to school, they will give you everything. Don't you see? Don't you know nothing, girl? You are cutting off your nose to spite your face."

I knew it, but I couldn't help it. I soon

became weak and confused. Once I awoke to see Mamma sitting in the wing chair by the window of my little blue room, holding my baby brother Michael on her knees. "Oh Mamma," I said in a rush, "I am such a bad girl, I didn't help you. It is all my fault." The minute I said this, I knew it was true, and I believed it absolutely. I should have told somebody, anybody — the nuns, the police, anybody who would have come and taken Mamma out of that apartment and put her into a hospital. I could have saved her life, and did not. Mamma looked up at me and smiled, in the old way, before she and Michael began to fade. "Don't go! Don't go!" I guess I was screaming, for people ran into the room.

"She's got to eat." I remember Mrs. Graves saying at one point. "She can't do this to us." Force-feeding was tried, disastrously, by a physician who came to the house, with a male assistant to help him. After they left, I burned my arm with matches I stole from the pantry.

Before I knew it, they were packing up my few belongings again, this time into a small leather suitcase provided by Miss Ella, who was to accompany me on the train to Memphis, where I would be met by a trained nurse who would take me on to Highland

Hospital, in Asheville, North Carolina. I remembered that the Graves owned a summer home somewhere in North Carolina. Perhaps this was how they had known about Highland; in any case, I am sure that Mrs. Graves wanted to send me as far away from New Orleans as possible.

"Get well," Mr. Graves implored me, "for the souls of your brother and your mother and for the love of God!"

"*He's* the one that ought to be going to that hospital if you ask me," Miss Ella whispered unexpectedly into my ear. The last thing I saw at Bellefleur was Alicia Graves sticking her pink tongue out at me as the car pulled away. We soon arrived at the station where several of the Graves servants helped us onto the train, which reminded me of a giant stallion, stamping and snorting on the track. I was filled with excitement, never having been on a train before. In fact, I had never left New Orleans. I was wrapped in a shawl and settled into a seat by the window of our private compartment. The engine roared, the whistle blew, and we were under way.

"There now," Miss Ella said, lighting a cigarette — something I had never seen her do at Bellefleur.

A porter came through the car to take our

32

tickets and then another man came through with a tray of food.

Suddenly I was ravenous. "Please, ma'am," I said to Miss Ella, for of course I had no money. "Please ma'am, a muffuletta."

"What?" Her eyebrows shot up as she dashed out after the man, coming back with two of the big sandwiches, which we ate with delight right there in our compartment, each bite bringing back to me the tastes and smells and sounds of the Quarter. How I enjoyed that muffuletta! Though it was too much for me, as I was immediately sick afterward in our tiny toilet, to Miss Ella's consternation. But I felt better. I tidied myself and settled down to watch the endless low-lying environs of the city at last give way to scrub pines and dark swamps, which rushed past us on either side, faster and faster, as we headed north.

I could not get away from Bellefleur fast enough.

Later, the curtain of our compartment was pulled shut; we slept. In the morning, we walked down the swaying train to the dining car for breakfast. There were linen tablecloths, and little pots of jam, and a cut glass vase of flowers on our table. I ordered toast, which "sat better" on my stomach.

"And no wonder!" Miss Ella said. "I can't believe I let you eat a muffauletta!"

In Memphis we were met on the platform by a tall, thin, twinkly sort of man, with a gold watch and round gold eyeglasses. He thrust a bouquet of red roses into Miss Ella's arms, and bowed to her.

"Never tell," she whispered into my ear, giggling.

Who would I tell? I wondered, for I knew I would never go back. Immediately I had a fantasy that I would live in Memphis from that day forward with these two as parents, Miss Ella and her boyfriend, yet of course this was not to be.

I was hugged and given over to Mrs. Hodges, a large Scottish nurse wearing a plaid cape. I expected I would like her, too. She looked just like a nurse in any number of those same English children's books that I had enjoyed immensely.

"Come right along, then," she said, grabbing my bag. "We've just enough time to make it!"

We flew down the platform through the grand, echoing station and then down another platform to board another steaming, clamorous train. I slept a great deal; it seemed as if I could not sleep enough. Mrs. Hodges kept a close, watchful eye upon me while knitting constantly, some mammoth thing large enough to fit a giant.

"For my husband," she announced at one point. "He's a big one!" We changed trains in the middle of the night; stars were out, and the brisk wind was chilly.

It was cold in Asheville, too, that early morning of our arrival, yet the air was sparkling, sharp and clean, shot through with sunshine and smelling of — what? Pine! Asheville was a city at the bottom of a bowl, a blue bowl of mountains. They encircled us on every side. Some of them were truly enormous, their tops obscured by clouds. We got into a waiting car, which bore us through the bustling downtown past large buildings and spacious parks, up a wide fancy street named Montford Avenue. We passed many big square houses with well-kept yards, inspiring confidence, though built in a style unfamiliar to me. A uniformed maid was out sweeping a spotless sidewalk.

"Who lives here?" I asked.

Mrs. Hodges said succinctly, "Rich people."

"Do they live here all the time or just in the summer?" I asked, thinking of Mrs. Graves. I was sure she was the one who had sent me on this long journey.

"Depends." She tied off a knot of yarn. "There's many comes up in the summer for the climate, don't you know, and others comes for the society, and still yet others that comes for their health. Oh, we are famous for it," she amplified in answer to my glance. "They comes here for the tuberculosis, for the vapors, the rheumatism, the aches and pains, and the alcohol, don't you know. Why there's more clinics than you can shake a stick at, it's a reg-u-lar industry."

Suddenly it hit me like a slap in the face: I was going to a mental institution. Highland Hospital was a *mental* institution. I would be a *mental* patient. Would they lock me up? Would they put me in a cage? I remembered the scary, wild-haired people high up behind the bars in the old Public Health Hospital on State Street in New Orleans. I was terrified.

As if she could read my mind, Mrs. Hodges patted my hand. "Now, now," she said. "You'll be fine here. We're a bit different."

"What do you mean, different?" I asked as we went through a handsome stone gate and passed the modest sign that read simply HIGHLAND HOSPITAL.

"Like a family," she said. "You'll see."

36

I rolled the window down and hung my head out to breathe in the piney, crystal-cold air and get a better view of the beautiful grounds, which looked more like a park than anything else, the gentle slope giving way to a wild ravine on the right-hand side, while the grassy hill to the left was topped by a cluster of buildings that to my eye resembled a resort such as I had seen only in pictures. Though winter had scarcely released her grip upon these high mountains, here and there a blooming tree — redbud, dogwood — was already to be seen. Stone walls accentuated various features of the landscape, but there were no fences, no locked gates. Driving slowly along the paved road up the slope, we encountered several groups of vigorous-looking people; most of them waved at me, and I waved back.

"Our Dr. C believes in exercise," Mrs. Hodges said. "He gets them walking, all of them, five miles a day. This is the cornerstone of his philosophy."

"But what if they don't *want* to walk?" I asked. I had never seen anyone walk for pleasure, or even exercise. I had thought walking was for poor people.

"Oh, they change their tune soon enough! Exercise, diet, and keeping busy! That's the ticket!" boomed Mrs. Hodges from inside the car. We were passing a huge and very unusual building on our left that featured turrets and towers and even a crenellated battlement, as in *Jane Eyre.* "That there is Homewood, the residence of Dr. and Mrs. Carroll themselves," she announced.

"It looks like a castle," I said.

"No, no, you'll see — it's also for music, and theatricals, and dances and games, and arts and crafts. You'll have your classes there, too. They keep the children quite busy, you'll see."

"But where *are* the children?" I asked. "I don't see any other children." I was panicking again.

"In the schoolroom, I daresay," Mrs. Hodges said cheerfully. "Dr. C always takes on a few, if he is interested in the case."

"Is he interested in *my* case, then?" I asked.

"Well, he *must* be, wouldn't you think? Or you wouldn't be here, now would you?"

I didn't know. I didn't know what to think, having no say in anything. Both these ideas — that anyone might be interested in me, and that I was a "case" — astonished me. But now we were approaching the grassy, open top of the mountain with its impressive buildings surrounded by gardens and shrubbery.

"That's Highland Hall." Mrs. Hodges indicated a huge fancy building with many verandas. "Offices on the first floor, patients' rooms upstairs. Next is Central Building, that's where the women patients live, and the assembly hall, and more offices, and then the treatment rooms on the top floor, and, of course, the kitchen and the dining hall downstairs. The dining hall's quite lovely, you'll see. Oak Lodge over there, that's for the men." She pointed out other, smaller structures as we came to a rolling stop before Highland Hall, where a tall, well-dressed man stood under the portico, shading his eyes to watch our arrival.

Instinctively I knew that this must be Dr. Carroll. He walked forward to open my door in a courtly manner. "So. Evalina," Dr. Carroll said gravely. "Welcome to Highland Hospital. You have had a long journey."

"I am not crazy," I said. "I am not a case."

"No," he said. "But you have been through a lot. You are much too thin, and very troubled, and very sad. I believe we can help you. We shall give you a place to grow up a bit, and keep you safe. Soon you will feel better," he promised.

"I doubt it," I said.

"Well, we shall see. Let us try." Dr. Carroll

had a nice smile, though he was a homely, awkward man, with jug ears and a big nose and gold-rimmed glasses. He held out a hand that was surprisingly hard — more like a workingman's hand than a doctor's. He must participate in these physical programs himself, I thought. He held my hand a long time, patting it as if it were a small wild animal. This was oddly calming. "Wait a bit, Margaret," he said to Mrs. Hodges.

"My wife would like to welcome you, too," he said to me. "Come in —" He opened the ornate door and led me through the wide entrance hall with its stained glass windows to the panelled drawing room on the right, where a beautiful blonde woman sat in a cozy chair by the fireplace, reading a book.

She looked up and smiled. "Evalina." She rose gracefully, closing the book. She was very tall. "It is such a pleasure to have you here. I, too, am a pianist." In fact, a gleaming spinet piano stood in the corner of that room.

"Allow me to introduce my wife, the world-renowned concert pianist Grace Potter Carroll," he said with a smile.

"You exaggerate, my dear." She smiled at him, and winked at me. "But I am a piano teacher as well, and I am hoping that we may work together, you and I, after a bit,

40

when you are settled. Would you like that?"

"No," I said, for I did not deserve this good fortune, which seemed to me like a dream come true. I deserved punishment, disaster, death. "Anyway," I said, "I thought this was a mental institution."

"It is," Mrs. Carroll said. "It is also our home."

At that moment I realized that I had no home at all, no place to go back to in New Orleans or anywhere else in the world. Would I have to live in this fancy mental institution forever? *I am not crazy!* I screamed at Mrs. Carroll, my loud, angry words immediately absorbed into the drawing room's thick rug and soft furniture.

"Why are you here, then?" Dr. Carroll asked with interest, while his wife continued to smile as if my behavior were completely normal.

"Because I killed my mother," I said.

At this, Mrs. Carroll knelt suddenly, unexpectedly, before me, taking my chin firmly in her fingers. She looked into my eyes. "I'm sure that is not true," she said. "Now, can you read music?"

"No," I said.

"Ah," she said, standing back up. "We have a starting point."

41

Mrs. Hodges sat waiting for me on a bench in the entrance hall. "Quite the pet, aren't you?" she said acidly after Dr. Carroll shook my hand and turned to leave. She put away her knitting and stood up.

"Am I?" I felt dazed, and dizzy again.

"Now, now, pay no attention to me," she said. "It's high time you had some care, if I am any judge, so come along, this way. Let's go round back, where your dormitory is."

The sun seemed too strong for me suddenly, the grass too green, the blooming forsythia too bright. Yet I followed obediently, or tried to. People streamed down the hill behind Highland Hall toward a wooded area where I could barely see a rustic building set deep in the forest, and then a long, sunny stretch of bare ground. "Brushwood." Mrs. Hodges jerked her thumb in that gesture I had grown accustomed to. "This is where they do all the gardening, hours of it, every day, all year round, mind you. You'll see. That there's the greenhouse, back in there. Oh, he's nuts about it, Himself is, digging in the earth, mind you."

Now I could tell that there was, indeed, something wrong with many of these people.

Several spoke to themselves as they came up the path, while others hung their heads, looking neither left nor right. Harsh words of argument came from behind a boxwood hedge; we reached the end of it in time to see an athletic-looking man, whom I took to be a staff member, walk away from a woman seated on a boulder, smoking a cigarette and swinging her foot disgustedly against the rock. Oddly — for it was still winter — she wore black tights and ballet slippers.

At that time, Mrs. Fitzgerald was quite mad. She had been a patient at Highland Hospital for almost a year, Mr. Fitzgerald having moved her there in desperation from Sheppard Pratt in Baltimore, following stays at other clinics in Europe. My first view of her is as clear to me today as it was then — etched in my brain as if by acid.

I could not move, transfixed by her ferocious gaze and weakened, I suppose, by hunger. I had a vivid, intense impression of bright flowers and blue sky, sunlight and piney air, before my own vision grew dark as hers and I fell to the ground insensible.

CHAPTER 2

I was placed directly into an upstairs hospital room in the Central Building, where several doctors and many nurses came and went, giving me pills that I later learned were barbiturates, poking me and prodding me, taking samples of blood and such as that. My tiny, rectangular room was like the interior of a shoebox, very white and very clean, with no pictures. Its one long window looked out upon the blue peak of a mountain, sometimes wreathed in clouds and sometimes shining in the sunlight so that I could still see high patches of sparkling snow. Or was it simply stone? But it was all I could do to merely notice this view; otherwise I lay totally still, exhausted, fingering the tiny balls on my pink chenille bedspread, often falling asleep even while the kindly nurses were still talking to me. I slept and ate; they seemed always to be feeding me, especially Cream of Wheat and oatmeal and applesauce, as if I were a baby. People came and went, their voices flying back and forth across my head like birds.

"She is *resting*." I remember Dr. Carroll's calm voice in response to someone's question. "This is her work now, her only work, and she is doing a good job of it, too. Yes, you are," he said directly to me, patting my hand in that way he had. "You are a good girl, Evalina" — though even in my nearly vegetative state, I knew that I was *not*. "Never assume that they cannot hear you, even while in coma . . ." he went on to say to the nurses in training assembled by my bed. "We understand so little about human consciousness. Never, ever, underestimate the human brain . . ."

Somehow, after several weeks, they had me sitting up and reading books, though I refused the first batch Mrs. Hodges brought me, as I had read them all. "Too babyfied, eh?" she said in surprise. "How old are you, then?" she asked, appearing dumbfounded when I answered thirteen, and doubly dumbfounded when I could not tell her what my birthday was, as no one had ever celebrated it. Mrs. Hodges reappeared with more books, including some Nancy Drew mysteries, which I had never heard of. Obviously, the nuns had not approved of them. I devoured book after book — *The Secret of the Old Clock, The Mystery at Lilac Inn, The Secret of Shadow Ranch, The Hidden Staircase* (my favorite!). I loved the way independent Nancy zipped around solving the mysteries in her blue roadster with her chums, boyish George Fayne and plump, easily frightened Bess Marvin. Another friend named Helen disappeared after the first few books, and I liked to imagine that perhaps she had been sent away to Highland Hospital in North Carolina and would soon appear as *my* chum.

"You're looking better now," Mrs. Hodges observed at length, bringing me another stack. Was I? How should I know, since we were all denied mirrors at Highland.

Though I resisted leaving my little white room in the clinic for a good while after Dr. C said I could go, it was finally the possibility of "chums" that coerced me into my dormitory room in the Annex of the Central Building at last. Here I found my poor belongings, such as they were, all unpacked and arranged and waiting for me, as well as six brand new Nancy Drew books along with an engraved note card from Grace Potter Carroll. "Ready for lessons?" she wrote in her elegant hand. This was the kindest thing anyone had ever done for me.

46

I burst into tears and threw myself onto my now-beloved chenille spread, which they had allowed me to bring over from the clinic.

Thus it began: my long tenure at Highland Hospital, my new life. And indeed I would have chums of my own, several of them, over the years I was to remain there, the first being the dark-haired girl whose room was just across the hall in the Annex from mine. Lily Ponder stared but did not speak; she had not spoken since the rest of her family was killed in an automobile accident in Mississippi almost a year earlier.

"Severely de-pressed, and little wonder!" Mrs. Hodges announced as we passed right in front of her.

"But she can *hear*," I whispered to Mrs. Hodges fiercely, remembering what Dr. C had said. "Just because she doesn't speak doesn't mean she can't *hear*."

Though that might be an advantage, I would realize soon enough, since another occupant of our small annex talked constantly, unable to shut up for even an instant. Virginia Day talked when others were present and when we weren't — it made no difference at all. This was a fat, excitable blonde girl who waved her hands and jabbed at the air to make her points.

"There is nothing wrong with me, nothing, nothing, nothing," she said over and over. "*She* sent me here! She hates me, that's all, and she has bewitched him."

"Who?" I had to ask.

"My father, the goddamn son of a bitch!"

I was fearful yet exhilarated to hear this language.

"*Who* has bewitched him? Your mother?"

"Not my mother." Now Virginia was hugging herself, rocking back and forth. "They have killed my mother, he pushed her off the pier. It was not an accident, not at all. I saw it. I saw it all, yet no one will believe me." Her diagnosis was dementia praecox, now called schizophrenia. But who was to say whether Virginia Day was telling the truth or not? Or telling, perhaps, a deeper truth? It was a mystery, beyond the skills of even Nancy Drew. I was to hear many such mystery stories at Highland; I shall spare you all the details. My new chums came and went, sometimes with such rapidity that I was tempted to try to gauge how long a promising new girl might stay before I went to the trouble of befriending her — rather like Alicia's cold attitude toward me back at Bellefleur. Some of these girls got better; some got worse.

But I loved school. I loved our castlelike

building, our big, airy schoolroom, and especially our English teacher, who was named Miss Tippin and wore her long brown curls pulled back in an old-fashioned bun. She loved poetry and could recite hundreds of poems, it seemed, aloud. She would close her eyes and lift up her face when she did it, rocking back on her heels like a person in a trance. Miss Tippin was a remarkable teacher as she faced the formidable task of reaching us all at our differing levels; her individualized assignments, I realize now, were both imaginative and therapeutic.

Dr. Broughton, our heavyset science and math teacher, looked rather like a monk with his bald head as round and shiny as a ball, and then the long fringe of red hair above his collar. While I had always been the smartest girl in all of my classes, here at Highland I was faced with a genius boy of my own age, Robert Liebnitz, so brilliant that he was already reading college texts; rather than classes, he simply engaged in "conversations" with Dr. Broughton and Dr. C and professors at the college in town. I couldn't even try to compete, which turned out to be a relief. The head of physical education, Mr. Axelrod, generally wore shorts and knee socks and a cowboy hat.

He was considered to be a real character. Our young music teacher, Miss Phoebe Dean, was a "flippertigibbet" in the words of Mrs. Hodges, but I liked her bobbed hair and her enthusiasm.

I liked them all, in fact, but it was my piano lessons that I lived for, revering Mrs. Carroll above all others — for her kindness as well as her brilliance, of which I had soon enough ample proof, accompanying Mrs. Hodges to see Mrs. Carroll perform Rachmaninoff, then Chopin's very dramatic "Grand Polonaise," and then a big Brahms "Ballade" in concert at the Asheville City Auditorium downtown. Mrs. Carroll wore a red evening dress and a boa; I saved the program.

My own classes with Mrs. Carroll were held at the grand piano in their private living quarters, filled with antiques, art, and oddities from their world travels — a Viennese crystal punchbowl containing postcards from every foreign country I had ever heard of, and several I had not, each with its exotic stamp; a life-size statue of a male dancer, miraculously balanced on one marble toe; six frightening African masks, lined up across one wall; a Tiffany lamp; a beautiful carousel clock, with moving horses, on the mantel, purchased on their honeymoon in Italy. I intended to have a honeymoon in Italy, just like Mrs. Carroll. In fact, I intended to *be* her.

A red silk fringed scarf lay across the top of the gleaming black Steinway. She always jerked it off with a flourish before we began, and flung it across a chair. Every little thing had to be done correctly, following the Diller-Quaile method. She was very strict. A child prodigy herself, Mrs. Carroll had once studied piano in Vienna with "the great Busoni," who had told her, "Music is freedom." She told me this again and again.

"Now you must sit just so, Evalina," Mrs. Carroll said, demonstrating. "No more of that slouching." She taught me to hold my arms straight between elbow and wrist, parallel to the floor, curving my hand as if I were holding a lemon, manipulating my fingers until they hurt. I was not to touch the pedals, nor to play by ear.

Every lesson began with about fifteen minutes of scales, then arpeggios. Soon we had advanced to simple Bach inventions, which I must learn one hand at a time, right hand first; I was not allowed even to try the left hand until the right was mastered. Imagine my delight when Mrs. Carroll sat next to me on the bench and played the left hand herself while I played the right — a duet! I adored her musky perfume, her dark red lipstick, the longish dresses and high heels she wore regardless of the elements. I loved it all — the diamond-paned windows that threw the light in rainbow prisms around the room, the sternly beautiful lines of the elegant notes marching across the staves, the rustle as we turned the pages.

I liked the theory sessions as well, held in the schoolroom with two town girls and one boy, where Mrs. Carroll walked around and looked at our hands on piano boards while she told us about the lives of the composers. We learned that Mozart was a prodigy; that Chopin had died of TB in his thirties, hunched over and bleeding at his keyboard; and that Bach had had twenty children. That was too many children, I thought. That might be almost as bad as being an orphan. After I learned to play some of his simple waltzes, it became my sole aim to play the "Minute Waltz" in one minute (*molto vivace!*) as demonstrated by Mrs. Carroll. I practiced and practiced, using a metronome, and was proud when I got it down to three. I learned to play Bach's "Little Prelude in C Major" and "Für Elise," by Beethoven, which I loved. Who was Elise? I used to wonder, playing. Was she his girlfriend? His wife?

A huge vase of fresh yellow roses always stood on the round marble top table at the center of the drawing room, the weekly gift of Dr. Carroll, we were all to learn, delivered like clockwork each Tuesday. He had met Grace Potter on a Tuesday and he had given her a dozen yellow roses every Tuesday since, for over thirty years. Robert Liebnitz did the math in his head and announced that this was 187,000 roses, which had cost at least $187,200 dollars. Dr. and Mrs. Carroll still called each other "darling" aloud, even in public, as if they were interchangeable, or a single organism. Robert said that their relationship was symbiotic.

In love with my study of the piano and with my classes, I cherished especially those early morning hours at the old piano in the little practice room on the second floor of Homewood — virtually the only time I was ever allowed to be alone during my entire time at Highland Hospital. Otherwise I was forced into the many activities that were so much a part of the program here: games, hiking, gardening, art. We *all* had to do it. We all had to do everything, thus "combating the damaging tendency of most illness to foster introspection," which was to be avoided at all costs. Dr C was adamant on this point.

■ ■ ■ ■

Thus I found myself face to face with the woman in the black ballet slippers and tights again, in the art studio at Homewood, several months after our first encounter. I sat at a long table, dabbling half-heartedly in watercolors, attempting a still life of the fruit that the art teacher, Miss Malone, had piled up in a wooden bowl before us. Yellow pears, red apples, dusky grapes. Padding softly from person to person with quiet words of encouragement, her thick gray braid hanging down to her hips, Miss Malone was somehow different, in a way I could not define, from the rest of the staff. She was a real artist, I would realize later, and a freethinker whose ideas sometimes differed from Dr. C's. Meanwhile a summer breeze blew through the studio, with its heavy leaded windows propped open, its doors ajar. I wanted only to be out of there, to be in the swimming pool, newly filled and opened, shimmering in the sunshine.

Miss Malone struck her hanging gong, the sign that the class was over. "Next time, we shall paint *en plein air,*" she announced.

These French words caught me unawares, bringing me back to New Orleans, where suddenly I could see the dusty summer streets, hear the clip-clop of the horses and the buggies down by Jackson Square, taste the multicolored ices the old man sold from a cart at the corner. I bowed my head to hide my tears as I washed out my brushes and packed my supplies away.

"There, there," a kind voice said, and I looked up in surprise to see the fearsome Mrs. Fitzgerald now changed entirely. She wore a loose-fitting artistic smock; her brown hair swung to her shoulders. She looked younger and prettier than she had before. "Now let me see." She smoothed out my "painting," which was terrible. "Not bad at all — though it must be boring for you, such a fuddy-duddy old assignment."

It *was* boring, though I hadn't thought of that. Determined to be a *good girl,* I did everything that I was told at Highland, as I had with the nuns, questioning nothing. I loved rules.

"I had a little girl, too, once upon a time," she told me gently, smiling. "A little pie-face girl like you. She was *awfully cute.*"

"Where is she now?" Too late I realized that perhaps I should not have asked this question, but Mrs. Fitzgerald's answer was calm.

"Oh, she's away, far, far away, away from

55

here, at a boarding school named Ethel Walker. She likes it there, she's better off." Her tone was wistful.

Better off than *what*? I wondered.

Others were leaving now. Miss Malone had come up to hover behind us, listening to our conversation, though she did not interrupt — according Mrs. Fitzgerald, as did the others, a kind of special respect. At that time, Mrs. Fitzgerald was spending almost all her time in the art studio, as much as Dr. C would permit.

"I know what little girls like." She was smiling at me. "Paper dolls!"

Inadvertently I clapped my hands, for I had never had any paper dolls, though I had always fancied them. "I would love that," I said sincerely. "But I'm afraid I am too old for them now."

"Well then, we shall make some very sophisticated *older* paper dolls for you," she said, "with very exciting lives. Look here." She hauled a leather portfolio onto the table and began pulling out big sheets of paper, all the colors of the rainbow. "Scissors?" she said to Miss Malone, who produced them without a word.

"Get the glue," she said to me, and I ran to do so, while the studio emptied out around us. She pulled up her chair; I pulled up mine, all thought of the swimming pool vanished.

Now the scissors began to flash in earnest as the silhouettes of girls — three, four, five, six, *ten* girls! emerged, fluttering out onto the table. They had very, very long legs and arms, big feet and hands, and breasts like tennis balls, which appeared to be just stuck onto their bodies, as if glued to their chests. Many of them seemed to be dancing, like ballerinas. Some of them had bobbed hair, some not, but all their little heads were tilted back, looking up. *What are they looking at?* I wondered, glancing up myself at the high, vaulted ceiling and wrought-iron light fixtures of the art room.

"Well, make them some clothes, then!" Mrs. Fitzgerald shot at me, and I did, clumsily at first, tailoring their skirts and jackets as best I could, Miss Malone appearing with bits of lace and cloth and sequins to glue on. Soon the table was filled with these girls and their rudimentary clothing, as the dappled sunlight shifted outside and the sounds of a faraway game floated in the window.

"Now look," she said, folding the biggest sheet of paper just so, then snipping quickly, expertly, before pulling them out suddenly — a string of six girls, then twelve more after that, holding hands, dancing. I was blissfully happy. It was all the chums I had ever wanted.

"But where will they all live?" I blurted out, for this was the question I worried about all the time.

"Draw them some houses, then," she said imperiously, pushing over another of the largest sheets, and I did so, an entire street of houses, something I was very good at, drawing houses with two stories, houses with three stories, houses with pointed windows in the eaves, some with balconies, some with chimneys, some little houses with picket fences surrounding them. I drew a grand house with a crenellated roofline, like Homewood, where we were, and then another, a real castle with a similar roofline and a tower with a flag flying from it. I cut out a piece of blue cloth for the flag, and glued it onto the flagpole. Then I took up one of our paper dolls and gave her a smiling face and blue eyes and a long blue dress and a yellow crown — this took quite a while; it was by far the most detail I had yet lavished upon any of my chums — I was working so hard, concentrating so intently, that I did not at first realize that Mrs. Fitzgerald had ceased her own fierce population of our town and sat quite still, observing me.

"Now she has been chosen princess by everyone in the country," I said, gluing the crown on her head, "and now she is going to claim her kingdom." I placed her up on the top of the tower, next to the flag, and drew a happy, smiling yellow sun in the sky above. "There now!" I said. "Ta-da!" imitating trumpets.

Mrs. Fitzgerald, saying not a word, reached forward in a lightning stroke to grab up my beautiful princess and crumple her into a ball, which she tossed under the table. I sat paralyzed, like a paper doll myself, feeling my own blood and all my volition draining out of my body.

"You have killed her," I whispered.

"Don't be such a silly little pie-face, Patricia," she said abruptly. Who was Patricia? "It is far better to be dead than to be a princess in a tower, for you can never get out once they put you up there, you'll see. You'll see. You must live on the earth and mix with the hoi polloi." At this she began gathering up all our other paper dolls and crumpling them up, throwing them into the air, where they were caught by the breeze and fluttered everywhere.

"Now, now, Mrs. Fitzgerald, let's save

these. Perhaps you and your young friend could create a fine collage," came the reassuring voice of Miss Malone, but I did not stay to see whether this suggestion had any effect or not. I grabbed up my chains of hand-holding chums and ran for dear life out the door, heart pounding, and did not look back.

Yet Mrs. Fitzgerald was perfectly friendly the next time I saw her in the art studio, and we did end up making that collage with the paper dolls Miss Malone had carefully saved, and also, miracle of miracles! a *dollhouse,* beginning with a cardboard shipping box and adding cardboard floors and walls, which we painted and papered, painstakingly. Everyone — patients and staff alike — got into the act on the dollhouse, fashioning little pieces of furniture for us. Mrs. Carroll brought in a fancy gold compact mirror from France; we hung it in the front hall.

Mrs. Fitzgerald often called me "Patricia" during the construction of the dollhouse, but I grew used to this and did not mind, once Mrs. Malone had explained to me that it was the original name of her daughter, now called Scottie, far away. I was happy to be a stand-in for anyone's daughter, though

I remained a bit wary after the incident of the princess in the tower.

But some of the things she said have stayed with me still, the sanest advice imaginable, though it came from a crazy woman. Or was she? Usually she hummed mindlessly, under her breath, as we worked on our dollhouse, but one summer morning she turned to me and said suddenly, rather formally, "It is excellent to have an interest in the arts, and to begin it early. The saddest thing in my life is that I am no good at it, having begun everything too late."

"Of course that isn't true," soothed the ever-present Miss Malone. "Why, Mrs. Fitzgerald is preparing an exhibition of her paintings right now, isn't that so? She is an extraordinary artist." Miss Malone always spoke slowly and with great conviction, after long consideration. She absolutely believed in Mrs. Fitzgerald's "genius," the word she used. I am sure that she did not agree with Dr. C's idea that women patients in general should be urged to give up their "unrealistic ambitions" and be "re-educated toward femininity, good mothering, and the revaluing of marriage and domesticity," as I would read later in his books.

Privately I went along with Mrs. Fitzgerald's own assessment of her talents. To me, her paintings were sort of scary, people's bodies that did not look like bodies mostly, with big blobs of muscles and mean faces. No one was smiling, not even the nursing mothers who seemed scariest of all, their tiny weird babies jammed into their huge breasts with no love, or even affection, evident. I preferred Mrs. Fitzgerald's floral compositions, for she truly loved flowers, and though these flowers did not look real either, at least they were better than those mothers. And I actually liked one painting of the pink and purple hollyhocks that grew along the stone wall by the entrance to Homewood itself. Perhaps Mrs. Fitzgerald had more aptitude for dancing — she was said to be a dancer — or for writing. She was forever scribbling in a black notebook, which she closed up immediately when anyone drew near.

Still, I loved the dollhouse, continuing to play with it long after Mrs. Fitzgerald had turned against it; for once it was done, she did not want to allow the dolls to live there, finally, rather like the princess in the tower. "This house will be the end of them!" she said, darkening in that way she had, leaving our table abruptly to go outside and smoke cigarette after cigarette on the stone bench under the blooming crepe myrtle.

"Why don't you go ahead and take the dollhouse to your own room now?" Miss Malone surprised me by asking, and surprised me further by helping to carry it over there herself that very afternoon, since it was too heavy for me alone. Later I wondered if perhaps she feared its destruction by Mrs. Fitzgerald — but in any case, its possession was a kind of turning point for me. It was the most splendid thing — the *only* splendid thing — I had ever owned.

The dollhouse stayed in my room, and Mrs. Carroll continued to bring me little items for it: tiny lamps, silverware and china, little scraps of carpet, from all their travels. I was totally devoted to her, and to my studies on the piano. Mrs. Fitzgerald's advice had sunk in.

Mrs. Fitzgerald was one of the few adults frequenting the large stone swimming pool that summer, one of Highland's true delights. Here we "children" could splash and swim without so much direction and regimentation as was found in all other areas of hospital life. We had the pool mostly to ourselves. Some of the staff were always on duty as lifeguards, but laps were not required of anyone. I have the fondest memories of this pool, for I had never been in one before, and was delighted by the sensation of *floating,* once our vigorous young Miss Quinn showed me how. Soon she had me swimming, too, kicking and flailing away in the shallow end. The huge trees arched over us; sunlight dappled the water. Here we all seemed less like patients than like regular kids, dunking each other and playing Duck Duck Goose.

On the hottest days even the shyest, quietest patients came, too, such as the frighteningly skinny Gould twin sisters from Baltimore, who appeared in huge black jerseys, so cumbersome when wet that they couldn't even swim. They sat on the stone steps submerged to their chins and spoke only to each other, in a private language.

"Why won't they take off those big sweaters?" I asked Miss Quinn. "Are they embarrassed because they're so skinny?"

"No," she said, "It's because they think they're too fat."

I looked down at my own legs, wavy and white and insubstantial in the water. Everything seemed changed at the pool, by the light and the breeze and the water — even my own legs, even my own body, for I felt different suddenly and had begun to suspect that I might be on the verge of developing breasts.

"Watch now," Miss Quinn said suddenly, quietly, and I looked up to see, of all people, Mrs. Fitzgerald alone at the deep end, wearing a white bathing suit, pulling a cap over her glorious hair, fastening the strap beneath her chin. Her body was long and deeply tanned, like a girl's, and as I watched — we all watched, in perfect silence — she climbed up the ladder to the high board where she stood poised for an instant, outlined against a patch of blue sky.

I gripped Miss Quinn's muscular arm.

"Ssshh," she said. "It's all right," just as Mrs. Fitzgerald went up on tiptoe, lifted her arms, and executed a perfect swan dive high into the air, then disappeared into the water below without a ripple, without a trace. She was down way too long, I thought, my heart in my throat, but then the rubber cap popped up, quite close to us now, and we all burst into spontaneous applause, Mrs. Fitzgerald then favoring us with one of her rare radiant smiles. She swam back to the ladder, climbed up and dove again, several more times, from the lower board. Though we all moved about in the water again, no one joined her at the deep end. It was as if she owned it. Finally she toweled off, removed her cap, shook out her hair, and lay back in the sun on a towel, smoking, at

65

a distance from the rest of us. She was always smoking.

"They do say she was quite a swimmer in her youth," Mrs. Hodges remarked another day that summer, as she sat by the pool fully clothed and knitting. "And I'd believe it, for sure. Then she married and they took to gal-i-van-ting all over Europe, mind you, her and Mister Scott Fitzgerald — France and Italy, la-ti-dah, oh my! Look there, how she loves the sun!"

In fact, Mrs. Fitzgerald was the only grown-up who came to the pool regularly, and the only person who lay in the sun like that, for hours on end. What was she thinking? I wondered. Why did she love it so much?

One beautiful July day Mrs. Fitzgerald brought a notebook to the pool and sat writing furiously at one of the old round cement tables before flinging down her pen and rushing over to the unoccupied deep end where she made dive after dive off the board. I shall not forget the last swan dive that day when she was momentarily poised in nothing but the air — arms open, head up, looking out at the trees and the sky beyond with wide fixed eyes. Then she wrapped her towel around herself and

66

exited the pool area abruptly, her pen and the notebook abandoned upon the table. Before I left, I picked them up and saw that she had been writing a letter to her husband. To my shame, I read what she'd written:

Dearest Goofo,

Summer has come round like a yellow cat sleeping heavily in the sunshine, purring and rubbing against our legs slow and inexorable in his passage, the purr and slink of days. Bright red burst of birdsong in the a.m. and the diamond counterpane of dew upon the grass punctuated by spiderweb cathedrals as insects go about their unfathomable tasks, complaining loudly. Then tennis that ridiculous game oh why does one love it so? To be followed by a wonderful sketching expedition down the hot white lane across the marching fields now filled with goldenrod and lavender asters and deep purple ironweed God's summer palette as we climb into the billowy mountains and arching blue sky radiant with His unfolding promise up and up and up we go into the very air, the world but a dream below spread out like a marvelous feast a buffet for the senses and I am so greedy for it all, the lovely things of this world, for life unlived and summers past on the Riviera. I already have a fine tan I should love to place it upon your shoulder Dear Heart and lick the salt from the crook of your neck and lie sleeping through the long hot afternoon at Cannes with the murmuring sea so blue just there, in the open window.

I know this place must cost a lot of money and it is a strain upon you who have always been the kindest and most generous of souls so I do not wish to complain, yet I am so lonely here DoDo in spite of people everywhere they are not real people and I am not a real person either though you will recognize me right away I dare say by the light in my eye to see you. I am counting the days in French until you come again un deux trois quatre cinq though I know forever after will not come again. The halcyon days of love and youth shone like a row of soldiers impregnable in their golden armor but we have killed them DoDo, we would have killed anything

Here the letter ended abruptly in a long jagged mark. I was frightened, and took it over to Mrs. Hodges who sat in the shade knitting. She merely glanced at it and patted my head and stood up heavily. "I'll see she gets it back. But not to fret too much, dear, it's good for her, all the writing, you know. The walking. The art. The swimming. It's good for her here."

The sun, the water, and the mountain air were working their magic upon me, as well. I had never lived in the out-of-doors before. Nor had I lived in my own body, which continued its development apace, once begun. My legs grew stronger, sturdier — sometimes I held them out from a chair in wonder, just to look at them. I found myself standing with my arms crossed, or holding my bookbag up against my chest, to hide my developing breasts.

Robert Liebnitz, the genius boy from Boston, took to walking with me from place to place around the hospital grounds. "Ooh, he *likes* you," Lily said, which threw me into a fit of embarrassment and discomfort, as well as a certain undeniable pleasure, for Robert was extremely odd. How can I explain it? He was caught back in his brain somehow, which was filled to bursting with strange facts and reams of history that he announced in his loud, halting voice at the most surprising moments. Even the shape of Robert's head denoted his intelligence, with its huge white bulging forehead.

Once when we had pancakes at breakfast, Robert passed the maple syrup along to me and then proclaimed, "The Great Molasses Flood of 1919 was one of the worst disasters of modern times, when a giant vat of molasses in Boston exploded, sending an eight-to-fifteen-foot-high wave of molasses through the streets at thirty-five miles an hour, actually picking up a train and tossing trucks and streetcars everywhere. Twenty-one people were killed and a hundred and fifty were injured. Can you imagine what that would feel like, to drown in molasses? They say the whole city smelled sweet for days." We sat with our forks in the air, looking at him. "My goodness," Miss Tippin said. Another time, when we were served fish at dinner, Robert told us that King Henry I of England had died from overindulging on lampreys, a parasitic fish that was one of his favorite foods. "But that's nothing, in terms of weird deaths," Robert went on, getting warmed up now. "Listen to this one! Aeschylus, the father of Greek tragedy, died when a flying eagle mistook his bald head for a rock and dropped a tortoise down on top of him in an attempt to break its shell. That's so the eagle could eat the turtle meat, see?"

I remember sitting with Robert beneath the great flowering smoke tree by Highland Hall, throwing out numbers at him one after the other, which he added up in his head. He could also do this with numbers on the license plates of passing vehicles on Montford Avenue. He had read everything, it seemed, though he disdained Nancy Drew. "Who *are* those silly people?" he'd ask. But in general he could not restrain himself from telling me the ending of whatever else I happened to be reading, so that finally I simply refused to tell him what book I was in, which drove him wild.

Dr. C's theories did not entirely work with Robert, who was very awkward and resisted all physical activity rigorously. He could not even swim, though he did come out to the pool sometimes, perhaps to see all the girls. Here he slouched moodily, whitely, in one of the Adirondack chairs with some of the staff. He liked to talk about sports with the staff, especially baseball; he loved the statistics, and knew them all. That summer Robert was very excited about Joe DiMaggio's hitting and Carl Hubbell's pitching. He used to badger Mr. Axelrod. "So whaddya think about King Carl, huh? He's got twenty-two games now — how much farther

can he go? He hasn't lost in two years —
you think he'll ever lose? Ty Cobb says
Carl's arm won't last, throwing those screw-
balls. Whaddya think, huh?" Yet once when
they had forced Robert to join in a big kick-
ball game, I saw him crumple to the ground
and writhe there wretchedly instead of
simply kicking out at the red ball when it
came his way.

He began bringing me odd presents at
odd times, things he found on the grounds
— a beautiful pebble from the creek, a silver
baby spoon, an army medal, a piece of shiny
white quartz, an animal skull, and once,
after a rain, a huge, ruffled orange mush-
room, which he plucked impulsively from
the woods near Brushwood and presented
to me with a little bow, as if it were a
bouquet. He started coming on hikes with
our group, wearing high black socks and
baggy green shorts with many pockets in
them, for putting things into, and a horrid
plaid shirt. I adored and despised him. Once
when Mr. Axelrod led us up a particularly
steep trail, Robert reached back to take my
hand, and did not release it once we reached
the rocky promontory, where we stood
catching our breath and looking out upon
space.

■ ■ ■ ■

Perhaps you feel that I am straying from my announced subject, which is Mrs. Fitzgerald. Yet it is impossible, as you see, for me to single her out from among all those others who composed the larger picture of our life as we lived it there upon that mountain at that time. Sometimes I see it as a vast painting rather like a diorama, yet in the style of Brueghel, densely populated with colorful people spread out over the rolling slopes, doing odd things perhaps, yet each one integral to the whole, and safe within the frame. At any rate this was how I experienced my life then: caught up, contained, and comforted by the routine that it had been Dr. C's particular genius to devise.

Of course dire things were always happening — some of these I knew about at the time; others I learned about later. There were several locked wards, as well as individual isolation rooms and a hypothermia chamber in which sedated patients were placed in "mummy bags" so that their body temperature could be lowered with a refrigerant. The frequently used metrazol and insulin shock treatments were administered on the top floor of Highland Hall, though

Dr. Carroll had now discontinued his controversial "horse serum treatment," in which equine blood had been injected directly into a schizophrenic's cerebrospinal fluid. Ambulances went screeching up and down the hill frequently in the middle of the night. People appeared suddenly with bandages, or bruises, while others simply disappeared from our midst with no warning and no discussion afterward — for life at Highland Hospital was lived strictly in the present tense. We were discouraged from asking about anyone else, we were never told what happened to anyone, and we were not encouraged to speak about ourselves, either, so that we knew only the most rudimentary facts about each other. Introspection was discouraged even in our consultations with the doctors, contrary to the in-depth analysis then taking place at other institutions, pioneered by Freud and Jung.

So my initial encounters with Mrs. Fitzgerald occurred within this larger — this very large and ever-changing — context, being significant, yet no more significant really than my interactions with a score of others, and always superseded in importance by my relationship with the Carrolls. It was only later, in retrospect, and in light of what was to come, that these scenes stand out.

And one of the most frightening of all, for me, stands out in silhouette against the vision of a leaping fire.

CHAPTER 3

This incident occurred in September when a good-sized group of us, children and adults alike, about thirty in all, including staff, took a picnic hike up to Point Lookout on Balsam Mountain. These outings were much sought after by us all, dangled like carrots before us, the "prize" for the effort we had exerted, the progress we were supposedly making. I was surprised to find Robert in the group, since he was so notoriously resistant to the program. Yet there he was, too, in striped shorts paired incongruously with a white dress shirt, knobby knees and fragile legs ending in those high black socks and big brown boots. He carried a rustic walking stick with the bark still on it and wore a silly straw hat too small for his head. His forehead gleamed hugely, whitely, in the sun. His blue eyes swam behind his glasses. He looked like a crazy professor out for an afternoon nature hike. Suddenly I realized that this was a picture of exactly who he would probably become. The wide smile broke across his face when he saw me. Lily Ponder was right, I realized: he *did* like me. And I did like him, though I also hated him a little bit, too, for his weakness, his oddness, his frailty.

I liked others on the picnic trip, as well: Lily herself, for she had turned out to be wonderfully outspoken and acerbic, once she began to communicate; fat, flushed Virginia Day, who was calming down; and of course Miss Tippin, funny and odd as usual.

Mrs. Fitzgerald, always an enthusiastic participant in any sort of athletic activity, was a part of this group, too. I had not seen her for a while. Someone said that she had been on a family vacation trip to Virginia Beach, which might be why she appeared somewhat moodier and more distant than usual that afternoon as we all waited for the van. Patients generally did not do well when they went to visit their families, returning to us disheveled and nervous. Perhaps I should be thankful to have no family at all, I thought — though I didn't really believe this, of course. Mrs. Fitzgerald stood apart from the rest of us, smoking and frowning and moving her mouth occasionally, as if she carried on a dialogue with herself.

Finally, the van and several cars arrived, followed by a truck carrying our food and other supplies. It would travel by another road, up the back of the mountain, so that our picnic would be ready when we arrived. Mr. Axelrod, the head physical education teacher, was in charge of this outing, wearing his customary cowboy hat and sunglasses as he read our names off a clipboard and directed us into the cars. "Come on now, put that out! No smoking in the van." He hustled the reluctant Mrs. Fitzgerald along. She got in last, up front with him. Robert went in one of the cars. I sat with Lily in the very back of the van, trying to ignore a new arrival, Melissa Handy, who sat weeping in the seat in front of us.

The wind from the open windows blew our hair about; it felt wonderful. Miss Phoebe Dean, the music teacher, came down the aisle passing out tangerines, a rare treat. Melissa Handy turned around and gave hers to us without explanation, then said, "Do you ever feel that there is another person, a different person, inside your body clawing at the inside of your head? Clawing to get out?"

"No," said Lily.

"Bitch," said Melissa.

We split her tangerine and ate it.

Miss Phoebe made us sing "The Old Gray Mare" and "Red River Valley," her own operatic voice jumping and vaulting over ours. She was also the Christian Youth Director at a large church in downtown Asheville.

"Showoff." Lily had an opinion about everything; I admired this.

Our van parked in a big lot at the foot of the mountain, which rose majestically into the clouds, far bigger than I had imagined when I had lain watching it from the window of my hospital room. A sign said RAIN-BOW TRAIL, which apparently began right there, disappearing into the trees.

"I think I'll just wait right he-ah," said a very Southern lady whose name I didn't know.

"Not on your life!" said Mr. Axelrod. "Up and at 'em, that's a girl!" He practically pushed her out of the van.

The lady turned to look at him, her eyes brimming over with tears. "I was the Maid of Cotton," she said hopelessly.

Robert was poking about in the dirt with his stick.

"Who's that?" Melissa Handy asked, pointing at him.

79

I didn't answer, embarrassed to be his friend.

Mr. Axelrod put us into a line, then marched to the front of it. "We're off!" he sang out, waving his red kerchief in the air.

"Jesus," Lily said.

We watched as Mr. Axelrod's hat and kerchief disappeared into the yawning green forest, followed by all the rest of us, Miss Tippin's bouncing brown ponytail, Robert's stupid hat, the bald pate of Mr. Pugh, the science and math teacher, the frizzy-headed Gould twins.

"I don't want to do this," Melissa said, pulling back.

"Nonsense!" Lily barked. She and I grabbed Melissa's bony hands and off we went, all of us, on the Rainbow Trail. At first the path was broad and nearly level, emerging from the forest to cross a natural meadow filled with beautiful flowers. "Bee balm, goldenrod, daisies, milkweed," intoned Mr. Pugh. All of these flowers were blooming as hard and as fast as they could, I realized, blooming their heads off because winter was on the way. They would die soon, all of them. It was autumn already, though they called it Indian Summer. I wondered why. I wondered if Indians had lived here, real Indians, on this mountain, walking up this trail where we were walking, putting their moccasins where my feet now trod. It made me feel important, even sort of holy, thinking this. The Rainbow Trail rose through giant pines, the mountain falling away on one side to a deep gorge where a loud creek came leaping down from ledge to ledge over enormous rocks.

"Snakeroot, yarrow, St. John's wort," said Mr. Pugh.

"That's a remedy for depression," Robert announced.

"Well pick us some then, honey," Mrs. Fitzgerald said, and everybody laughed.

The piney smell was overwhelming now, brisk and healthy in my nose, making my eyes smart. It reminded me suddenly of getting off the train with Mrs. Hodges ages and ages ago. It was jarring to realize how different I felt now from that pale, thin little girl standing on the platform in the cold January wind, clutching a leather suitcase that wasn't even her own. I could see her as if in an old photograph, like the photographs on the walls of that house in Metairie — someone I didn't know.

A wooden bridge took us over the creek to a platform where we stood to observe the Rainbow Falls, a great sheet of water that plunged into a deep pool creating a spray of mist that turned all colors in the sun. We couldn't talk or hear; the noise of the falls was deafening. We jumped back, too late to avoid the freezing spray that had already covered us, head to toe. *This is me,* I thought suddenly. *I am alive, and I will remember this.* I have, too. That moment, that diamond shaft of sunlight piercing the canopy of trees to shoot through the Rainbow Falls, our entire ragtag company jeweled and beautiful. Miss Phoebe made us sing "On Top of Old Smoky" as we continued up the mountain. "Now courting's a pleasure, and parting is grief, but a false-hearted lover is worse than a thief!" Lily and Melissa and I sang at the top of our lungs, holding hands.

Robert and Mr. Pugh discussed nature versus nurture, endlessly.

At last we reached Point Lookout, our destination — not the top of the mountain, but a rocky bald overlook with a 180-degree view, the land below us a living quilt so pretty that it took our breath away. Sky was everywhere, boundless sky, with here and there a crow or eagle, weaving and dipping or soaring, borne up on the brilliant air. Blue upon blue, the mountains stretched into distance until finally they became a part of the sky. Here and there a steeple rose from the little quilted towns or communities below, or a thin line of smoke that soon disappeared. Fluffy white clouds sailed past, like a flock of sheep.

My chums and I drank dippers full of ice-cold water from a spring over by the tree line, then flung ourselves down, panting, on the smooth rocks still warm from the sun. Their heat filled my body with an indescribable sense of well-being.

"Look!" Lily cried, pointing up at the clouds. "That big one, right there — it's an elephant!"

"I see a dragon," Melissa called out.

I saw it, too, then; it reminded me of a float in the Mardi Gras parade, and I imagined my mother, riding atop and waving.

"Look, there's the Buddha." Robert was the only person who would have thought of this, but sure enough, there was the Buddha up in the sky, with his huge round stomach.

The staff built a fire and lit it, while Henry and Johnson, two black men who worked in the kitchen, unpacked the food. Suddenly I was starving, but we all had to wait while Miss Phoebe, who loved to pray, said a long blessing, and then Mr. Axelrod said he wanted to say a blessing, too, which was: "Good food, good meat, praise God, let's eat!" Everybody laughed and finally we got to open our boxes of cold fried chicken, deviled eggs, and ham biscuits. For dessert, we were instructed upon the making of "some-mores," which required us to toast marshmallows on long sticks prepared and handed out by Mr. Axelrod, then put the marshmallows all hot and gooey into a graham cracker sandwich containing a Hershey bar. These were indescribably delicious — even more so since Dr. Carroll was usually quite strict about our dietary restrictions, with very little sugar allowed.

Miss Phoebe sang "Shenandoah" and then the lady from Memphis did "Hardhearted Hannah (the Vamp of Savannah)," belting it out like a nightclub singer. I liked that one better.

Robert, who had wandered away from the fire, came back with his hat off, all squashed up in his hands. "For you," he said, holding it out to me.

"Whatcha got?" asked Mr. Axelrod, drawing near, but Robert looked only at me.

"Open it," he said, and I did, very slowly, after straightening the brim. A beautiful orange and black butterfly fluttered out into our midst.

"Monarch," announced Mr. Pugh definitively.

"Danaus plexippus," Robert said. "One of the few insects capable of making a transatlantic crossing."

"Good-bye, good-bye," I screamed with my chums, watching my butterfly flicker out across the bald then shoot straight up into the air until it was lost in the sky.

"Atypical behavior," Mr. Pugh muttered.

"Thank you," I said directly to Robert, who ducked his head and stumbled away.

"What next?" Miss Tippin smiled, watching him go.

It grew chilly up there as the afternoon wore on, winding down. We drew close around the fire, lounging on the old blankets they had brought for us. People were dozing off. It was an unusual time, a precious time for us all. Then Johnson began to move about purposefully, putting things back in the truck. Henry stirred up the fire and put a big pot of coffee on a grate directly above it.

"Better wake up!" Mr. Axelrod clapped his hands. "Time to get going! It'll get dark before you know it."

This seemed odd, as the bald was still bathed in sunshine. Henry and Johnson poured hot black coffee into tin cups and handed them all around, to us as well as the adults. The strong, acrid coffee almost

85

burned my tongue, but it was wonderful. I held my cup out for more, as did Mrs. Fitzgerald, now seated beside me in the great circle around the fire.

"Evalina?" Suddenly Robert was standing behind me. He leaned over and thrust his hat, crushed again, into my lap.

"Oh, brother," said Mrs. Fitzgerald.

Everyone looked on while I opened the hat slowly to reveal a wet green lizard, iridescent in the sunshine as it twisted and turned, breathtakingly beautiful. "Oooh!" we all gasped as one. It was the loveliest gift I have ever received, then or now, though Lily, on my left, was afraid of it, scrambling to get away.

But Mrs. Fitzgerald muttered, "Stupid, stupid." She grabbed the hat from my hands and flung it into the fire.

It was gone in an instant as new yellow flames leaped up to engulf the straw. Pandemonium ensued — several people screaming, others running away from the fire into the woods with staff members in pursuit. Robert and I stayed right where we were, eyes fixed upon the fire. So did Mrs. Fitzgerald. When all traces of hat and lizard were gone, I turned to find Mrs. Fitzgerald staring intently, almost hungrily, into the flames.

"I don't understand why everybody is so upset," she said petulantly. "It didn't hurt it. Salamanders *live* in fire, don't you know anything?"

"That is not true," Robert said. "That is only a legend, a myth. This was a real salamander, genus Plethodontidae, and you have killed it."

"It *is* true, you little idiot," she snapped at him, darkening.

"How do you know it, then?" Lily asked.

Mrs. Fitzgerald turned to face us. "I *am* a salamander," she said. "I have lived in the fire for years, yet here I am." She held out her tanned arm, palm up. "Touch me," she whispered. "I am still alive, as real as you are."

We drew back, horrified, yet again I felt that awful closeness, that familiarity I had felt when I saw her for the very first time, sitting on the rock. I started to cry.

"Fools!" Mrs. Fitzgerald spat at us. "Silly little fools!" She started laughing. She flung back her head, laughing.

"Come along now, we'll give you a ride back, easy does it . . ." Suddenly Mr. Axelrod and Mr. Pugh were hustling Mrs. Fitzgerald along, one on either side of her, over to the food truck. Miss Tippin hugged me, wordlessly, stroking my hair. She held me like that while Henry and Johnson and some of the others doused the fire and scattered the ashes about. Mr. Axelrod returned to lead us off down the mountain immediately, single file, urging us to move along as rapidly as possible, to beat the lengthening shadows. Robert stumbled along somewhere ahead of me. The Maid of Cotton was crying. Nobody sang.

I got my first and only glimpse of Mrs. Fitzgerald's famous husband later that November, when Mrs. Hodges took me on a long-promised visit to the Grove Park Inn, where two of her daughters worked, one as a chambermaid and one as a hostess in the lobby. Moira, this one, was a big, buxom girl with a ready smile and a headful of carrot curls. She waved at us from her desk in the middle of the cavernous lobby, which took my breath away, as had the grand entrance out front.

"She'll join us later for a bite, when things slow down," Mrs. Hodges said. "Now what do you think, eh? Quite the spot, isn't it?"

I was too overwhelmed to answer immediately. The Grove Park Inn had been built on a grand scale, as if it were a hotel for giants. The lobby in which we stood was by far the largest room I had ever been inside, as big as an athletic field, all wood and stone, with immense stone fireplaces blazing at either end. The rocking chairs lined up before the fireplaces were filled with people talking and sipping from cups or glasses, while uniformed waiters and waitresses moved about. Groups of comfortable furniture filled the lobby itself, as if there were many little living rooms, each with its own leather sofas and upholstered armchairs and tables and lamps, then a bar area over near the windows that featured tiny round tables, all of them occupied by chatting, gesticulating people. Beautiful people. A man with slicked-back hair, in a tuxedo, played tinkly jazz on a grand piano.

"I'll bet you'd like to get your hands on that now, wouldn't you?" Mrs. Hodges said as we crossed the lobby past the piano.

"Yes, I would," I said sincerely, though I felt that I would never be able to play as well, or be so much at ease, as that smiling man.

We went through the tall, many-paned doors out onto the wide stone terrace that overlooked a pool area and a long golf course sloping down toward the bowl below that was Asheville. "There we are," Mrs. Hodges announced, pointing over to the right, "that there's the hospital," as indeed it was, also overlooking Asheville from its different vantage point, its own mountain. I could see all the familiar buildings as if they were dollhouses, but we were too far away to spot any people. "Fore!" a man's voice called out.

"They serve lunch and dinner out here on the terrace in the summertime," Mrs. Hodges said. "Aah, it's lovely then, the view. The sunset and the moon and the stars, don't you know. Why, everybody has been here, everybody, politicians and movie stars . . ." Back inside, we looked at autographed pictures of Mae West, Charlie Chaplin, Clark Gable, Herbert Hoover, and many others hanging on the corridor walls.

Our lunch in the grand dining room, with its view out over the mountains, was by far the fanciest meal I had ever had, surpassing even my breakfast in the dining car on the train. An elegant older man — I thought he looked like a count! — handed us the heavy menus as Moira slipped into her chair.

"Lo, Mum." She leaned over to kiss Mrs. Hodges on the cheek. "Hi, Evalina, don't you look pretty!"

Did I? I was wearing a pink matched sweater set, shell and cardigan, the unexpected gift of Mrs. C. I fingered my pearl-tone buttons.

"Now, Miss, order anything you'd like," Mrs. Hodges directed grandly. "It's on *her*!" pointing at Moira.

"Sssh! Hush, Mom," Moira said. "Or you'll lose your privileges." She winked at me.

I read the menu from start to finish, as if it were a novel. It contained many items that were entirely foreign to me, such as Welsh Rarebit and Tomato Aspic.

"I'll take a nip of the sherry," Mrs. Hodges said when the aristocratic waiter came back. "Against the cold, you know."

"I'll bet you'd like the hot chocolate," Moira said to me. "It's quite famous."

I nodded, then followed their lead in ordering the club sandwich as well, though I wasn't sure what it was. I was delighted when it arrived in four triangular pieces with a fancy gold fringed toothpick stuck through each one, spearing all manner of meats and cheese within, curvy chips and tiny pickles to the side. "Oh my," I said without meaning to. "And this hot chocolate is delicious, thank you so much," I told Moira.

"She's coming along now, isn't she?" Mrs. Hodges said to her daughter as if I weren't there. They launched into a long conversation about the financial problems and disastrous "love life" of yet another of Mrs. Hodges's daughters while my attention wandered to the other tables, well-dressed and prosperous people such as I had never seen, really, except for our long-ago outings with Mr. Graves. But as I could not bear to think of that time, I began to make up scenarios in my mind for these other diners, their histories and personal lives.

She is an actual princess, that brunette, from Europe, and her husband is so much in love with her, look at him holding her hand across the table. Of course! They are on their honeymoon! While those awful crabby old lady sisters dripping with diamonds have nothing to say to each other, they have worn out all their topics, they are too mean to talk, just staring out hatefully at the rest of us. And that young man eating alone is so handsome, handsome beyond belief, maybe he is a movie star, though obviously he is heartbroken at the present time, perhaps because he has fallen in love with someone unsuitable, and knows he can never, ever have her . . . or maybe she has a wasting disease, or maybe she is crazy, maybe she is over at Highland Hospital right now, taking a rest cure . . . I ate my club sandwich as slowly as possible, savoring every bite, while Mrs. Hodges and her daughter talked on and on. The other diners conversed in hushed tones and the silverware shone and the glasses tinkled all around us and the waiters glided back and forth gracefully through the beautiful room like skaters until suddenly I realized that in fact I was staring straight at Mrs. Fitzgerald, and that man with her — *that very man!* — must be the famous Mr. Fitzgerald, the author, her husband. By then, I had heard all about him.

The Fitzgeralds sat together on a banquette next to a giant fern in a giant planter, both of their backs against the wall, looking out across their table at the vast dining room before them, and did not speak.

I touched Mrs. Hodges's sleeve. When she did not respond, I grabbed it. "Isn't that . . . ?" I started to ask, looking over at them.

"Hush now, Evalina, why yes it is, don't stare. There's a good girl."

But I could not take my eyes off them for they seemed so odd, so unlike the others there in that lively, lovely company. He was much smaller than I had expected, and very pale, though he was undeniably good-looking, with sharp, fine features and glittering green eyes. She wore her stoic, secretive Cherokee face, and toyed with her food. He was drinking a beer directly from the bottle. While I watched, the waiter brought

93

him another, taking that bottle away.

"*Thirty* a day, they say!" Moira leaned closer. "Thirty bottles a day, and that's when he's on the wagon, off the gin! Oh, it's sad, sad. Such a talent, such a loss."

"They look so unhappy," I said inadvertently.

"I should imagine!" Mrs. Hodges snorted. "They've worn it all out, I daresay. What a life they've led! Dancing all night and jumping into fountains and drinking like fish all the while, mind you. Living in hotels and receiving guests in the bath. Frankly I don't know what Himself is thinking, imagining that she should ever get well again, and make a proper wife! Who would want her, after all this?"

"Well, who would want *him*?" Moira asked. "Look at him. He's up all night, can't sleep, he's got the insomnia, you know. Sick as a dog, never eats a thing but a bit of rice or potatoes and gravy, no wonder, imagine the shape his stomach is in! And that room, Lord, Lord. A pigsty!"

"But I heard he has a lady friend . . ." Mrs. Hodges scooted nearer her daughter.

"Oh he does, he does. She's real nice, a young married woman from Memphis that comes up here by herself, rich as Croesus. She's mad for him, you can tell. God knows what she thinks she's doing. It will end in a disaster, of course. But that's not all. Why, he's even had fancy ladies up to his room, right here in the Inn, I am not kidding you, Mum" — in answer to her look of disbelief. "You just ask Ruthie, if you don't believe me. Why, Ruthie's passed them in the stairwell, close as you and me! And there's one in particular that's been up there visiting numerous times. You know that girl down at the Biltmore, the one that gets so dolled up and tells the fortunes, Lottie Stephens her name is, well they say she's a *mulatto . . ."*

The red heads merged — the one dulled by grey, the other a riot of wild curls — as the conversation continued in whispers now, punctuated by Mrs. Hodges's occasional "Why you don't say!" or "Blessed saints in heaven preserve us!"

Meanwhile I could not keep myself from staring at the Fitzgeralds, though I knew it was rude to stare. I also knew instinctively that they would never notice me anyway, just a skinny little girl in whom they could have no possible interest, lost in a sea of people. I was beneath their notice. Mrs. Fitzgerald wore a purplish coat and a gray cloche hat. She looked dull and almost ugly. He wore a tweed jacket and a white shirt and a red bowtie, incongruously jaunty. Neither one of them ever spoke. They sat like dolls in a window staring out upon the world beyond them, a world they no longer owned. She was smoking. Their waiter came with beer after beer.

"Pity, pity, pity!" Mrs. Hodges concluded with a certain relish, pushing back her chair. Our own waiter returned with the bill, which Moira signed in a fancy, definitive hand, and then we left, the three of us, as unlikely a trio as any in that elegant dining room that day — Moira back to her post in the lobby, Mrs. Hodges and I back to Highland Hospital in a taxicab. I craned my neck to view the stone arch at the entrance one more time as the taxi bore us rapidly down Sunset Mountain.

"Please, mam, can we come back at Christmas to see the tree?" I asked, and Mrs. Hodges said that we could, if I promised never to tell any of the other patients — my chums! — or anyone else about our lunchtime visit to the Grove Park Inn, since it was strictly against the rules. (Everything was strictly against the rules, unless Dr. C himself ordained it.) I gave my promise, of course, and I never told a soul — perhaps this is the reason that Mr. and Mrs. Fitzgerald, as I viewed them in the dining room that afternoon, made such an impression upon me; the scene would be permanently etched in my mind.

For there was the oddest thing about Mrs. Fitzgerald, then and always, and this is when I first realized it: she never looked the same, from one day to another. Truly she *was* like a salamander, or a lizard, shedding its skin, or like a chameleon, changing its color constantly. She never, *ever* looked the same. It was the oddest facility, almost as if she were empty, her face as blank as those paper dolls we made, that anyone could draw upon, giving them whatever features and expressions they desired . . . or like a lump of clay on the pottery table in the Art Room, that others could take and form to fit the shape of their dreams.

I have thought a lot about this, for even the photographs taken of her vary radically one from another; they appear to be photographs of different people. And in almost none of them can be seen her extraordinary beauty, that quality of intense and shimmering life that animated her when she was truly "on," especially when she was dancing.

In fact, in the clearest image I have of Mrs. Fitzgerald from this period, she is dancing

— dancing, dancing, dancing ecstatically — in a performance at a masquerade ball held at Highland Hospital in 1938.

Not only had she choreographed the entire performance; she had also designed the costumes, such as they were, drawing feverishly in the black notebook she carried about everywhere that spring, when she was again more animated and talkative than anybody, urging all to help with the paper masks and hats, the net skirts and funny costumes that took over the Art Room during this period. Every patient able enough to participate was enlisted, and there we all sat for weeks, making paper moons to hang from the ceiling on strings, and cows to jump over them, for the theme was "Mother Goose." A big old book of nursery rhymes had appeared in the Art Room for inspiration. I paged through it, fascinated, as I had never heard any of these odd and charming little poems. I don't know who came up with the idea — Miss Malone perhaps, or perhaps Mrs. Fitzgerald herself — but it truly *was* inspired, as everyone except me, grown-ups and children alike, seemed to have some familiarity with Mother Goose, and this theme gave everybody the chance to dress up, to become somebody other than the broken, sick people we really were . . .

or, at the very least, to put on a silly hat!

And we made silly hats by the dozen in the Art Room, colorful cones with puffy balls of cotton at the top and ribbons hanging down all around, or top hats created by making a black tube of construction paper, then setting it down on a hollow circle carefully cut from cardboard. The average person could never understand, I believe, how *boring* it is to be crazy — to be unable to live a regular life, unable to have a regular family or friends or a job, for instance, unable sometimes even to read or think or do anything except smoke, perhaps, on a veranda, staring into space. How wonderful it is, then, to make a cardboard hat, or a giant paper flower! To have, even for a moment, even if it's all make-believe, a happy childhood.

Mrs. Fitzgerald herself chose to be "Mary, Mary, Quite Contrary."

"I shouldn't wonder! She'll be grand at it!" Mrs. Hodges snorted when she heard this news.

Mrs. Fitzgerald chose a half-dozen others, young women and girls, to be the "silver bells and cockleshells and pretty maids all in a row" in "Mary's" garden; each was fitted with a loose, silvery blouse and pink net skirt, worn over a leotard and tights. "Mary" was the soloist — *prima ballerina* — as well as choreographer and director of the grand finale, a "Flower Dance."

And I — I was directly involved in this ambitious project, too, for Mrs. Carroll had pushed me into playing the piano for the entire production: first, the march of all the nursery-rhyme characters into the ballroom, then an appropriate musical interlude between each performance, then the "Waltz of the Flowers," from the Nutcracker.

Our few rehearsals of the "Mary, Mary, Quite Contrary" dance were disastrous, as one or another of the "flowers" always burst into tears or ran offstage in a fury, though really all they had to do was kneel in artful positions upon the stage while Mrs. Fitzgerald recited her own poem and danced, after which they were to rise and "bloom" in turn, finishing up with a simple step in unison before their twirling finale. But my goodness, the fireworks!

"She kicked me, on purpose!" Virginia cried out on the very afternoon of the ball. "That little bitch!" flailing out at Grace Barker, a new girl, who doubled up and fell forward weeping onto the stage.

"Oh, for Pete's sake," Lily muttered.

"Get up now, dear, this won't do," said Mrs. Fitzgerald. "No temperament. You don't have time for it. You have a performance tonight."

Miraculously, Grace obeyed her.

We all marveled at this new, calm Mrs. Fitzgerald with her black notebook — "Cool as a cucumber, she is!" Mrs. Hodges pronounced.

As for myself, I was more excited than I had ever been; *anticipation* was not an emotion I had had much cause to feel. Apprehension, yes, even fear — but not anticipation.

"Hold Still," Mrs. Carroll said, buttoning up the back of my blue silk frock herself, a hand-me-down from her grown daughter. Mrs. Hodges stood by with her needle and pincushion, prepared to alter the fit if need be, but "Perfect!" Mrs. Carroll breathed, smoothing the liquid silk down over my nonexistent hips. "Look now." She led me to the long mirror on the back of the door that opened into her own private dressing room, where I had never been before, and suddenly there I stood, a thin, unrecognizable girl in fashionable new shoes called "French heels" and a long shiny dress as blue as the sky, with flyaway curls down to her shoulders and big blue eyes and rosy red dots on her cheeks that looked like

rouge, though I wore none. Mrs. Carroll grabbed my chin and tilted it up to the light. She smoothed pink lipstick on my lips. It felt good, and tasted delicious, like strawberries. "There now. What do you think?"

"I think I look beautiful," I said sincerely.

They both burst into laughter, though Mrs. Hodges dabbed at her eyes.

"Don't you get nervous out there now," she said as she helped me into my old coat.

"You don't have to worry. Evalina will *not* be nervous," Mrs. Carroll announced grandly, arranging her own evening cape around her shoulders just so. "Why, Evalina doesn't have a nervous bone in her body, isn't that right, honey?" She smiled at me. "She is already a professional, Mrs. Hodges, with a brilliant career ahead of her. I knew it the moment I first heard her play. She's the real thing." I was to repeat this phrase, doggedly and sometimes desperately, over and over in my mind in the years to come.

But in all truth, she was right. I was not nervous at all, despite the fact that we had not had a dress rehearsal. I seated myself at the grand piano onstage and warmed up the crowd by playing "Tiptoe Through the Tulips" and "Mighty Lak' a Rose" by ear while viewing the Great Hall, now hung with glittering suns and moons, while cows,

dogs, cats, fiddles, and real spoons borrowed from the dining hall dangled at the
ends of their strings. These decorations
came from my favorite nonsense rhyme of
all:

> Hey, diddle, diddle, the cat and the fiddle,
> The cow jumped over the moon;
> The little dog laughed to see such sport,
> And the dish ran away with the spoon.

Such silliness astonished me — I had had
no chance at silliness, so I had not much
aptitude for it, either. Still, I was delighted.

The Great Hall was transformed utterly,
as were the partygoers, all in fancy dress,
patients and staff and townspeople alike.
Looking out upon this crowd from my
perfect vantage point at the piano onstage, I
really couldn't make any distinction among
them. They mingled and chatted, a vibrant
sea of color beneath me. I played "Bye Bye
Blackbird" and "Moonlight Bay." Unobtrusively the flowers and maids slipped out onstage and knelt or sat and bowed their heads
in their dormant positions — all nine of
them! even the obstreperous Grace.

I hit five stirring major chords — the
prearranged signal — and the golden curtains parted as the Grand Parade began.

Here they all came, the characters from the nursery rhymes marching in ragged step as I played "The Parade of the Wooden Soldiers." They crossed the stage, came down the steps, and made a full tour of the ballroom, to continuing applause, then tramped back up on stage to form a semicircle behind the still motionless flowers. I finished with a commanding flourish as Mr. Pugh himself stepped forward first — a surprise to all of us, even the other performers! — elegant in a top hat, wearing a suit with an enormous flowing purple silk tie and a yellow waistcoat stuffed with a pillow as he declaimed:

Humpty Dumpty sat on a wall
Humpty Dumpty had a great fall,
And all the King's horses, and all the King's
    men
Could not put Humpty together again.

Everybody clapped, and I played a little interlude as he bowed and went back to his place. Though improvised, it was easy, easy, my fingers filled with a power I didn't know I possessed.

The Gould twins followed, skittering out in bright polka-dot sacklike dresses, each carrying a pail, to recite "Jack and Jill." They blinked in the stage lights and seemed totally surprised by the applause.

Enormously fat Mr. Lewinski stepped forward with a pie to proclaim, in his funny accent, "Little Jack Horner sat in a corner, eating his Christmas pie . . ." He gave a big wink as he held up his plum, and left the stage in a funny skedaddle walk.

Mean, bossy, and universally despised Mrs. Aston Archer came out as Little Bo Peep wearing a long green silk dressing gown and a ruffled cap that, I knew, had been made in Art, from one of Mrs. Fitzgerald's sketches. The idea that this pompous lady could be "little" anything was extremely amusing.

But I was unaccountably upset by one of the nurses, pretty Miss White, who cradled a big glassy-eyed baby doll in her arms as she sang,

Rockabye baby, in the treetop
When the wind blows, the cradle will rock,
When the bough breaks, the cradle will fall,
And down will come baby, cradle and all.

We all gasped when she dropped the baby, catching it just as it hit the floor. Perhaps it was because she wore her own real nursing uniform, but this performance was entirely too realistic for me, calling back certain nightmares from which I still suffered.

Three young men wearing big mouse ears and whiskers and sunglasses — two patients, one staff — began running around the stage in circles while Mr. Axelrod, in his accustomed cowboy hat and kerchief, brandished an enormous knife. He shouted out "Three Blind Mice," before chasing the others off the stage and right out through the crowd, overturning several chairs and creating a hubbub.

The "garden" stirred restively, complaining. I didn't blame them one bit, realizing how hard it must be to hold one position for so long. Virginia, in fact, sat up. But there were a few more performers — a black sheep, a baker — and then, finally, here came Robert, moving forward in somebody's big flannel nightgown to generous applause, for he was a favorite of all, having actually lived at Highland Hospital for three years by then.

Robert went out to center stage and froze, his huge white forehead glistening with sweat. Was he supposed to be Wee Willie Winkie? Or Diddle Diddle Dumpling, my son John? We were never to know. Robert took his glasses off and mopped his face with his sleeve, then put his glasses back on and grinned a big goofy grin at the assembly before shambling offstage, waving good-bye, to laughter and friendly cheers.

Now only Mrs. Fitzgerald was left for the Finale, perfectly poised in a graceful attitude, utterly still. She seemed to swell up, growing larger before our very eyes as she waited for silence and attention. Alone among the participants, Mrs. Fitzgerald was clearly a real performer, every inch the prima ballerina in her flowing costume and her pink satin toe shoes, carrying a gauzy silver wand with streamers. A hush fell upon the hall.

I begin to play softly, almost tentatively, as "Mary" wanders out into her garden — bending, peeping, searching for her flowers, then whirling across the front of the stage in a pique because she cannot find them. Now the music sounds vexed as well, glissandos and arpeggios, and "Mary" is contrary indeed, stamping, leaping, whirling, searching furiously everywhere, to no avail . . . I play more softly now. She stops, still as marble. She is not even out of breath, holding a ballet position to recite, "Mary, Mary, quite contrary, how does your garden grow?"

I play a tinkly harp-chords introduction to the "Waltz of the Flowers" as she touches the "silver bells and cockleshells" one by one with her wand. They stretch and rise, then leap up to "bloom" vigorously. Finally the "pretty maids all in a row" jump up, too, executing their funny little jig step in perfect synchronicity. Now the music is happy and jubilant, the major chords of springtime in a floating melody over the three-four time, as Mrs. Fitzgerald leads her ensemble in a "flower dance" similar to the one that she performed herself as a young girl in Alabama, where she grew up.

"Oh I was the prima ballerina of Montgomery," she had told us. "I could have gone anywhere, and done anything. But then my husband saw me perform a solo at the Beauty Ball for officers during the war, and could not take his eyes off me, and that was that. He fell in love with me at first sight. So that was the end of it, or the beginning. He looked so handsome in his uniform. I was not yet eighteen. We danced all night and then walked out into the moonlight together, among the honeysuckle." Her eyes had looked through us, past us, as she remembered.

Now arranged in two lines upon the stage, her pretty maids sway in unison to and fro, to and fro, to and fro — one can easily imagine a springtime breeze wafting through this "garden." They dissolve into groups of three to dance a charming step, my favorite, holding hands and prancing round like little children in a game. Led by Mrs. Fitzgerald, they form up into a line across the front of the stage again, twirling one by one and then all together before joining hands to sink to the floor in a graceful bow . . . somewhat ahead of my final chord, but I make do. They rise and bow again, now in delight and disarray, as the applause swells.

Suddenly Mrs. Carroll appeared at the edge of the stage and gestured to me — *me, Evalina!* — and I came out from the piano to curtsy deeply, instinctively, though I had never done this before, and did not know that I could do it.

Then we all melted into the crowd as a professional dance band took the stage. Chairs were cleared away. Couples began to foxtrot. We had been learning to dance, too, all those who would agree to participate — in exercise class, instead of basketball or volleyball. Most of us did not dance that evening, however; we sat in folding chairs and drank the red fruit punch and ate the usually forbidden cupcakes and looked at each other, and at the dancers.

"Evalina?" Someone touched my bare back. I jumped a mile, but it was only Robert. I had been looking about for him in vain, but he had rushed off into the darkness after his appearance. Now he had taken off the nightgown, but he looked ridiculous anyhow, in some sort of black suit at least a size too small.

"Do you want to dance?" He made a crazy little bow.

"I don't know how," I said honestly, for I had been too timid to try it. "Do *you* know how?"

"Oh, I had to take lessons," he said.

I kept forgetting about Robert's privileged childhood.

"Well . . ." I began.

He held his elbow out at an angle and I grabbed on to it and stood up, then pitched forward to fall flat upon the floor. Somehow I had forgotten to take my new French heels off the rung on my folding chair. There was a nervous hush, then a titter, and finally a smatter of applause as I finally got up off the floor, my face burning.

"Let's go outside," Robert said with utter tact, leading me out the diamond-paned door and onto the cold stone porch. Globe lamps made pools of light all down the sidewalk; partygoers were already leaving.

"I didn't know you could play the piano like that." His voice came out of the dark.

"I didn't either," I said. Actually I felt

wonderful, glowing, every nerve on fire, in spite of — or maybe because of — my embarrassment. Out beyond the slope of the mountain, the whole dark sky was filled with stars, the Milky Way in a huge arch, the clearest I have ever seen it.

Robert came up behind me in the dark and lifted my hair from my neck and put his lips there, a kiss that ran all the way down my body, creating a shimmering, lovely sensation that I have never forgotten in all these intervening years . . . if not passion, then the *promise* of passion: the salamander, twisting and shining in the sunlight.

"Ev-a-*lina*! Ev-a-*lina*!" my chums burst out the door — Lily and Virginia and Melissa — and Robert stepped back. In fact, he disappeared, and it was over. The moment, my triumph . . . it was all over.

It was as if we were in a turning kaleidoscope — everything changed. Everybody went back to being sad, or crazy, or got better and went home . . . Mrs. Fitzgerald to Montgomery for a visit, Lily to Mississippi, Robert to Cap d'Antibes where his mother was getting married for the fourth time.

I made a new friend, Ella Jean Bascomb, one of the cooks' daughters, who came to work with her mother when school was out.

She surprised me one day by singing along when I was playing "Blue Moon" in the music room at Homewood. Ella Jean had a high, thin, pitch-perfect mountain voice, and she knew lots of songs. Soon she was seated on the piano bench beside me. She taught me all the sad verses of "Barbara Allen" and other ballads they sang up in Madison County, north of Asheville, where she came from, and I began teaching her to play piano. In no time at all we could play a duet on "Heart and Soul," belting the words out over and over, as loud as possible, until we collapsed in laughter. I taught her "Shenandoah," which she sang beautifully, even Mrs. Carroll agreed, though she disapproved of this friendship because Ella Jean "did not come from a nice family," by which Mrs. Carroll meant a family in town.

And actually, Mrs. Carroll didn't know the half of it.

For Ella Jean was a tomboy through and through. She thought it was silly to hike, unable to imagine why anybody would want to just walk through these mountains she'd been walking in all her life. Instead, she taught me to swing on grapevines in the deep forest up above the hospital, climb the rocky cliffs (which she called "clifts"), find caves and old Indian graves, and strike fire from two rocks.

"I'm part Cherokee," she declared one time.

"Which part?" I asked. "Your hiney?"

She chased me through the trees. We built a fort and painted Indian signs on our arms and legs with pokeberry juice, then smoked rabbit tobacco she'd brought tied up in a rag from home. Unfortunately I got sick after this escapade, which caused Mrs. Hodges to declare Ella Jean "too rambunctious!" and limit our activities to the hospital grounds. Mrs. Hodges seemed relieved as, increasingly, Ella Jean had to stay home to take care of the younger children in her family.

After several false starts, spring finally came to North Carolina. Along with the rest, I spent long hours in the gardens under the direction of old Gerhardt Otto, weeding around the perennials as they popped up in the beds near the buildings, clearing dead brush away everywhere, planting early lettuce in the covered beds at Brushwood, then seeds and tomato plants in the garden. I came to love the smell of the soil itself; my arms grew strong and brown.

In June, a pool of scary red blood appeared without warning on my sheets, terrifying me. Nobody had ever told me that this would happen. Nurse White was dispatched to "show me the ropes," as Mrs. Hodges put it, "the belt and pads and such."

I was out in the garden again, wearing this apparatus as I separated irises at the edge of the forest late one afternoon, when I heard laughter back in the trees. I stood up and peered into the woods to glimpse Miss Quinn, our PE instructor, and my beloved old art teacher Miss Malone actually *kissing each other,* of all things! Miss Malone's back was turned to me; her long gray braid swung back and forth, back and forth, like the metronome on my piano. Across her shoulder, Miss Quinn winked at me — I'm sure she did — but she said nothing, and neither did I.

Summer fled past, a beautiful summer. In June, Mrs. Carroll took me to Mrs. Grady's Country Day School, all dressed up in a new dress with a sailor collar, for an interview. I played Debussy's "Clair de Lune" on the piano for Mrs. Grady, who closed her eyes and swayed to the music. In July, my chums and I were taken out in boats on the French Broad River. Miss Quinn taught me to swim several different strokes in the Highland pool. Mrs. Hodges taught me to play bridge, which I was very good at. My period came and went again, twice more, my own bright blood, and I did not die. I learned a monologue, "To a Drunken Father," though I had no father. Monologues were sweeping the country, said Phoebe Dean.

In August, the staff and patients of Highland put on an outdoor performance of *Midsummer Night's Dream* that starred Dr. Carroll himself, in puff sleeves and embarrassing white tights. Everyone got lost in the forest and then came out with someone else, holding hands, and then got married. By that time, I was coming to understand that there are all kinds of love. And there is no telling whom we may love, or when or why, or vice versa — for love is the greatest mystery of all. *The Kiss in the Garden,* I thought, smiling to imagine this book among my other Nancy Drews on their special shelf in my room, as I remembered Miss Quinn and Miss Malone's long kiss. I pictured Mrs. Carroll and Dr. Carroll in a similar embrace, surrounded by yellow roses; Miss Ella on the train platform with her twinkly old boyfriend and his bouquet; Mr. and Mrs. Fitzgerald waltzing all night long in Alabama when they were young; and my own beautiful young mother, how she brightened when Arthur Graves appeared at our door, back when he loved us so. Robert's face rose before me unbidden, like the sun.

Finally, the good news came: I would attend Mrs. Grady's Country Day School beginning in September. I would move into a room at Homewood, *almost* with the Carrolls! I counted the days, weeding the gardens and gathering tomatoes, ripe and warm from the sun.

"Now then, Evalina, I'd say you are finally *on your way*!" Mrs. Hodges announced with no small satisfaction as she drove me over to Mrs. Grady's on that first day of school. It was early September, a bright blue blowing day. Leaves skittered about our feet as we got out of the car. "Hold still, now." She yanked my collar, gave my blouse an extra tuck, smoothed back my hair, and then surprised me with a brisk, firm kiss on the cheek. "Pretty as a picture you are," she said. "There'll be none finer, not to worry."

But I wasn't worried, oddly enough. Nothing about school had ever alarmed me; I was good at school, placed a year ahead into ninth grade. I welcomed the regularity of Mrs. Grady's, which was much calmer than our classes had been at Highland — no one ever burst into tears or fits or ran from the room crying or attacked anyone else. I loved the uniforms at Mrs. Grady's, the bells and books and teams: everybody was on the Blue team or the Gold. I was to be a Gold. Now my time at Highland stood me in good stead, especially for athletics. Though I had never played some of these organized games, such as basketball or field hockey, I had grown strong walking up and down those hospital slopes, and I could run like the wind. I learned fast. The other girls had somehow gotten the idea that I was the Carrolls' granddaughter, and I did nothing to enlighten them. Nor did Mrs. Grady herself, a formidable maiden lady who actually winked at me once when this came up. As a "new girl," I was briefly the darling, courted by all. Everyone wanted to share her lunch with me, to be my partner in the relay races, to swing with me on the wicker swing in the arbor.

It was a heady, sunny time for me, which somewhat offset my greatest disappointment: for Robert Liebnitz did not return to us. Mrs. Hodges and I sat side by side on the horsehair loveseat in the Carrolls' apartment while Mrs. Carroll read his mother's letter aloud to us. She wrote informing the Carrolls that her new husband, named Dr. Jerome Livingston, was an internationally acclaimed professor, a don of philosophy.

"That's rich!" snorted Mrs. Hodges. "He'll need some philosophy, he will, dealing with the likes of that woman! She'll run him ragged in no time, that she will. Mark my words."

Mrs. Carroll raised an elegant eyebrow at Mrs. Hodges, then continued. Apparently Dr. Livingston was also a famous educator who was very interested in Robert's "case," and had "taken him on."

"It's about time, I'd say!" Mrs. Hodges seemed mollified. "Nothing *wrong* with the child, I always said. Just too smart, that's all. Too *in-tell-i-gent.*" She made it sound like a curse, or an illness.

Robert's mother had bought a grand house for Dr. Livingston, a widower with several daughters of his own, in Cornwall, England. I was immediately jealous when I heard this news. Robert was already attending Oxford University under some sort of special dispensation arranged for him by his new stepfather. He was said to be "adjusting well" to all these arrangements. In fact, he was "in his element," according to all.

Mrs. Carroll put the fluttery *avion* letter down on the porcelain back of the elephant table next to her chair. "So we shall all miss him, yes?" She touched my hand.

"I daresay," answered Mrs. Hodges, while

I nodded, unable to speak.

"And yet, it is what we hope for above all things, Dr. Carroll and myself," Mrs. Carroll continued quite seriously, leaning forward to cross her thin ankles. "That *all* our children shall be healed and strengthened, and go on to live successful real lives of their own, beyond our beloved mountain."

I nodded and tried to smile, though tears were running down my face. I understood that her words were meant for me, too, that the kaleidoscope was taking yet another turn, and I had better adjust to this new pattern.

Of course I continued my music lessons with Mrs. Carroll, sometimes along with several other town students, including a black girl named Eunice Kathleen Waymon who would later be known as Nina Simone. Mrs. Carroll had first heard her sing at a gospel service downtown. Now Mrs. Carroll was very interested in Eunice Waymon, more interested in her than she was in me, I felt. I was jealous of Eunice in the same way I had always been jealous of Mrs. Fitzgerald, who had sometimes been taken on trips with the Carrolls, once to Sarasota, Florida, for instance, where she studied art and they all went to the circus. I had been terribly upset about this; I would have given anything to see the circus! And now Mrs. Carroll was giving Eunice Waymon private singing lessons. Still, Eunice was very sweet to me and to everyone, and I was pleased to accompany her at the Carrolls' afternoon soirees, when Eunice leaned up against the piano to sing "Night and Day" with all the assurance of a born performer. It was funny to see such a little girl with such a big voice, and to hear her sing those grown-up songs.

"Pizzazz!" Mrs. Hodges crowed. "That girl has *got it*!" Everyone clapped and shouted "Bravo!" when we were done, and Mrs. Carroll gave us cupcakes and little cucumber sandwiches on white bread with the crusts cut off, and fruit punch in tiny green glasses from Italy.

My old chums had dispersed over the summer, along with Robert. It was as if they had all walked into the forest as in *A Midsummer Night's Dream*. Lily had stayed on in Mississippi, where she liked living with her Aunt Dee Dee in a big house brimming over with smaller cousins, four of them. I wrote to her, worried that she might be like Cinderella in this situation, but Lily wrote back saying no, there was plenty of help, and she was very excited because she was going to make her debut in two years' time. Lily wrote to me on pink stationery with her name engraved on it in raised rose lettering.

Miss Lily Ponder
Summerlin Grove
Greenville, Mississippi

Virginia Day had gotten better and had gone to a boarding school named Chatham Hall, though Mrs. Hodges told me privately that she wasn't sure Virginia was quite ready for this, and she was *quite* sure that Chatham Hall was not ready for Virginia. Melissa had been transferred to another hospital back home in Tennessee. "Cheaper," Mrs. Hodges said succinctly. Always discouraged by Mrs. Carroll, my friendship with Ella Jean Bascomb had now become nonexistent. An occasional hurried wave across the hospital grounds was about it, now that my activities at Mrs. Grady's kept me so busy. Before I knew it, Ella Jean had disappeared from my life.

CHAPTER 4

It would be two years before I saw her again. I was walking down the path toward Brushwood on a changeable, windy August day. I was almost seventeen, and had already been accepted into the Peabody Institute of Music, in Baltimore. I was to leave in a few weeks' time.

"Black is the color of my true love's hair . . ." Suddenly Ella Jean Bascomb's high, unearthly voice floated out on the fragrant breeze. Nobody else in the world sang like that. I stopped walking and shaded my eyes as I looked all around. Groups of patients and staff were walking up and down the paths, as always. *"The prettiest face, and the neatest hands, I love the ground whereon he stands . . ."* I got chill bumps on my arms, but I couldn't see her anywhere. Then I noticed the long lines of flapping sheets on the hillside out behind the Central Building, where the hospital laundry was located.

I left the path and ran across the grass. "Ella Jean!" I called. "Ella Jean!" I couldn't see her yet. The sun was in my eyes, and all I could see was the sheets, like a company of cheerful dancing ghosts.

"Evalina?" Here she came, running out barefooted between the rows, wearing a long white utility apron over her dress. "Lord, have mercy! Why, you have *growed,* girl! I wouldn't have hardly knowed you."

"Well, I would have known you anywhere," I said, which was true, though her thick black hair was pulled back now into a ponytail, and she had grown considerably taller and sturdier, with breasts. But her big dark eyes and wide grin were just the same. "Why didn't you come find me?" I asked her. "Are you just working over here for the summer? When did your school get out?"

She frowned, digging her toe in the grass. "I ain't in school no more," she said. "Mama had us some twins, and then she took real sick, and she liked to never got back up on her feet. So I stayed home to help out, and hit's been just one thing after another. You know."

I didn't, having no such family experience of my own to draw upon. But I felt embarrassed to realize that I hadn't even noticed that Ella Jean's mother was gone from her

123

place at the stove. Living now at Home-wood, I scarcely ever got over to the cafeteria in the Central Building anymore. "So, your mother must have gotten well, then?" I asked. "Or you wouldn't be over here working now, I mean." I had never been able to understand Ella Jean's family situation very well.

"I reckon," she said noncommittally, flashing that big quick grin.

"Ella Jean, *why* didn't you come find me?" I asked again.

"Lord, I figured you'd be too fancy for the likes of me, now," she said. "You being a town girl and all."

Am I a town girl? I wondered. *Sometimes I feel like a town girl, and sometimes I feel like an impostor,* I wanted to say.

"Hey, what was that song you were singing just a minute ago?" I asked her instead. "That was pretty." I hummed the lines back to her.

"Oh, hit's just one of them mournful old songs from up on Sodom, one of them old tunes that Granny sings," Ella Jean said. "Hit's a girl what loves this man with black hair, but he's dead and buried in the ground. Somebody is always dead, and somebody else is always singing about it."

Just like opera, I thought. Recently, Mrs.

124

Carroll and I had been studying *Aida.* I was very glad to see Ella Jean again, who stood out there in the sunshine grinning at me just like old times, her big apron pocket filled with wooden clothespins.

"I got me a banjer now," she announced. I was struck by her mountain accent, especially after talking to all those girls at Mrs. Grady's, where we were given "elocution" lessons as a matter of course.

"Ooh, I'd love to hear you play it!" I clapped my hands.

"Ella Jean? Ella Jean Bascomb!" the short fat woman in charge of the laundry called from the back of the building. She stepped out the door and peered over at us. "Oh, I'm sorry! You take your time then, honey," she yelled, seeing who I was, for everyone at Highland knew my special status.

"I've got to go," Ella Jean said to me. "Coming!" she hollered as she started back up the hill.

I couldn't stand to see her leave. "When do you get off?" I called after her. "Can't you come over to Homewood sometime and we can sing some more? Nobody is ever in the music room after about four thirty or so."

"Tomorrow," she yelled back down to me. "They can't pick me up till real late tomorrow anyhow, so I reckon I could come then."

I did a quick calculation: I would have to cancel a shopping trip with Stephanie Patterson and her mother. I would say I had cramps, I decided. "Okay. I'll see you over there." I waved and Ella Jean waved back before she vanished into the billowing sheets.

The next day she had the banjo. This was a primitive-looking long-necked thing with a rawhide face and a leather strap on it. I took my seat at the grand piano at Homewood while Ella Jean stood behind me, tuning the banjo and plucking at it.

"Slow or fast?" I asked.

"Fast," she said. "You know me!"

I started right in on Camptown Races, which we had done together years before. "Camptown racetrack's five miles long, doo-dah, doo-dah," we sang as one. Other people suddenly began to appear from everywhere — the art room, the practice rooms, the open door from outside, drawn by the music — especially the banjo, I believe, for a banjo has a naturally happy sound that no other instrument possesses. Everybody joined in lustily on "Oh, doo-dah day!"

■ ■ ■ ■

A week later, Ella Jean held the banjo carefully between her knees as we jounced about on a pile of old tobacco sacks in the back of the most beat-up truck I had ever seen, heading toward Sodom Laurel, Ella Jean's hometown up in Madison County, north of Asheville. Finally, after much pleading and bargaining on my part, Mrs. Hodges had agreed to this overnight visit, so that I might "hear Granny sing" myself. I am sure she would not have done so had Dr. and Mrs. Carroll not been off on one of their "jaunts" — this one to Chicago, where he was to address a worldwide conference of psychiatrists, as I recall.

I still wasn't exactly sure who our driver, Earl, was — relative or neighbor, I supposed. He had not yet spoken. A little old man in a shapeless black hat, Earl hunched so low in the seat that whenever I looked ahead through the cab's cracked window, it appeared unnervingly as though no one was even driving. The smoke from his cigarette floated out the window of the truck past my face, almost sweet, and somehow intoxicating. The wind blew my hair into my eyes. I had to give Ella Jean credit, because somehow she had had the sense to get Earl to park down by the gate, out of sight. Mrs. Hodges would never have let me get into that truck if she had seen it. The last thing I saw as we left was Mrs. Hodges standing out in the middle of the road in front of Homewood with arms akimbo, a worried frown on her face, as the two of us raced down the hill. Ella Jean grabbed my overnight case and hoisted it up over the side of the truck, then the sack she'd been carrying, then finally the banjo, before jumping up herself and leaning back down with hand extended to pull me up. I had clambered over the top to land sprawling among the sacks and straw and old cans and boxes and trash that filled the back of the truck.

"Lord!" Ella Jean exclaimed. "I never thought I'd see *this* day come, did you?"

"No," I said honestly, trying gingerly to make myself a little nest, for I feared we'd go flying out once the truck picked up speed.

"You ever been in the back of a truck before?" Evalina asked me over the rattling.

"No," I said.

She grinned her jack-o'-lantern grin at me as Earl turned out of the Highland grounds and into regular Asheville traffic. We headed north, out of town.

"You wanna dope?" Ella Jean rummaged around in her sack.

"What?"

She held up a strawberry Nehi pop. "Hand me that there church key then," she directed, at my nod.

"What?" I asked.

She pointed at a kind of bottle opener hung on a screw at the back of the truck with twine; I grabbed it and passed it over. That sweet hot soda was the best thing I had ever tasted, the carbonation going straight to my brain.

"Here, now." Ella Jean was down in the bag again.

Next came saltine crackers in little cellophane packages, filched from the dining hall. They were delicious, too, and we ate them up ravenously. Ella Jean still had that special quality about her; she was simply more *alive* than anybody else. We rumbled on through Asheville past tall office buildings, then houses with yards, then farms and open road.

Up and up we went, into that far countryside I had only seen as framed by the windows of Highland Hospital and the literal frames of the landscape paintings in the Art Room, where several of my favorites were watercolors by Mrs. Fitzgerald. First we came to the little farms and pastures and churches on knolls, each with its own graveyard, then the piney foothills, and finally those high, solemn blue mountains themselves, traveling up and up on roads so twisting they took my breath away and caused the truck's engine to sputter until I thought it would surely die. Earl turned off the main road into a forest so thick and dark it was like a tunnel, then steered us back out into the sunshine, where the gravel road narrowed to a scary ribbon as it hugged a cliff side. The drop on our right was perpendicular. I could not even see what lay beyond the miles of empty air below. I shut my eyes and clutched Ella Jean's brown arm.

"Aren't we almost there?" I asked.

"No we ain't," she said, with evident satisfaction. "You just hold your horses."

I shut my eyes. The truck climbed to the top of that mountain, then another, and crossed a creek on a rickety wooden bridge with no guardrails.

"Now?" I asked.

"Yep." We had come to a high narrow valley — or "holler," as Ella Jean called it, looking out upon yet another range of rolling blue peaks. A dirt road ran up the holler, where several cabins were visible back in the trees, with their outbuildings.

"But where's the town?" I said.

"Ain't none."

I smiled to imagine Mrs. Hodges's re-action to *this* news.

The truck turned, forded a smaller creek, and made the last steep, short drive up into a clearing, where stood a large misshapen boy — or was he a man? — leaning against a kind of small barn to watch our approach without any emotion at all on his wide, flat face. Several little dogs were playing at his feet.

"That's Wilmer, he's real sweet," Ella Jean said. "He lives in that there barn."

"Hey Wilmer," she called. A smile broke over his whole face. Earl stopped the truck and people came running out of the log house like the figures in Mrs. Carroll's Austrian cuckoo clock. In addition to Wilmer, there were two little blond twins named Billy Ed and Mister. "He's the one that was so sickly when he was borned," Ella Jean explained, "so we just called him Mister instead of give him a name, that's what we always do, in case they up and die on you, but he didn't, and this time it stuck."

"Sissie, Sissie!" the twins ran to Ella Jean and hugged her legs.

"Now this here is Evalina," she said. "Can you say that? Eva-*li*-na."

"Ev-a-*li*-na!" they chorused, and I had to kneel right down and kiss them. I was very startled by their presence somehow, though I'd been told there would be children up here. They were wriggly and dirty and very *real*, like Ella Jean was — certainly more real, I felt suddenly, than my own life at the hospital. I knelt and hugged them tight, along with an older girl, maybe seven or eight, named Baby Doll, though she certainly did not look like a baby doll, dish-faced and sallow. Nobody here looked anything at all like Ella Jean.

"Y'all come on."

I glanced up to see a tall, long-faced woman standing at the open door, holding a pie pan. She crossed the porch and threw the contents of the pan out into the bare "yard" below, where the dogs began yapping and fighting over it.

"Them's little fice dogs," Ella Jean said. It seemed they would tear each other to bits over this food, which did not look all that good to me anyway, mostly bones. Why were they fed like this? Where were their dog bowls? The woman threw the pan itself out in the yard and they fought over it, too, and licked it clean.

"This is Aunt Roe," Ella Jean said of the woman, who did not look any too pleased to see us. Probably because I am one more mouth to feed, I realized, resolving to eat as little as possible.

"Very pleased to meet you, ma'am," I said.

She nodded at me curtly but said nothing. Her nose was sharp, her eyes too close together.

We trooped up onto the porch, where I was surprised to find that the pile of quilts in the corner actually contained Ella Jean's Granny, the one she was always talking about. "Granny has got the sight," she had said. Surely this was the oldest person I had ever seen, the oldest person in the whole world.

Ella Jean pulled me over there. "Granny?" she shouted. "Granny? This here is Evalina, the one I've been telling you about."

The old eyes opened, bright as buttons. She reached out a skinny claw to grab me. Her hand was warm, and as she stroked my own, I felt a warm sense of well-being flow throughout me.

"I'm so glad to meet you," I said sincerely.

" 'Bout time," she said in a voice surprisingly clear. She continued to look straight at me while holding my hand, now smoothing my palm again and again with her light, papery touch. Ella Jean stood uncharacteristically still, watching intently. I found myself closing my eyes for a minute, completely at peace. I opened them just in time to see a change come over Granny's face, a grave sort of settling as she leaned back among her quilts. "Honey, honey," she whispered fiercely then, balling my hand up into a fist and squeezing it so hard that I almost cried out in pain before she released me. Ella Jean grabbed me and pulled me back. I felt relieved, and a little scared.

"Is she your grandmother or your great-grandmother?" I asked, jealous because I had neither, but Ella Jean just laughed at me. "One or t'other," she said. "I don't reckon it matters, does it?"

"I don't reckon it does," I said.

Inside, the log house was a jumble, with no regular furniture in the front room save for a giant handmade wooden wardrobe and Granny's iron bed, pulled right up to the only window. Homemade mattresses — bedticks, they called them — were scattered across the floor beyond, along with several wooden chairs, trunks, and haphazard piles of clothing. A calendar from a funeral home and a long rifle hung on pegs above Granny's bed. I could see why Wilmer might prefer to live in the barn! We threaded our way through the clutter, following Aunt Roe's summons into the added-on "kitchen," such as it was. She stood at the black cookstove dishing out food from two black pots and a skillet; Baby Doll already sat at the big wooden table, reading a comic book while she ate from a battered tin plate before her, along with the little boys, Billy Ed and Mister, who perched together on a sort of high homemade bench and ate their beans and cornbread with their hands from a single plate, literally shoveling it in. Long-haired, sweet-faced Wilmer appeared at the back door to receive a heaping plate of steaming food, then stumbled back out with it. Or at least I thought he stumbled — later on, I would realize that this was the way he walked.

"Isn't he going to eat with us?" I asked Ella Jean.

"He don't never eat with nobody," she said.

Aunt Roe did not even look at us as she handed Ella Jean and me our plates of green beans, cornbread cut from the skillet, and something mysterious from the other pot. I had a special plate — blue and white china. Ella Jean grabbed us two dishrags for napkins and we took our seats at the bare wooden table just as Baby Doll got up. Aunt

Roe gave her a plate to take out for Granny.

"She won't eat hardly a thing, though," Ella Jean remarked to me. "Lives on music and air."

I, on the other hand, found that I had turned into a glutton; this was the best food I had ever put into my mouth, and suddenly I was ravenous. Ham and onions had been cooked along with the beans, for hours it seemed, by their smoky, salty taste. The cornbread was crisp and crusty outside, chewy and moist within. "And what's this, exactly?" I asked, eating the other dish, a piece of something with thick gravy on it.

"Meat," Aunt Roe said.

I did not pursue this topic, but ate every bite.

"It really is good, Roe," Ella Jean said, confirming for me that this was indeed a special supper.

"Everything is just delicious!" I added sincerely, and Aunt Roe nodded, once. She herself ate standing up, though there were chairs at the table. I sensed that she preferred to take her meals this way.

Suddenly we were joined by a barefooted girl in a flowing sort of nightgown, I believe, and a fringed, flowered shawl that dangled almost into my plate as she stood behind me and stretched her arms out over the table. She was very pale and very beautiful. Her eyes were shut; her silvery hair cascaded all down her back.

"Mama, Mama!" the little boys chanted, pulling at her gown. Without her kitchen uniform and hairnet, I would never have recognized her.

Never opening her eyes, their mother began, "May the Lord bless this food before us, may He bless and keep us every one, especially these sweet little children, and make His face to shine upon us all the days of our lives, so that we may go forth and do His bidding in the wide world, and live each day in such a way that we may enter into His kingdom, where we shall all be blessed to eat His heavenly food forever, and sing with His heavenly angels and say with them this heavenly prayer, 'Our Father, who are in heaven, hallowed be Thy name . . .' "

I joined in the Lord's prayer, as did Ella Jean. Aunt Roe did not.

"In the name of the Father, and the Son, and the Holy Ghost, Amen," we said loudly, and Ella Jean got up to pull out a chair for her mother, who was hugely pregnant again, I realized. Aunt Roe gave her a plate of food as she reached over to take my hand.

"Now, I'm Trula," she said. "Ella Jean has been talking about you coming up here for the longest time, and I love you, and God loves you." Her eyes were as simple and blue as the sky.

"I love you, too," I said, surprising myself. This remark seemed to please her, and she began to eat. I looked at Ella Jean but she was looking down, not looking at me on purpose, I felt. Clearly, there was a lot she had not told me. The little boys tumbled off their bench and out the door, leaving a mess behind. The dogs were barking in the yard.

"Where is Mister Bascomb?" I asked, for I was dying to know.

"Why, he's off doing the Lord's work," Trula said sweetly, in unison with Ella Jean, who said he was playing music at a honky-tonk in Tennessee. Finally Ella Jean looked at me, and we both burst out laughing, Trula along with us, her laugh like little bells ringing. I got it, all right. I wondered if she had always been like this, or if it was more recent, the result of too many babies, or too much Jesus. I got up and cleared off the table and washed the tin plates in a basin of water that Aunt Roe had heated up on the woodstove so hot that it almost scalded me. I didn't mind. I wanted it to scald me, the same way I wanted to eat what they did and do what they did.

"Show her the garden, then," Aunt Roe

said to Ella Jean, who took me out the back door through the pecking chickens, past the "back house," and up a dirt road toward the great overhanging mountain, where darkness and mist were already gathering.

"There it is," Ella Jean said, pointing at the large garden, which was as tidy as the house was messy, row on row of corn and glossy green plants such as squash and beans and potatoes, ripe red tomatoes neatly staked. "Aunt Roe got here just in time to help us put the garden in, thank God," Ella Jean said. "Or else I don't know what we would of done."

"You mean she doesn't live here all the time?" I was shocked.

"No, she don't live noplace, I reckon, just goes where she's needed. I was mighty glad when she showed up, I'll tell you."

A big stuffed scarecrow in jeans and a black frock coat stood in the midst of the pumpkin vines, presiding over all. "Who's that?" I asked.

"That's Daddy," Ella Jean said, not laughing. "Leastways, that's his old coat. Daddy is something else. I wouldn't of let you come up here if he was home."

"Why not?" I asked. "What would happen?"

"Well, that's the thing of it," Ella Jean said.

"He might be sweet as pie, or he might take drunk and start sworping around. You just don't never know."

"Is he really a preacher, then? Like your mother said?"

"Well, more or less. He's been *known to preach,* let's just leave it at that." Ella Jean's quick grin flashed white in the gathering darkness. "Up there's the tobacco field," she added, pointing out a patch of ghostly-looking little white tents that didn't look like tobacco — or anything growing — to me, and I said so.

"That's just how it gets when you go to cut it, all droopylike," she said. "We'll be getting it in the barn this week."

"*You'll* be getting it into the barn?" I stopped walking and looked at her.

"Yes mam." She did not look back. "Along with a passel of otherunses. People around here are real good to help each other out when hit's a job of work to do."

"Then what?"

"Then we'll hang it up, and let it get good and dry, and then we'll take it to market. That's good money and a good time," she added. "Music and everything." We turned back toward the house, where the sound of music already came drifting from the porch as if on cue. "Down there's the privy," she

140

said. "We better go on down there and use it, fore it gets plumb dark," and so we did, one after the other. There was a choice of dried corn cobs or old catalogue pages for toilet paper. When I came back out, Ella Jean took my hand and led me up the path to the front porch where several neighbors had gathered, including Earl, who was now playing a guitar almost as big as he was, while Granny strummed the "dulcimore" on her lap and Trula fiddled. Ella Jean grabbed up her banjo and there we stayed, all of us, singing the moon up, as lightning bugs rose from the brush into the trees and Wilmer came out to hunker down in front of his barn and listen.

At one point, Ella Jean and her mother put their instruments down and stood together at the porch rail, almost touching but not quite, as they flung back their heads and closed their eyes and sang "Barbry Allen" in the old way, with that flip of the voice at the end, their high tremolo voices quivering out over the holler. The last note still hung in the air when there came the sound of a loud car engine — with no muffler, it sounded like — and then it was there below us, with slamming doors and voices raised. The dogs started barking like crazy.

"Oh Lord," Ella Jean said.

"Who is it?" I asked. "Is it your daddy?"

"Not hardly. And he ain't *my* daddy, anyhow," Ella Jean said, leaving me to ponder that as I watched the arrival of Ella Jean's older sister, Flossie, who had *not* come back to stay, she told everybody at once, tossing her yellow ponytail. She just wanted her clothes, that was all, she was moving to Knoxville, and this was Doyle — the boyfriend who stood back by the treeline smoking a cigarette and wearing a snapbrim straw hat with a green feather in it.

"Oh no, honey —" Trula flew down the steps to envelop her oldest daughter in tears and recriminations, but Flossie said she didn't care if she was going to hell or not, she was going to Knoxville first, if everybody would just get out of her way and let her get her stuff.

While Flossie made her way into the back house, trailed by all the rest, I decided to venture back down through the woods in the moonlight to the privy by myself. I found my way all right and was coming back up the path when suddenly I was grabbed from behind, one strong arm around my waist and another around my neck, a hard fist in my mouth.

"Now don't be scared, honey. I don't want nothing but a little kiss." Flossie's boyfriend

142

had a deep, insinuating voice. "I've always had a hankering for a city girl." The bristles of his beard scraped my neck, and I could smell his awful hair pomade. I could not speak, for now he was choking me as his other hand moved under my blouse. It was pitch dark, with that woodsy smell all around. I could not move or breathe. I tried to struggle, but lost my footing on the dark path.

"God damn it!" the man said, and suddenly I was thrown off to the side, into the bushes, as a dark furious struggle of some sort occurred, punctuated by the noise of blows and grunts, "Oof! Ugh! Ah!" like the balloons of speech in cartoons. Then it was over, and the man was gone, and Wilmer was leaning over me. He picked me up and set me on my feet. He smelled terrible.

"Thank you," I said, clutching the back of his rough wool shirt as I followed him out to the clearing where the man, seeming not much the worse for wear, was piling Flossie's bundles into the car, cursing all the while. Crying now, Flossie herself got in and slammed the door. Granny still sat in her corner, in her quilts, watching — or not watching — it all from her high perch. The car rattled off down the mountainside.

Trula picked up her fiddle again. She and

Ella Jean sang "The Demon Lover," and I
soon joined in on the chorus. *"Well met, well
met, my own true love, Well met, well met,"
says he. "I've just returned from the salt water
sea, and it's all for the sake of thee."* The
demon lover talks the young wife into running off with him, leaving her husband, who
is a "house-carpenter," and a "tender little
babe" behind. At the end of the song, both
lovers drown in the "salt water sea" and
then go to Hell. All the ballads ended tragi-
cally, and all the women died, or so it
seemed to me, especially in the terrible
"Omie Wise," and yet I felt a pure, undeniable exhilaration upon learning these old
tunes. Granny strummed her dulcimer in
darkness with her eyes closed, yet she never
missed a note or a single word when she
sang solo on "The Wagoner's Lad" in her
strong old voice. That song seemed to go on
forever, verse after verse in the night.

The moon rode high in the sky, so bright
it cast shadows behind every tree, when
everybody finally drifted off to bed. As Ella
Jean and I made a final trip down the path
to the privy, I could hardly believe what had
happened there; I did not tell her about it,
for some reason I did not understand. We
slept up in Ella Jean's little loft in the back
house, where I found a number of my old

Nancy Drew books — I did not mention this either. Ella Jean's breathing instantly grew slow and regular, her warm heavy arm flung across my stomach; but as for me, I was too excited to sleep, lying awake far into the night breathing the cool, scented mountain air and gazing out through a pie-shaped chink at the starry sky.

In the morning we ate anything we could find and then sat out on the porch in the sunshine playing checkers and drinking black coffee out of tin cups while we waited for Earl to come back and get us. Granny sat in her corner as if she had never left it — maybe she hadn't! — picking out a fast little tune on Earl's guitar. The little boys wrestled in the dirt yard below while Trula sat on the steps painting her toenails pink. She could scarcely reach them over her big stomach. Up the hill, Aunt Roe was already out working in the garden. *"I'll fly away, oh Lordy, I'll fly away,"* Granny sang. *"When I get to heaven by and by, I'll fly away."* We joined her.

"Y'all sound good," Trula said.

"King," I said to Ella Jean, crowning the black disc. I had scarcely slept yet felt strangely rested and alert, with every nerve on edge. Mist still hung in the trees though the sun shone hot and bright already; the deep blue sky was cloudless.

"Don't y'all want to do your nails too?" Trula asked, offering the little bottle of nail polish.

Ella Jean and I had just finished painting each others' toenails when Earl's old truck rumbled into the clearing. We grabbed up our shoes and bags and ran barefooted down the warm stairs and across the yard to jump in the back of the truck. "Bye! Bye!" the little boys cried, waving. Trula waved, too, and even Baby Doll, who came out to sit sullenly beside her mother. Granny dozed in the sun in her corner. We bounced down the hill past the barn where Wilmer suddenly appeared in the door with a big smile on his face, wearing his familiar overalls and wool shirt and that snap brim straw hat with the green feather on it. He touched the brim and nodded, once, as we rode past.

Earl dropped us at the stone gate and we set off up the hill, swinging our bags. The grounds of Highland Hospital had never looked more beautiful — the long green slopes of perfect grass punctuated by flowering oak-leaf hydrangeas and crape myrtles, stone benches and birdbaths placed here

146

and there, the bright, orderly flower beds as we neared the top. Everyone we encountered waved or spoke to us, and we spoke back. But suddenly Ella Jean grabbed my arm, jerking me off the driveway with such force that I almost fell down.

"What are you . . ." I began, but stopped as I saw the Carrolls' long, black, shiny Lincoln shoot past us like a bullet, with Johnson at the wheel.

"Something is wrong," I said.

Instinctively we both slowed down as we continued on up the hill, achieving a literal snail's pace as we neared the top in time to witness the Lincoln slide to a stop in front of Homewood. Its huge front door and the car doors sprang open at the same time. Out came Mrs. Hodges, almost falling down the stone steps as she rushed to envelop Mrs. Carroll in such a hug that Mrs. Carroll's red pillbox hat went spiralling down along the pavement. *"Ai-eee, ai — eee!"* Mrs. Hodges wailed. Her hair stood out from her head in big clumps. Miss Malone and Mr. Axelrod appeared in the open door behind her with serious expressions on their faces.

"Come *on,*" I said.

But Ella Jean hung back, pulling me into the honeysuckle arbor. "Maybe we ought to wait awhile," she said. "They ain't seen us yet."

Through the trellis we watched Dr. Carroll himself, tall and grave, climb out of the car and take off his navy blue suit coat and his hat and hand them carefully to Johnson. Then Dr. Carroll stood in the hot sun in his brilliant white shirt with his hands on his hips, surveying the two women as if they presented a job of work to be done — a familiar stance I had often witnessed as he surveyed a new garden plot to be put in or a flagstone walk to be laid. Mrs. Hodges kept on talking and waving her arms while Mrs. Carroll covered her face with her hands.

"She's crying," Ella Jean said.

Mr. Axelrod and Miss Malone moved forward awkwardly. Johnson carried the Carrolls' suitcases inside. Ella Jean and I stood like statues in the arbor, watching through the vines. The smell of the honeysuckle was overpowering. Now Dr. Carroll had put his arms around Mrs. Carroll in a tight embrace while Mrs. Hodges stepped back, still speaking and wringing her hands.

"Look," Ella Jean said, pointing. We were both transfixed by a sudden influx of yellow butterflies that fluttered down to land in a bed of orange day lilies just beyond our hid-

ing place. They stayed for only a second before flying up again in a yellow cloud that rose erratically into the cloudless sky. I rushed out into the sunshine to see them go, shading my eyes with my hand.

"Well, you've gone and done it now," Ella Jean said from the arbor.

"It's Robert," I screamed. "Something has happened to Robert. I know it has." The minute the yellow cloud of butterflies disappeared over the brow of the hill, I set out toward Homewood, at a dead run.

But it took me forever to get up that hill, for the closer I got, the slower I seemed to go, running now as if in a dream. The Carrolls stood locked in their embrace like a statue, but Mrs. Hodges opened her arms wide to catch me up in a stifling hug.

"Oh honey," she cried, "he's gone and kilt himself."

"Evelyn!" Mrs. Carroll said to her sharply.

But Mrs. Hodges could not stop herself from telling it, again and again, her jumbled recital punctuated by those odd cries, *"Ai-eee, ai-eee!"* The facts were these: Robert had been on vacation from Oxford, at home with his new family at the grand house his mother had bought for Dr. Jerome Livingston on the coast of Cornwall. There had been a nature hike that afternoon, led by

Dr. Livingston, then croquet on the lawn, then a jolly dinner for everyone, including the three stepsisters and several of their friends, with two visiting uncles thrown in. Nothing unusual had occurred at this dinner, according to all. Lamb, potatoes, peas, and carrots had been served. Robert had been pleasant and talkative, excusing himself just before dessert.

"But he loved dessert," I said.

"Ah yes, remember how he used to steal my sweeties? *Ai-eee!*" Mrs. Hodges had always kept cellophane-wrapped hard candy in her pocket for him.

No one had thought anything of it when Robert left the table, assuming of course that he had gone to "the necessary," as Mrs. Hodges called it. Nor was Robert missed when he did not immediately return, for one of the uncles chose the interval between courses to perform a few magic tricks, and everyone was enthralled. Robert had simply folded his napkin, excused himself quietly, and walked down the hall and out the front door where he circled the house to take the "Cliff Walk" which ran through the woods to the great red cliffs above the sea, continuing in a circuitous fashion down to the "shingle" or stretch of sand where the family swam and sunned at low tide only. Robert did not take the lower path. He climbed out onto the rocks, into the sunset, then "cast himself into the sea," as Mrs. Hodges told it. No one in the world could have shut her up at that moment.

The family might never have known what happened to him had not a kitchen boy, taking a smoke break on the lawn, seen him go. There was something about the way Robert was walking, the boy said later, something about the way he looked back before ducking into the woods on the cliff path, that bothered him. The boy ran in to sound the alarm, which took a moment, for he was a stutterer. When those at table realized what he was saying, the entire company threw down their napkins and leapt up to follow him down to the cliffs, where they found only Robert's wristwatch, which he had left for some reason on the rocks, and the gorgeous sunset, and the huge waves crashing on the rocks below.

"But he couldn't swim!" I cried, remembering Robert out by the hospital pool, fully dressed.

"Well, that was the point then, wasn't it?" Mrs. Hodges snapped. "Suicide, it was, and now he's gone straight to Hell in a hand basket, he has, there's the pity of it, there's the shame."

"Evelyn, this is rubbish, and you know it. You are overwrought. Let's step back to the office. I'm going to give you something for your nerves." Dr. Carroll spoke firmly.

"And Evalina, you must come with me, dear. Let's get out of this blinding sun." Mrs. Carroll was disengaging me from the overheated Mrs. Hodges, trying to draw me away. "We have a lot to do," she said, "and a lot to talk about."

But I was unable to talk about Robert then, or for years to come. He had been my most precious friend, my most private memory, purely my own amidst my oddly public adolescence at Highland Hospital. He was the still point at the center of the kaleidoscope.

In only ten days, I would leave for Peabody. In the meantime, I was supposed to shop, pack, and practice — practice the piano above all — but I could not. I crumpled into a ball when I sat upon the piano bench. Nor could I eat any supper later. Finally I was allowed to go to bed, where I pretended to sleep so that they would let me alone while I watched the terrible film that played over and over in my mind, Robert's body smashing against the rocks, his head broken apart in pieces like

Humpty Dumpty, that huge head crammed too full, too full of dreams and facts and lore and bits of odd knowledge . . . and *love,* I thought, for Robert had loved the world, and all the facts and bits of it, every name and every living thing.

Finally I slept, waking later in the night to see a crack of unaccustomed light beneath my door and hear voices — Dr. Carroll's, Mrs. Carroll's, and another man's voice which I did not immediately recognize. They had been checking on me. I was surprised by this, as the Carrolls normally retired to their own apartment unless they had an engagement. The voices continued, now coming from the sitting room down the short hall. Some instinct made me get up, open the door, and creep in darkness, shrinking against the wall, right down to the corner where I could hear them clearly. The other man was Dr. Raymond Levy, a young doctor newly arrived from Duke University.

"But the rest cure was successful before, darling." Mrs. Carroll's voice had an argumentative edge to it. "Don't you remember what sort of shape she was in, the little waif, when she arrived?"

Me! They were talking about *me.*

"I've told you, Grace. There just isn't time now for the rest cure." Dr. Carroll spoke impatiently. "It takes several weeks, as you well know, at a minimum. Evalina has to go to Peabody, and she has to go now. Within a fortnight."

"But surely her matriculation could be postponed," ventured the young Dr. Levy, "under these circumstances. This kind of thing must happen with some frequency, I'd imagine, due to illness, or a death in the family. Schools have to make allowances. Evalina is very young, anyway. Can't she go next year, or at the beginning of the winter term?"

"*Yes,* Robert." Mrs. Carroll had a note of pleading in her voice. "Let's keep her here with us, darling, until she is stronger."

"No," Dr. Carroll said. Instantly I could see his craggy face in my mind's eye, the big nose, the jut of the chin. "Absolutely not. I am in the business of discouraging weakness, and encouraging strength. Banishing illness and enabling wellness, this is what we are about here at Highland Hospital." Dr. Carroll spoke for the benefit of Dr. Levy, I could tell. "Coddling is not kind. Coddling fosters neurasthenia, hypochondriasis, hysteria, and paralysis of the will."

"But darling . . ." I could imagine Mrs. Carroll's beautiful, pained face, how she would be leaning forward in her chair.

154

"Enough!" I knew Dr. Carroll had held up his hand in the familiar traffic-cop gesture. "Sometimes a physician must simply make a judgment call. I take full responsibility for my decision. Evalina is the most fortunate of children, for she has a true talent, and the capacity for real and important work. Thus, despite her unfortunate birth and the sorrows of her youth, Evalina possesses every capacity for achieving that highest of all our goals here at Highland, that which I refer to as the Victorious Self. But timing is all, as we are well aware."

"Robert, I implore you. At this moment, Evalina is scarcely speaking. She can neither practice nor eat. Who knows whether or not we shall even get her out of bed in the morning?"

"This is precisely why I am prescribing a course of metrazol convulsion therapy for our Evalina, beginning as soon as possible. I shall speak with Wilfred Terhune about it first thing in the morning. One or two may do the trick."

"Oh, I just don't know, dear." Now Mrs. Carroll sounded really worried.

"You need not know, dear, nor worry your pretty head about it. But your participation will be important — crucial, in fact. Do not allow the faintest shadow of doubt, or indecision, to cross your face or enter your voice as you discuss this with her. We *must* be in concert on this, Grace. We must act as one."

"But what about Evelyn?"

"Don't worry. I will put the fear of God into Evelyn Hodges," Dr. Carroll said grimly. "She shall not scotch this project, I can promise you that. And she is not to tell anyone outside this hospital — *anyone* — about Evalina's treatments. Mrs. Grady is not to know, nor are Evalina's friends, nor their parents. This moment, too, will disappear into Evalina's buried past, and she will go forward into the useful future which awaits her."

"Well, if you are sure, then . . ."

I could tell by Mrs. Carroll's voice that the conversation was over. She always did whatever Dr. Carroll suggested — or decreed. "Good night, then, dear," she said. "Good night, Dr. Levy."

Trembling, I pressed myself flat against the wall, but she took the other hallway, thank goodness.

"A point of information, Dr. Carroll," Dr. Levy began seriously. "At Duke, the insulin coma treatment is currently preferred; I am wondering why you have chosen metrazol for your ward."

Ward? I was thinking.

Dr. Carroll said, "Here at Highland, we administer the insulin treatments — usually for longterm schizophrenia and depression — over an extensive period of time. Thirty or forty comas would not be uncommon. But with a trauma-induced state such as Evalina's, I have found metrazol to be quicker and more effective. Sometimes a sudden jolt or two is all that's needed. I am hoping that this will be the case here."

Dr. Levy went on to question Dr. Carroll about electroshock, a new treatment which "shows much promise," as Dr. Carroll agreed.

But I had heard enough. I crept back to my room and lay down in darkness. Something Dr. Carroll had said kept coming back to me. What did he mean, my "unfortunate birth"? What could he possibly mean by that? Finally I closed my eyes and surrendered to my terrible waking sleep, watching the film of Robert's suicide over and over. There was a part of me that did not want to take the metrazol, that did not want to get better, that wanted to stay here in this darkness with Robert, no matter how hard it was, so long as I could see him at all. Yet there was another part that did want to leave Highland, to go to Peabody, to fly away, fly away like the butterflies, like Granny's song, *I'll fly away, oh Lordy, I'll fly away. When I get to Heaven by and by, I'll fly away.*

It was still early the following morning when I was awakened by one of my favorites, the pretty young nurse Dorothy Rich, and escorted up to the top floor of the Central Building, through double steel doors that clanged shut behind us, one after the other. "Oh, that's for the patients' safety," she told me with her bright pink lipstick smile. "They are at first so disorienting, these treatments."

"Then what?"

"Then they prove very helpful," she said reassuringly, squeezing my shoulder as she led me into a tiny room where I was to take off my clothes and put on a terrycloth robe and some paper slippers and "rest" until my turn came.

Another young nurse came in with two tablets and a glass of water on a tray. "Here, honey, go ahead and take these now," she said, putting the bag down on the little table by my bed. "Then you can take a nap, and when you wake up, you'll feel a lot better."

"Oh Diana, I tried to call you last night,"

Dorothy said to her. "Some of us are going out to Lake Lure on Saturday, don't you want to go with us? *Bert* is going," she added, giggling.

"Really?" Diana said. "But . . ."

I turned my back and slipped the tablets into the pocket of my terrycloth robe, then faced them again, drained my glass of water, and lay down on the bed, surprising myself. I am still not sure exactly why I disobeyed. Hands at my sides, I lay flat on my back and closed my eyes. The two young nurses continued to whisper and giggle. I heard the words "big band."

Then Dorothy came over and put her cool hand on my forehead. "She's gone," she said, and the two left my cubicle.

I sat up, possessed by nothing so much as a sudden terrific curiosity. I opened my door and went out into the narrow hallway to find the bathroom, where I flushed the tablets away immediately. Some of the doors along the long corridor were open, and some were closed; I knew that these rooms contained patients in varying stages of insulin and metrazol shock therapy, either drugged and waiting for their treatments to be administered, as I was supposed to be doing, or still "sleeping it off" from the day before. Nurses flitted in and out. The big door down at the end of the hall swung open as a patient, prone and still on his bed, was wheeled inside; the doors closed behind him. I ducked back into the bathroom as another gurney with a large sleeping man on it came down the hall past me, pushed by an intern I did not know. The metal doors clanged shut again behind the unconscious giant, then opened for yet another patient on a gurney. Soon they would come for me.

I looked both ways, then walked quickly (and calmly, I hoped, though my heart was beating fast) down the hall. I turned the large knob, then pulled it; the door swung open easily. Without even thinking, I slipped inside, to hover just there, by the back wall.

The large ward was in semidarkness. Six or seven patients already lay in place on the gurneys to which they were virtually bound, I realized, by carefully folded sheets and raised rails, so that they would not roll out. But it was only later that I would fully understand everything I saw. A little table holding a glass of orange juice, a bottle of dextrose, and several syringes filled with different amounts of insulin on a clean white cloth had been placed next to each. Patients just commencing their course of treatment were given low doses of insulin, which would increase with time until the dose was quite high by the end of therapy. Usually the injections were given in the buttocks, though I saw two patients receiving injections in their arms instead. The insulin shock treatment was given five days a week, with the weekend off, and might go on for weeks and weeks. On a few tables there lay only one syringe, which was destined for the metrazol shock patients such as myself. We, too, would be thrown into a spontaneous convulsion, like an epileptic fit.

Some of the treatments were already in progress. They started early each morning, so that the patients could be carefully monitored all day long for any delayed reactions. Highland was a famous, progressive hospital, remember — this was the most effective and humane treatment for mental illness to be found in America at that time. While I watched, yet another patient — a woman I recognized from Art, a good sculptor — was wheeled in sound asleep and placed in an unoccupied space beside a table.

Now the reactions were beginning all around the dim room. Soon after their first shot, the patients began to perspire and drool; already, as I watched, the ones who had had the higher doses went into coma and began to toss and moan, their muscles twitching. Some grabbed at the air — hands were shooting up all around the room. Four or five nurses moved among them continuously now, like fish in an aquarium, checking pulse and respiration. Dr. Terhune and an intern monitored them minutely as well; only Dr. Terhune could decide, on an individual basis, how long each coma should last. This decision was the key to the success or failure of the treatment. The coma must be long enough to be effective; yet patients left in coma too long could suffer brain damage or even death. Usually a treatment lasted for several hours before being terminated by a drink of glucose or by a glucose injection.

I was not present long enough to witness the completion of any treatment, of course; for no sooner had the convulsions begun in earnest than Dr. Carroll himself stuck his head in the door, looking a great deal less calm than usual, and strode over to whisper something to one of the nurses, who went to speak to Dr. Terhune immediately. The large door closed.

Realizing that I must make my escape, I waited only a moment or so before opening it myself and slipping out, despite a nurse's cry from behind me as the door shut soundlessly. I was in luck! Dr. Carroll had gone elsewhere.

I don't know what I intended, really, as I ran blindly down the corridor toward, I hoped, freedom — only to collide with Mrs. Fitzgerald as she emerged from one of the rooms at the other end, dressed in regular clothes and carrying a little red leather overnight bag. I imagine that her course of treatment had been completed the day before, and she was then being released. In any case, I hit her head-on, pushing her up against the wall and knocking her bag to the floor where it fell open, spilling its contents at our feet.

"Oh, I'm so sorry!" I gasped.

"Why, Patricia Pie-Face!" she said immediately, her own face appearing puffier though prettier than I recalled, despite a large bruise on her cheekbone. Had she hit it on a guardrail, during a convulsion? She had a new haircut, too; I might not have recognized her. Mrs. Fitzgerald always looked different, and always younger than she was, as if caught back in some perpetual girlhood. It had been ages since I had seen her. And now suddenly here she was, hugging me tight, tight, sobbing into my hair.

"I heard about the salamander boy," she said. "I am so sorry."

I hugged her back.

"There she is. Evalina!" called Dr. Carroll as he came flying through the double doors with Dr. Levy in tow. "Hold on to her, Zelda," he instructed, which was completely unnecessary, for I wasn't going anywhere. I stood still while Mrs. Fitzgerald hugged me, an embrace I recall vividly to this day. Mrs. Fitzgerald felt soft and warm and mommy-ish.

Dr. Carroll halted, panting, a few feet from us.

"Leave her alone, Robert," Mrs. Fitzgerald said to him in a quiet yet commanding voice, oddly intimate. "Just you leave her alone." They were facing each other.

I raised my head to look at him, too. "I will go to Peabody," I said. "I am ready to go now." I bent to retrieve Mrs. Fitzgerald's belongings — her black notebook, her colored pencils that had rolled everyplace, a few toiletries, and a fancy blue silk night-gown. I stuffed them all into her little red case and snapped it shut and handed it to her, and we walked down the hall together. Dr. Carroll shook his head as we went past him.

Back at Homewood, I found Mrs. Carroll and Mrs. Hodges in my room, already putting linens into into my trunk — the same steamer trunk, with stickers all over it, that Mrs. Carroll had taken to Vienna as a student herself. She squealed like a girl now as she stood up to hug me. I still wore the terrycloth robe from the top floor of the Central Building.

"What in the world has happened, then?" Mrs. Hodges asked, hands on her ample hips.

"Dr. C changed his mind, and I did, too. I'm going. I'm ready to go to Peabody."

"Of course you are!" Mrs. Carroll clapped her hands. "I knew you would not fail me, Evalina," she said. "Go, go. Go — you must go, for me. Music is freedom, never forget it." How many times had she repeated these words of "the great Busoni?" Yet she was *not* free, Mrs. Carroll, I realized, her grand career secondary to her famous husband's. Nor was Ella Jean free, even with her own music, even up on her own wild mountaintop. Yet somehow, through nothing I had ever done to deserve it, I was being given this chance. Suddenly the voice of Matilda Bloom came into my mind clear as day, and the words she had said to me at Bellefleur years before: *I know you, honey, and I know you are a smart girl, and you have gots to realize this is the chance of a lifetime here. Your mama would want you to take it. She would want you to grab that brass ring that she never got aholt of herself.*

I hugged them both, hard. "I'll write to you," I promised. "I'll send postcards for your collection."

Intermezzo

*The Peabody Institute of the Johns
Hopkins University, Founded 1857*
Sept. 10, 1940

Dear Mrs. Carroll,
  As you see, this Institute is huge, like a
grand monument! But inside all is lively,
a beehive of music. I had no idea. This
is a world. Thank you, thank you.
>   Love from your overwhelmed
>   yet happy student,
>   Evalina

The Peabody Library
Sept. 12, 1940

Dear Mrs. Carroll,
  This where I do my work study, for
the Scholarship. They call it the "Cathedral of Books," you can see why, with its
wrought-iron stacks soaring many floors

up to the skylight. It is a place like reading itself.

Your inspired,

Evalina

Seagulls, Chesapeake Bay
Sept. 17, 1940

Dear Mrs. Carroll,
   To answer yr. question in haste, I am
taking Italian, humanities, music theory/
musicology, ensemble arts, and piano of
course. And no, thank you, I do not want
for a thing. And yes, there are concerts,
every day.

Love from yr

Evalina

Baltimore Harbor at Twilight
Sept. 22, 1940

Dear Mrs. Carroll,
   A group of us ate softshell crabs here
in a café hanging right out over the
water, lights everywhere. And guess
what? Mr. and Mrs. Fitzgerald lived in
Baltimore, too, quite near Peabody, in a
house named La Paix. They are VERY

famous here! I had no idea.

> Hello to All from your
> Evalina

Fort McHenry, Baltimore, Md.
Oct. 15, 1940

Dear Mrs. Carroll,

No everything is fine, I have just been so busy, that's all. To answer yr question, my roommate is Susanah Knox (oboe) from Ohio. She is very serious. Today it is raining and I miss you, and Mrs. Hodges, and the mountains, and all.

> From Evalina

P.S. It is very intense here.

The Capitol, Washington, D.C.
Oct. 18, 1940

Dear Mrs. Carroll,

I am sight-seeing! We came on the bus, we are having a picnic on the mall, ducks are swimming in the big pool. All this grass reminds me of Highland, say hi to Mrs. Hodges and Dr. C for me, and all.

> Your Evalina

Mount Vernon
Oct. 27, 1940

Dear Mrs. Carroll,
   I went on a weekend visit with my friend Barbara Scott (clarinet) to Orange, Va., out in the countryside. Their house is very old. We rode horses! And gave a little concert in the parlor together for all her family and all the neighbors, like at Homewood.

Love from yr
Evalina

The Peabody Conservatory Choir
Nov. 1, 1940

Dear Mrs. Carroll,
   There are more crazy people here than HH! And Susannah Knox has had a nervous breakdown and gone back to Ohio. I hope I do not have to have another roommate. I stayed up all night reading Neitzsche for humanities, now I may have a nervous breakdown myself!

Yr Evalina

A "Mess" of Maryland Blue Crabs
Nov. 21, 1940

Dear Mrs. Carroll,
I have a new job playing piano for Mrs. Hretzsky's private vocal lessons. Also Barbara and I are in a quartet together in Ensemble Arts, my favorite course so far. I love it. Also Italian, I am getting the hang of it now!

Ciao from yr
Evalina

Joyeux Noel
Dec. 15, 1940

Dear Mrs. Carroll,
Please don't worry. Of course I understand that it would be too expensive for me to travel back and forth for every holiday. In fact we have many international students who will be staying here for Christmas, too. I have sent a box, I hope it arrives before you leave for Italy. Please understand that I am forever yr grateful

Evalina

Snow Scene, Virginia Skyline Drive
Dec. 28, 1940

Dear Mrs. Carroll,
Actually Christmas was very jolly. Dr. Twomey took us all out to his house, a huge barn filled with children and pets and his beautiful wife (cello) plus a whole roasted pig with an apple in its mouth! Music and singing far into the night. There is a boy here from Sweden, we have gone to the cinema and several concerts during this holiday. He is a tenor.

Happy New Year from yr
Evalina

Ludvig van Beethoven 1770–1827
Jan. 6, 1941

Dear Mrs. Carroll,
Surely not ALL tenors are homosexual! And I AM working hard, believe me! This term it will be more Italian, piano, ensemble arts, early music, and vocal accompanying, which is very helpful since I have also been hired to play for the Peabody Children's Chorus at practice sessions, I am very excited

about this!

> Yr very busy,
> Evalina

Frederic Chopin 1810–1849
Jan. 16, 1941

Dear Mrs. Carroll,
I am surprised by your note, though I do see what you mean, and yes, piano remains my focus of course, though I am not brilliant, Mrs. Carroll, not like these others. I know that now. We have prodigies here. I shall work very hard, however, and hope I shall not disappoint you. Be assured that I remain

> Yr diligent,
> Evalina

The Norwegian Lady
June 14, 1941

Dear Mrs. Carroll,
This Norwegian Lady looks out over the boardwalk of Virginia Beach where I am thoroughly enjoying my summer job playing for Mrs. Ruth Gardiner, a vocal teacher, and for the quaint Seaside Church upon occasion. Barbara's job

with the Starlight Dinner Theater is much more glamorous. Our boarding house is filled with such characters!

Yr Working Girl,
Evalina

The Historic Cavalier Hotel, Virginia Beach, Va.
Aug. 5, 1941

Dear Mrs. Carroll,

Guess what? Mr. and Mrs. Fitzgerald came HERE, too! Along with many others such as Will Rogers, Mary Pickford, and Betty Grable. It makes me think of the Grove Park and Mrs. Fitzgerald and I wonder how she is now, and all. How are YOU? Right now Highland seems very far away from this hot sandy beach. Please write to me,

Yr Evalina

The Maryland Zoo, Baltimore, Md.
Sept. 18, 1941

Dear Mrs. Carroll,

It is français, français, et plus de français this term! I am taking French language and diction/voice and also opera accompaniment. I love Massenet, do you? especially "Manon."

Au revoir,
Evalina

"Autumn Leaves"
Oct. 2, 1941

Dear Mrs. Carroll,
  Now I have learned the most important skill of the accompanist — learning
to breathe with the singer! That means
playing on the vowels and breathing with
the singer's every breath, in and out,
Mme. LeBlanc calls this the "shared
intimacy of breath and being," isn't that
beautiful?

Yr thrilled,
Evalina

The Training Choir
Nov. 11, 1941

Dear Mrs. Carroll,
  Here is my darling Children's Chorus
and there is my favorite, little Alex
Chadbourne, 4th from the left in the
third row. His hair is flaming red and his
eyes are robin's egg blue though you
cannot tell that of course from the

photograph. He has a hard little life but a heavenly voice, like an angel.

Yr Evalina

Wolfgang Amadeus Mozart, 1756–1791
April 18, 1942

Dear Mrs. Carroll,
After much soul-searching and many conversations with my teachers here, I have chosen ensemble arts/vocal accompanying and music education as my primary fields, for after all I must earn a living, must I not? And I am proud to do so, and eternally grateful to you and Dr. Carroll for this miraculous (for so it still seems to me) opportunity.

Yr ever grateful,
Evalina

"More Than I Can Say"
Aug. 27, 1942

Dear Mrs. Carroll,
Thank you and Dr. Carroll very much for the lovely visit back to North Carolina, it meant so much to me to be among my beloved mountains again and to see all of you, though now I wonder if I have done anything to offend you,

perhaps? If so I assure you that it was entirely unintentional as I esteem and appreciate you and Dr. Carroll above all others in the world, and so, IF so, forgive me.

Mi dispiace,
Yr Evalina

Franz Peter Schubert 1797–1828
Nov. 8, 1942

Dear Mrs. Carroll,
I have hesitated for weeks to pen this note, yet must now inform you that I have not been chosen for a solo piano recital as my senior performance, instead I shall accompany soprano Lillian Field, the star of our class, in a program to be presented Feb. 10th at 7 o'clock in the Great Hall. This is an honor. A proper invitation to follow. I hope so much that you and Dr. C can come!

Yr Evalina

"Thank You"
Feb 11, 1943

Dear Mrs. Carroll and Dr. Carroll,
Finally, a proper letter to thank you for the graduated pearls, they are just

beautiful. I wore them at the performance with my new black taffeta dress, a gift from Barbara's family. I was so surprised to look out at the audience and see Mrs. Hodges, Moira, Ruthie, and Miss Tippen along with her nice new husband, all sitting there. Oh, how I wish you could have come too! I still can't believe that Lillian Field asked me to play for her, she was just brilliant! She chose a really hard Richard Strauss program, which included my absolute favorite song in the world, "Morgen!," Op. 27, No. 4. Do you know it? The words go something like

> In the morning the sun will shine
>   again
> As we walk the happy path together
> Across the sun-breathing earth.
> And all around us will sing
> The muted silence of happiness

And I want you to know that I am happy, Mrs. Carroll and Dr. Carroll, and I am proud to say that I played well, all thanks to you.

Soon to be yr graduate,
Evalina

Wild Ponies, Assateague Island
October 16, 1943

Dear Mrs. Carroll,
 I disagree with you! I love my work here at Peabody, both with the little chorus and with Mrs. Hretsky's singers, and also the living quarters where I now reside as dormitory counselor, a privilege, I assure you! I am proud to be yr working girl,

Evalina

Felix Mendelssohn
1756–1791
Jan. 21, 1944

Dear Mrs. Carroll,
 Perhaps you will feel better to learn that at a recent recital I was asked to fill in for Jules Brunhoff who had fallen ill at the last possible moment (!) accompanying Joseph Nero, a visiting Fellow, he is *very* Italian, all swagger and flash, as if straight from Rome. He received a standing ovation, and I believe I performed creditably.

Evalina

The Eastern Shore
Mar. 6, 1944

Dear Mrs. Carroll,
   Don't worry, nothing is wrong. Joseph Nero has selected me as his personal accompanist and assistant — so, along with my other duties, I am yr VERY busy,

                                    Evalina

Lyric Opera House, Baltimore, Md.
June 2, 1944

My dear Mrs. Carroll,
   Au contraire I have left Peabody in order to establish my own career and accompany my fiancé Joseph Nero who has recently joined the Baltimore Opera at the urging of Rosa Ponselle herself. Perhaps you have heard of her.

                              Best wishes,
                                    Evalina

Carmen, Georges Bizet
June 18, 1944

Dear Mrs. Carroll,
   In answer to yr question, Joseph spent his childhood in Italy, coming to

180

America at age 9 with his family. He was trained in Philadelphia at the Academy of Vocal Arts founded by Helen Corning Warden. His mentor is Edgar Milton Cook, perhaps you have heard of him.

Best Wishes,
Evalina Toussaint

Harbor Lights, Baltimore
Aug. 23, 1944

Dear Mrs. Carroll,

While Joseph and I do appreciate yr kind invitation, we cannot plan a visit to Asheville at present as we shall be relocating to San Francisco immediately. The San Francisco Opera has made Joseph an offer he cannot refuse. So we are heading West! I hope it pleases you to imagine yr old steamer trunk embarking upon such a journey.

Au revoir,
Evalina

Fisherman's Wharf, San Francisco
Sept. 30, 1944

Dear Mrs. Carroll,

For your information, we are certainly

engaged to be married! Joseph presented me with a beautiful diamond and emerald engagement ring just after his debut performance as Pollione in Bellini's "Norma," do you know it? And I continue to work simply because I enjoy it.

Our best wishes,
Evalina

Église Saint-Eustache, c. 1637, Place du Jour, Paris
Sept. 10, 1945

Dear Mrs. Carroll,
   Our new address is 5 rue Coquilliere in Les Halles, the marketplace. It is very colorful, quite near the Cathedral of St. Eustache, with its great organ. Have you heard of it?

Evalina

The Statue of Liberty, New York City
June 9, 1946

Dear Mrs. Carroll,
   As you see, we are stateside now as Joseph has joined Fortune Gallo's San Carlo Touring Company with recent roles in "Tosca" and "Pagliacci" — plus his Tristan, of course. I find myself

thinking of you; I hope that you and Dr.
C are well.

Evalina

Hotel des Fleurs, Vieux Carre
Aug. 11, 1946

Dear Mrs. Carroll,
Look! Fortune Gallo has deposited us
in New Orleans of all places, with perfor-
mances at the Municipal Theater and an
actual address: Hotel des Fleurs (above).
How I should love to hear from you.

Evalina

CHAPTER 5

Or to hear from *anyone,* actually, since by
that time even I could no longer pretend
that Joey loved me — or, that is, that he
loved *only* me, for he had grown so large in
his appetites that he was becoming legend-
ary even among his peers. And New Orleans
is a feast for the senses, of course. With the
temptations of the street added to an ever-
increasing intake of alcohol, Joey lost all
vestige of scruples and caution. Even his
beloved work suffered. Mr. Herbert issued a
warning, then a strong rebuke.

Often alone, I found myself thinking back
to that fateful night at Peabody when it all
began, for Joey, whom I had yet to meet,
was sitting in the dark audience when I accompanied Lillian Field in our senior
recital. Lillian went on from there to sing
with several of the leading orchestras in the
United States before being struck and killed
by a taxicab outside Severance Hall in

Cleveland only two years later, when she was engaged to be married. The knowledge of this tragedy has always underscored my memory of our Strauss duet that evening, for it has a size to it, a sense of true performance, of grandeur even, from the dark wintry night outside to the gleaming chandeliers and mirrors within the hall. Wearing my new black dress and pearls, I scarcely recognized the girl I glimpsed in one of those gilded frames. Barbara had helped me fasten my hair up high on my head in that little knot that is traditional among accompanists. My neck looked somehow disturbing to me, so private, so long and so white as it rose from my low-cut neckline.

"You were like a little swan," Joey told me later, "gliding across dark water."

Dark water indeed. Yet we did not meet until the evening when I filled in for Jules Brunhoff and accompanied Joey for that first amazing time. He was still surrounded by admirers when I slipped out unobtrusively, as was my wont, and headed across the cold dark campus with its antique lampposts bearing frosted globes, which shone at intervals along the sidewalk. Halfway to my dormitory I heard "Miss! Miss!" behind me and turned to see Joseph Nero himself rushing out of the darkness like a great black bird, long coat flapping out behind him, carrying a sheaf of music foolishly exposed to the elements. His gait was both impetuous and halting.

"Miss!"

I paused in a pool of light beneath one of the lamps, and waited for him.

It had just begun to snow; a few snowflakes were already glistening on his unruly cap of dark curls. He caught up to me then paused, hand on lamppost, like a figure from a melodrama — a big, hefty young man well over six feel tall, looming out of the elements, out of the very night, breathing hard. He reminded me of a bull, the bull in the Europa myth, perhaps. His breath made white plumes in the air.

"Why did you run away?" he asked — to my great surprise, for why would I have stayed? "I wished to thank you," he continued, with a funny, almost archaic little bow. "So, thank you!"

This was so awkward as to be charming; I burst out laughing.

He laughed, too. "How can I find you again?" he asked. "For I will need you, I know. Please write it down for me how to find you, though I will lose it, and you will have to write it down many times more. As for me, it is easy, just ask them . . . ask that terrible woman, she will know." Miss Turnbull was the administrative secretary in the opera division.

I smiled as I scribbled the information down on the little pad I always kept with me. "I am easy to find, too," I said, "for I live at Peabody itself, in the dormitory, where I am a counselor for the girls."

"Oh dear God!" He seemed to consider this situation intolerable, snorting out a cloud of frosty air. He jammed my scribbled note deep into his coat pocket, where I assumed it would stay forever. But "I shall need you," he continued. "Peabody is a waystation for me, a distraction, yet a credential, do you see? In the meantime I must practice, do you understand? Can you do this? Are you available? I will need you."

The words I could not refuse. "Oh yes," I said, immediately reconsidering my crowded schedule.

Thus it began, in a circle of light in the chilly, dark Baltimore night, as the snowflakes began to drop silently, now in earnest, all around us. Joey stood completely still, looking at me. His was the perfect face for opera: the great dark liquid eyes, the bristling black brow, the strong cheekbones and sad, mobile mouth. He appeared to embody sadness, loss, and tragedy, an emptiness that could never be filled, a pain that could not be assuaged. Without another word, he turned and lurched off into the falling snow. Later I would learn that his left foot had been crushed by a streetcar in early childhood, an injury which kept him out of the War.

Waking in my narrow bed the next morning, I felt that I had dreamed the entire encounter, conjured him up "out of whole cloth," as Mrs. Hodges used to say. I was distracted all day long, smiling a goofy smile that I was unable to wipe off my face.

Then, nothing. Ten days passed. Eventually, I plunged back into my work, chiding myself for my silliness.

Until that Sunday evening when the dreadful Miss Turnbull herself came pounding upon my door at 9 p.m., wearing red galoshes. "Can you come along then, Evalina?" she asked abruptly. "He is asking for you."

"Yes," I closed my book. "Of course."

Soon I was indispensable to him, my duties rapidly expanding beyond the piano to errands, laundry, shopping, and even housekeeping. I could have walked with my eyes closed to his third-floor flat in an old brownstone rowhouse several blocks from

Peabody. For such a rundown edifice, it boasted a surprisingly ornate stoop and entry — beautiful rose marble steps that appeared to change color depending upon the time of day, or the weather — they seemed entirely magical to me, an entry into another world.

I did not bat an eye the first time I encountered a disheveled woman coming down the narrow stairs as I climbed up to Joey's apartment. She murmured an apology as I stood aside, with lowered gaze, to let her pass. Another time I slipped upon some tiny silk panties as I entered the apartment carrying groceries, and once I found "PIG! PIG!" scrawled in scarlet lipstick across the mirror in his bathroom.

All this seemed quite natural to me, for Joey drew women the way honey draws flies, through no will of his own it seemed, moving through the world like another order of being, one of the gods and goddesses of mythology who were not bound by earthly laws. I also realized that this was ridiculous, such power held by a big, undisciplined immigrant street kid from Philadelphia whose father was an Italian butcher.

Of course my own work suffered — I who had been appreciated and rewarded for my reliability now drew looks askance, raised eyebrows, as I arrived late for certain responsibilities and refused other requests. Such a good girl all my life, I felt my own identity crumbling, yet I did not care.

May arrived, the most beautiful springtime I had ever seen — or perhaps I was only noticing it, in the heightened sense of awareness that had come to me with Joey. One day I traveled down to Richmond for a noontime concert with my beloved choir, leaving in the predawn darkness and returning at dusk with our bus full of children . . . then waiting even longer for several tardy parents to pick up their exhausted little singers. I sat playing XO's and Hangman with them until their parents finally came.

Though I had been absent from my post in the dormitory all day — and was exhausted, to boot — I felt that I must, *must* go by Joey's apartment before returning to my room. I can't even remember what my pretext was. Soon I was running up the rosy steps. I turned my key in the lock. "Hello?" I called. "Hello?" At first, stumbling through clothes and books strewn across the floor, I thought he wasn't there.

Then, "Who is it? I am outside, just here —" His booming voice echoed through the little rooms, and there he was, out on the fire escape amid the flowering trees, shirtless, suspenders dangling over his striped trousers, waving a big bottle of red wine. "Evalina!" He sounded delighted, as always. He held up a wineglass full. "Join me!"

I scurried to do so, first rinsing out another wineglass in the kitchen. My tiredness vanished the moment I stepped through the bedroom window onto the narrow iron fire escape. I was taken aback by his closeness and by the mat of curly black hair on his wide chest. For a moment I thought to run. Yet I held out my glass.

He filled it, then raised it aloft. "To Evalina!" he cried out. "My little swan!"

No one had ever toasted me before.

I had to sit one step above him on the narrow iron fire escape, which was nothing more than a ladder, really. The setting sun shone through the flowering dogwoods all around us; streetcars clanged somewhere below; and the silly tune from an ice cream wagon came wafting up to us on the little breeze that lifted my wispy hair. "Have some more, my Evalina," Joey entreated, and I did, and yet another glass.

As dusk came, everything took on a heightened, mysterious intensity. Now streetlights shone through the trees. And it was *I* — I, Evalina! — who leaned down in the darkening shadows to kiss his neck, thick and salty, to touch the hair that grew in clumps upon his shoulders, to receive his waiting kiss, which was everything I had somehow known it would be. He picked me up like a rag doll, and lifted me back inside.

I woke before Joey, lying with him in silence while the first faint light of dawn crept through the open window into the bedroom, breathing with him, in and out, in and out, as he lay curled around me, sleeping like a child. Reluctantly I rose, then hurried through the still-dark streets hoping to make an inconspicuous return to the dormitory.

I arrived instead to find a scene of horror in the early morning light: all traffic blocked from entering our cul-de-sac by uniformed policemen; the blinking red lights of an ambulance and two police cars drawn up before the building; several staff members and many students milling about on the sidewalk, most of them still in their pajamas or gowns and robes. The ambulance pulled out just as I reached the group. One of the police cars followed, siren shrieking.

"Now, now girls, not to worry, she will be all right," screeched old Miss Barnstable, the counselor from upstairs, still wearing her ugly black hairnet. Several of my girls were hugging each other and crying. They looked at me curiously. I could not even imagine how I must have appeared to them at that moment, considering the night I had spent. Surely, all could tell!

Dr. Humboldt, dean of students, turned to me as well, dark circles under his sad, bespectacled eyes. "Miss Toussaint," he said, "at last."

We shepherded the girls back inside, past my own locked door with its several missives still taped or tacked to it: some of them sealed, with my name written on the front of the envelopes, then one sheet of paper that read simply in bold print MISS TOUSSAINT WHERE ARE YOU? MARY STILL WON'T MOVE WE DON'T KNOW WHAT TO DO PLEASE COME, SUSAN ROYSTER

After leaving Baltimore, Joey and I traveled constantly (San Francisco, Vancouver, Toronto, Montreal). Wherever we were, I found jobs in churches or schools, gave lessons, or worked in music libraries or stores. Though Joey's career flourished, his habits and tastes grew ever more expensive — silk shirts, restaurant meals, fine wines, late hours, and taxicabs. Usually I had been asleep for hours when he came in. And yet I was always thrilled to wake and find him there beside me, like a miracle — and glad enough to slip out to the early morning bus or metro while he slumbered on, rosy mouth open, breathing in and out, in and out, lying hugely across the bed in whatever rented rooms in whatever city we inhabited at the time, sprawled out on his back like a great broken statue or a giant angel fallen to earth. Of course I had no ring!

How happy we were in Paris in those heady days following the end of the War — hugely happy — and here it was that Joey first sang Tristan, the role that would make him famous. O, the Rue Coquillière! Soupe à l'oignon at midnight in the Pied de Cochon just down the street from us, always open for the delivery men who arrived in their clanging trucks filled with all manner of fresh foodstuffs for the stalls, which did a bustling business all night long. Frequently we walked to our building through running blood from the butcher's on the corner, crowded with its hanging slabs of beef, whole lambs, and pigs. Everybody spoke to us; everybody knew Joey. Sometimes, too keyed up after a performance to sleep, he'd drink at the bar of the Pied de Cochon until dawn, finishing up with dozens of oysters (huîtres de Bretagne) and champagne, paid for by somebody else. Joey and I had a private reference to the "great organ" of

Saint-Eustache, and I remember how he stood behind me pushing his erection against my coat at mass in the vast, chilly cathedral with the glorious deafening music booming from every side, filling the nave with exaltation as I swooned with desire.

But here our troubles began as well, when Madame du Maynadier, our landlady, suddenly evicted us, claiming that she had not received our rent payment for four months, though Joey swore that he had paid her . . . but in cash, so it could not be proved. There was a horrible scene, and a rage, and a broken lamp, followed by our sudden surreptitious move to a smaller set of rooms in the rue Gay Lussac, near the Luxembourg Gardens.

The pattern was established long before our move to New Orleans. Incidents occurred, which I was not to know about, so I did not know about them, concentrating instead upon every moment I had to spend with Joey, for he was still mine then, though not all mine, I suppose . . . but I did not care. I would take what I could get.

Thus arrived the day that I left work early, feeling slightly ill, and opened the door to our rooms in the Hotel des Fleurs to find him in bed with twin chorines, the Fabulous

Fouche Sisters, who beamed at me identically above their round, pink breasts. Joey did have the grace to pull up the covers, though he elected to brazen it out, speaking to his companions instead of me: "Allow me to introduce my little swan, my Evalina."

This was entirely the wrong thing to say, as suddenly I saw myself for the creature I truly was: Joey's pet, his servant, and nothing more. Surely my face must have changed in that instant, yet he took no notice, blundering on, with a grand sweep of the hand. "Come Evalina, and join us —" As if it were a tea party! I really don't know what he intended by this remark, for I turned and fled, returning only when I knew that Joey would be at the Opera.

I found the bed made — clumsily — and a long-stemmed red rose laid across the pillow — *my* pillow! Along with a note which read "Rember Morgen" in his almost illegible hand, for Joey was virtually illiterate as well as intemperate.

Of course I stayed. What else could I do? By this time, I was nearly three months pregnant, according to my own calculations, though I could not, simply could *not* bring myself to tell him. And Joey mended his ways somewhat, or at least exercised greater discretion. He was tender and solicitous, even taking me on several outings. We went out on a riverboat for lunch one Sunday, as Mama and I had done years before with Mr. Graves, and I remembered every detail of the outfit she had worn on that day: the pink-and-white-striped dress, the straw hat, the white sandals. I remembered how she laughed when the flame on our bananas Foster would not go out. Joey and I also went to the Audubon Zoo, where he was fascinated by the big cats, the lions and tigers. Remarkably, he had never been to a zoo before. I put on my black dress and went to the opening of *Siegfried* to hear him in the title role; he was magnificent. The Fabulous Fouche Sisters did not reappear, nor any other woman.

Instead, much of Joey's free time was taken up by a young man named Hubert Huffman, the new music critic at *The Times-Picayune* who had raved about Joey's *Siegfried.* It was suddenly "Hubert this" and "Hubert that." Hubert had been raised in San Francisco and educated at Harvard before beginning his career at *The Boston Globe.* Now Joey was bent upon introducing him to New Orleans. When I finally met Hubert, I liked him, too, a thin, blond boy with spectacles and a wide open smile and beautiful manners. He grabbed up my two hands and pressed them, saying, "Ah yes, Evalina. Joseph has told me so much about you" — a lie, I knew, for what was there to tell? Joey did not know my past, nor the link I had with this city.

During those days, I often found myself sitting at the window, gazing out upon the busy square at the beautiful fountain and the clanging streetcars or a group of nuns like a flight of birds hurrying across the street. I thought of my mother, who must have looked out such a window herself when she was pregnant with me — perhaps the GIRLS GIRLS GIRLS window in our old apartment above the Bijou on the rue Dauphine, or perhaps another, earlier window, or even a screen door, down in the bayou country. What did she see? What did she hope for, or dream of? Was she dreaming me?

We had supper with Hubert Hoffman, just the three of us, at the Court of Two Sisters, beneath a giant banyan tree in the leafy courtyard. I was wearing a black lace stole Joey had bought me in Paris. I ate every bite of my delicious crab étouffée, then my crème brûlée. The men drank Armagnac with their coffee. By candlelight their faces were beautiful, one so dark and one so light, as they spoke passionately about opera.

Suddenly I knew they would soon be lovers. I remembered what Mrs. Carroll had said about tenors so long ago. After Hubert bid us adieu outside the restaurant, Joey and I walked hand in hand back to our hotel, where he made love to me.

The next morning I lay watching him sleep for a long time, watching him breathe, and when he finally awakened, I gave him his café au lait and croissant and told him about the baby. What was I thinking? What did I expect? I can no longer remember. What I got was an explosion of operatic proportion.

"Evalina!" He hurled the little china plate against the wall, where it shattered. "What have you done? How can you do this to me? To *me*? It is not possible, not possible. I will not have a child, not at this point in my career, not never. *Never!* You hear me? You hear me, *mi senti*?" He called me *puttana, stupida*. He grabbed my shoulders and shook me like a ragdoll, until I feared my neck would snap, my teeth would be broken. "How dare you? You who are nothing, nothing, to myself. Do you hear me? Nothing!"

Finally he let me go, throwing me back against the bed, where I lay in terror, heart beating like a drum in my ears. Joey stood at the window with arms outstretched, as if in monumental prayer. *"Tesora,"* he said. At length he turned and came back to me; he sat on the edge of the bed where I lay very still, too frightened and exhausted to move even though I had bitten my lip badly. Blood soaked the pillow and matted my hair. *"Mi dispiace, cara."* Joey got up and went to the sink where he ran water on a towel and then came back with it to kneel, now, beside the bed, wiping the blood off my face gently, even stroking my hair. "Little swan," he whispered. "You were with me at the beginning, you were here always. I will never forget."

Then he stood up abruptly, or as abruptly as his lame foot and considerable bulk would allow. He placed his hands on his hips, a magisterial pose, then clapped them, surprising me. "Enough!" he decreed. "This little problem will be taken care of immediately. I go now, and I will find a way. You will stay here. When I come back I will tell you, and you will do it. You will do what I say to you. Then it will be over. The end. *Fine.*"

I closed my eyes.

The door slammed.

Quickly I rose and gathered all the belongings I thought I could carry, stuffing them into an old satchel, and left the apartment, looking carefully left and right before darting to a taxi. I ordered him to drive me out to Arabi, where I easily found a room in a boardinghouse named Temps Perdu, a peeling old mansion near the river, surrounded by magnolias and inhabited mostly by circus and carnival performers who were odd and kind, ever more solicitous as my condition became apparent to all. My baby would be a girl, announced Madame Romanetsky, a fortune-teller. I determined to take *such* good care of her!

I was fortunate to find a little job playing piano at the ancient church school around the corner, for chorus and assemblies and music classes; to my surprise, I found myself playing with my old light touch again, though it had been over a year since I had sat down at a piano. I moved freely about the new neighborhood, never once concerned that Joey would find me. I knew he would never try. As far as he was concerned, I was dead, and my baby with me. In fact I felt lucky to be alive, and as the gorgeous autumn progressed I grew more and more excited, vaguely planning to have her at the charity hospital over by the park. I would just appear at the emergency entrance, I thought, when it was time. My neighbors began to bring me things — a special healthy soup, with cabbage in it, from the Hungarian tumblers upstairs; a pink blanket, soft as angels' wings, from the dwarf lady, who had knitted it herself.

One day, coming back from work, I chanced to notice a poster affixed to the kiosk on the corner — LONG JOHN LIGHTNING, it read, the KING OF THE BLUES, soon to appear at a club named Snug Harbor. I kept looking at the keen narrow face, the big white grin, the bright eyes . . . surely this was Mojo, the boy who'd played piano at the Bijou, all grown up!

On the appointed night, I stood waiting in the alley outside the club, and when he emerged from a taxi, nearly seven feet of him, I stepped forward and touched his arm. "Mojo?" I said.

He was still a beanpole, though now resplendent in a shiny purple suit, with high, pomaded hair. "What you say?" He looked down at me.

"I am Evalina Toussaint," I said. "My mother was Louise Toussaint, the dancer."

"Oh my lord, honey!" he said instantly, throwing off his girlfriend's protective grasp as he bent down, limber as a pipe cleaner, to peer at my face.

"Do you remember us? over the Bijou?" I

asked with my heart in my throat.

"Remember you? Remember you? I sure do, honey, I sure do remember you. In fact many is the time I have sat up late wondering about you, and where you ever got to, and what happen to you. Your mama — your mama — well, I know she have passed on now, to her reward. But I want to say to you, child, you had the sweetest mama on this earth, I hope you know that. And fun? And beautiful? My gracious. Why, folkses use to come from all over . . ."

But now two men from the club were pulling him away from me, gently but inexorably, one on either side.

"What I remember the best, though, is how crazy your mama was about *you,* Evalina, why, you never saw nothing like it. Seem like the sun rose and set on Evalina! And you used to play some piano yourself, am I right? Lord Lord. What are you doing here, girl? I tell you what, these folks is going to give you a real good seat for the show, and then we will talk afterward, you and me. What you doing, little Evalina? What is your story?"

The iron door closed, leaving his gorgeous girlfriend to glare at me once, dismissively, before stomping up the alleyway toward the front entrance. Though a man darted back out immediately with a ticket for me, I did not stay, slipping back to Temps Perdu instead, to sit rocking in the chair that the landlord had recently brought for me, clutching the Snug Harbor ticket against my stomach and thinking about my mother, who had loved me. No matter what else had happened to us, she had loved me; this was all that mattered.

Yet the more I thought about her, the more curious I grew, for my own baby was coming soon. What could I tell her about her grandmother, or myself, or the people we had come from? Was it possible that we even had some *family,* somewhere? I determined to visit Mr. Graves's Bellefleur.

Though most places in New Orleans had seemed smaller to me upon my return — since I had been but a child when I left — Bellefleur appeared grander than ever, almost invisible now behind its high pink stucco wall, beneath its immense canopy of live oaks a century old. To my surprise, the side gate was unlocked. I lifted the latch and walked quickly up to the massive door flanked by potted ferns and twelve white columns. I rang, then waited. No one seemed to be about. Dry leaves rattled across the portico. I rang again. Ten years had passed since I left there, yet it could have been a hundred — or only a fortnight — for Bellefleur seemed timeless, captured beneath a bell jar.

Alicia herself opened the door. She, too, appeared unchanged in all essentials — thin, but not elegant — rather more like a bird of prey now, her makeup too heavy, her avid mouth a slash of red. She was dressed in a black suit I recognized as French, with large (too large) pearl earrings and choker.

I started to speak, but she interrupted me immediately, holding up her red-nailed hand as if to ward me off.

"Never come in this house again!" She all but shrieked. "I know exactly who you are!" She stepped backward as if in fright, one hand fluttering up to the pearls. "You are that crazy girl, the whore's daughter — Oh, what was your name?"

"Evalina Toussaint," I said.

"It may please you to know, Evalina Toussaint, that you ruined my family, you and your mother, that horrid slut. Ruined us! My father was never the same again after his . . . breakdown. He hanged himself the next Christmas, on Christmas Day. How's that? Merry Christmas to the family. Love, Dad. Of course he was insane."

205

"I am so sorry," I whispered, for I had loved Arthur Graves, too, as much as circumstances had allowed.

I was further unnerved by the appearance of Matilda Bloom, who moved silently, slowly, to stand in the shadowy hall just behind Alicia. White-haired and very heavy now, she did not smile or acknowledge me in any way, her face a dark mask, her black eyes filled with something deeper and harder and more sorrowful than I could bear.

Alicia went on. "We can do without your condolences, Evalina Toussaint. But I want you to know, it has been a disaster. The business gone, my brothers haywire, a rogues' gallery of failures and fools — luckily I have been able to stay here and take care of poor Mother who has never been the same again either, as you might imagine, though we pretend. Oh yes, we all pretend —" Suddenly Alicia looked at her diamond wristwatch. "Actually Mother is out having lunch at Commander's Palace right now," she announced, "and you shall not be here when she returns."

Alicia looked me over more closely now, her eyes narrowed to slits as she took in my gray wool cape and pretty boots, French, too, and my pregnancy.

"Ah," she said. "I suppose you want money. Well, you won't get it from me. In fact, I'd like to get back just half of what my father paid to get rid of you — but that's long gone, I suspect. And now look at you, just like your mother! I'd hope you'd have more sense, that you'd have thought of the child, at least. How can you do this to another child? But I suppose you people just can't restrain yourselves, can you?"

Turning to leave, I had to ask: "What do you mean, about the child?" pulling my cape close about us.

"Why, it will be a monster, won't it? Just like you, Evalina — the child of your mother and her own father, don't you know that? Don't you know *anything*?"

CHAPTER 6

Thus I found myself in the place I had perhaps been heading all along, the top floor of the Central Building of Highland Hospital, being administered a course of insulin shock treatments, which I did not resist. How could I? for during that time, I was nobody — a husk of a person, the shape and shell of a person, the skin of a salamander girl — all emptied out. Nobody home. Shock treatments do that, they rob you of your immediate memory, and in my case, this was a blessing.

I knew Dr. Carroll immediately, though now I am not certain how long I had been back in the hospital when he arrived; perhaps it was hours, perhaps days. I was in a little cubicle of a room, coming out of a treatment, when I heard the deep, familiar voice rolling in from a great distance somewhere above me, like thunder.

"Evalina, Evalina, can you hear me?"

I fought to open my eyes, which seemed to be glued together, and tried to raise my hand, but this I could not accomplish either, even though the restraints had been removed.

"Evalina, this is Dr. Carroll."

I know it, I thought furiously, heart pounding. *I know you* — with a curious mixture of dread and relief as I struggled to come back to myself. I tried but could not control the muscles of my mouth.

He laid his hand, dry as paper, lightly on my forehead.

"Now, now," Dr. Carroll said. "Your job here is to relax, Evalina. To rest. You may leave everything else to us. You have been very ill, but you are safe now. You are here, you are home." His voice came down to me through shifting layers of fog. "We do not intend to let you go again. We do not intend to lose you." Threat or promise, the words sank in.

Suddenly my eyes popped open and there he was above me, blocking the light, his head a dark shape I would have recognized anywhere — those big ears sticking out! I could not see his face. Was it day or night? I could never tell, in that place. I struggled to gain a slight purchase on one elbow and tried to speak to him, but only horrible sounds would issue forth from my mouth.

"Never mind." His words floated like clouds above me, out of reach. "Trust me, Evalina. It is better this way."

What way? *What* is better? What did he mean? But I could not speak.

The door closed. I heard steps and voices outside in the hall, then nothing. I lay exhausted in utter darkness and finally slept, to wake much later upon a cold wet sheet, humiliated. Yet somewhat restored — now I could open my eyes, sit up, even get up and stagger to the door to call the night attendant, who came running. She was a strong, bouncy Negro girl who clucked and cajoled and went to work on me immediately: "Why my goodness, look a here at you, poor thing, ain't nobody put you to bed proper nor took you to the toilet neither one. I tell you what, you come along with me now. Just come on —" half carrying me down the hall to the communal bathroom, though it was still pitch black outside the windows.

This girl, whose name was Gloria, ran the big, old-fashioned claw-footed tub in the corner full of hot water and put me in it, then ducked out briefly to reappear with a little blue bottle of Evening in Paris bath salts, which she sprinkled liberally all about me, so that soon I was surrounded by iridescent bubbles up to my chin. "Now just lay back," she commanded, and I did so, each cell of my body letting go. "Ain't that better now?"

It felt wonderful. I had never seen this tub in use before. Usually we were led into the washroom by the nurses, who sometimes had to assist — or force — those in the worst conditions into the showers. Often I had to look away. Now I reveled in the luxury and warmth of my bubble bath, with time to notice the pink and maroon tile rosettes on the floor, repeated on the border running around the pink tile walls, halfway up. Out the barred window, I saw the first light fall upon the autumn foliage outside.

"Where in the world did you get this bubble bath stuff?" I asked Gloria.

"Kress's," she said, "on Patton Avenue, you know?"

I did know, as suddenly Asheville itself came flooding back to me — Pack Square, with the Vance Monument in the center of it, the lunch counter at Woolworth's on Haywood Street where they made the vanilla cokes, the Grove Park Inn up on its mountain, and us up on our own, at the end of Montford Avenue, at Highland Hospital. *Highland Hospital.* I remembered the crenellated roofline of Homewood, the greenhouse gardens behind Brushwood. I knew exactly where I was.

I lay back in my bubbles and swore not to tell as Gloria opened one of the windows and lit an illegal cigarette, blowing smoke out into the rosy dawn. She ran some more hot water into my tub and left me again while she raced over to escort an older woman into one of the toilet stalls, a thin, gray woman bent into the shape of a question mark, who shuffled along looking down all the while and mumbled to herself and did not notice me. By then I would have been glad to get out of the tub, but as my soiled gown had disappeared, thank goodness, and there was not a towel within reach, I resisted the idea of walking naked and dripping down the hall past all those others who were undoubtedly waking up now, too.

So I was still there when a truly frightening woman stomped in. Wild, red-gray hair stuck out in clumps all over her head, huge breasts swung to her waist beneath her hospital-issue gown. She wore big, dirty, untied men's brogans, shoelaces flapping on the white tile floor. Her eyes darted everywhere, fastening upon me. She approached my tub, hands on hips, then began jabbing at the air with a fat, pointing finger.

"Get out! Get out!" she screamed. "Who do you think you are?"

I shrank back, alarmed — for she was *strong,* this woman, I could tell, and suddenly Gloria was nowhere in sight. But then the woman made a disgusting sound with her mouth and rushed out, the open back of the hospital gown exposing her huge red buttocks, such a sight that I couldn't help laughing.

"Good grief!"

For the first time, I noticed the pretty, dark-haired woman about my own age standing before one of the stalls. She was laughing, too, though gingerly, as if it hurt her.

"What are you doing in that tub, anyway?" she asked. "How'd you rate that bubble bath? You'd better get out of there, or we'll have an insurrection."

"I'd love to get out," I said, "if I had a towel. Do you see one anyplace?"

Bath towels were always in short supply, given out carefully by a nurse or attendant when one entered the bathroom for a shower, then taken up again afterward. Apparently they feared that we might somehow hang ourselves with them.

"Oh Lord." Now she was giggling, for all

the world as if this were a dormitory at Peabody instead of the locked floor of a mental institution. Was she a patient, too? This seemed highly unlikely, especially as she wore a pretty two-piece "sleep set," a lavender gown and matching robe sprigged with violets, instead of a hospital gown. "Just a minute." She darted around the maroon and pink tile wall divider into the shower area and came back with a damp bath towel, which she handed me none too soon, as the heavy door opened again. I wrapped myself up in it entirely, easy to do since I was very thin.

"Thanks *so* much," I said.

"It's okay, it was nothing." She had a soft, Southern voice.

Then she smiled and I could see it, what was wrong with her. Beneath the perfect, arched brows, her wide violet eyes were flat and dead. Nobody home there, either.

Her eyes were like the eyes of the fish laid out in rows on ice in the French Market in New Orleans, down by the river, where I went with my mother in the past, some time ago. In the past. My who? My mother, in the past, some time ago. My mind wavered, then stilled.

"What's your name?" she was asking.

"Evalina Toussaint," I said automatically,

though I didn't feel I owned it anymore. I didn't feel connected to it in any way. It could have been something I'd just picked up from the basket of toiletries by the door, like a little green bar of soap.

"What a pretty name," the woman said. "My name is Mary Margaret Stovall." She shook her head as if to clear it. "*No.* Mary Margaret Stovall *Calhoun.* Dixie, for short. My name is Dixie Calhoun."

Then she smiled, and I realized how beautiful she was, really beautiful. Even that morning, in a hospital where she was undergoing a course of shock treatments, Dixie looked like a lingerie model who had just stepped from the pages of a fashion magazine, with her jet-black hair curling naturally all around her heart-shaped face. Perfect skin. Though it wasn't quite adequate, just like mine. Dixie, too, needed a carapace. A what? A *carapace.* This word, straight out of Robert's vocabulary, came into my head from no place. Nowhere. Who knew what else was out there?

"Now girls, really! This is not a gab session." An older attendant, all business, had taken over for Gloria. The new shift — morning in the asylum.

"Bye," Dixie said, with a fluttery little wave of the hand. Instinctively I knew that she had learned that wave from riding on floats, in parades. I could hear a parade in my head, with a Dixieland brass band. A *krewe*. At Mardi Gras. Glancing back toward my claw-foot tub, I saw day stealing in though the bathroom windows — pink clouds in the sky and golden sunshine on the mountaintops, reflected in the iridescent bubbles fast disappearing in the tub. Only a few were left. Now I could smell breakfast — and I was starving.

Gradually, over the next few weeks, the world kept coming back to me in halting, unrelated images or words or even sudden overwhelming feelings for which I had neither name nor cause. The sweet taste of a sugary doughnut in my mouth, for instance; or a vision of white dogwood blossoms all around me as I sat in the open somewhere, in some city; the majestic swell of Bach's Toccata and Fugue in D Minor on a cathedral organ, filling me with exaltation and then shame as I woke in orgasm to find the young lady physician, Dr. Gail Schwartz, patting my arm.

"It's all right, Evalina," she said. "Don't be embarrassed. This is all right — this is normal. You are beginning to recover."

But the next morning I woke up racked

by sobs and could not stop weeping for hours, though I did not know the source of my sorrow. If this was recovery, I wanted no part of it. Why couldn't I just simply *remember*?

"Because the insulin shock treatments cause coma and convulsions, which are scrambling the connections in your brain, Evalina," Dr. Schwartz told me. "This is how they work. Nobody knows exactly *why* they work — and any of these doctors who tell you they do is lying — but they do work. They are working now. You are better. You were sent to us in a virtually catatonic state, the result of severe trauma, injury, illness — who knows? We don't know exactly what happened — we have only a few pieces of your story. Our first task has been to jolt you out of the condition in which we found you. Next, we may be able to help you form new connections and ways of thinking that are not so painful for you, not overwhelming. So don't worry, you will remember when you are ready to remember. The brain is an astonishing organism in which nothing is ever lost. Nothing! Not even you."

I liked Dr. Schwartz's calm, quiet manner, the little gold glasses perched down on the end of her long, thin nose, her tidy bun of dark, frizzy hair, even her practical, let's-get-down-to-business Northern accent. She seemed very young to be a doctor.

"This may take some time, but what else do you have on your calendar right now?" She smiled at me, and I smiled ruefully back, knowing already that this was so; for in the world of the mad, time is not a continuum but a fluid, shifting place, relative to nothing.

"Don't *try* to remember," Dr. Schwartz said. "Concentrate on the day at hand. Just do what we tell you." She flashed me a quick grin, and I imagined being her friend, her chum, in other circumstances.

Dr. Schwartz vanished, carrying her clipboard, to be succeeded by a host of others, each with an agenda. Thus I found myself walking up and down the long halls several times a day with a fresh-faced young man wearing a whistle who said, "How ya doin' now, honey? How ya doin'?" unnervingly, at every lap; making bead necklaces with an art group in the day room; tossing a large red medicine ball about a room in which one woman screamed and dived for the floor whenever the ball came in her direction; and singing "Row, Row, Row Your Boat" lustily in a music therapy group led by Phoebe Dean, who was still on the staff, wider in the hips but just as enthusiastic as ever.

"Why, Evalina!" she cried in her ridiculously cheery way. "I'm so glad to see you. Now let's do it again, everybody, but this time as a round — Evalina, will you lead the second group, please? Here, come on up here to do it."

I stood up and went forward to face the group.

"Okay. Now, let's go!" Phoebe struck her tuning fork to get the key. I led my group lustily in song, remembering every word, to my surprise. Clearly, Phoebe's high expectations of me had a therapeutic value. We did "Dona Nobis Pacem" and "Music Alone Shall Live" in rounds, too, with Phoebe mugging as our groups competed against each other. My friend Dixie, in Phoebe's group, could scarcely sing for laughing.

"Hurry up and get well," Phoebe said to me when the others had left and she was gathering up her songbooks. "I could really use you to play piano for me. My assistant is going on maternity leave the first of the month."

What month? What month was it now, for that matter? I wasn't even sure. But indeed, my fingers had been moving against my skirt as we sang; my fingers still knew every note of the songs.

"I'd like that," I said.

Passing by in the hallway, Dr. Schwartz turned back to wink at me, amused.

Dr. Schwartz was part of the new management that had gradually taken over Highland Hospital since Dr. Carroll had deeded it to Duke in 1939. Evidently this was the reason Dr. Carroll had not come to see me again while I was on the top floor; though still involved with the hospital, he no longer took an active role in patient care. A Dr. Basil T. Bennett was the medical director now. I studied his photograph on the cover of *The Highland Fling,* our weekly newspaper. Clearly, things had changed. I could not imagine this Dr. Bennett, with his cropped hair and upright, military bearing, ever donning tights and doublet, for instance, and acting in a play! The article about him said that since he had come to Highland directly from the army, Dr. Bennett was an expert at dealing with the many men who had suffered mental breakdowns as a result of their war experiences. I had already noted a number of such veterans receiving shock treatments along with me.

Another article in *The Highland Fling* profiled Dr. Billig, who had replaced Dr.

Terhune as the new clinical director of the shock treatment unit in complete charge of the top floor. He had worked with the great Dr. Sakel himself, the physician who had originated this "miraculous" new treatment in Vienna. Dr. Billig dealt directly with us all in a calm, businesslike fashion, asking quiet questions, monitoring us constantly as we went into and out of insulin shock, taking measurements and making notations and calculations in a series of numbered gray notebooks, rather like we were test tubes instead of human beings. Oddly enough, such minute documentation actually produced a comforting effect, for it made our bizarre, grotesque treatments seem scientific — more like common, everyday hospital procedure. Electroshock treatments were conducted on this floor as well, in another locked area, which I had never entered.

And we *were* getting better, many of us. It is a funny thing but you can actually *see* improved mental health in the eyes, the face, the very gait and bearing. Even I could tell. Dixie, several weeks ahead of me, was moved out of our locked ward and onto the floor below, where patients were given more privileges, such as personal items in the rooms, permission to see visitors, and eventually a pass for the rest of the campus or even a trip into town — while finishing up our prescribed number of treatments, of course. We still had to spend one night on the top floor following each session.

But it was heaven when I, too, was finally moved down to the next floor, to find myself in a lemon-yellow room with a lace-curtained window that had no bars — and a view! And even a painting of buttercups in a blue vase. I scarcely recognized myself in the bathroom mirror, the insulin had made me gain so much weight. I knew I had been too thin, *but still* . . . I peered at my round cheeks.

"In the pink, I'd say!" crowed Mrs. Hodges, my first visitor.

First there'd been a commotion out in the hall, as Mrs. Hodges had not signed in properly at the office below. "Oh bother!" Her accent was unmistakable. "Oh, rubbish!"

I stuck my head out the door to watch in delight as she padded her way past two of the younger aides, swatting them aside like flies. Mrs. Hodges, too, had grown much larger in the intervening years. With the addition of a mammoth purple coat, she filled the whole corridor, wall to wall. But of course she was carrying several large, bulky bags as well.

"There you are, God love you!" she exclaimed, dropping everything to surround me in a stifling hug. "My little Evalina, all grown up, but whatever did they do to you, child? And what's become of your hair?" She made that familiar tsk-tsking sound as she took my face in her hands, turning my head side to side for a proper examination.

"But you're recovering nicely all the same, aren't you, dear?" she went on. "Just look at these roses in your cheeks!" She pinched my cheeks, hard. "Where there's life, there's hope, as the good fellow said."

"Who was this good fellow?" I had never had the nerve to ask her before.

"Never you mind!" She plopped down on the bed and set to unwrapping her scarves, then removing her voluminous coat.

The supervising nurse appeared at my door with two aides right behind her. "Twenty minutes!" she said sternly, then smiled at me and disappeared.

Mrs. Hodges ignored her entirely. "Here now," she said to me. "Made you a African, I have!" drawing an enormous knitted afghan from one of her bags.

I burst into laughter. "Oh, it's just lovely!" I cried. "And so warm! How did you ever remember that blue is my favorite color,

Mrs. Hodges? Thanks so much."

"Well, you *sound* all right, too," she announced somewhat grudgingly. "We've been that worried, I'll tell you. Me and the girls, such a drama when they brought you in, hospital transport and whatnot. It gave us a turn, I will tell you. Last we heard, you had up and married a opera star and gone traipsing all over Europe. Where's he now? This famous husband of yours?"

"He's gone," I said quietly.

She peered at me. "I see. Well, Mr. Hodges is gone, too, dead and buried, bless his soul, though I must say it's simpler without him, no more 'What would you like for supper, Dear?' nor hairs in the sink nor listening to all those baseball games so loud on the radio."

"I'm so sorry," I said.

"Well, life does go on!" She slapped her thighs. "I'm still here, and so are you. Might as well make the best of it!"

The longer she stayed, the better I felt. "I am just so glad to see you," I told her sincerely. "I wish you had come sooner."

She snorted. "Ah, no chance of *that* around *here* these days, dearie. They run this hospital like the army, they do. Gates and badges, rules and regulations, patient plans and whatnot. You have never seen so much red tape! I'm well out of it, I'll tell you."

"Out of it — what do you mean?"

"Oh, they sacked me first chance they got, them of the new regime. Said I don't have the required *degree,* the proper *credentials.* Credentials!" She spat out the word. "As if working here for a quarter century added up to nothing! Why, the minute Himself stepped down, I was out the door before you could say 'jack sprat.' And he did nothing to contradict them, nothing to save me — nothing! Of course now, *she* may have been the one behind it, the culprit; she's been jealous of me all along, she has . . . but we'll never know the truth of it, will we? It's a mystery, as the good fellow said. Oh, they held a little reception in my honor, gave me a silver bowl and a steam iron. A silver bowl and a steam iron, for twenty-five years of service! It's an uncaring bunch, I'll tell you, a gang of accountants. I'm well out of it, I expect, Missy, if the truth be told, yet there's times I miss it, too — the old days, I mean."

"Is everything changed, then? What about the gardening, and the walking, and the recitals?"

"Oh, they go on right enough, now we've got famous for them. This new gang can't change his program through and through. He's still around, you know, still right here in Asheville with Mrs. Carroll, when they're not sashaying off to Florida, that is. Oh, they like the sunny sands these days, the tropical breezes, they do. She's got a hat with a red hibiscus on it, still putting on airs, same as ever. You watch yourself, Missy, when you go over there. She's put out with you something terrible."

"She *is*?"

"Just you be careful," Mrs. Hodges intoned. "Watch yourself."

Something clicked in my foggy mind; I knew she was right.

"You're retired, then?" I asked.

"Heavens no, child." She drew herself up on the bed. "On the contrary, I have become in-dis-pen-sa-ble!" She stretched the syllables out one by one. "At the Grove Park Inn, no less," she added, enjoying my surprise. "Oh yes! It was Moira's idea, but I must say they pounced upon it, the management, popped me right into Housekeeping where I run a tight ship, I'll tell you. A ton of laundry we do every day. A ton! And that's not counting holidays, mind you. 'I don't know how we ever got along without you, Evelyn!' That's what Mr. Potts, the Manager himself, said to me just last week.

226

He's a prince, I will tell you! And Moira's admirer, as well."

I began to see how all this had transpired. I remembered my first lunch at the Grove Park years before, that lengthy lunch in the grand dining room where I had seen Mr. and Mrs. Fitzgerald sitting together at the banquette against the wall, like dolls in a store window. Suddenly my mind filled with questions.

"What about Mrs. Fitzgerald?" I asked. "She was moving back to Montgomery, I believe, about the time I left for Baltimore."

"Ah, now there's a sad story!" Mrs. Hodges announced. "A regular trag-e-dy!" She made the *tsk-tsk* sound with her mouth.

"Why, what do you mean?"

"He died, you know."

I leaned forward in my chair. "Who?"

"Mr. Scott Fitzgerald, the drunkard himself. The whore-monger, the adulterer, the seducer of rich young wives. The *famous writer.*" Her scorn for him contorted her face. "Oh, it was in all the newspapers, very prominent, I'm surprised you missed it."

"But when did this happen?" My heart was racing now.

"1940," Dixie said from the doorway.

Her clear voice surprised me so much that

I nearly tumbled from my chair. Caught up as I had been in this terrible news, I did not know how long she had been standing there, listening.

Now Dixie moved swiftly and gracefully across the room, offering her hand to Mrs. Hodges in a practiced gesture, with a little bow. "I am Dixie Calhoun," she said, "from Thomasville, Georgia. I am a patient here as well. In the short time I have known her, Evalina and I have become great friends."

"You don't say! Pleased to meet you then, I'm sure!" Always impressed by any display of manners or class, Mrs. Hodges grasped Dixie's slim, elegant hand.

"And I just love F. Scott Fitzgerald. I am his biggest fan!" Dixie seated herself right next to Mrs. Hodges on my bed. "So now you have to start over, right from the beginning, and tell me all about him. You didn't like him much, did you? I can tell by your voice. Oh, I know he was a drinker, everybody knows that. But *everybody* is a drinker, aren't they? I mean, everybody Southern, everybody smart. They all drank and drank, Zelda and Scott and all their friends. I've read all about them. And I knew that Zelda was insane. But I certainly didn't know that she'd ever been *here,* at Highland, my goodness! I just can't believe it." Dixie clapped her hands and scooted closer to Mrs. Hodges. "Now, *tell*. Tell, Evalina." She turned to look at me. "I can't believe you didn't even know about his death." Dixie took my hand and held it, as if we were little school friends. "It was 1940," she prompted Mrs. Hodges.

Mrs. Hodges opened and closed her mouth several times, but finally she couldn't resist Dixie; nobody ever could. "Oh yes, well, he'd been out there in California for some time, not a penny to his name, living in sin with a chorus girl, a real low-life, a *Brit* she was —"

"A journalist," Dixie added primly.

"A gossip columnist," Mrs. Hodges corrected her, "who looked exactly like our own Zelda when she was a young girl. I've seen the photos, mind you, exactly like poor little Zelda when he appeared in that uniform and plucked her up from the bosom of her family and married her. Oh quite dashing, he was! Why Zelda never even had the benefit of an education, poor thing! Plucked her up and married her and dragged her off to New York City and got her on the bottle just like himself. She didn't know what hit her, is what I think. Fast company and no fixed address. Receiving friends in the bath and swimming in the nude. She never had a chance."

Dixie raised her perfect eyebrows. "Now wait just a cotton-picking minute. I'll bet Zelda didn't *want* to go to college. Belles don't go to college, everybody knows that being a belle is a fulltime job. First she was the wildest girl in Montgomery, and then she was a belle — and this is something I know something about, believe me! — being a belle alone is enough to kill you . . . or ruin you, if you survive, which I'm trying to do right now."

We both stared at her.

She blushed and went on. "And then *he* appeared, Scott Fitzgerald, like a lover from a dream, like the answer to a question, and that was it. That was just *it.* They were a pair, like this." She held up two fingers, pressed together.

Mrs. Hodges snorted. "I'd say he ruint her. He ruint them all. Criminal, it was. Just criminal."

"But he was a wonderful writer, you must admit," Dixie said. She turned to me. "Didn't you just love *The Great Gatsby*?"

"Actually I've never read it," I said. Somehow — in Canada, perhaps? — I had lost my early habit of reading, enslaved by my love for Joey and exhausted by my jobs. Suddenly I was filled with longing for books again. "But I will read it," I said. "Right away." At that very moment, a part of myself flew back to me, landing as gently as a butterfly on my head. I touched my hair, short as a boy's.

"Well. As I was saying —" Mrs. Hodges wanted to get on with it; she wanted to be the expert. "We did hear all about it here, of course — the details of Mr. Fitzgerald's death, you know. And it *is* sad, I suppose, though no more than what you'd expect, a man like that. The facts are these. He was out there writing movies, and books, and whatnot, and then he had his first heart attack in a drugstore, Schwab's, I think they said it was, fell out in the floor like a tree. But they doctored him up after that until he was all right for a time, though dizzy, mind you. That's when he moved in with the floozy, in a first-floor flat, so that she could take care of him. And it wasn't long before he suffered the next attack, after taking her to see a film. I don't know what the film was, mind you. But the very next day he was just sitting calmly in a green armchair eating a chocolate bar and waiting for the doctor to come when suddenly he jerked up, staggered across the floor, and grabbed at the mantelpiece, then fell flat down in the floor, looking elegant as always. Wearing a gentleman's cashmere sweater and the customary bowtie. Forty-four years old, dead as a doorknob."

"Doornail," Dixie said.

Mrs. Hodges peered at her.

"The expression is, 'dead as a doornail,' " Dixie said.

"You're a pert one, you are!" Mrs. Hodges said to Dixie. "Smart, too. Wouldn't think it to look at you neither," she said as if to herself.

Because you're so pretty, she did not say, but I already knew this. Smart girls didn't look like Dixie; they looked like me, big-eyed and thin and pale.

Dixie flushed a deep pink, which made her look even prettier. "I'm sorry," she said.

"What about Mrs. Fitzgerald?" I asked. "Wasn't she in Alabama? How did she take it?"

"Ah yes, there she was down there in the hot Deep South with that mother, reading her Bible, painting her paintings, working with the Red Cross and digging in the dirt — oh, she still loves her gardening, mind you, her flowers, always has, always will. She got onto it here with old man Otto and never did give it up. 'Tis a great source of strength for her somehow. Himself was correct about that. Camellias and roses in

232

Alabama, peonies here — peonies big as plates! Bone meal, this is her secret. That bed of peonies out by the entrance, that's all due to her."

"Wait a minute! She's still here? Still? After all this time?" Dixie asked.

"Oh, she's been in and out, back and forth, of course, poor thing. She will never leave this hospital entirely, not that one. She was back here in 1943, as I recall, after her daughter got married. Now that was just too much for her, a quiet lady by then, New York City and all that, and who can blame her? A city is hard on the nerves. She stayed with us till February of 1944, that time, and was back again in 1946. I remember the date for she was here when her first grandchild was born, Tim, it was, ah, she was that excited. I remember it well. I knitted him a little yellow robe and a cap with a tassel on it and took it to her and she said, 'God loves you, Mrs. Hodges, and I do, too.' "

"My goodness," Dixie said. "She'd gotten very religious, then?"

"And is to this day, I'd expect. They all do, after a while, the mentals. It overtakes them all."

"Why is that, do you think?"

"I couldn't rightly say, Miss," she answered. "It's a good question, mind you."

"You like her, don't you?" Dixie said. "You like her a lot better than you liked him. But I have a question for you. Let's put her husband aside for a minute. Don't you think Zelda was sick, then, I mean really sick? You make her sound like she wasn't sick."

"Oh, she was sick, all right," Mrs. Hodges said darkly, "and she's still sick, I'll wager. She'll be back, mark my words. But I don't think she was schizophrenic, not for one bloody moment, pardon my French, I don't. I think she didn't fit in, that's all, and they didn't know what to do with her. Not her family, and not Mr. Fitzgerald either. None of them knew what to do with her. She was too smart, too or-i-gin-al. She was too wild and she drank too much and she didn't fit in. That's the bare bones of it. And that's enough. That's the case with half of them, the women that comes here. They're too privileged, too smart . . ."

The color disappeared from Dixie's face.

Mrs. Hodges stood up, groaning and heaving. "But you will be out of here right enough, both of you, not to worry. I can tell. I can always tell."

"How's that?" Dixie asked.

"Ex-per-i-ence!" she hooted. "There's no substitute for experience, a thing they do not know, them with the little clipboards and memos and such." She put on layer after layer of her wraps. We stood up, too.

"It's a pleasure to meet you, ma'am," Dixie said, recovering herself and her perfect manners. "I hope I will see you again."

"Oh, you will, Miss. There's no doubt about it. And in the meantime . . . the inter-im, mind you, why don't you see what you can do with our poor little Evalina's hair?"

Dixie smiled. "I'll do my best," she said.

"Good-bye, then." Mrs. Hodges half smothered me in her woolen hug. "I'd best be on my way. I've got my duties waiting at the Grove Park Inn — you'd better believe it — with two big weddings coming right up this weekend!"

"What did you mean, exactly?" I asked Dixie the very next afternoon as we made our way down the sidewalk along Zillicoa Avenue to the bus stop, arms linked for balance, bundled up against the cold. I was not sure where my own coat had come from, a green wool loden that I rather liked.

She glanced sideways at me, a question on her pretty face beneath her fur-lined hood.

"What did you mean when you said that

being a belle is enough to kill you, or ruin you if you survive?"

Dixie laughed her tinkly, self-deprecating laugh. "Why, I was more of a belle than anybody!" she said. "Don't you know it? I made my debut at the Gone with the Wind Ball in Atlanta when the movie came out. They had this great big premiere."

I stopped dead still to peer at her. "You're kidding!" Even caught up in my own world as I had been then, I had seen the famous film; a whole gang of us from Peabody had gone down to New York on the train for it, then ended up sleeping in the station overnight because it had lasted so long — four hours! — and we had missed the last train back that evening.

"Oh yes," Dixie went on. "I won a contest. Well, I *almost* won it." She was smiling. "I was the first runner-up in the Scarlett O'Hara look-alike contest. This girl named Margaret Palmer won first place, so she got to lead the Grand March — escorted by Clark Gable and wearing one of Vivien Leigh's Scarlett costumes from the film — but I walked right behind her."

"Who was *your* escort?"

"I swear, I can't even remember his name!" Again, the tinkly laugh. "He wasn't a real date, I'd just met him five minutes before it started. He was the son of the lady who ran the Junior League, so it was all a put-up job. But you do see what I mean — it don't get more belle than tha-yat!" She was using her fake, ironic Southern accent.

I had to laugh. "I guess not," I said.

The chilly wind blew at our backs, pushing us along. Two men were up on ladders attaching Halloween decorations to the streetlights, a black cat or a witch on a broomstick beneath each globe. Holidays were taken seriously at Highland, where we celebrated everything we could.

"Good afternoon, girls!" one of the men called out. I knew he had noticed Dixie.

"Y'all be careful up there!" she called back, and we all laughed.

I envied Dixie her belle's charm, a quality very useful in the world, I had noted, having none. In fact, this was the reason I had invited her — dragooned her, to be exact — to come along for tea with Mrs. Carroll this afternoon. I needed all the moral support I could get. The engraved notecard had been delivered to me two days ago, with its familiar handwriting, precise as calligraphy. I had been expecting it. I might as well get it over with, I knew, even though I was terrified, remembering Mrs. Hodges's warning.

We ran for the bus and then enjoyed the long ride up Merriman Avenue past Beaver Lake to an exclusive-looking neighborhood. I was not surprised to find the Carrolls' large home one of the most imposing, all glass and dark wood in the modern style of Frank Lloyd Wright.

The huge door flew open just as I lifted the heavy brass knocker.

Mrs. Carroll had been waiting.

"Evalina! My little Evalina! My dear! I am so glad to see you. Come in, come in —" Here was a new tack; all her former coldness and disapproval seemed to have vanished overnight. Mrs. Carroll had dressed to the nines for this mandatory occasion, in a tailored midnight blue wool suit with a diamond brooch and earrings — and of course, the ever-present high heels, her legs still beautiful in sheer silk stockings. Her pale blonde hair was perfectly coiffed in a new, bobbed fashion; her makeup was flawless.

I should not have worried so, I realized then, nor expected less; for above all, Mrs. Carroll was a public person, as was Dr. Carroll himself. Appearances would be kept up, civility maintained.

"And I am so very glad to see *you*!" I had practiced saying this again and again in my

room before leaving. "Please let me introduce my good friend, Dixie Calhoun, who
is also a patient at Highland —"

"A *guest,*" Mrs. Carroll interjected.

". . . a guest at Highland as well," I
concluded.

Dixie offered her hand and inclined her
head in a little bow. "Oh Mrs. Carroll, I
have seen you play the piano, and I have
heard so much about you and Dr. Carroll,
and I am just so happy to make your acquaintance at last. It is a real honor!" The
hundred-watt smile, the widening of the
violet eyes that said, *Yes. You. You are special.*

Mrs. Carroll narrowed her own eyes ever
so slightly, registering Dixie, as she smiled
back. "Well, my goodness, it is so lovely to
have you both here on such a cold, dreary
afternoon. Come in, come in, let's just hang
up your coats right here in the hall so that
they can dry out, and you must come in
and sit by the fire . . ." leading the way into
the drawing room.

"Oh heavens, what gorgeous roses!" Dixie
exclaimed, for there they were, the famous
yellow roses, beautifully arranged on their
round marble top table. Inadvertently I
wondered what Robert's tally would be
now, after ten more years? How many roses,

how many thousands of dollars . . . a fortune in roses. So many roses, so much love — or perhaps not. For if I had learned anything at Highland in my youth, it was how mysterious love is in all its ways, its guises and disguises. In fact, I had loved the Carrolls deeply, and I thought they had loved me . . . I had believed that they loved me . . . but perhaps not. In my mind's eye, I saw the cast of "A Midsummer Night's Dream" disappearing into the forest, only to reemerge all changed and new, shining and smiling, each with a new partner.

The special drop-leaf table had been brought in and laid for tea, which Mrs. Carroll poured from a silver teapot into fragile rose china cups, meanwhile entranced by Dixie who oohed and ahhed over all the beautiful and unusual furnishings and art. Mrs. Carroll told about purchasing the carousel clock on their honeymoon in Italy forty years ago, and how the African masks had been presented to her, a gift, after a concert in Johannesburg. We sat before a leaping fire that crackled merrily behind a most unusual fire screen, a golden peacock spreading its wings. Now that was new, I believed, wondering where it had come from, and with what miraculous story attached. I glanced all about the spacious room searching for the crystal Viennese punchbowl, which had disappeared from its spot on the sideboard.

Noticing my silence Mrs. Carroll turned to me. "And how are you, Evalina?" she inquired kindly. "Beginning to feel better, I trust?"

To my horror, I suddenly collapsed into wracking sobs. "Oh, Mrs. Carroll, I'm sorry, I'm just so sorry —" I upset my teacup onto the pink linen tablecloth. Dixie leapt up to rectify the damage with her own napkin, while Mrs. Carroll came over and knelt to hug me. I stiffened instinctively; she had not touched me in many years.

"Now then, dry those big eyes, dear." Mrs. Carroll dabbed at them herself. "Your eyes have always been your best feature, you know."

They *had*? I didn't think I'd ever had a best feature.

Mrs. Carroll touched my cheek and gave my shoulders another squeeze before returning to her chair, where she crossed her legs at the ankle and composed herself again. She fixed her regard upon me directly. "It is not the end of the world, you know. You are not the first, my dear, nor shall you be the last, to have an adventure. Even I — even I —" but here she stopped herself, and poured the last of the tea all around. "Of course you must have been to Europe, as well," she said, turning to Dixie, who launched into a description of her own art tour in France, with private sketching lessons and lectures at the Louvre.

I sat looking into the fire — an *adventure*, rather than a debacle?

Mrs. Carroll seemed genuinely kind now, no longer jealous or competitive, perhaps because I had turned out to be such a failure. And who knew? Perhaps she had had a European adventure herself, perhaps Dr. C had saved her from something, too, perhaps even from herself. There must be some reason she had stayed at Highland with him instead of seeking out the fame and fortune that clearly could have been hers. For the first time I saw the battlements of Homewood as a fort instead of a castle, though I also remembered what Mrs. Fitzgerald had said about the princess in the tower. But now, at Dixie's urging, Mrs. Carroll was enumerating the famous people in the framed photographs on the piano, including herself with the great Busoni, beside the Danube. Looking at the dark, polished Steinway, it seemed improbable to me that I had once played four-hand arrangements on it with her, "Mountain

Tune" and Bach's "Sheep May Safely Graze."

"And this is one of my own students, the jazz singer Nina Simone. She is making quite a name for herself." Mrs. Carroll held up a framed photograph of the little girl I had played for, now all grown up and beautiful.

"Dixie made her debut at the Gone with the Wind Ball in Atlanta," I blurted out.

"Really!" Mrs. Carroll focused her formidable attention upon Dixie. "And did you see Clark Gable?"

"I danced with him," Dixie said. "But he couldn't get very close to me because of my hoop skirts, nobody could —"

Mrs. Carroll put the picture of Nina Simone back on top off the piano, then drew Dixie down upon the curvy horsehair loveseat. "Describe your dress," she breathed.

"Well, it was a rose taffeta evening gown with jet beading at the neckline. The skirt went over crinoline petticoats and hoops and it was trimmed with black velvet bows and black net lace and streamers all around. Oh, and I wore jet earrings, too, and a black velvet ribbon around my neck, this was all my idea. And I wore my flowers in my hair."

"What kind of flowers?"

"Camellias. I didn't want to wear a hat," she added. "A lot of the girls wore big hats."

Mrs. Carroll had her eyes closed. "No," she said. "Quite right. Not for evening. And what did your mother wear?"

"My mother wasn't there," Dixie said simply.

We both stared at her.

"Oh, but there were fifty of us, the debutantes," she said. "We sat up on stage before the dancing began, with our escorts standing behind us. We filled up the whole stage! And Vivian Leigh wore a special gown that the costume designer for the movie had created just for her to wear to the Gone with the Wind Ball, though I didn't like it much. It had cap sleeves made of feathers, if you can imagine that! She looked as though she might just fly away." Dixie rattled on, with all Mrs. Carroll's attention trained upon her like a spotlight. I found this to be a relief, I realized, rather than a loss — perhaps I could get out of my role now, in this cast in this play that I had never auditioned for in the first place, for I had never, *ever,* wanted to be a star. While Mrs. Carroll and Dixie talked on — vividly, exaggeratedly — I looked around the room until I spotted the crystal Viennese punchbowl sitting at the foot of the petticoat mirror, filled

with little hand puppets. From Czechoslova-
kia, I guessed.

As we were leaving, Mrs. Carroll pressed a
packet into my hands, wrapped in newspaper, tied firmly with twine.

"What a character! What an old bat!"
Dixie said the minute the door had closed
behind us.

I started laughing and couldn't stop as we
ran down Merriman Avenue to catch the
bus. It was already dark by the time we
reached the Highland stop.

"Oooh, what's this?" Dixie grabbed at my
package as we set off up Zillicoa Avenue.

I shrugged and shook my head.

"Well, let's open it up, then!" she exclaimed.

I pulled the parcel back, sticking it firmly
under my arm. "Not yet," I said. I knew it
contained my postcards. A vision of Joey
Nero came to me then as real as the very
flesh, Joey with his sad dark eyes and sloppy
grin hanging onto one of these holiday
streetlights, arm flung out in a grand gesture. Dixie and I walked back up the hill
through cone after cone of falling light.

That afternoon marked the real beginning
of my recovery. My sense of welcome release

continued into the next day, and the next, and the next, as I followed my appointed schedule. Plus the required walking and gardening, everyone had to take at least two kinds of occupational therapy. Several new sorts were available at Highland now: hairdressing, for instance, which doubled as a free beauty salon where "students" could practice on other patients, sometimes with hilarious results, all under the supervision of a wise-cracking, gum-chewing beautician named Brenda Ray. Dixie loved working at the Beauty Box and had become Brenda's unofficial assistant; she was a "natural," Brenda said. Most of the men took Woodworking, where they hammered, sawed, planed, and polished away earnestly in the big basement workroom under the low-hanging lights and close supervision of old Cal Green, who had been at Highland for years, working as a caretaker. Cooking classes took place three afternoons a week in a workroom next to the big industrial kitchen in the Central Building. This class was very popular, for the cooks got to sit down and gobble up the results of their labor, or sometimes serve it publicly.

"Let's sign up for cooking," I suggested to Dixie, as squares of gingerbread still warm from the oven were passed out to us all at the afternoon "social" on Halloween.

"Not me." To my surprise, Dixie shook her head so vigorously that I could see the bluish shaved spots at each temple where they affixed the electrodes for her still-ongoing electroshock treatments — which had never been a part of my own prescribed regimen, though electroconvulsive therapy was usually alternated with insulin therapy for long-term patients. Dixie always arranged her pretty curls very carefully to hide those shaved spots. By now I was getting a sense that my own "case" was not deemed as serious as many others, though no one had actually told me this.

"Why not?" I was surprised by Dixie's vehemence. I polished off the rest of my gingerbread, which was delicious, and took a dark chocolate "black cat" cookie with orange icing.

"Are you kidding? I had to cook all the time when I was a little girl, and that was enough. I swore I would never do it again, and I haven't. Our Lilybelle does it all now, out at the farm. It's *her* kitchen, really, not mine."

I tried to pick through this information, which seemed to contradict itself. "Why didn't your mother cook?" I asked finally.

"Never mind," Dixie said, flushing. "Let's

just stick with Art." Which we did, though my own personal favorite was Horticulture, as it had been called before, when old Gerhardt Otto was in charge. Now it was "Hortitherapy," which Dixie avoided at all costs, save for the requisite two hours per week of grounds care required of all, which she could not get out of. "Who wants to muck around in the dirt?" she asked. "And ruin a perfectly good manicure?"

Yet she didn't mind covering her hands in clay or paint as we worked at those familiar tables in Homewood under the calm tutelage of Rowena Malone, whose long braid was white now, her face softened by age but even more beautiful, with its strong features.

"And not one bit of makeup!" Dixie marveled. "Can you imagine?"

Dixie pooh-poohed her own artistic talent, which seemed remarkable to me as she turned out realistic rural landscapes of wide fields and fencerows, with towering thunderclouds in the distance, or still lifes, bowls of peaches and vase after vase of flowers. "They're not original," she said. "Now *that* is original!" She pointed her brush at Miss Malone's ever-changing "gallery" wall, where the patients' work was displayed. "Look at those. My goodness!" A new exhibit had just gone up.

"All by Zelda Fitzgerald," Miss Malone said proudly. "I have saved them over the years, everything I could, for her and her daughter. But this is just a tiny fraction of what she's done. Most of it is gone now, sent off to art shows or taken by friends and relatives or destroyed by Zelda herself when the mood hit her. That's the worst of it. Of course we at Highland have no right to any of these, but while they are in my keeping, I will keep them safe. I take it as a sacred trust."

"Well, no wonder." Dixie got up and walked slowly along the display of perhaps ten pictures. "These are just *remarkable,*" she said.

"Ah yes." Miss Malone nodded. "She has real talent for art, a lucky thing, since her husband stole all her stories. Quite an original style, too, though of course her illness gets in the way. But then perhaps it contributes as well."

I joined Dixie in perusing the exhibition. Most of the paintings were gouache or watercolor on paper, rather small. *Hospital Slope,* one was named, though I could not recognize the actual slope or location of the subject, two blowing apple trees loaded with fruit, approached by a dirt road that disappeared into a fanciful, cloud-filled sky. All the shapes were fluid, filled with wind and life. A vibrant blue and green watercolor entitled *Mountain Landscape* featured that same dirt road again, now running straight up a green mountain into the distant blue peaks and the sky beyond.

"Very impressionistic," Dixie remarked. "Does she paint quickly?"

"Why, yes," Miss Malone said, looking at her.

Several of the paintings of flowers reminded me of how much Mrs. Fitzgerald had liked gardening, way beyond Dr. Carroll's requirements. I remembered her kneeling in the dirt for hours with old Gerhardt Otto, weeding or planting, tan and strong. The flowers in these paintings were close-up, pastel and glowing — blue morning glories, pale lilies on a salmon background, yellow roses.

"Would you call these still lifes?" I asked. "Because they are anything but still." In fact, there was a great deal of movement in all of the paintings, a kind of rushing upward, out of the frame.

I paused before a fanciful pink watercolor of Paris at dusk, which appeared to be actually *happy*, I thought, in contrast to all the others. It gave me the strangest feeling to look at it.

"She did a whole series of these soon after her husband died," Miss Malone told us. "Mainly European scenes, to remember all the traveling she did with him back in better times."

I still hated the way Mrs. Fitzgerald drew people, especially these ballerinas, so tall and weird, with such large, ugly, muscular feet and legs. But everybody's feet and legs were too big — even the characters in the fairy-tale pictures, such as Old Mother Hubbard or the Three Little Pigs. And all the figures were looking up, often with their eyes closed, and no ground at all beneath their feet.

"Why, they're dancing," Dixie said. "You can tell she was a dancer, can't you?"

"Ah, that was her big dream," Miss Malone said. "Yet she started too late and worked too hard and it broke her health."

"I just read *Save Me the Waltz,* or tried to read it, I should say," Dixie announced. "It's impossible to buy it now, Tony told me at the bookstore. So I borrowed it from him. It's obviously autobiographical, all about a girl who is training for the ballet."

"And?" Miss Malone was looking at Dixie with great interest now.

"Well, it's heartbreaking at the end. And very hard to follow because of the way she

251

writes. The language is so unusual, the way she mixes everything up — flowers might *think,* for instance, or have emotions — but it's wonderful, too. Finally it's about obsession, which I envy." Dixie sat back down with a grim face and resumed her own painting, and did not explain herself. Both Miss Malone and I stared at her, but she spoke no more until the end of the hour, when she laughed and tossed her head and said in the old way, "Oooh, I wish I could have met Zelda Fitzgerald, all the same!"

"You probably will," Miss Malone said. "They often come back after the holidays, you know. I wouldn't be surprised."

I was not artistic. But Miss Malone had introduced me to the making of mosaic pottery using tiny brilliant glass tiles, which I enjoyed, as I have always enjoyed completing jigsaw puzzles. In general, I have always liked to fit things into things, to create a pleasing order. Not for me the huge blank canvas, the tubes of oily brilliance. Working carefully, I finished a little bowl in shaded circles of red, ochre, and gold tiles, which Miss Malone placed upon a wooden stand. Everyone admired it.

"What are you going to do with it?" asked an intense skinny woman at my table.

"Maybe I'll give it to somebody for Christmas." I was thinking of Claudia and Richard Overholser, who had been very kind to me since my return.

"Ah yes," Miss Malone said, "Bye and bye we shall turn into Santa's workshop here, so that anyone who wants to make a gift can do so. I have ordered beads for necklaces already — and maybe we shall make some funny sock dolls for children? Tell me your ideas, everyone, please. And now it is time for us to put away our supplies for today —"

But Dixie was already gone, overturning her easel, running out the door without her coat, flashing past the window, leaving a half-done vase of roses on her canvas and her paints in a mess behind her, one jar overturned to make a vivid red spreading stain on the wooden floor. Miss Malone ignored it all, helping the rest of us to put our things away, bidding us all her customary calm, fond adieu. Nothing ever seemed to surprise the quietly smiling Miss Malone as she padded about in her great smock like some sort of nun or priestess.

Dixie vanished for a week, her room locked. She returned a bit paler, a bit thinner, and never mentioned this perplexing incident again, nor did I ask her about it.

CHAPTER 7

Though at first I missed old Gerhardt Otto's gruff presence terribly, I still loved "Hortitherapy" where there was more going on than ever, even in late autumn. It seemed that it had taken half a dozen people to replace Doc Otto! I had been watching them out my window for weeks. Under the direction of several experienced groundskeepers, teams of three or four patients were cutting back and mulching the perennials and roses; dividing and transplanting irises, daylilies, and the like; and planting the bulbs for spring. The greenhouse itself had been expanded, with a multipurpose activity building adjoining it.

I had wandered over there shyly the first time, early for my appointment. Sunlight flowed in through a row of big new windows looking out upon the kitchen gardens and across to the woods beyond. Sturdy rough-hewn ceiling beams held swags of flowers, hung to dry: purple statis, golden yarrow, delicate white baby's breath, those lavender asters that grew in great drifts on the bank behind the Central Building. All their names came flooding back to me. They looked beautiful hanging there. A man came in stomping his feet with the smell of the woods about him and an armful of bright-berried holly and evergreens; he placed them carefully on a wide shelf. Several people were working around a big potting table with a pile of dirt in the middle of it.

"Evalina?" An older woman detached herself from the group at the potting table and came toward me, stripping off her gardening gloves to hold out her arms. "Welcome. I am Mrs. Morris. I have been looking forward so much to meeting you — I can use your help." She surprised me with a hug, instead of a handshake. Though Mrs. Morris actually held a doctorate in psychology, she did not look or act like a doctor at all, but like a grandmother, or someone's ideal of a grandmother, with her gray curls, dimply wrinkled face, and plump figure — even her fingers were pudgy, and stained with dirt. Nor did she ever dress like a doctor, always wearing slacks and a smock or a big green apron with pockets containing the tools of her trade. "Here, put this on." She handed me a man's soft old shirt. "And come, sit down —" She led me toward a group of comfortable wicker chairs set in a circle. "Today we shall all start a project together. Come, have a seat. Let's wait for the others . . ." Oh no, I thought. A *group*! Nothing of this sort had ever occurred in Horticulture with old man Otto in charge. He had just put us all to work.

But they soon arrived, all women in our group of six: three who seemed to know each other well, falling into instant conversation. The spinsterish one named Myra was a bore who began all her remarks with "Mama always says . . ." while Amanda and Susan, younger, might possibly be belles, I thought, newly aware of this category. Helen, also new to the group, was older, thin and downcast; while black-haired Ruth was an angry, fidgety woman about my own age who said she didn't see why she had to come here at all, she was a city girl and this wasn't what she had expected at this hospital, this wasn't what she had signed up for, plus she had never had a green thumb, she had the opposite of a green thumb, she had a black thumb, so there!

Mrs. Morris laughed merrily. "Oh honey," she said, "Don't worry — no one else has a green thumb either. In fact there is no such thing as a green thumb." She sat smiling at us all. "Plants and people have a lot in common," she suggested. "Both need a harmony of society and environment within the natural laws of biology and chemistry. They need care and food. There are certain things they must have, such as water and sunlight, and certain things they must not have —"

"Oh, I see what you're up to!" dark-haired Ruthie spat out furiously. "Jesus Christ, how dumb do you think we are?"

"Mama always said that cursing shows a weakness of vocabulary," Myra said primly.

Mrs. Morris continued, unfazed. "Both plants and people make their way through a life cycle as single individuals, yet both are actually dependent upon their relationships with other plants and animals for survival. These interactions and associations between individuals vary from the casual or superficial to ties that are so close that the death of one partner may threaten the existence of others."

Helen, the downcast woman, began to cry at that moment, soundlessly and hopelessly. I wondered if perhaps she had just lost her husband.

Mrs. Morris leaned forward to take her hand, and went on. "Today you will each pick a bulb to plant and nurture throughout this winter season. We shall begin the process of forcing bulbs now, so that each of you will have a potful of beautiful blooming plants in the darkest, coldest part of the winter when the snow comes to cover our mountains all about." Mrs. Morris had an almost Biblical way of speaking, though her Southern voice was so soft that we all had to pull our chairs forward and lean toward her a bit to hear. "Of course it is unnatural, forcing bulbs to grow out of their season. This is a special project to bring us cheer for the upcoming holidays. In reality, plants, like people, need room in order to spread and grow and sink their roots — in order to thrive."

"And now, look!" She opened the huge old book upon her lap, turning it upside down so that we could all see the botanical prints marching in full color across the pages: cheerful orange and red tulips; lacy spikes of blue, violet, and pink hyacinths.

"Those always smell so good," I said involuntarily, pointing to the hyacinths. I was rewarded with a smile.

"Yes they do, Evalina, and so does this paperwhite narcissus and also the freesia — it's heavenly, just like perfume, does anybody know it?" Mrs. Morris indicated the extravagant lavender and white blooms.

"And then, of course, our most dependable and sturdy flowers of all — daffodils! Does anybody know the Wordsworth poem?"

I wandered lonely as a cloud popped into my mind, from the little book of poems that Mr. Graves gave me.

"Jonquils," Helen said. "Mama always called them jonquils."

"Oh, who cares what anybody calls them?" Ruth snapped. She jumped up and went to stand at the big window, jiggling her foot.

Mrs. Morris stood and smoothed her apron down over her stomach. "Now you must each one be deciding upon the flower you would most like to grow, as we proceed over to the potting table where I shall introduce you to your bulbs." We moved as one to line up on either side of the table. "Now look at this." Dr. Morris held aloft a big, lumpy, dirty clod as if it were a jewel. "Can you believe it? *This*" — pointing at the bulb — "will turn into *this.*" — pointing at the picture of a giant red amaryllis. She looked at us carefully one by one. "But it will happen only with your care."

"Oh brother," Ruth muttered. Nobody took any notice of her as she stepped tentatively toward us, then retreated, then finally rejoined our group as we all chose bulbs and pots and began — gingerly, in most cases — to break up the soil and put several inches of it into our clay pots, then place the bulbs just so upon it ("No, this way," Mrs. Morris said gently, upending several, "so they can reach straight up for the sun. We must all reach for the sun.") Then more soil, then sphagnum moss to hold in moisture. We crammed several bulbs into each pot. I picked daffodils for my pot. Ruth picked the showy amaryllis; I knew she would.

Afterward I found myself walking back up the long, grassy hill between Amanda and Susan; both would be leaving Highland soon, I gathered from their conversation. Susan, recovering from a broken heart, was looking forward to the holidays, but Amanda dreaded her return to an older, domineering husband whom she referred to as "The Judge" and described as a "sex fiend."

A sudden gust of cold air brought us a shower of brittle leaves.

"Oh well, at least it'll be warm down there," Amanda said. "I don't think I could stand a winter at this place."

"Where do you live?" I asked, and she said, "Tampa."

"That sounds nice," I offered.

"You don't know anything," Amanda said.

The sound of sudden cries and exclamations erupted from the edge of the woods to our left, where a teenage grounds crew was working on beds at the tree line — cutting back the ever-encroaching forest, pruning and separating the perennials, I imagined, for I had worked on these borders myself in the old days.

"Oh man, you ought to see that thing!" a tall, skinny redheaded boy tossed his hoe high in the air as he burst out onto the grassy lawn, followed by a shrieking blonde girl. But the others gathered closer to the tree line, jabbering excitedly, as a man appeared in the forest's mysterious opening and then stepped forward carrying something in his arms.

"Kill it! Kill it!" The redheaded boy started the chant.

We stopped on the path to watch, but couldn't see what it was due to the excited clot of jumping teenagers.

I found myself transfixed — as my companions appeared to be, too — by the scene and the man himself — dark, small, yet finely made, with handsome features — utterly calm in the midst of all the uproar and consternation. A white dog followed at his heels. He smiled broadly, sweetly, as he walked forward into the group with arms outstretched, as if with an offering.

"Lord, it's a snake!" Susan whispered, seizing my arm.

The teenagers quieted down and gathered around him, blocking our view, then radiated outward to form a circle with the man in the center of it, kneeling.

Without a word, the four of us left the path and moved down the hill, closer, to see.

It was a thick-looking thing, like a snake but clearly not a snake, more primeval and misshapen than a snake, despite a recognizable head at one end, with sleepy eyes and a mouth that turned up curiously in a sort of smile. Its blackish-gray body was highlighted with yellow spots on the head which continued down its back toward the wedge-shaped tail. It was about a foot long. Now the man moved back from it a bit, still on his haunches, a position that seemed absolutely natural to him. We all watched in utter silence as the animal began to move very slowly — so slowly that it seemed to ooze across the grass and back into the brush at the edge of the forest. I stared in fascination until it was gone — then looked up to find that the man had disappeared as well, along with his dog.

The kids headed toward the greenhouse,

carrying their tools and talking loudly, as if they had all been on a grand adventure.

"Mama always says, 'Snakes are our friends,'" Myra announced as we joined the lunch line entering the dining hall in the Central Building.

"Oh for God's sakes, who cares what your damn mother says?" Ruth snapped, and Myra's mouth fell open, as if this were a brand new idea.

"I don't think that was even a snake," Susan said thoughtfully. "I grew up on a farm, and I never saw a snake that looked like that."

"But who was the man?" I asked, trying to sound casual, surprised at the catch in my voice.

"Oh!" They turned to me. "Haven't you heard the story? Don't you *know*?"

The animal was a spotted salamander, a mole species of amphibian native to the area but rarely seen except by foresters and gardeners digging in deeply wooded locations.

What a shame, I thought, that Robert had missed it.

The man was, indeed, another story, which I pieced together by diligently questioning Mrs. Hodges, Dr. Morris, Mr. Pugh, and the Overholsers, who had all worked with him ever since his arrival.

His name was Pan Otto, though this was a name he had acquired only since he had been brought to Highland Hospital eight years earlier. I had not missed him by much, actually, a fact which fascinated me, as well as the fact that we were about the same age, twenty-six or twenty-seven, so far as anyone could tell, in both cases. He had lived here continuously ever since, and was now a familiar and beloved figure about the grounds, seen usually in the company of his dog, Roy, a gentle though wolflike creature.

But I am getting ahead of myself! Mrs. Hodges told me the whole story.

He was born William Raymond Moss — called Billy Ray — over in the deep mountains west of Asheville. The family had lived up a long, rutted road in an old homestead on Crabtree Mountain that had always belonged to his mother's family. Considered "slow," his mother Lorena had seldom left the mountain, and then only for brief trips into town with her parents. Here she attracted some considerable attention, for she was beautiful, but no one came calling until her fearsome father's death, which left Lorena up there on the mountain with her ailing mother to care for.

Now the neighbors and townsfolk ventured forth to bring what was needed, food and clothing and even wood. It was not long until they came up to tend the body and bury the old woman in the Crabtree cemetery at the top of the mountain.

This is when a no-account man named Dwane Moss first set eyes on Lorena, or so it was believed. He married her two months later over in Sylva, before a drunken magistrate. Lorena bore him child after child. Dwane Moss had no known profession other than selling off Crabtree land he had gained through marriage. Shameful, they all said in town, though no one could stop him so long as Lorena signed the papers. People were scared of him, for he was a violent man, hot-headed and alcoholic. But when he shot the wrong man in the groin at a roadhouse fight, the sheriff made him a deal. Since Dwane liked to fight so much, the sheriff sent him off to the army instead of prison.

Lorena kept chickens, and sometimes people left food in the shed down at the end of the rocky road for her and the children — a bag of cornmeal, perhaps, or potatoes — for some still remembered her and who her people were. In their father's absence, the older boys ran away, hopping a freight out of Asheville, never to be seen or heard from again. ("And who could blame them?" Mrs. Hodges said, throwing up her hands as she told this part.) Dwane's brother Roman showed up out of no place and moved in with Lorena to help out, though it is not clear exactly what he did, beyond taking her into town once a month to pick up the check from the army. The older girl, Ava, "smart in school" when she could get there, just didn't come home one day, staying in town with a classmate's family.

And then Dwane got out of the army and came back a hero, with a wooden foot, a lot of medals, constant pain, and a chip on his shoulder. Soon there was a terrible accident up on Crabtree Mountain, and Dwane's brother Roman got killed some way or other, bringing the high sheriff and his deputies up the long rutted road. Charges were never placed against Dwane, but the county went back two days later and took the twins. Another baby gripping her skirt, Lorena stood weeping at the door to watch them go down the mountainside. After that, folks left them alone. Dwane made regular trips into town for the checks and the drugs he required from the pharmacy, sometimes accompanied by Lorena, who spoke to no one, shopping with her head down at the grocery store.

Time passed, and more time.

Then came the blizzard of 1928, which brought two feet of snow followed by an ice storm that left a solid sheet of ice on top of it. When that finally melted, making a river out of the road, Lorena put her coat on and wrapped little Millie up as best she could and they walked all the way down the mountain and just sat down in the snow, the two of them huddled together holding hands by the side of the road until somebody came along and found them.

This turned out to be a Church of Christ minister named Rudy Swink and two of his deacons, on their way to a prayer breakfast. Crazed, emaciated, and babbling, Lorena pulled at them until they parked the car and walked back up the mountain. She led them first to Dwane's body, face down in the snow at the side of the house, where he had fallen coming back from the woodshed. He had been dead for several days.

But that was not all. Tugging insistently at the Reverend Swink's sleeve, she took them into the house, which was "filthy something awful" as the Reverend described it later in the newspaper articles that Mrs. Hodges had saved all these years. The stove had gone out; you could see your breath in the air. Lorene kept on pulling at Reverend Swink's sleeve, taking him into a makeshift pantry off the kitchen, which had ladder steps at the back of it leading down into a kind of a root cellar that contained the boy, Billy Ray Moss, in a slatted cage fashioned with chicken wire. At first, in the dim light, they didn't even see him. Then "Lord God have mercy!" the Reverend had hollered, flinging out his hand in the old gospel style to pray before stumbling forward to open the latch, but the boy drew back into his rags and blankets and would not look at the preacher, or at anyone.

He was taken to Broughton Mental Hospital in Morganton, where he was the subject of great interest and much attention by the entire medical establishment, who came from far and wide to view him. Although about eight years old at the time of his discovery, he weighed only forty-eight pounds, walked on all fours or maintained a crouching posture, ate with his hands, and did not speak or make eye contact, flinching when anyone approached him.

"How do you all know all this?" I demanded of Mrs. Hodges one afternoon. "These details, I mean?"

"Why, my goodness, it was in all the

papers, you had better believe it. Worldwide! Everybody knew about it. The Boy in the Cage, they called him. It was terrible, terrible. But he improved, with time. They made him their special pet over there at Broughton, they showered him with attention, and affection, don't you know, as much as possible, and he improved, he did, quite a bit, to where he could stand up, and walk and run and speak, too — though he has never liked to, mind you — and eat with a spoon and a fork and all that, and even throw a football, and play a harmonica. Oh, he took to the harmonica! But he was still different from other children, of course, and the time came when he reached a plateau, they called it."

"What did that mean?" I asked.

"They came to a point where the boy did not need to be in hospital any longer, and certainly not the state hospital, where all beds are nec-ess-ary. Yet he got booted out of the Oxford orphanage, and then no other orphanage would have him, nor any foster home either, he was just too . . . too different, too un-u-su-al, or so they said. He was removed from placement after placement, which had a damaging effect, don't you know."

"Like what?"

"Regression," she said darkly, clicking her needles. "My, yes. Finally they sent him back to Broughton, and this is when Himself got involved."

"How?" I asked.

"The head of child psychiatry at Broughton, a Dr. Spiegelman, had heard Dr. Carroll speak at Duke, and so he came to call upon us, and of course the Carrolls were fascinated to learn what had happened to the boy in the cage, and went immediately to see him, and the upshot of it was that he was brought here, where he has lived ever since, as you see. He has not progressed as far as Dr. C had hoped, I daresay — it soon became clear that he'd never go to university! He's not got the intellect for schooling, nor the temperament either. Too odd! But he has got a job and a home here now, at least."

"All thanks to the Carrolls," I murmured almost to myself, wondering how Billy Ray felt about that, for I harbored conflicting emotions of my own when I contemplated the overwhelming debt of gratitude I owed them.

But Mrs. Hodges glared at me. "Indeed not!" She snipped off the yarn with a huge pair of scissors. "All thanks to Gerhardt Otto, to be sure."

This part had never been in the papers. But as soon as the "caged boy" Billy Ray was introduced to the greenhouse and let loose upon the grounds, he abandoned the studies the Carrolls had set out for him. ("You might say he was stubborn, as a student," Claudia Overholser told me, smiling. "Intractable!" pronounced her husband.) Billy Ray loved the out-of-doors and took to the work, following old Gerhard Otto everywhere. No task was too long or too hard. Dr. Carroll took to calling the boy "Pan" ironically, in jest, and the name stuck. Old Gerhardt built him a little partitioned room off the greenhouse itself, and gave him his first puppy, a stray they found in the woods. The boy became more expressive, evidencing pleasure and sometimes mirth. He began to work in groups with the others upon occasion.

When old Gerhardt was diagnosed with lung cancer, he officially adopted the boy, whose last name was then changed to Otto. Upon the old man's death, a small inheritance was settled upon him, in a trust he himself would control upon reaching the age of twenty-one.

"And that, I'd say, has been the making of him," Mrs. Hodges concluded.

When Highland Hospital changed hands

and Mrs. Morris arrived to head up the Hortitherapy program, she kept him on. "I have never known anyone so tuned to plants and animals — and sometimes people," she said, surprising me.

"People?" I repeated.

"Oh yes, our most psychotic patients respond to him in a way that they do not respond to the rest of us, a way that we cannot understand. He knows more than you think. In fact, sometimes I feel that he may know more than we know. Just watch — you'll see."

Mrs. Morris's prediction turned out to be true, I learned, as I found myself spending more and more time down at the greenhouse or out on the grounds with Pan Otto and his crews whenever possible, despite the encroaching cold weather. I enjoyed the work, quite simply. I liked the cold on my cheeks and the ache in my muscles at the end of a task. I felt that I was getting my body back, my strength, after whatever had happened to me. Apparently Dr. Schwartz agreed, for the rest of my insulin shock treatments were abruptly cancelled. I began to play the piano for several of Phoebe Dean's groups and programs, too, but it was Hortitherapy I took to.

I don't recall that I was ever actually introduced to Pan Otto, not formally. I just seemed to know him after a while, spending as much time in his presence as I could, for he made me comfortable in the world in a way I cannot explain. I felt at home with Pan Otto — I, Evalina — who had never had a home of my own on earth.

But here, let me try to describe him for you exactly as he was that autumn afternoon when we met.

He is not particularly tall, due perhaps to all those years in the root cellar, though they say he grew rapidly, once released — eighteen inches, Mrs. Hodges claimed, in the first year alone. We can stand shoulder to shoulder, and our eyes meet instantly when we face one another. Pan's eyes are a light, light blue — almost the color of his dog's eyes. This dog is named Roy Rogers, for Pan delights in Westerns, sitting in the front row whenever they are shown at Movie Night in the Assembly Hall. Roy Rogers follows Pan everywhere, always watchful and polite, though he does not play. I have never seen him fetch a stick, for instance, or jump up on anybody. He just watches, patiently. He is not waiting for anything. Nor is Pan. Pan has no plans, beyond the demands of the season. Instead he is simply living in the present time, all the time, rather like an animal himself.

When he is in the woods, you cannot see him — you really can't, for he is camouflage itself, wearing old, nondescript clothes that blend right in with the forest and look like they came straight out of a Salvation Army box someplace — perhaps they did! His skin is more brown than white, whether from natural pigmentation or the effects of the sun, I do not know. His hair is dark and thick. Mrs. Morris cuts it with shears as he sits in a straight-back chair, I have seen her do this many times, putting a towel around his shoulders and letting the hair fall around him onto the cement floor, to be swept up later. I have swept it up myself, saving several locks of it, thick and wiry. Pan must shower and shave in the greenhouse bathroom, after hours — I find his razor there, in the medicine cabinet, and hold it up against my own face as I look in the mirror hanging above the sink. I cannot say why I do these things. But in any case I deduce that there is no running water in his own living facility, the hut which he is reputed to have built for himself in a "laurel hell" of the deepest woods, moving there after Gerhardt Otto's death. Oh, how I would love to see it! To go there, where he lives, myself . . .

As often as possible, I joined expeditions of

one sort or another where Pan would be present, such as the memorable occasion when I went along on one of the teenagers' "nature hikes," obviously designed to wear them out as well as show them the various flora and fauna. Old Mr. Pugh identified the plants and trees and animal droppings and pontificated upon the ecosystem, but it was Pan we followed single file on a trail across a high sere meadow with its rustling weeds and dried wildflowers rattling in the wind that swept unceasingly across the long curve of the earth. Perhaps that unceasing wind is what made the boy so nervous; wind has that effect upon me, too. In any case, one of the teenagers toward the back of the line — Randall Cunningham, a big boy, a troublemaker — suddenly spat out a curse and grabbed one of his fellow hikers from behind, throwing him down upon the ground and slamming his head again and again upon a rock outcropping while the boy screamed. Now everyone else was screaming or yelling, too, as they closed in — but the attacker jumped up and zigzagged across the meadow toward the cliff beyond.

Instantly Pan was after him, not seeming to run so much as flow through the waist-high weeds, effortlessly and silently, like the wind itself. He caught the boy a good way before the mountain's edge, tackling him, and then both were lost to us for a time, down on the ground in the weeds but finally emerging — wonder of wonders! — with their arms around each others' shoulders. Pan kept his arms around the boy's waist from behind as Randall stumbled, sobbing, back to the rest of us, then sat with his head in his hands next to the injured one, who was still unconscious though moaning.

Mr. Pugh directed the making of a kind of litter from several long saplings crisscrossed by brush tied with twine from his pack. They lifted the hurt boy onto it; I looked away from the pool of blood on the rock where his head had been. Then Pan touched Randall Cunningham on the shoulder just once, lightly, jerking his head toward the stretcher; without a word, Randall stood up and grasped a limb and helped to carry the stretcher all the way down, though the rest of us took turns. I shall not forget our slow progress back across the mountain as the sun began its colorful descent behind us. I remember having the sensation, which I had had before at Highland, of being in a painting.

This incident, interestingly enough, was the making of Randall Cunningham, who became a model patient on the spot. He was released at Christmastime, and returned to his own school in January. Maybe he had just needed to hit somebody . . . or maybe he had finally scared himself, gotten his own attention.

When I asked Dr. Schwartz later what she thought about all this, she threw up her hands and laughed. "Who knows? Pills are not everything," she said. "Spontaneous remission can certainly happen, especially with young people. Sometimes their symptoms are situational, a reaction to certain stress, but not internalized, not real illness. It's impossible to predict."

It was impossible to predict *anything;* I was realizing this more and more.

CHAPTER 8

I had trouble believing that Dixie had never been to college, for she seemed to know everything about everything, not only painting but books, too. She and Richard Overholser fell into long literary conversations whenever we went over to their house for dinner. I especially remember one Saturday night when I was helping Claudia clear the dishes while he and Dixie discussed existentialism, "a philosophy that emphasizes the uniqueness and isolation of each individual in a universe that doesn't give a damn," as Richard explained it to me. I had never heard of it. "So each person is solely responsible for giving his own life meaning and for living that life passionately and sincerely," he finished up.

"But what about God?" asked I, the product of all those nuns.

"He doesn't exist," Richard proclaimed. "It's all up to you girls."

"That's sort of what Hemingway is saying, isn't he?" Dixie said.

"Well, yes. An even better reading choice would be Albert Camus."

"Albert who?" Dixie had her pencil out.

"C-A-M-U-S. And look here, Dixie," he added in his emphatic Northern way, "why not enroll in some college courses when you get back to Georgia? You'd enjoy them. Be damn good for you, too, I'll wager."

"Now Richard, you know that's not allowed, we're not supposed to get involved here —" Claudia tossed over her shoulder as she headed back to the kitchen.

"Well, why not?" He pounded on the table. "This is a brilliant woman, why shouldn't she go to college? For God's sake!"

"Oh no," Dixie said quickly. "Frank wouldn't like it." I perked up; she never, *ever* mentioned her husband's name. "A, there's no college back home, for miles and miles around. I'd have to drive all the way down to Tallahassee, a day's trip. Assuming he'd let me drive at all. Assuming he'd let me spend the night. And B, you do know that's not the purpose of therapy at Highland, don't you? That's not why he sent me up here. I am being 'reeducated, retrained' . . ." Though she used the mimicking voice, her smile was sweet and resigned.

"Retrained for what?" Richard pushed back his chair.

"For marriage, I guess," she said. "I wasn't very good at it before."

Richard picked up the serving plates and abruptly left the table. "You know what I think of all that," he called back over his shoulder.

"Well . . ." Dixie said calmly, vacantly, playing with her hair as she looked away, into some distance we couldn't see.

I sank down at the table beside her.

Claudia came back in to join us. "Why not sign up for a correspondence course, then, honey? I know they have them at Goddard College, where I went to school — I can find out for you. You would enjoy it, and then perhaps you wouldn't be so bored by the routine at home. I am sure that your husband wants you to be happy, doesn't he?"

"Lord! He's such a busy man, that's the furtherest thing from his mind!" Dixie laughed and shook her head *no,* vehemently. Again, the flash of skin, the bald patch at the temple. "He just wants me to shut up and quit being sick and do what I'm supposed to and quit bothering everybody. I don't know what we would have done if it hadn't been for his mother, that's Big Mama, to take over for me. Now don't get me wrong. Frank loves me, he really does, or he sure wouldn't have put up with me all this time. He just wants me to calm down and be satisfied. That's what I want, too. I'm sick of myself!" The rueful smile.

Back in the kitchen Richard Overholser was washing the dishes, singing "Is You Is or Is You Ain't My Baby?" at the top of his lungs.

"But changes *can* be made in a marriage, you know," Claudia suggested carefully, leaning across the table to take Dixie's hand. "Old roles can change. Even little things can help a lot. How old are your children now?" she asked, completely jolting me, for Dixie had never once, in our month-long friendship, even mentioned their existence.

"Margaret Ann is seven and Lissa is six." Tears stood in the violet eyes. "I miss them so much," she said.

Over the following weeks, Dixie's story came out in bursts and whispers, which I shall attempt to piece together here. I was very surprised to learn that she had not grown up in circumstances such as she clearly enjoyed today. In fact her mother, Daisy Belle, came from a family of share-croppers in rural Georgia, and her own tragic past had determined the whole family's life — in my opinion.

"Oh, she never stopped telling it!" Dixie cried, stamping her foot. "She used to go on and on — it was like she just *couldn't* stop."

"Well, what was it?" Of course I asked.

"It really *was* awful," Dixie said. "Mama was real good in school, and just beautiful, the most beautiful girl in the county" — this part was no surprise to me — "so she got picked to be Homecoming Queen, and then Miss Magnolia at a contest over in Waycross, and that's when she started running around with a banker's son named Lynwood Small, staying out all night drinking and whatnot. He even gave her his grandmother's ring, right before he drove his car through the guardrail of a bridge over the Tar River. The car hit some kind of a big concrete post before it sank.

"Somehow he only broke his arm, but Mama's beautiful face was completely destroyed. She ended up with one eye a whole lot lower than the other one, so she was always staring off to the side, and she got this big, jagged white scar which ran from her hairline down to her chin. She broke her back, too, so she always had a limp. Lynwood Small took back his grandmother's ring, and then Mama's reputation was completely ruined in that town, according to her. When she finally got out of the hospital, she was real different, real serious. She took a room in a boardinghouse in town and became a seamstress. She joined the Methodist Church, where she met my sweet daddy, Dudley Stovall, who was a lot older, and he married her. He worked for the power company."

"And then what?" I asked.

"And then all they did was work, I reckon, with a little time out to have me and my little sister, Estelle. That's when we moved into a bigger brick house with a patio and a garage. Mama used to say it was perfect in every way. She made all the draperies and the upholstery herself. She turned the front parlor into a sewing room, with her big Singer right there on its own table and swatches of material to choose from and this raised platform where her ladies turned around and around real slow, like ladies in a music box, while Mama knelt at their feet to pin up their skirts for hemming. She used to keep the straight pins in her mouth. I had to do the cooking while she worked.

Daddy used to try to get her to stop working so hard, but she wouldn't, because she said we had to have all the advantages. We had to take piano lessons and dance lessons, we had to have braces — I even had to take elocution! I think Mama got all these ideas from her ladies.

" 'Look at them! My little dolls!' she used to say when we ran out the door in our matching clothes, which she made, which were always perfect. I guess she was living vicariously through all this, but she never would go out to any kind of public meetings or events at our schools."

"But how did you and your sister *feel* about all this?" I asked her.

Dixie grinned at me. "Estelle rebelled the minute she was old enough, but I kept on going. Maybe this is awful, but I was glad to get out of there! So I kept on going to everything. When they offered me a scholarship to Dover Academy in Atlanta, I took it and went, even though Daddy had a lot of misgivings about it. Then I won the scholarship to Agnes Scott, and that's when I got invited — after a *lot* of interviews, I'll tell you — to make my debut at the Gone With the Wind Ball. It was because of my girlfriends at Dover. Mama was tickled to death. She stayed up night after night sewing those ruffles onto the skirt of my ball gown. Finally Daddy just exploded. I remember him saying, 'My God, Daisy, this thing has gone far enough. It will break us!' "

But nothing could stop it by then, the great rolling ball of Mary Margaret's social success, which left her jealous sister and her awestruck family behind. With her new nickname, "Dixie," she traveled from debut to debut of her girlfriends, house party to house party, taken up by the girls and their families, courted by their brothers and their friends. Now part of a vast network that seemed to cover the whole South, Dixie was way too busy for college.

Nothing could stop it except for Dixie herself, who got unaccountably pregnant by somebody's older brother in a boathouse while attending a wedding in Sea Island, Georgia. "I'm not sorry, either!" she insisted. "I've never been sorry. I swear, that was the most important night of my life. And it was the most magical, too. I was wearing this long baby-blue satin sheath dress with spaghetti straps and a little bolero jacket, made by Mama, of course, and a camellia in my hair. That camellia used to be my trademark. Two boys at this dance claimed to be in love with me, so I was dancing with first one, then the other. I remember they had this hot Negro band from Macon, it was all so much fun . . ."

Finally Dixie had to slip outside and catch her breath. She walked down the crushed shell path into the garden, away from the white-columned mansion, and sat down on a wrought-iron bench looking back at it, the whole mansion fairly pulsing with music, each window lit, with the flitting forms of the dancers inside. Suddenly it seemed like a stage set to her, like the way they had decorated the outside of Loew's Grand Theatre to make it look like a plantation for the Gone With the Wind Ball. It seemed fake, all of it, and suddenly Dixie felt fake, too, and very separate from the house and the party and everything else in the world, sitting on her curlicue bench in the moonlight. She had a headache from drinking Champagne, and her face hurt from smiling so much.

"Smoke?" A thin boy with long black hair emerged from the shrubbery, not dressed for the occasion.

"Sure," Dixie said.

In the flare of the match, Dixie saw his big beaky nose, his twitchy mouth, and the dark, serious eyes behind his gold-framed glasses, glasses like an old man would wear.

"Thanks," she said. Then she said, "I know who you are." It was Genevieve's older brother Duncan, the brilliant one, now attending graduate school at Harvard.

"I know who you are, too." He smiled a long slow smile at her. "You're the lucky one, aren't you?"

"Am I?" She thought about this.

"Want to walk down and see the water?"

"Sure," Dixie said, suddenly wanting to do this more than anything, leaving the path to follow Duncan down to the glittery, slapping water filled with stars. She ran forward to stand at the edge of it and he stood just behind her.

" 'The sea is calm tonight, the tide is full, the moon lies fair upon the straits; on the French coast the light gleams and is gone,' " he recited.

" 'The cliffs of England stand, glimmering and vast, out in the tranquil bay. Come to the window, sweet is the night air!' " Dixie finished the verse, and then he put his arms around her and squeezed her tight, and then he turned her around and kissed her full on the lips, not a groping, sloppy kiss such as she allowed her beaux, but a solid, real kiss. She opened her mouth to him.

"Come on," he said, taking her hand and walking her along the edge of the beach to the old boathouse, where a beautiful wooden motorboat named Miss Dolly's Folly rocked in its slip and the upstairs loft contained only a mattress pulled right up to the huge triangular window propped wide open, looking out over the harbor. Duncan drew her down upon it.

"You like English poetry, then," he said to her, and Dixie said, "Oh yes," telling him her favorites, "Ode on a Grecian Urn" and "La Belle Dame Sans Merci." She went on and on, she just couldn't believe herself. He nodded gravely, fiddling with the spaghetti straps on her shoulders. He had majored in English literature himself; in fact he would be leaving for England in a few days, headed for the Lake District and then for Oxford, where he would study for the next two years, soon to be joined by a woman from Boston, his lover. His family didn't know this part. "And you're going where, to school?" he asked.

"Agnes Scott," she said, "but not right now. I've put it off a year."

"Don't do that. Don't put it off." He turned her around to face him. "You're not like these others." He took the camellia out of her hair, carefully, then laid her back against the mattress where she forgot in an instant everything her mother had always told her about leading them on, then making them stop — always making them stop — and hanging on to your most precious possession. Suddenly she didn't care about that anymore, and she was not sorry then, or later when they watched the moon set, dropping down like a glowing opal into the water, the most beautiful thing Dixie had ever seen, or at least *noticed.*

At one point he drew back a bit, to look into her face. "You are protected, of course," he said.

"Of course," she said, not having a clue what he meant.

It was her sister Estelle who broke the news, coming into the bathroom to stand silently while Dixie, on her knees, retched into the toilet, not even caring that her long dark hair trailed down into the horrible water.

"Oh my God," Estelle said flatly. "Oh my God." Then, "You're pregnant, Mary Margaret, I'm going to tell Mama!" almost crowing as she ran off, her bare feet slapping down the hall.

"Mary Margaret Stovall, I just can't believe you would do this to me!" Dixie's mother dragged her head up out of the toilet and slapped her face, laying her flat out on the bathroom floor, sobbing.

"What?" Dixie remembers asking. "Do what to you?"

"This baby!" her mother shrieked. "You cannot have this baby!"

A Lysol douche followed, right there on the bathroom floor, with Estelle holding her down. When that didn't seem to work, Daisy Belle pushed her into the car for a trip out into the county to visit an old black woman who poked and prodded and then patted Dixie on the head and said, "Yes, girl. You go on home and have this child and love it to pieces. That's all you can do, that's what I'm telling you. This child gone be a blessing in the world." Whereupon Daisy Belle started to shriek again. The scar stood out white in her red face. "Drunk!" she screamed. "Whore!" Dixie had to drive back home, with Estelle giggling in the backseat.

Dixie wouldn't tell them, then or later, not ever, who the father was. She could not say why exactly, except that seemed to be the one thing she might keep out of this whole experience, the secret of the father, and the sound of the little waves, and the moonset over the water.

So instead of Agnes Scott, she went to the Florence Crittendon Home outside Columbus. Her parents made her duck down in the backseat as they drove out of town, and no one said a word. They smoked cigarettes on the long ride, all three of them. It was nearly dark by the time they turned down a long unmarked drive that led to a tall Gothic building with heavy pointed doors, like church doors.

One of the matrons opened the door. She was large, mannish, and grave. It all happened very fast. Her father handed the matron an envelope, and the matron shook hands with him. Dixie's father kissed her on the cheek, while her mother sobbed into a handkerchief. Then they were gone. The matron pointed down at Dixie's small suitcase, and Dixie picked it up.

"Come on, then," the matron said.

"I don't want to stay here," Dixie said.

"You should have thought of that earlier then, shouldn't you, dear? Instead of opening up your legs to any Tom, Dick, or Harry who came around. But at least you have made the right choice now, at least you will be giving your baby to good people, decent people who want it, who will love it and take care of it since there is no way you could ever provide for it yourself," the matron said in a voice that was neither mean nor nice. "Too late now," the matron said.

Dixie followed her up two flights of stairs,

dark woodwork everywhere, to the third floor dormitory where the girls slept four to a room. Finally they stopped before room number 303; through the cracked door, Dixie could see three girls moving about within.

The matron put a restraining hand on Dixie's arm. "Wait. Pick a name for yourself," she said.

"What?" Surely Dixie had heard wrong.

"A *name*. Everyone assumes another name here. You'll be glad about this later. No one will ever know who you were — it will be as though this dark chapter never happened in your life. You may choose your new name now."

"Annabelle Lee," Dixie said immediately.

"Oh. Ha, ha. A little joke, I see. We shall go with Anna, then," the matron said, pushing the door open to clap her hands and announce, "Girls! This is your new roommate, Anna." They gave Dixie a cautious greeting, then a real welcome when the matron had left, closing the door behind her.

All the girls had to do chores, such as washing dishes, cleaning, and helping in the kitchen, Dixie's permanent job as soon as they realized she knew how to cook. "Biscuits," she said. "They all loved my biscuits,

I had to get up at the crack of dawn to make them."

"Wasn't that hard?" I asked. "Didn't you mind?"

"No." She shook her dark curls. "I didn't care. I was just so glad to be away from home, away from Mama and Estelle. I didn't want to be Mary Margaret anymore. And I was sick of being Dixie, too — I didn't even realize that until I left."

So Dixie liked being Anna, who was nobody, measuring out the flour and the buttermilk in that great big shadowy kitchen at dawn. She taught the other girls to fox-trot and waltz, all of them laughing at how hard this was because of their big stomachs, and helped them with their schoolwork, for she was far beyond them all. Some could scarcely read, and these became Dixie's special challenge. To her surprise, she liked being pregnant, too, feeling her stomach stretch and pull, feeling the swell of her breasts.

"The first time he kicked, I got so excited I almost died," she told me. "I used to lie awake with my hands on my stomach so I could feel him moving around in there, which filled me with the strangest, strongest feeling. It was like a deep, deep joy. The baby still didn't seem exactly real to me,

293

but he made *me* feel real."

When Dixie's water broke (in the kitchen of the Florence Crittendon Home, while she was making biscuits) they rushed her to the hospital and then shaved her and gave her an enema, which was a horrible shock. Nobody had told her anything about having the baby, what it would be like. By then the pain was so bad, she asked the nurse for something to take, but while the nurse was gone the baby started coming, and then they were wheeling her out of that little room into the delivery room with its big blinding lights in her eyes. When Dixie woke up, she had already had the baby, a boy they said, and he was already gone.

A social worker came in and said, "Here, sign this paper. It's your choice — do you want to see your baby or not? We advise against it." Dixie said no and signed the paper giving him up to his adoptive parents, giving up all rights. And the social worker said, "Good. That's the best. Your parents will be coming for you in a few days."

But then Dixie cheated. In the middle of the night, she walked out to the baby room and saw him. A young nurse was giving him a bottle, right in front of the window. Then an old nurse noticed Dixie, and went into the baby room and whispered something to the young nurse, who looked up and then on some impulse held the baby straight out to Dixie, right on the other side of the glass, so that she could see him up close, his long head, his funny squashed nose, and dark fuzzy hair. Then the old nurse grabbed the baby up and whisked him away to the back of the baby room where he turned red and started crying and then Dixie couldn't see him anymore.

When Dixie's parents came for her, she started telling them what the baby had looked like, but her mother said, "Hush. You never had a baby. That never happened. You went off to college, but then you got tuberculosis, and so you have been staying with your aunt Julia, in Thomasville, to recuperate. In fact you are still recuperating. We are going there now."

Dixie had never met her father's younger sister, since Daisy Belle had always refused to have anything to do with his family. Julia, a plump, blowsy blonde, handed Dixie a glass of whisky the minute her parents left. "Well, you've been through hell, haven't you, honey?" she said. "I know all about it, believe me. You can stay here as long as you need to. First thing you'd better do is lie down."

When Dixie began to feel better, she

didn't want to go back home. So Julia got her a job at the candy counter up at the front of the dime store where Julia herself worked in the office; she had been the proprietor's mistress for twelve years. Here Dixie thrived, talking to everybody who came in the store, especially the boys from the nearby military academy who came in droves to buy her candied orange slices and nonpareils. Soon she was out every night with one or another, "dancing up a storm, and drinking . . . Lord! Seems like I was drunk half the time. I didn't care. I didn't care what I did, I didn't care about anything. And Julia didn't care, either. She was a drinker herself. Her Mr. Gordy was sneaking in and out all the time, Ernie Gordy, I got used to him. Hell, I *liked* him! Mr. Gordy was real nice."

Some of the cadets were nice boys, and some were not nice boys, and one of these had tried to do something bad to her one night and she had jumped out of his car in a clearing in the woods and he had roared off, furious, and that's when she met Frank Calhoun, who came along and stopped his car and was such a gentleman. He never even asked her what she was doing out there barefooted on that road in the middle of the night, wearing a party dress. A light rain had just begun to fall. He got out of the car and took off his seersucker jacket and put it around her shoulders before settling her into the passenger seat and asking her where she needed to go.

Frank Calhoun had been a soldier himself, it turned out, stationed in San Francisco, but then his father had died suddenly of a heart attack and he had been released from the navy and sent back home to run the farm. "And I'm still here," he said, smiling at Dixie, who was desperately trying to sober up enough to take all this in. She liked what she could see of him, the big square pleasant face in the dashboard lights. "Where is the farm?" she asked, and he said, "Here. Right outside of town here," and when she asked, "Is it a big farm?" he just grinned at her. "Yep," he said. He drove her back to Julia's, then got out and went around the car to open the door and hold an umbrella for her in the rain, which was pouring down like crazy by then, but this didn't matter because Dixie was a mess anyway, and all of a sudden she was crying so hard she couldn't see. Frank Calhoun was the perfect gentleman, escorting her up on the porch to the front door.

"Are you going to be all right now, Missy?" He lifted her chin to look into her eyes in the porch light.

She swallowed, tasting gin. "Yes. But nobody has ever been so nice to me."

He grinned, touching the tip of her nose. "You ain't seen nothing yet."

Which turned out to be completely true. Frank Calhoun was the nicest young man in the world, capable and calm, running El Destino, his family's plantation, which covered 400 acres and contained his embittered mother, who became furious when Frank dropped his childhood sweetheart, Raynelle, on the spot and married Dixie who came from trash whether she had actually made her debut at the Gone with the Wind Ball or not. Big Mama Calhoun turned out to be the only person in the world who didn't like Dixie on sight, and she never liked her, not even in the early years when Dixie was trying so hard and learned to ride the horses that Frank loved and joined the Junior Woman's Club and served on committees and gave big parties and had such a hard time with her first pregnancy, toxemia, that she had to be on bed rest the last three months. Dixie felt like an impostor in this life, and she always felt like Big Mama knew that she was an impostor.

But nobody knew her secret except Frank,

who loved her to distraction anyway, and always called her "Missy," and adored the little girls, too, riding first Margaret and then Lissa everywhere on his horse with him. Soon they both had little ponies of their own. Dixie had all the household help in the world. But none of that mattered. And somehow, having children of her own didn't matter, either. Somehow, that made it worse. Dixie knew what she had done, and she knew that she didn't deserve Frank, or her beautiful daughters, or her wonderful life. She was not worthy of any of it. She suffered from migraine headaches, colitis, and neuralgia. She stopped riding, she stopped seeing friends.

And then came the day when she just couldn't get out of bed.

CHAPTER 9

The first day of November dawned unseasonably warm and sunny. Somehow, the moment I woke up, I remembered to say "Rabbit, Rabbit" out loud, a superstitious practice taught to me by Mrs. Hodges years before, these words to be spoken first thing in the morning on the first day of each month to ensure good luck for all the days of the month ahead. And I even *felt* lucky as I skipped out after three sessions of playing piano for Phoebe Dean's groups and ran down the hill toward the greenhouse, looking for Pan.

"Where is he?" I asked, finding Mrs. Morris doing her crossword in a wicker chair she'd dragged out into the sunshine.

She looked up to smile at me. "Listen," she said. "You can hear him."

I followed her gaze up the hill toward the Central Building, then followed the music to the wide-open kitchen door, where a group of apron-clad workers had spilled out onto the lawn, some on wooden chairs and stools, some kneeling or seated on the cold, wiry grass. Most were singing along. Pan's harmonica wailed out above the voices. And there he sat, knee to knee with a blonde girl who was playing a small, handmade, and very old guitar. I could not see her face for the fall of her white-gold hair, but her high voice vaulted and arced over all the rest, sending a sudden chill to my heart, for I knew that voice somehow, as I knew the song, which I had learned from Ella Jean Bascomb years before. I drew closer and began to sing along.

Pan was playing the harmonica furiously and stomping his right foot on the ground, the way he always did. When he looked up and saw me, his eyes lit up and a big grin crept around the edge of his "harp." He nodded then threw his head back in a gesture of welcome, and my own heart soared with the music. Others greeted me as well. "Hey, little Liza, little Liza Jane," we sang. I sat down on the grass. From this perspective, I could see the girl guitar player's face, and then it came to me. She was Flossie, Ella Jean's sister who had gone off to Knoxville in the car with that horrible man, the one who had tried to kiss me in the dark woods. *Flossie!* She looked almost exactly like her mother now, though she was paler and even more beautiful.

When they were done with "Liza Jane," they did not stop but picked up the pace as they moved into "Orange Blossom Special," leaning in toward each other until their heads touched, his shaggy dark hair and her wild light curls that caught all the sunshine, as they played faster and faster, playing up a storm. For a moment on that bright sunny day everyone else fell absolutely silent; we knew we were hearing something rare, something wonderful. It was a moment caught in time and space that would not come again. Oddly it reminded me of my own senior recital accompanying Lillian Field at Peabody, years before. Then Pan went into a big long train whistle, going away, going down the track, around a curve and then another curve, and she kept up with him, all the way down the mountain. "Oh Lord!" Flossie hollered as she hit the last lick. "Woo woo!" Pan yelled as he jumped to his feet, harmonica still in one outstretched hand.

It was over. They were dispersing, headed back to work, when Mrs. Morris called from the edge of the group: "Pan, I hate to break this up, honey, but Cal needs you to go down to the station with him right now to pick up a shipment."

Pan touched my shoulder — just once, lightly, as he took off down the hill.

I got up and went to sit on his empty chair next to Flossie. She had appeared possessed, playing, but now she looked drained, slumped back in her chair as if exhausted, every bit of color bleached out of her by the bright winter sun. For a minute I wondered if she might be albino, or part albino, if such a thing were possible; yet I remembered how fair her beautiful mother was. Flossie sat gazing out at nothing, with no expression at all on her perfect paper-white face.

"You are Flossie Bascomb, aren't you?" I said. "I'm Evalina Toussaint, and I was a friend of your sister Ella Jean, a long time ago. She brought me up to your house one time to spend the night, and I met you then, and your family, and your granny, too. We sat out on the porch and sang the moon up." I smiled, for this was one of my favorite memories, and in all that had happened to me since, I had never lost it.

Her pale, glittery gaze moved back toward me very slowly, as if across the years. But I could tell that she remembered me.

"Where is Ella Jean now?" I asked. "And the rest of them? Do they still live up on that beautiful mountain?"

She stared at me. "Don't you *know*?"

I shook my head no. "I have lived away from here for a long time," I said.

"Shit." The word seemed doubly obscene, coming from such a pretty mouth. "Ella Jean's gone and got famous. I thought everbody knowed it. Famous and rich and *mean*! Won that National Banjo championship and got on Jimmy Dean's show and done made three records already. They call her the Cherokee Sweetheart these days. She was up in Cincinnati on a radio barn dance, the last I heard. She's done got too good for the likes of us'uns."

"Oh I'm sure that's not so," I said almost automatically, though what I said was true. For I remembered Ella Jean as forthright, honest as the day is long, and totally dedicated to her inexplicable family.

"And you —" I inquired more delicately. "You were on your way to Knoxville . . ."

"Well I got there," she said, "But it didn't work out. Ain't nothing ever worked out since, neither. That's the God's truth. You think I want to be over here working in this here kitchen? You think I don't want to be riding around in a custom-built silver tour bus with all the boyfriends and hundred-dollar bills I can handle? She wasn't the one

— I was the one. She didn't have no talent to speak of. I had the talent. And the looks. I was the one! I was the talent! And now look at me, here I am, slopping up soup for crazy people, just like Mama."

"How is your mother?"

"Dead." She turned to look straight at me, squinting her eyes to silver slits in the sunshine. "Mama's dead, and Mamaw's dead, and Wilmer's in Broughton, and Daddy's gone, along with the rest of 'em, and the house gone, too. *Burnt,*" she said in answer to my look. "Burnt to the ground, all gone, but let me tell you, honey, I am *still here*! Why, you just ask any of them, they know me. They know me around here. And I've got me a boyfriend, too. Yes ma'am. You might not think it to look at me, but I'm telling you, Miss Whatever-Your-Name-Is, I'm doing all right. I'm doing just *fine.*" Her speech became more rapid, more incoherent and hostile, as she spoke. I found myself drawing back, as if for safety. Inadvertently I rubbed my palm, which had begun to itch, for no reason I could think of. I remembered how Flossie's granny had held this hand so long ago, and the strangest feeling came over me. I shook my head to clear it, very relieved when Flossie suddenly jumped up, putting an end to our conversation.

"I'm glad to meet up with you again, Flossie," I said carefully. "And I really enjoyed the music."

"I'm the talent," she said, absently scratching her thigh as she stared off vacantly into the distance beyond me. I was chilled to the bone as I watched her turn and go back into the kitchen, shutting the door behind her. It struck me that Flossie might well be crazier than many of these hospitalized here at Highland, and I wondered what she meant when she said that she had a "boyfriend." Surely she didn't mean Pan.

I was very excited when told I could move into Graystone, the new women's halfway house. I would be a sort of hybrid, part patient, part staff. Though officially hired to help Phoebe Dean with music classes and all musical events, even teaching piano, I would still be required to continue my personal counseling with Dr. Schwartz and my group therapy sessions with the new young Dr. Sledge.

"For how long?" I asked Dr. Schwartz.

"For as long as it takes," she answered, smiling.

Graystone was an appropriately entitled

old bungalow on a tiny side street off Montford Avenue, almost but not actually on the hospital grounds. This made an enormous psychological difference. Graystone was an experiment — a residence intended for people in the final stages of "transitioning" into regular life outside the institution. A similar "halfway house" for men had already been operating for about six months, several blocks away on the other side of Highland's extensive grounds — too far away for socializing with us, or so it was hoped. A big, cheery social worker named Suzy Caldwell was present every morning to make coffee and get us going for the day. Suzy referred to herself as a "troubleshooter." She'd check our plans, reminding us of hospital events and appointments, sometimes giving us rides into town for errands, though we were encouraged to use the city buses whenever possible. They stopped right at the end of our street.

Everybody's schedule was different at Graystone, some combination of "day hospital" and work. I probably spent more time at the hospital than anybody else, since my job took place there, too. Well do I remember hiking up and down the icy hill in that winter's freezing rain or falling snow. Sometimes they took pity upon us and gave us a ride to and fro. Whenever we were all expected to attend the same program or event, the big green van arrived, always a welcome sight. Sometimes Suzy Caldwell came back again in the evening to check on us, often making popcorn or hot chocolate in the kitchen.

Left to Highland Hospital in an old lady's will, Graystone was like a time warp, homey as could be, with its flowered carpets, puffy old sofas, and antiques galore. China figurines, old framed photographs, and lacy antimacassars covered every available surface. It was like living in your grandmother's house — if you had had such a grandmother. I was willing to bet that most of the women and girls who would pass through these doors — such as myself — did *not,* so in a way, Graystone was like a kind of wish fulfillment, or fantasy, or stage set. Still, this was a play I was glad to have a part in, for once. I had lived beyond those hospital walls for years, and was more than ready to do so again.

I was issued a corner room upstairs, other bedrooms having been already taken by Myra, who was "learning to live without Mama," and black-headed Ruth, now taking phenobarbitol, and so much calmer and friendlier that she really seemed like a different person. Myra had been placed in a volunteer job at the public library. But Ruth had landed an impressive part-time job on her own, working at an exclusive designer clothing shop downtown near the bookstore. Ruth dressed to the nines every day, then caught the bus. I remember a red bead necklace she often wore, and her big lustrous pearls. I could not imagine such a job as hers, dressing up like that or dealing with the public so directly, convincing rich women to buy dresses.

"But sweetie, I've always been in retail," Ruth said when I expressed my admiration. "My parents were in retail, even my grandparents were in retail! They had a little shop on Seventh Avenue. Besides, what about you? You were playing the piano in front of about a hundred people at that program last night."

"Oh, that's different," I tried to explain. "That was background music. I'm just an accompanist, that's all."

Ruth's laughter floated out behind her as she clicked off down the hall in her high heels.

My last piano student of the day had failed to show up, so I was sitting in the alcove window seat reading, out of view, when the front door of Graystone burst open and a number of people came in with a rush of cold air, loud voices, and the general stamping of feet. Except for Dr. Bennett, I did not know the men's voices, though I recognized Dr. Schwartz, of course, and Mrs. Morris's calm tone. I was surprised that Mrs. Morris had left her accustomed realm of Brushwood and greenhouse and ventured all the way to Graystone. And why was Dr. Bennett here, anyway?

"Gentlemen," Dr. Bennett said in his clipped, commanding style. "Mrs. Morris will escort our new patient upstairs and help her get settled into her room while we take this opportunity for a brief chat."

"I'm staying right here." Soft but steely, the girl's flat Southern voice hung in the room.

I put my book facedown on the window seat.

"Now wait just a cotton-picking minute, young lady, who do you think you are, telling us what to do, when we've done brought you all the way over here?" a man's deep voice exploded. "Hell fire, I'd just as soon take you straight back to jail. That's where you belong anyhow, in my opinion. This here is a bunch of damn foolishness."

"Now, now, Officer Gillette," a more

neutral male voice interposed. "We are here to do the court's bidding, of course. And as a personal favor to Judge Ervin. *Annie Jenkins Feeney,*" the same man continued pointedly, louder. "You go on upstairs with the nice lady now. This is your big chance, as we discussed in the car. It may be your last chance."

I perked up my ears, as you might well imagine, for I had once heard these words myself.

"I ain't moving. I ain't about to move. I want to hear what you're going to say about me." The girl's flat little voice remained unperturbed. "Those papers are full of lies. I'm going to stay right here."

"Miss Feeney." Dr. Bennett adopted his most military manner. "The law requires us to conduct an intake interview with the referring authorities, under these circumstances."

"I can talk for myself," the girl said.

"That's the goddamn truth!" the deep voice was raised. "And won't shut up, neither!"

I decided he must be a policeman. Probably the other one was some kind of police social worker.

"Of course you can speak for yourself, Annie," Dr. Schwartz said, "and you shall have

311

every opportunity to do so. At Highland Hospital, we are here to listen and to help. We hope that we can help *you*. But before we can do that, we have to admit you, don't you see?"

"Come along, dear. I think you'll like your room." Mrs. Morris's reassuring voice was followed by her heavy tread on the stairs. The girl said nothing more, and soon I heard their steps and voices above me. I was dying to go up there, too, but at this point I could not show myself, of course, or all would be lost. I shrank back into the pillows to listen.

"Gentlemen," Dr. Bennett began, "this is an unusual situation. You have brought us a new patient, remanded by the court."

"Sent by Judge Ervin hisself," the deep voice agreed. "She up and wrote him a damn letter, damnedest thing I ever heard of. So then he taken her out of jail and sends her over *here*." The man made a sound of disgust. "Seems like he knowed this Dr. Carroll in college or something."

"I'd like to read that letter," Dr. Schwartz remarked.

"It's in her file, I'm sure," the other man said, "which I might as well give you right now."

"Dr. Carroll has stepped down as head of

312

this hospital," Dr. Bennett said in a smooth, formal voice, "though he remains closely involved, as a member of our governing board. However, as he is in Florida for the winter, Highland Hospital will be pleased to honor the judge's request for a thorough evaluation and treatment or whatever." There was a creaking sound as he stood up.

"*Excuse me,* Dr. Bennett." Dr. Schwartz's voice surprised me in its firmness. "I am sure you've got other, much more important fish to fry. But as the Director of Psychiatry for adolescent girls at Highland Hospital, I shall be in charge of Miss Feeney, and I am personally requesting that you listen to her history as presented in these transfer papers from Samarcand Manor, the reformatory where she was incarcerated before being sent to jail in Statesville, thence to us. I want you to understand exactly what we will be dealing with."

"Yes, Gail." I heard the sigh and then the creaking noise as he sat back down. I imagined him glancing at his watch; with Dr. Bennett, the schedule was everything.

"Thank you," Dr. Schwartz said crisply, rustling the papers. "My goodness, this is quite a file for such a young person. Since your time with us is so limited, Dr. Bennett, I shall try to concentrate upon only the most pertinent facts, at this point. Let's see . . ." At length, she began:

"Name, Annie Jenkins Feeney, age seventeen. No fixed address; ward of the state. Birthplace unknown. Over-sexed female adolescent of the high moron type; a moral imbecile. Mother, Catherine Jenkins Feeney, died in the Virginia State Mental Hospital in Staunton, Virginia. Girl raised by father Kirvin Feeney, drunkard, tinker, and carpenter, primarily at Pocosin, N.C., until his death. Girl then taken into the good Christian home of her aunt and uncle, Mary Ellen and Royster Biggs of Warsaw, North Carolina. After two years of defiance, rude behavior, and disruption including arrests for drunken and disorderly conduct, girl ran off with a Negro, finally apprehended in a Blue Ridge tourist cabin. Whereupon Mr. and Mrs. Biggs were forced to seek the services of the state. Girl declared 'unmanageable . . . incorrigible . . . dual personality.' " Dr. Schwartz was clearly skimming along now. "Morally defective . . . suspected of prostitution . . . my goodness!" she exclaimed before going on. "Girl admitted to Samarcand Manor where necessary therapeutic sterilization was performed for the public good. Gentlemen, this is outrageous!"

"Now wait a cotton-picking minute, Doctor," came the deep voice. "You gotta understand, these morons breed like mink. And she had ran off with a Negro, remember that. The duty of the state is to protect the race."

"Oh, is that so?"

I could just imagine Dr. Schwartz's face, the way she drew her mouth into a tight straight line.

"Yes ma'am," came the milder voice. "Working in a high-class situation like the present, you may never have encountered such a type, meaning no disrespect, of course. But in our line of work, we deal with plenty of them, believe me, and I want to make you aware that this particular girl, this Jinx Feeney, is a special case. I have never seen such a one as her, I'm here to tell you. It's been one reckless act of defiance after another. Why, she even set her mattress on fire over at Samarcand! That's how she got herself out of the reformatory and into prison. That's the history here. I urge you to be careful, doctor, that's all. Never trust her. This girl has unusual language and musical abilities, physical coordination, and great cleverness, but she has no sense of right and wrong, and no soul either. Mark my words. No matter how much she fooled the judge, Jinx Feeney is a dangerous girl."

They hate her, I realized, chilled. *They really hate her.*

"Wait a minute. What did you just call her?" Dr. Schwartz asked. "Not Annie, but . . . ?"

" 'Jinx,' " he said. "That's what she goes by, and believe me, it's appropriate."

"Thank you, gentlemen, for these insights." It was Dr. Bennett's rising good-bye tone. "It sounds to me as if you will, indeed, have your capable hands full, Dr. Schwartz, and even your famous compassion may be tested. Girl trouble is not my bailiwick, of course, so I shall leave you to it. Gentlemen, we thank you for your services, and wish you a good day."

It was over. A rush of cold air poured into the parlor in the men's wake.

Dr. Morris came back downstairs. "She's sleeping now," she told Dr. Schwartz. "Out like a light."

"I'm sure she's exhausted," Dr. Schwartz said. "I'm exhausted myself, just from reading her file! But we'd best get on back, hadn't we, Maureen? I've already missed two appointments this afternoon."

"I wonder if it's wise to leave her here like this, Gail."

"We are not operating a prison," Dr.

Schwartz said lightly. "And Mr. Dobson was right, you know. This is her last chance. She ought to be on her best behavior. Besides, the other girls will be back within the hour. In fact, I'll try to intercept Evalina."

"I still think the girl should have been placed in the adolescent wing."

"She's too experienced, and too smart," Dr. Schwartz said. "As well as thoroughly sexualized, from the sound of it. Besides, Jinx Feeney will not be with us long, unless I miss my guess entirely. Despite that nickname, her luck may be about to change."

"Be careful, Gail," Mrs. Morris said, the last bit of conversation I overheard. "Don't forget what that awful man said. Sometime you really may be too trusting for your own good."

"Well, *you're* one to talk!" Dr. Schwartz exclaimed.

The door closed behind them.

A few minutes later, I found our old beat-up pot with a lid and popped some popcorn in it, then dumped it into the basket and took it upstairs. I knocked on our new resident's door.

"Come in." That odd little voice.

I pushed the door open to find her sitting

straight up in bed, cross-legged and obviously wide awake. Had she really been sleeping?

Or had she fooled Mrs. Morris . . . and if so, why?

"Ooh, I thought I smelled popcorn!" she said. "I was just sitting here hoping it wasn't a dream and hoping I was going to get some of it. I'm about to starve."

"Didn't you have any lunch?"

She gave a disgusted snort. "*Hell* no! Them cops wouldn't stop for nothing. They like to starved me to death, I'm telling you. They done it on purpose."

Warily, I thrust the basket across the bed; after all I'd heard, I was a little bit scared of her. She grabbed the basket and started eating the popcorn ravenously. She didn't look at all like I'd thought she would. I had expected a large, belligerent person, but this girl was a waif: pale, wiry, freckled, with a mass of curly red hair and light green eyes, small and hard, shaped like almonds.

She looked up from the popcorn once to ask, "Have y'all got anything to drink?"

"Sure." I ran back down to the kitchen where I poured her a tall glass of milk, then carried it carefully up the steps. The girl drank half of it in one long swallow. She licked her top lip and looked me square in the eye.

"I'm Jinx," she said.

"I'm Evalina," I said.

She nodded. "Are you a lady or a girl?"

I had to smile. "A lady, I guess." I was ten years older than she.

"Are you a nurse?"

"No, I'm a patient," I said. "Or a resident, I guess I should say, on my way to getting out of the hospital. I've got a job playing the piano for their programs."

She lit up. "I can sing," she said. "Dance, too."

"Well, you just might get a chance to do that," I told her. "They're big on that here."

Still sitting straight up on the bed like an advertisement for perfect posture, Jinx stared at me intently. "You are going to be my friend," she said. "I need one. I have to make friends and have increased socialization and pass a lot of tests to get out of here. And not set fire to my bed and not hit anybody. You think I can do it?"

"I don't know," I said.

"You want some of this popcorn?"

"Sure." I perched gingerly upon the edge of her bed, and we finished it up together.

Jinx was dying to tell her own story, which

was completely different from the police record I had overheard in the alcove at Graystone, though in a way, both stories were true. Her mother, had she lived, might have offered another; certainly her aunt and uncle had stuck to their own angry narrative. Perhaps any life is such: different stories like different strands, each distinct in itself, each true, yet wound together to form one rope, one life. I couldn't say. I don't know why they all told them to *me,* either. Dr. Schwartz suggested that I'm a good listener — maybe that's like being a good accompanist.

Anyhow, this is Jinx's version.

Though born into a "good family," Jinx's mother was "never right," causing that family no end of trouble and embarrassment before she ran away with the Irish tinker and musician Kirvin Feeney, traveling all over the South in his specially built wagon, like a little house, pulled by two horses named Dan and Grace, stopping only for their child Annie Jenkins's birth. So Jinx's earliest and happiest memories are of life in the tinker truck, pulling out all the little hand-built drawers one by one, hundreds of drawers, each containing its own nails or bolts or tools; sitting on her mother's lap before a campfire deep in the woods; feeding hay to the greedy horses, who grabbed it right out of her little hands; and kneeling down to drink from running creeks. Her mother used to laugh a lot in those days and sing endless songs to the tune of Kirvin's fiddle. Those were the good times, before old Dan died and Grace went lame and a rich widow, one of Kirvin's favorite customers over the years, up and gave them a place to stay.

The old white frame house sat deep in the pinewoods at the edge of blackwater swamp. Jinx had her own room with no bed but a mattress on the floor with a velvet crazy quilt flung across it and a sky-blue chest of drawers where she kept the little dolls that her mother crocheted for her, an entire village of little dolls. She cannot remember the kitchen, where no one ever cooked, or the parlor, where no one ever sat.

What she does remember is her father's workroom, the shed beside the house where people came to get things repaired, such as engines and threshers and stoves and hand mills and even radios — or the handles of pots and pans, or the blades of knives or saws, or anything that needed sharpening. Her daddy could fix anything. While they waited, men played cards or checkers at the long table he had made of a single board from the big tree that fell out by the ice-house. Or they gossiped and talked or played music with Daddy joining in, for it was always easy to get him to quit working and fiddle a tune. Even as a tiny tot, Jinx learned to sing "Danny Boy" and to dance a jig with the best of them. Liquor was sold from under the floorboard, where it was hidden when certain people were present. The liquor was brought by a black man named Noah Dellinger and his son, Orlando, who became Jinx's best and only friend, a skinny, solemn boy who could play the banjo like nobody's business, joining right in with the men.

By the time she was three or four, Jinx knew to stay out in the workroom and not in the house where her mother spoke often to those who were not there, sometimes obeying their instructions to set off on a little trip with her daughter — hitchhiking into town, say — which Jinx enjoyed — or all the way to Edenton; or moving into an abandoned bread truck out in the woods where there was nothing to eat but blackberries. Jinx stopped going when she grew old enough to resist. Then her mother went off traveling alone, and then she was put into a hospital somewhere up in Virginia. Jinx knew her mother died there, but instead she likes to imagine her still riding on a bus, looking out the window at the passing scenery.

Kirvin Feeney had girlfriends, nice girlfriends who cooked sometimes, or cleaned up, and gave Jinx clothes and taught her to dance and wear makeup when she was just a little girl, a "little fancy girl" they called her. Everybody got a kick out of her. The only problem was that these women tended to leave pretty quick once they realized they were not going to change her daddy. Though Jinx went to school for a while, she soon stopped trying. It was hard to get there, and it was more fun to hang around the shop with the men anyway. The older she got, the nicer they were.

Soon she was going off with some of them to do things that were mostly fun anyway and didn't mean a damn thing to her anyhow. If Kirvin Feeney knew about these things, he never said so, but his health was so bad by then that he had pretty much stopped working, and he must have been glad for the kerosene and coffee and food that she supplied, though finally he wouldn't eat hardly anything, living on grits and liquor brought around by Orlando Dellinger and his daddy, the only ones of all that crowd who continued to come to the house at the end.

Jinx was sent to live with her mother's sister, whom she had never even seen. This was her aunt, Mary Ellen, and her uncle, Royster Biggs, who ran a big hog farm out in the country near Warsaw, North Carolina. The man from the state drove her over there. The highway ran straight as a ruler across the dry red land that lay flat in every direction, laid out in different kinds of fields like some kind of big board game.

Her aunt and uncle's two-story brick house sat out in the middle of a yellow field as if it had been dropped there. Out behind the house were the hog barns, long low structures, lots of them, and several big scummy ponds that looked suspicious. "Damn," the man said. "I can smell it already." He rolled up his window, which did not help. To the left sat a brick garage that was nearly as large as the house, with space for five vehicles. A gleaming white Cadillac with fins was pulled up in front of the house. The door of the house opened up, and there stood her uncle and aunt, who looked like hogs themselves.

"Oh, they did not!" I exclaimed at this part of the story, but Jinx swore they did, from their fat pink hands and arms right down to the hairs in his nose and ears and her aunt's plump cheeks and rosy complexion, the diamond rings she always wore cutting into the flesh of her pudgy fingers.

"I would have known you anywhere, you poor little thing, you!" Jinx's aunt Mary Ellen exclaimed, smothering Jinx in a hug, which Jinx hated, she said, even when Aunt Mary Ellen burst into tears and cried, "Oh Royster, she looks just like Catherine!"

"Well, that don't sound too good to me," Uncle Royster said, carrying Jinx's bag into the house, where all the furniture looked like big dark crouching animals. Up they went, one, two, three flights of stairs to a stifling attic room with a fan in it at least. The bedside table held a Bible, which Aunt Mary Ellen picked up and presented to Jinx. "It is never too late," she said, her cheeks quivering.

The Bible turned out to have a bookmark in it, open to the story of the prodigal son. Uncle Royster turned out to be a deacon in the church, as well as a member of the Ku Klux Klan. Jinx found the box holding all his regalia in the crawl space at the back of the attic closet, along with several boxes of guns, carefully oiled and shiny.

They bought her some new clothes in Kinston and made her go to church on Sunday, Sunday night, and Wednesday. The minister's son, Troy Merritt, had a big crush on her. They made her go to the consolidated school, too, but the kids made fun of her, how ignorant she was for her age, so soon she was skipping out and playing hooky with some of them, and then they all got caught and her uncle disciplined her by spanking her with a hairbrush on her thighs where no one could see the marks. "This is our duty," Aunt Mary Ellen told Jinx. They knelt and prayed for her, making her kneel, too.

Then she ran away with Troy Merritt in his parents' car, and all hell broke loose. They stayed gone for two days. Jinx was brought back to the farm by the sheriff himself. A sweet old man, he came into the parlor where he stood with his hat in his hands and surprised them by counseling kindness and mercy. "This girl has already been through a lot," he said. "It's time for this family to come together and make a new start." Jinx hated for him to leave. She stood at a dining room window watching him drive off down the driveway, kicking up a plume of dust that grew smaller and smaller.

Her aunt went, too, out to the grocery store. Uncle Royster made her take off her panties and bend over the sofa while he whipped her with his belt, raising welts on her butt with the buckle which had his initials on it, REB. Her aunt came home and fixed chicken and biscuits, Jinx's favorite dish, in honor of the brand-new start, the three of them holding hands for the blessing.

That night Uncle Royster came up to the attic and into her bed, and when she fought him, he said, "Why, you're one little hellion, you are!" almost approvingly. "But how are you gonna like this?" holding the cold gun against her temple so that she would get down and do what he said. Such things happened many nights afterward, so long as Jinx stayed in that house, but she didn't care anymore, or fight back, or react in any way, which made him "madder than fire," she said. She made Fs at school, which Troy Merritt no longer attended, having been sent away to a military academy.

One day Jinx got off the bus and came in to find her aunt waiting for her, seated on the floral sofa with an even higher color in her cheeks. "Dear," she said — this is how she had addressed Jinx ever since the new start — "in doing the laundry today, I noticed stains in several pairs of your panties. It looks to me like they are *bloodstains*, Annie, and I believe it's time for you to tell me what is going on."

"Nothing." Jinx slung her bookbag onto the marbletop coffee table. "Not a goddamn thing."

"Don't you swear at *me,* young lady. I am trying to help you. This question is just between you and I, dear. Are you having menstrual problems? Or perhaps, er, *relations*?"

Jinx looked her in the eye. "Why, yes I am," she said. "With your husband, my uncle Royster Earl Biggs. He pulls a gun on me to make me do it."

Jinx's aunt turned bright red, then white, then red again. She stood up and started screaming and pulling at her hair, which came loose from its ugly clamps and clips and stood out all over her head like snakes. "Liar!" she screamed. "Whore!" beating at her own face with a Guidepost magazine.

"I couldn't believe she even *knew* those words!" Jinx told me, gigglng.

When her aunt stumbled off to lie down, claiming palpitations of the heart, Jinx stuck her few belongings into her pillowcase and grabbed a set of keys to the old green Ford from the secret drawer in the mudroom. For weeks now, she had been practicing on it. She picked up Orlando Dellinger in Greenville two hours later. He wore a maroon felt cap and carried his banjo and a valise that contained, among other things, several bottles of whisky and a .45.

Dear. Judge. Irven.

If you think you are doing me a faver to let me out of jail here at Carthage and send me back to Samarcand Manor I want to tell you Dear Judge you are NOT. The Moore County Jail is Heaven in my opinon. I will stay in this Jail a hunnerd years before I go back over there.

It is True I set my bed on fire, I am not sorry ether, I do not care. I will do it agin in a minit, anything to tare that place down to the ground so No One will ever go there agin. It is not fit for a soul. I have been chased by dogs over there, and bit in the leg, and made to lie down nekid on the dirty floor and beat with Whips until bloody, I have still got the scars on my legs to show for it, and been locked up for days in a filthy room to sleep with rats, and also with a girl that had the dipthery but I did not catch it ha ha. I am STILL ALIVE and I beg you do not send me back over there.

If you think it is a Reformatery it is NOT they do not reform any one over there but make us mean and sad and turn into Bad girls that do not give a dam, as I was before I landed in this nice jail where Sheruff Tate and his wife treats you good like a real Person and has give me a white Bible for my Own. This Bible is a humdinger with the words of Jesus wrote out in red. I love to read and the Bible above all, I want to be Good above all in fact I will be so good and cook or clean or help out in any way even slops I mean it. Do not send me back over there for the Love of God do not. O please Dear Judge I am a child of God like your own children if you have got any, do NOT send me back over there for the love of God do not, let me stay in the Moore County Jail I will be So Good I sware it.

SIGNED ANNIE JENKINS FEENEY

JINX

I believed Jinx's story, told to me over several baskets of popcorn during late nights sitting up before the electric grate at Graystone. And I read the letter she wrote to the judge, because Dr. Schwartz shared it with the staff, including Phoebe Dean. Yet I was never certain that this letter was completely sincere, though it had obviously been effective. For one thing, I never saw that precious white Bible. For another thing, I soon realized that Jinx lied constantly, almost reflexively, and often for no reason at all. She once told Suzy Caldwell that we had taken a bus to the neighboring town of Black Mountain, for instance, when we had not; she told Dr. Schwartz that I was sick when I was not; she told Phoebe Dean that I was mad at her, when I was not, and on and on. I began to wonder if Jinx could even tell the difference between the truth and a fib. I overheard her telling Mr. Pugh that she couldn't do her homework because she had lost her history book, when I had seen her stick it in the garbage can myself, and later remonstrated with her about it, telling her how expensive textbooks are, to which she made a face, cutting her green eyes away from mine. "I don't care," she said.

This disturbed me, as did some pretty little pearl earrings that tumbled out of her book bag another day. It was hard to tell what Jinx did care about, if anything, other than getting out of Highland. But after all she had been through, who could blame her now for anything she said or did to save herself?

CHAPTER 10

"I told you she'd be back," Miss Malone remarked one dark afternoon in November as we were cleaning up the Art Room. I was the only group member yet remaining.

"You mean Mrs. Fitzgerald," I said. It was not even a question. I stopped picking up my little mosaic tiles to look at her.

She nodded. "Arriving next week, I'm told. For another *rehabilitation and reeducational program*" — Miss Malone's expression told what she thought of this — "plus deep-shock insulin, of course."

"I imagine she'll be in here painting again?" I ventured.

Miss Malone shook her head, the long gray ponytail swinging. "Not immediately. Not till they've got her well under way up there on the top floor. Though it would do her more good than any of that other. Her husband may have stolen her words — and her life, for that matter — but he can't steal her art. She's safe here. We'll see her soon enough, I imagine."

I couldn't wait to tell Dixie.

The two of us were headed for lunch on a freezing though sunny morning. I had just had a session at the Beauty Box with Dixie and Brenda Ray, who were still working on my unruly hair, now growing out wispy but curly.

"Wait. Slow down." Dixie put her newly manicured hand on my arm.

Sure enough, a sort of assemblage, with everyone in winter coats, was gathered there before the grand entrance to Highland Hall, and a car driven by Mrs. Morris's husband was just pulling away from the curb. I stopped walking, along with Dixie.

"It's *her*," Dixie whispered in my ear. "Isn't it? It's her. She's back."

For now we could see the woman who was being escorted into the building with Dr. Pine on one side of her and Dr. Sledge on the other. Between the two of them she appeared as small and frail as a child, in a long, nondescript gray coat that was clearly too large for her, and a funny brown knit hat that nearly hid her hair, dull and graying now. Mrs. Fitzgerald looked neither left nor right but kept her eyes down, mouth moving all the while, as they passed through the group on the sidewalk and entered the building. The door shut behind them.

"Oh, my goodness, she looks so *old*!" Dixie remarked. "She's only forty-eight — I remember because she was born in 1900 — but she could be seventy, I swear! She doesn't look anything like her pictures."

"She's really sick right now," I said. "But she looks different all the time anyway, and she'll look different the next time you see her, too. You'll see."

Except Dixie wouldn't see her again, I remembered suddenly, biting my lip. For Dixie was going home to stay, at the plantation out from Thomasville, Georgia, if everything went as smoothly during Christmas as was hoped.

The group was dispersing as Dr. Schwartz came over to hug both of us. "Sad, isn't it?" she said. "But she'll be much better soon."

Tall, shy Dr. Sledge emerged from the entrance hall, shaking his head but smiling to see us. "Ladies, let's get some lunch," he said in that old-fashioned way he had.

"Hold your horses, now! Just hold your horses!" Suddenly Mrs. Hodges had lumbered in amongst us, out of breath, wearing a huge red hat. "Where's that Dr. Pine? Where's he got to? I've got an important message for him. From Minnie Sayre her-self," she snorted with emphasis, her breath making puffs in the air as she spoke.

"Who's that?" Dixie asked me, just as Dr. Schwartz said, "Oh dear, he's not here right now. I imagine he is still escorting Mrs. Fitzgerald up to her room."

"Mrs. Sayre is her *mother*," I told Dixie. "Mrs. Fitzgerald's mother. The one she lives with when she's in Montgomery."

"Lord, *she* must be a hundred then," Dixie whispered back.

"Well, Minnie Sayre called me up on the long-distance tel-e-phone just as I was finishing up my breakfast this morning," Mrs. Hodges announced loudly and impor-tantly to any who might be listening, "with some important information, and so you'd best give him this message, Miss —" which was what she always called Dr. Schwartz.

Dr. Schwartz hid a smile, nodding. "I'm all ears, Mrs. Hodges, please do go on."

Mrs. Hodges put a gloved hand to her heaving breast as she continued dramati-cally: "Well, Minnie Sayre wanted me to know that Zelda — Mrs. Fitzgerald — had suffered a pre-mo-nition just as she was leaving Montgomery, and she wanted us all to know the circumstances of it, and what it was exactly."

"Yes?" Dr. Schwartz said as we all drew around, Dr. Sledge leaning in, too.

"Apparently they were all gathered together on the porch of Rabbit Run — now that's Minnie Sayre's little house down there in Montgomery, that's what they call it, don't you know, on account of it's so small, all those little rooms right in a row. Well they were all gathered there on the porch to wait for the taxicab to come for Miss Zelda — now this is Mrs. Minnie Sayre herself, and Miss Marjorie, she's the other daughter, Miss Zelda's sister, don't you know, and yet another one of their friends down there, a lady named Livvie Hart, I believe it was." She stopped to catch her breath.

"So *what happened,* ma'am?" Dr. Sledge asked gently.

"I'm telling you, don't rush me, I'm getting to it in my own sweet time. Just kindly remember that you wouldn't know one thing about it if it wasn't me telling you, for she never would have called the rest of ye, Minnie Sayre would not, what with the Carrolls gone off to Florida and all of the rest of ye perfect strangers to her, of course. So! Of course it is me she'd call, Mrs. Hodges, that she has known all these years. She knew she could depend upon me. So! It seems that they was all gathered on the little porch there, and the taxi pulls up, and Miss Zelda she begins walking down the walk toward the taxi and she was almost in it when suddenly she runs back and throws her arms around Minnie and says, very composed, 'Don't worry, Mama, I'm not afraid to die.' Just like that. 'Don't worry, Mama, I'm not afraid to die.' "

The color drained right out of Dr. Schwartz's cheeks, and Dixie's hand on my arm suddenly felt like a claw.

"And then? What happened next, ma'am?" from Dr. Sledge.

"Well, then, she turned around and composed herself like the fine lady she is, and walked back down the walk and got in the taxi and thence the train, and here she is. A trip she has made a hundred times. But her mother wanted you to know this, don't you see, Miss Zelda's pre-mo-nition and all the circumstances of it."

"Yes, I can see that. We thank you so much, Mrs. Hodges," Dr. Schwartz said. "But now, won't you come and join us for lunch? Our new Dr. Sledge will be your escort."

Dr. Sledge smiled and nodded, extending his arm like a dance partner.

"Well, he's a big un, ain't he? But ah, no,

I've got God's own amount of work to do over at the Grove Park. They cannot exist for long without me, don't you know. My daughter is a-waiting for me right now, she drove me in the car there."

"Oh yes, I see her now," Dr. Schwartz said.

I turned and waved at redheaded Ruthie, who waved back.

"We certainly do appreciate your making this visit, then, and I will be sure that Dr. Pine receives the information," Dr. Schwartz called out to Mrs. Hodges as Dr. Sledge walked her over to Ruthie's car and put her in it.

"My goodness!" he said, coming back. "And that was — ?"

"Mrs. Hodges!" we chorused, laughing, and then all went in to lunch except for me. Pleading ill health, I excused myself and went to my own room instead. I sat on my bed, unable to get this odd little scene out of my mind, where it has remained as clear as if I had seen it myself. My palm itched fiercely and I remembered what Ella Jean's granny had told me about "the sight." Perhaps it is true that I have always had "too much i-mag-i-nation for my own good," as Mrs. Hodges once claimed, but her report unsettled me, all the same.

And it was the oddest thing — not only

we few, but everyone at Highland Hospital seemed to know that Mrs. Fitzgerald had returned, in that indefinable yet immediate way that knowledge travels in even the most carefully guarded of institutions. And somehow, this knowledge was exciting — even gratifying — to the rest of us. I know there is something wrong with this — and I am stating it badly — yet it is a fact, an uncomfortable truth. Mrs. Fitzgerald completed us, perhaps. And now she was back, one of us again.

I dreaded group therapy, even with the very popular Dr. Sledge. Perhaps due to the solitary, almost secretive nature of my own childhood, I have always been uncomfortable speaking about personal matters, especially in groups. I'd rather listen to others. I do not wish to have the spotlight focused upon me; I really do prefer to be the accompanist. It was not that I could not remember — many things, as time went on — it was simply that I did not wish to divulge these things to perfect strangers whom I would not see again, I knew, once the kaleidoscope had made another quarter turn. I had a longer perspective on this process than the others.

I tried to explain all this to Dr. Sledge

when he characterized me as "resistant to therapy." He said he understood my feelings, and I felt he did, for he seemed shy himself, smiling hesitantly in his gentle way behind his thick glasses. He was a very large young man, nonathletic, with curly brown hair. ("Mama's boy," Jinx pronounced scornfully, and "pansy" — though even she liked him.) But for a psychiatrist, Dr. Sledge seemed oddly lacking in communication skills, a failing that was almost a technique. Often he seemed at a loss for words, letting a silence fall and extend itself if no one volunteered an immediate answer. These long silences settled upon us like snow, producing sudden, explosive, surprising results.

I remember one session when the announced topic was "home." No one spoke. Blushing determinedly, Dr. Sledge did not push us; instead he got comfortable, stretching out his long legs, crossing his ankles and putting his hands behind his head, looking out the window toward the snowy peaks. The moment grew, expanding.

Suddenly Dixie burst out. "I didn't have a home at all, it was just a shell, a doll's house, and I was Mama's doll, that's all, just a pretty doll to dress up and sew for . . ." Dr. Sledge continued to lean back, nodding, listening.

Charles Winston, a young veteran, spoke about the cruelty of his father, a tobacco magnate who had shot the family dog to death right in front of the children when it misbehaved, and then in the next breath announced that this was nothing, because he himself had shot a child during the war, a girl about eight years old, as she ran from a barn in France. "She fell over and crumpled up like a rag doll and her blood made the snow red all around her." Charles choked it out. "They were shooting at us from the farmhouse." He put his head down between his knees, rocking and sobbing.

Jinx told about the little drawers in the tinker truck, then went on, "You can give me a truck anytime, over a house, I mean. I ain't kidding. Once somebody gets you in a house, they can lock you up in there and do all kinds of things to you, and nobody knows it. You can just forget about home. I don't want no home." For once, I felt she was telling the truth. But her outburst caused a kind of eruption in the entire group. When we had quieted down, Dr. Sledge turned to me.

"Evalina?" he asked gently, and I was amazed to find my own face wet with tears.

"This is my home," I said.

"It is not, either," Jinx said. "It's a mental institution, in case you ain't noticed."

Everybody laughed.

"I'm sorry." I went to Dr. Sledge's office later that day to apologize. "I just can't talk about these things in the group, that's all. But Dr. Carroll put my entire childhood in the record, I'm sure. You can look me up if you want to. My mother was an exotic dancer in New Orleans, a courtesan, and my father was a rich man who sent me here after her death. That's all."

Dr. Sledge put a large, soft hand on each of my shoulders, and looked me in the eye. "Thank you, Evalina," he said gravely. "Thank you." He acted as if I had given him a gift, and I felt, oddly, as if I had, though it turned out to be a gift for me, too, as that very afternoon I took the bus downtown to Woolworth's, where I purchased the first of these notebooks and began jotting down all the details that suddenly came into my mind — the big bed, the mirror, the beignets, and the neon GIRLS GIRLS GIRLS sign outside the window, for instance.

I took a deep breath. "Dr. Schwartz says you play clarinet. Would you like to play with us sometime? We have a little jazz group here — me, and Phoebe Dean, and Mr. Pugh, and whoever else wants to play, really. Sometimes we have Louis Lagrande on drums — when he's well enough, that is. He's a patient here."

Dr. Sledge turned bright red, like a child. "I'd like that very much," he said.

He turned out to be good, too, adding a great deal to our group, which got together every Wednesday evening in the great room at Homewood, something I always looked forward to. Often, as I played, I'd feel Dr. Sledge's eyes upon me; several times I turned abruptly and found him staring at me.

"He likes you," Dixie said after attending one of these sessions. "He's going to ask you out, just wait and see."

"Oh, he is not," I said, "They're not allowed to get involved with the patients, anyhow. He's just being friendly." But when Dr. Sledge stopped me in the hall and said, "Evalina, you know you're right, you've been here longer than anybody. I wonder if you'd like to be my tour guide around Asheville one afternoon?" I was quick to accept, to the subsequent crowing delight of my roommates at Graystone, who hid behind the curtains to watch us leave, exactly as if we were all thirteen. Illness infantilizes everybody, even if it doesn't paralyze or wreck us forever. It holds us back, it keeps us from being adults. I believe this is especially true when *children* are ill, or have been damaged during their childhood or adolescence — all those crucial stages of development are missed. But I am thinking aloud now, thinking of us all upon our snowy mountain, and wandering from the moment of my story.

Doctor Sledge is picking me up. He parks at the curb in front of Graystone and gets out wearing a red muffler, a huge tweed coat, and a plaid cap with earflaps. He's driving a blue station wagon, the kind with wood along the sides. It is meticulously cared for, scrupulously clean. It looks like the family car of some family in the Midwest, the kind of family you see in advertisements. This is not far from the truth, actually.

On this and subsequent rides, I learned all about this family, consisting of Mrs. Sledge, the mother whom he adored, his three older sisters, and his identical twin brother, Rupert. Two key facts drove this narrative. The first was that Mr. Sledge, a businessman, had dropped dead from a heart attack soon after the twins were born. The second was that Dr. Sledge's twin had turned out to be schizophrenic, though "the sweetest and gentlest of men," thus determining Dr. Sledge's own story — his empathy, his gravity, his eventual vocation. Dr. Sledge postponed college and took a job at home in order to help his mother take care of Rupert, until Rupert killed himself at twenty. Then Dr. Sledge enrolled at Ball State, followed by medical school at the university, and an internship at the Mayo Clinic. This story also explained Dr. Sledge's somewhat princelike aura, for he was not only loved but virtually worshipped by his mother and all those sisters back in Indiana. This was of course a burden, though a gift. It explained everything. If ever a man were trustworthy, it would be Dr. Sledge.

I took him to see the Biltmore House; the French Broad River; Thomas Wolfe's grave at Riverside cemetery, which has a regular tombstone, not the angel everybody expects; and the Old Kentucky Home, his mother's boardinghouse downtown, which Wolfe had made famous in *Look Homeward, Angel.* The following Sunday we went for a drive along the breathtaking Blue Ridge Parkway, built by the WPA. We stopped at an overlook to look out at the dreamy, quiltlike landscape below, then stopped again at Mabry Mill to watch dried corn being ground up into meal by the giant turning stone water wheels. It was a very cold day, I remember. Dr. Sledge's red muffler exactly matched the red spots on his cheeks. He bought a cloth bag of the freshly ground cornmeal to send to his mother, Dorothy — called "Dot" — back in Indiana. While he paid the mountain girl at the counter, I checked my watch. "Too late," I announced, for I had been planning to take him by Fat Daddy's for a barbecue sandwich before our return to Highland, where I had to play for the glee club concert late that afternoon.

"You know, you weren't kidding, were you?" Dr. Sledge said when we got back into the station wagon. "Asheville actually is home for you, isn't it? I certainly picked the right tour guide."

"Oh, I was just talking, I guess. But I've certainly lived here a long while, off and on — exactly like Mrs. Fitzgerald." I realized this only as I said it. "We even arrived at Highland about the same time, a little over ten years ago. Of course I was scarcely more than a child myself, and she was a grown woman . . ."

"Only in a manner of speaking, from what I understand," Dr. Sledge said. "Remember that she was still in her teens, no real education, when she married Scott Fitzgerald and fell into that fast world of constant drinking and parties and travel — perhaps she never had a chance to grow up any further than that, emotionally. Alcoholism is an illness in itself, you know, and it's amazing how much they drank, the two of them. I've been researching this since I got here and met her. But I think Mrs. Fitzgerald may have been misdiagnosed, too." Dr. Sledge was warming to his topic. "Actually I think she may have had lupus, early on — there's all that eczema in the records. I don't think she was ever truly schizophrenic, though. With lifelong schizophrenia, there's permanent damage from every big break. Brain lesions. Loss of affect, loss of IQ, what we call blank mind. Mrs. Fitzgerald has 'come back' too far, too often. Look at all her writing. Look at her art. It's very impressive. Why, she's still painting. I'm pretty sure it has always been manic-depressive illness, not that it matters now." He bit his lip; I realized he was telling me too much.

"But Mrs. Fitzgerald improves every time she comes back to Highland," I said, and he nodded. "And she's kept coming back, all these years. So maybe she thinks of it as home, too, like me. Just a little bit, anyway."

"Why don't you ask her? She likes you." Dr. Sledge was navigating his way so slowly around the hairpin curves down the mountain road that the cars behind us were all blowing their horns, which didn't appear to bother him in the least, if he even noticed. I didn't mention it. These Blue Ridge mountain roads were still new to him, of course.

"Oh, she'd say Montgomery." I was sure of it. "Because the house is still there, remember? Rabbit Run. With her mother still alive, still in it. So Mrs. Fitzgerald is stuck in Alabama, really, don't you think? Still in the past. No matter how much she and Mr. Fitzgerald traveled the globe."

"Well, Mrs. Fitzgerald is a special case by now, of course," Dr. Sledge said gently. "So many, many treatments at so many different clinics have undoubtedly harmed her as much as they have helped her, at this point. So much medication, so many different kinds of shock treatments. I think she's suffered some serious brain damage. But it's not that her earlier doctors were negligent, you understand. There's a lot of new thinking on this now." Sometimes I forgot that Dr. Sledge was part of the new regime. "Psychoanalysis would be wasted on Mrs. Fitzgerald now, of course. But for the rest of us," he went on with some emphasis, "we *must* go back into the past, we *must* try to process the trauma of our earlier lives, if we are to move forward at all."

I made a face at him. "Dr. Carroll didn't even believe in therapy, except for gardening and walking. And remember what Thomas Wolfe said, 'You can't go home again.' I'm with *him.* Because it's all gone the minute you leave, even if it ever existed at all. Like New Orleans, or Montgomery, or wherever. It's just the past. It's all different. And we're different, too," I said almost to myself. "There's no going back."

"Spoken like Thomas Wolfe's dark angel, my brilliant Evalina," Dr. Sledge said, reaching over suddenly to take my hand, which lay on the bag of cornmeal between us.

The station wagon swerved suddenly to the right, almost hitting the vertical cliff, then rocked from side to side down the mountain as both of us burst into sudden laughter. I am still not sure why. But I'll bet that Freddy Sledge was as astonished as I, though he did not relinquish my hand.

More and more, whenever I could get the time, I found myself haunting Hortitherapy, where Mrs. Morris was coming to depend upon me, too. One cold, bright morning in December, I went on the annual expedition to gather greenery for holiday decorating. A light frost lay on everything, for all the world like the silver spray we were using in Art to make Christmas ornaments. Fences and branches and weeds glistened in the sun as we walked back into the woods with our clippers, following Pan and old Cal, who carried a shotgun to shoot down mistletoe, if we encountered any. We were all encouraged to look for it, high in the tops of the hardwoods, as we walked along. Our breath made silver puffs in the air, like characters' speech in the cartoons that Pan adored, which the Morrises saved for him (though it was somewhat unclear to me whether he could really read them, or just liked the pictures). In any case, here we all went, a goodly group of us, down into a ravine where fir and hemlock hung over the icy rushing waters of Balsam Creek; its song filled the glittering air. Soon we held armfuls of the fragrant greenery, including holly, two or three kinds of it, galax and grapevine, and a real find, the bright orange bittersweet berries on their long, bare stalks, almost Asian in appearance, which Mrs. Carroll loved. She used to keep a Chinese urn filled with bittersweet on her piano for the holidays.

The piano! Suddenly I felt like playing "Deck the Halls," "Away in the Manger," "Hark the Herald Angels Sing," and all the carols of the season. As we trudged back up the hill toward the hospital, I could hardly wait to get my hands on the keys.

But we all stopped obediently when Pan held up his hand. Some of us put our heavy branches down; I did, shading my eyes as several of the men pointed up into the highest branches of the huge old oaks and sycamores we stood among. Mistletoe! Round clouds of it hovered in the highest branches, against the deep blue sky.

"Okay, here goes," Cal said, raising his gun; yet still it was a shock when the shots rang out in the cold, clear, quivering air — one, two, three, four of them. Three bunches of mistletoe fell to the ground.

Yet so did the nice-looking man just ahead of me, crying out incoherently, drawn up into a ball, rolling this way and that like a crazy person — which he was, I suddenly remembered; it was so easy to forget, him in his tailored tweed jacket with the leather patches on the sleeves. His checked wool hat rolled off down the hill and then I could see the blue bald spots on his head, too, where they attached the electrodes. Though Dr. Pine arrived first at his side, it was Pan who was suddenly all over him, covering him up like a bear, rolling with him until he stopped and there they lay together, panting, like one huge animal.

"My God, how stupid of us!" Dr. Pine said, almost to himself, slapping his own thigh.

For of course this man was one of the shell-shocked veterans, though he'd been a very high-ranking officer, it was said.

Somehow we got him back to the hospital, along with the rest of us, and our greenery.

Later, festive wreaths hung on all the hospital doors, and fragrant evergreen bouquets filled all the vases. A garland lined the grand stairway, and a great ball of mistletoe hung from a red velvet ribbon in the fancy entrance of Highland Hall.

My new part-staff status allowed me to drive the Hortitherapy truck on errands about the grounds. This was a big help, I judged, from the number of times Mrs. Morris asked me to do it. I remember her riding with me one day as I drove to pick up a load of rocks from workmen on a road at the back of the property and deliver them to an area near the old swimming pool, where they would be used eventually to build some sort of little pavilion. Together Mrs. Morris and I stood at the side to watch two of the grounds crews swing into action, handing the rocks off from one to another in a relay line, piling them up where the new structure was to be located.

At the end, a number of the workers clambered into the truck bed for the ride back to Brushwood. I popped Pan a quick slap on the rear as he jumped up last, onto the bumper. Through the back window, he gave me a grin and a wave in response.

With difficulty, Mrs. Morris hauled herself back into the seat beside me; she leaned over to place her hand over mine on the gearshift, so that I was forced to pause before starting the truck.

I looked over at her.

Her warm eyes, often puffy and rheumy, looked straight into mine, bright and intent. "He *is* a man, you know," she said, squeezing my hand hard before she released it, before I started the engine.

Perhaps I most enjoyed the unscheduled moments in the greenhouse when we were between groups or events — sprawled out on the wicker furniture drawn up around an old gas heater, absorbed in the newspapers, usually several days old by the time they made it to Hortitherapy — Mrs. Morris chewing on a pencil eraser as she did one of her beloved crossword puzzles, Pan chuckling over the comics, or fixing something — he was forever fixing something, often with the help of Carl Renz, a huge, slow-witted lobotomy casualty. Several of these unfortunates had ended up at Highland, where lobotomies were not performed, though they were very popular at that time. Currently lobotomy was being promoted nationwide by the famous Dr. Walter Freeman, who had simplified the procedure by using a home ice-pick through the eye socket and was now traveling the country in his "Lobotomobile," as he called it, performing his "transorbital" lobotomies at mental hospitals and doctors' offices everywhere. Thank goodness he was never invited to Highland! Our own Carl Renz was a familiar and even beloved part of Brushwood. He liked to stand rather than sit, pacing in the background as we all busied ourselves around the stove.

Often I took this time to scan the news, especially the news from Europe, which seemed impossibly far away to me now. "Look." I held a crackling page out toward Pan. "Look at this." It was a picture of the Eiffel Tower.

"That's Paris," I said, my heart pounding, holding my breath. "I lived there. In Paris."

He glanced at the picture and then at me, his gaze both alert and uncomprehending.

Mrs. Morris looked up from her puzzle. "Perhaps you should go and check on the poinsettias," she said to Pan.

"Why, where are they?" I asked, as none were to be seen among the shelves of flowering plants and bulbs being forced into bloom.

Pan took off in answer, me following. He darted outside and over to the larger toolshed, which I had never entered, assuming it was merely a storage space, for there was no end of grounds equipment at Highland to be stored. He threw the latch and hoisted the big garage door up along its tracks and we ducked inside; I paused to get my bearings in the semidarkness. I couldn't imagine what we were doing in *there*! But Pan turned back to pull at my sleeve, and I crept forward, though cautiously. It was not the first time I had had the sense that he could see in the dark. Beyond the tractors we came to a nondescript door, like a closet. He opened it, pushing me forward. I stumbled over the sill to stand amazed.

In the soft red light, I could barely make out the dozens and dozens of poinsettias, starting to bloom. It was beautiful, like being inside a heart.

"Oh my God!" I said involuntarily.

Behind me, in the darkness, Pan was laughing. Like a vine, his arm snuck around my waist, pulling me back against him; before I knew it, his warm breath was in my hair, his lips on the back of my neck. A feeling that I cannot describe swept over me, down to my very feet. I felt his lips on my neck, his tongue.

"Evalina, are you in here? Pan?" Mrs. Morris stood in the open space beyond the tractors, her voice sharp. Carl Renz loomed behind her. "Are you there? Answer me. Answer me!"

We stepped back, closing the secret door.

Later, the blooming poinsettias would be brought out and placed all over the hospital for Christmas. Every time I saw one, I thought of that moment with Pan.

For weeks I had been promising Freddy that I would show him the fabled Grove Park Inn, yet it was nearly Christmas when we finally got there. "Good God!" he exclaimed upon first glimpsing the hotel itself, banging his hand upon the steering wheel so that he inadvertently blew the horn, which tickled me. The better I got to know Freddy, the funnier he became — he was not at all the serious man he seemed at the hospital; and in some ways, after all my time in

Europe, I was actually more sophisticated than he.

Initially he refused to relinquish his keys to the doorman at the Grove Park Inn, for instance — one of a bevy of such doormen who met all arriving and departing cars. "How do I know they won't lose them? It's my mother's car, you know."

I knew. "They never lose them," I said, then enjoyed his reaction as we entered the cavernous lobby with huge fires burning in the fireplaces at either end. The tree stood at least thirty feet high, so bedecked with ornaments and lights that one could scarcely see its green needles. The rockers before the fireplaces and all the chairs in every group were taken. A holiday tea dance was in progress. Looking at these festive folk, I felt underdressed, even though I was wearing my good black dress and Ruth's pearls for this occasion. A jazz version of "White Christmas" came from the grand piano, played by a tuxedo-clad old man, clearly a master. Couples were dancing on the shiny dance floor in front of the piano. Others sat at the little round tables, waiters and waitresses moving among them. I looked for Moira at the hostess station — or Mrs. Hodges — and felt oddly relieved to see neither on this occasion.

"Should we try to get a table over there?" Freddy asked, but I said, "No, not yet, there's more to see," pulling him toward the grand arcade where all the photographs of famous guests were hung — presidents, movie stars, and kings, as well a photograph of Mr. and Mrs. Fitzgerald in evening dress, which we looked at for a long time.

We continued to an exhibit of gingerbread houses, a holiday contest in which the gingerbread constructions were truly works of art — not only the usual cottages from fairytale lore but also castles, mansions in the Newport style, and feats of whimsy, defying gravity. We wandered down the line slowly with the others, marveling.

"Speaking of Mrs. Fitzgerald," I said, suddenly remembering, "You know I made a dollhouse with her help once, in Art Class," and then I told him all about it, in every detail.

Freddy was extremely interested. "Where is it now?" he asked.

"Lord, I don't know," I said. "Maybe it's over at Homewood someplace. I can ask Mrs. Carroll, I guess, when they get back, though I doubt she'll know either. Somebody probably threw it out."

We moved on down the row. I enjoyed the gingerbread houses themselves and also the children who had been brought to see them, especially the little girls all dressed up in velvet and silk dresses, with their white stockings and patent-leather shoes. I remembered how my own mother used to dress me up in white organdie. In New Orleans it was so seldom cold that I had had only one fancy winter dress for church, gray velvet with a white lace collar.

Later, after we had ordered our tea, I leaned across the table toward Freddy, who sat there smiling in his nice navy jacket and a tie with little reindeer all over it, and said, "After my mother's death I learned that I am the child of her and her father — her father was my father — and now I believe this is why she fled the parish and never went back. Someone came to our apartment for money, though, every week until we moved, and then they couldn't find us, I suppose — it was a woman, I remember that much, I remember seeing her from the back, though I don't know who she was — a cousin? A sister? Perhaps the money was for him, our father, or her mother, or perhaps it was blackmail money, for somebody else . . . what do you think?"

If he was stunned, Freddy did not betray it. Instead he simply reached across the embroidered tablecloth and took both my hands. "I think your mother must have loved you very much," he said.

I can't remember anything else about our tea, though afterward, as I nibbled the last macaroon, he said, "Let's dance!" surprising me mightily.

"I don't know how." I remembered the French heel fiasco with Robert, the only time I had ever tried.

"It doesn't matter," said he with utter confidence. "I'll show you. Come on" — leading me onto the shiny circular floor where a mirrored globe turned slowly. Freddy grasped me firmly and said, "Now just do what I do. Follow my lead. Right foot forward, that's good, now left, now back . . ." and somehow, with his hand pressing firmly on the small of my back, I could do it — even twirling about beneath his arm held high in the air. For years, I had watched other girls performing this step. Freddy explained that his sisters, needing a partner to practice with for dances and dates, had pressed him into service as a child, with this result. He was a grand dancer, and I found that I had a knack for it myself, something I had never suspected, always having been the accompanist at every such occasion. I stepped and spun until I was dizzy and out of breath.

"Let's get some air." I led him past the piano to the long French doors that a doorman opened for us, and then we were out on the wide terrace facing the vast sweep of open air and the mountains beyond, on every side. We walked over to the low stone wall and stood looking out at Asheville below us in the bottom of the bowl of mountains. Somehow, it had gotten to be twilight already. Long shadows slanted across the wintry plain of the golf course. The weak sun was mostly caught now behind gray clouds massing at the horizon, the entire scene a darkening palette of somber hue. Lights came twinkling on like stars in Asheville below.

Someone opened the door for a minute so that we heard the music and the laughter inside. Then it cut off abruptly. Now I was freezing.

"I guess it's time to go back," I said.

"Just a minute." Freddy put his arms around me as firmly as he had on the dance floor. "Evalina, you have told me something important today, and now I have something important to tell you."

"What is it?"

"You cannot be in the therapy group any longer," Freddy said, "because I am falling in love with you."

But when I closed my eyes at the moment of our kiss, I was dismayed to see a clear vision of a princess peering over the battlements of a gingerbread castle, looking down a mountainside like the mountain we were on, still searching anxiously — for what? for whom? Nevertheless, I was not a fool. I kissed him back soundly.

Promptly at noon on December 20, Brenda from the Beauty Box, the Overholsers, Dr. Schwartz, and I joined Dixie to stand under the Highland Hall portico and wait for her husband Frank to arrive. He had driven all the way from Georgia to pick her up himself. His mother, Big Mama, was at home with the children, who were said to be very excited about their mother's return. So was Frank Calhoun, apparently; he had planned two nights in a big Atlanta hotel — plus a shopping trip! to Dixie's delight — on the way back home, a sort of "second honeymoon," he'd called it. Dixie was all ready: every dark hair curling perfectly in place, wearing a sky blue wool coat and matching blue beret that I had never seen before. She had pulled the beret down rakishly on one side, just so. Dixie was literally sparkling, herself — her white teeth, her bright blue eyes, her shiny red lipstick, "Fire and Ice," I knew, for she had bought me some, though I had not had the nerve to wear it. In fact I knew that a lot of Dixie's total effect was caused by makeup, but she was good at it, and it didn't *look* like makeup. She was the most beautiful living person I had ever actually known, or even seen. Her matching red luggage was lined up along the curb like some small, uniformed army standing at attention.

Back inside the hospital, papers had been signed and good-byes had been said. Perhaps because of her "missing carapace," everybody who knew Dixie or had worked with her seemed to love her, not only me. Even Dr. Bennett started to shake her hand, then unexpectedly embraced her, wiping his eyes as he went back inside his office. I had been witnessing such phenomena for days. Truly, it was as though Dixie really was a princess, or some kind of royalty, a special person. Everyone had to touch her as they told her good-bye. All were sad, but I was devastated.

Suddenly a ripple ran through our group — here he came! Dixie stepped forward, putting up a hand to shield her eyes from the sun.

"Don't forget," Richard Overholser blurted out, *"college!"*

"Hush, Richard," Claudia said.

"Lord God, would you look at that big old car!" Brenda cried as Frank Calhoun came into view driving the longest, whitest, shiniest automobile I had ever seen, like a vision from another life.

"Oh, that's Frank!" Dixie cried. "Here he is —" running lightly down the steps and straight out into the road to greet him. If there had been another car, she'd have been hit.

Brakes squealed as her husband slammed them on, not parking but just stopping dead in the middle of the street. He leapt out, leaving his door wide open — we all got a glimpse of the red leather interior with wrapped gifts piled high in the backseat. Frank Calhoun was a big, vigorous man with a rugged, deeply tanned, and beaming face beneath his wide-brimmed leather hat, the hat of an outdoorsman.

"Missy!" He swept her up in his arms and twirled her around and around until they looked like a spinning top. Then he set her down and gave her a big, long kiss. "Are you ready?" he asked, pulling back to look at her, and she said "Yes," laughing, adjusting her beret.

"Let's do it then," he said, bowing in the most courteous way to the rest of us, whom she introduced one by one as he moved among us shaking hands and thanking everyone for "taking such good care of my girl." He gave Brenda and me special hugs. When he said, "Oh, *you* are Evalina! I know all about Evalina," I could feel myself blushing.

"All right, boys," he said to Bernard and Marcus, two hospital workers who hovered at the edge of our group, "Let's load her up." They put all of Dixie's red luggage into the trunk, then brought the wrapped gifts from the backseat and placed them carefully on the steps of Highland Hall. "Now a few of these have got a tag on them," Frank said, winking at me, "but as for the rest, y'all can just give 'em out however you want, to everybody that's been nice to my baby."

"That's everybody," Dixie said, twinkling.

"There's some fudge and some fried pies in those two baskets." Frank pointed at them. "So y'all had better get right on with it. Honey?" He opened the passenger side door.

But first, Dixie ran over to whisper her parting advice in my ear. "You hang on to the doctor, now, you hear? And just forget all about that retarded yard boy!" Then she jumped in the car.

Frank Calhoun got behind the wheel and slammed the door, tipping his hat to all.

"Good-bye, good-bye!" we chorused as the car pulled out; he blew the horn in response, several long, musical blasts as they drove down the hill and out of sight.

"My goodness!" Claudia Overholser said.

"Well, what did you expect?" her husband asked peevishly.

"But he's so genuine, so much charm and goodwill, so generous . . ." Dr. Schwartz mused as if to herself.

"And she absolutely loves him, doesn't she?" I said. I had known this, but hadn't understood it. Now I did.

"Yes, and that's the main thing, that's the kind of thing we can never understand about a patient's real life, those of us who only see them for one short hour here and there during what is just a short and removed period of time in their actual lives, an interlude —"

"Intermezzo," I interrupted.

"Yes," Dr. Schwartz said, glancing at me. "An intermezzo. How can we ever expect to understand a whole life? Or to influence it in any way? How arrogant of us, really . . . This is an absurd enterprise." Dr. Schwartz caught her breath sharply as she turned away.

Bernard, one of the hospital workers, looked at the rolled bill that Frank had apparently slipped him, then grinned as he pocketed it again, saying, "Now that man, he *somebody,* ain't he? And ain't he got a great big car?"

CHAPTER 11

By Christmas Eve, anyone who had anyplace else to go had already gone, including
Freddy, who was driving his station wagon
across the country — all those big, square,
orderly states — to Indiana, where six little
nieces and nephews eagerly awaited him,
along with his mother and sisters and their
husbands. Freddy and I had had dinner
with the Overholsers and several others the
night before he left — a huge roast cooked
by Richard, much too rare for my own taste,
though acclaimed by all the rest.

"I guess you'd like my mother's cooking,
then," Freddy told me. "She cooks everything all day long. If we had a big roast like
this, she'd make pot roast out of it. In fact,
we probably *will* have pot roast!" Beneath
the tablecloth, his hand closed over mine. "I
wish you were going with me," he blurted
out, sotto voce, in my ear.

Amidst all the hubbub, I hoped that no

one would notice, but Dr. Schwartz chose that moment to smile at me across the table, and I worried that perhaps she'd heard him after all. This bothered me on two counts. Not only was Freddy very close to breaking the rules for doctor/patient relationships, but also I knew — we all knew — that Dr. Schwartz's marriage had just ended. This was not her choice; her husband, a therapist in private practice in Asheville, had "fallen in love with someone else," as she'd put it delicately.

Richard stood up, glass in hand, to offer a toast, "To Indiana and her fair-haired boy!" and everyone drank, myself included, though I never took more than a sip, instinctively wary of what might happen should I take too much. I didn't like the tongue-in-cheek way Richard had said, "To Indiana and her fair-haired boy!" as if it were somehow a joke, as if he were almost but not quite making fun of Freddy. Richard was a bit hard to take in general, I had decided, so opinionated — though it was clear that Claudia adored him.

Richard Overholser was the very opposite of straightforward Freddy, who stopped by the next morning to envelop me in a huge bear hug before he left. "This courtship will resume when I return!" he announced, his words floating out as white puffs in the chilly air. He looked ridiculous in that silly hat with the ear flaps. Yet tears came to my eyes as I watched him drive off on his long journey home, so far away.

The next day was Christmas Eve. The hospital grounds looked empty and forlorn, though beautiful, as I hurried over to Highland Hall, where I would play for the traditional candlelight vespers service in the drawing room. This had always been my favorite event at Highland, though it would be different now, without Dr. Carroll's long prayers, for he had fancied himself a preacher as well as an orator. Only the very sickest among the patients and those who had nowhere else to go, plus a skeleton staff (what a horrible expression! I realize as I write these words) remained at Highland now. The severely ill were housed as always on the top floors of the Central Building. I noticed the lights up there burning brightly — though there were lights in all the buildings, an attempt at cheer, I suppose, Christmas being an exceptionally emotional time for all.

Though only late afternoon, it was already dark, or almost dark, that lovely gray twilight of French impressionist paintings, with the lightly falling snowflakes as dabs of white on the canvas. *Pointillisme.* Oddly dislocated by the snow, I felt a kinship with those painted ladies in Mrs. Fitzgerald's city-scapes who had no ground at all beneath their dancing feet. But they didn't seem to care. They were always gazing up, up, up, at something beyond the picture frame — what? When I looked up myself, the rushing snowflakes fell like soft, cold kisses on my face. As I crossed our beautiful campus, all the streetlights along Zillicoa Avenue came on at once, each globe casting a lovely round silver glow filled with falling flakes — for all the world as if the streetlights had been transformed into big snow globes, the sort that you turn upside down to make it snow upon the little scene within. Mrs. Carroll used to collect those, too.

Light-headed, I had to stop and catch my breath, which made me nearly late. Every-one was already seated when I slipped into the drawing room to take my place at the spinet piano, starting off with "Deck the Halls," for we were to keep this service upbeat, short, and "not religious," accord-ing to Dr. Bennett, who had decked himself out in a red plaid vest with a green tie for the occasion. His wife looked like an enor-mous cream puff in ruffled beige lace. Phoebe Dean, large herself, could have been a Wise Man in her long purple frock, which buttoned up the front, like a robe. She led them vigorously in singing "Jingle Bells," and then we all listened to old Mr. Pugh's vigorous recitation of "T'was the Night Before Christmas."

Everyone who *could* come had been encouraged to do so, I believe, for all the regular chairs had been pulled forward and were now filled, as well as a number of additional folding chairs. Most people had dressed up a bit, too, as much as they were able, with varying results. Another thing about being crazy is that you are not self-conscious, but totally unaware of how you look or how you might appear to others. Old Mr. Crowninshield, sitting on the front row, wore a blue velvet smoking jacket with his red-striped pajama pants and monogrammed bedroom slippers. A more recently arrived lady was the very picture of elegance in a long pink satin evening dress that Cinderella herself might have worn to the ball. It made me sad to note that four of the men had chosen to wear their military uniform jackets — medals, too — honoring that which had harmed them so badly.

Phoebe handed out song sheets that I had mimeographed earlier, and we started in upon "The Twelve Days of Christmas."

As they sang lustily through the turtle doves, French hens, and calling birds, I looked around the beautiful drawing room, transformed by the glowing candles, the red poinsettias we had grown, and the greenery we had gathered in the woods. Mrs. Carroll's collection of manger scenes covered every available surface. Some of them I remembered, such as the primitive stone Inuit group from Alaska, nestled into their own stone cave; the colorful Russian egg set; those bright tin Haitian figures; and the minimal Swedish stick people. I remembered Mrs. Carroll showing me the small painted terra-cotta set from Provence called a *santon,* with its various characters from village life — the scissors grinder, the fishmonger, the chestnut seller, everyday people. It had always been my favorite. They used to roast chestnuts on the street in Paris; Joey Nero and I ate them right there, out in the bitter cold, wearing our overcoats. There was also a menorah on the sideboard, and an Islamic star and crescent display.

No doubt about it: Mrs. Carroll had broadened my world, as well as determined the course of my life. It is a complicated thing to be broadened and determined, of course — not to mention saved and abandoned! But as I sat playing the piano in that beautiful room on Christmas Eve, I was able to thank her for all of it.

I smiled to recognize the crude little nativity made with popsicle sticks, a recent Christmas project for staff children that I had helped Miss Malone conduct in the Art Room. There sat Miss Malone and Karen Quinn now, shoulder to shoulder in the front row, Karen wearing one of those Scandinavian knit hats that made her look like she had pigtails. In fact, she could have been Miss Malone's daughter. Mrs. Hodges was there, too, having coaxed her own reluctant-looking daughter Ruthie into bringing her over. Mrs. Hodges always said she wouldn't miss this service for the world.

Dr. Schwartz looked like one of the Murano glass figurines, thin and almost transparent, yet singing beautifully on the "five golden rings," her small, perfect soprano quivering above the rest. They all sang out on "five golden rings," holding the notes as long as they could while I ran arpeggios up and down the keys. Mrs. Fitzgerald, seated with the Morrises, looked the best I had seen her in years, laughing as she tried to keep up the pace on the repeated verses, which grew speedier and speedier as the "days of Christmas" progressed. I knew that Mrs. Fitzgerald was expecting another grandchild soon, to be produced by her beloved daughter Scottie Lanahan, the real "Patricia Pie-Face," now living in New York with her husband and little son Tim.

The Morrises had brought several young people and two small children (grand-children?) along with them, a fact that I somehow resented — it seemed so odd for Mrs. Morris to have grown children I did not even know, for her to have an entire life away from the greenhouse, away from us. Huge Carl Renz hovered in the back of the drawing room, standing, pacing, turning his hat in his hands — he never sat down. We were all used to it. But where was Pan? I wondered. Down in his mountain lair, beneath the falling snow that must be accumulating seriously by now? Or out playing music somewhere, perhaps in an Asheville tavern? But I didn't really know, did I? I didn't have any idea of where he went or what his life was like, any more than I knew what the Morrises' life was like. Or the Overholsers'. Or anybody's, really . . . all of us a collection of snow globes.

On the seventh day of Christmas, my true love gave to me seven swans a-swimming, six geese a-laying . . . There was the pretty receptionist Sharon Green, and Dr. Pine with his flowing moustaches and his cheerful elfin wife. And *he* looked like Einstein, as everybody said. On we marched, through maids and pipers, though the pink lady cried out, "How many goddamn verses are there, anyhow? I've had about enough of this!" prompting general amusement. And finally we were done, with the last resounding major chords of "a partridge in a pear tree!" They all shouted it out, then collapsed in laughter.

Having achieved, I imagine, the mood he'd been aiming for, Dr. Bennett was adjourning us all to the dining room when old Mr. Crowninshield, wild-haired and white-bearded, jumped up and croaked, "Sir! Sir! I beg you! at least, a prayer, a blessing — for it *is* Christmas, after all!" his voice breaking. It was a voice that bespoke culture, refinement, an entire life of public speaking — perhaps he was a minister himself, in his real life outside these hospital grounds.

I thought Dr. Bennett might cut him off, but he, with a courtly gesture, said, "Please, Sir — proceed!" and bowed his head. Most bowed their heads but I did not, looking around the lovely room as the old man prayed, calling for peace in the world as in our troubled hearts, and asking God to "bless us every one."

I continued to play a soft little Christmas medley of my own devising as everybody headed to the dining hall for a cold meal left by the kitchen staff, who had been given this night and most of tomorrow off for the holiday. Christmas Eve supper always featured picnic fare and forbidden sweets: thick ham sandwiches, deviled eggs, potato salad, red and green jello salad, fudge, and pecan pie, with bowls of hard candy and tangerines for treats. Suddenly it crossed my mind to wonder if Flossie had had a hand in any of this — a chilling thought, for some reason, though surely she had.

"Merry Christmas, Evalina!" Claudia called out to me. "We're heading on home now, while we can still *get* home!"

"Oh! I didn't even realize you were here," I called back, very surprised to see the Overholsers present, as Richard was a self-proclaimed atheist, and they were not churchgoers — unlike Freddy, a Lutheran. But the Overholsers wanted to give their daughter Ellen a religious sense, Claudia came up and whispered to me, a sense of drama and mystery, and this service was just perfect, wasn't it? Wasn't it perfect?

It was.

In fact, it had been so perfect that I couldn't bear to leave the drawing room, even after Mrs. Hodges had said "Merry Christmas" and hugged me good-bye and the Overholsers had wrapped themselves up and left. I played "Silent Night" as the room cleared out, then "Ave Maria" once all were gone, losing myself in the rippling, emotional music, imagining Lillian Field's voice as she might have sung it.

"Evalina, this is beautiful, but you'd better come along and have some supper now before it's all gone," Mr. Pugh remarked, startling me. I don't know how long he had been standing behind me.

"Oh, I'm not very hungry," I announced, to my own surprise. "I'll just stay here a minute, if you don't mind, and finish this piece, and then I'll come along. Don't worry, I'll blow out the candles," I assured him.

"It's time to go, honey," Mr. Pugh said. "Come on, go over to the dining hall and grab a sandwich, and I'll close up here. I always do."

"I just hate to leave all these little pietàs," I said, still playing. I really didn't mean to be obstinate, I just couldn't stand to leave.

"Pietàs? What do you mean, pietàs?" Mr. Pugh sat down next to me on the piano bench, and I moved over to accommodate him.

"The *santon* from France," I said, "and that painted tin one from Haiti, I remember those from when I was a child. All these little pietàs. She got them out every Christmas."

We both knew who "she" was.

"Evalina," Mr. Pugh said in what I knew to be his "instructive" tone, "You have confused your terms, my dear. These are not pietàs. They are crèches, manger scenes, nativities."

I was confused. "Well, what's a pietà, then?"

Ever the pedant, Mr. Pugh did not hesitate. "A pietà is a depiction of the Virgin Mary cradling the body of the crucified Christ, the dead Christ. Such as Michelangelo's famous sculpture at St. Peter's, or Titian's last painting, or El Greco's famous depiction . . ." Dr. Pugh always went on longer than he needed to.

"Robert would have known that, wouldn't he?" I mused. "The difference between a pietà and a crèche."

"Yes, I expect he would." Mr. Pugh patted my shoulder awkwardly. "And we still miss him, don't we? I expect we always shall."

"Yes." I slid into "Silent Night" and went on playing — I could not have stopped if my life depended upon it.

"It's a well-known fact that the infant Jesus is frequently stolen from crèches," Mr. Pugh went on, sounding like Robert himself. "Many of them can be purchased with two or three Jesuses, in fact, for that very reason."

"Jesus triplets!" I had to laugh.

Mr. Pugh cleared his throat as if to speak again, and then did not. He stood up. "You take your time, then, Evalina," he said. "I'll just have a cup of coffee and another piece of that pie, and check back here later." He squeezed my shoulder and lumbered off, an old man, a good man. I was alone in the beautiful room with the glowing candles, the poinsettias, the piney scent of evergreen, and all the little crèches, each with its baby Jesus. Or not.

My own baby was born in the middle of one of the worst thunderstorms anybody had ever seen in New Orleans, that city of afternoon thunderstorms, an unusual September storm that produced fallen trees, flooding streets, and accidents. In fact it was only by accident, the sheerest chance, that I went back outside at all that afternoon.

My own school day over, I had taken off my shoes and put my swollen feet up on a pillow as I rested upon my bed at Temps

Perdu. My room was stuffy and humid, even with all the shutters open. Not a breath of air was moving, outside or in. I felt as if I could scarcely catch my breath, though that was the way I had been feeling for several weeks now. But of course I had forgotten to turn on the overhead fan. I had just decided to make the effort to get up and do it when Sasha, the sword-swallower's daughter, came running in with a note written in a spidery hand I well knew. Sister Anna Louise, the sweet, small nun with the buck teeth, asked if I might return to play for the five-fifteen mass this afternoon at St. Catherine's, the ancient little chapel connected to our school. Sister Eugenie, the organist, had been taken ill after eating a redfish. Somehow that redfish made me smile. Of course I would do it, for it was Sister Anna Louise who had interceded for me when I began to "show," convincing the others that it would be an act of mercy to keep me on. And certainly I needed all the money I could make. No — *we* needed all the money I could make.

I was already eight months pregnant, by my own reckoning, though I had not yet visited a doctor, only Auntie Tonton, the old gris-gris lady on LeMaire Street. But I planned to take a taxicab to the charity hospital when the time came. I was determined that my baby should be born in a hospital, that all the official papers would be signed, and that she should have a birth certificate, and know when her birthday was. I already had the money saved and placed in my new petit-point overnight bag over there on the chifforobe, a gift from the fortune-teller Madame Romanetsky and her son, along with a new gown and robe and baby layette donated to me by the Sisters. More baby clothes, free from the Mercy Mission, filled the bottom drawers. She had a whole wardrobe waiting for her! So I was ready, but not ready — though the baby was dropping, I could tell. And Sasha was waiting for my answer, a narrow ribbon of a girl. I had seen her hang by her teeth from a leather strap, whirling around and around and around, with one toe pointed and the other leg bent at the knee, just so.

I sat up and swung my legs off the bed. "Tell her I'll be right there," I said. I was struck by the sight of my own face in the big gilt mirror of the rather grand bathroom I shared with several other residents — my cheeks round and glowing, utterly unlike myself in those last months: *happy.* Everybody at Temps Perdu had taken a fancy to it — to me. They felt I brought them luck, and they were people who needed luck, they lived by luck; they were always touching my stomach, and bringing me gifts and food. I think they felt that my baby would be their baby, too. I pushed my hair back into a knot suitable for church, snapping the barrette in place, then got my shoes back on, with difficulty.

When I opened the front door, something about the atmosphere outside gave me pause, and at the last minute I grabbed an old gray raincoat off the coat tree in the hall, a coat I had previously liberated from the "lost and found box" at school. As I left our densely shaded yard and stepped into the lane, I was struck by the light — yellow, turning the lush vegetation a sickly iridescent green. Though no breeze had yet arisen, all the plane trees along the sidewalk were rustling mysteriously, the leaves showing their silver sides, which I had never seen. It was spooky. Once I rounded the corner and entered the square, I could see that the day's bright sun had disappeared into a hazy, sultry sky, clouded over yet glowing. People were looking up, remarking it. Trash appeared from nowhere to swirl about my feet. As I walked the two long blocks above the river, I saw that the Mississippi was gunmetal gray, swelling and agitated. I could hear water crashing against the revetments. And there was not a boat or barge to be seen — strangely, as it was not yet four in the afternoon. The boatmen knew how to watch the river; perhaps they knew something we didn't.

I was glad to enter the chapel where my sheet music, marked, awaited me at the organ, along with a little girl, one of ours, to turn the pages. Would my own little girl be musical? Would she perform this task for me? Or I, later, for her? At least it was cooler in the church, though there were few parishioners, mostly old women in black, filling not a quarter of the seats.

The most remarkable thing about this old chapel is the big rose window behind the altar, which catches all the light, almost as if it is a light itself. As the mass continued, I watched that window turn from a vibrant pink to a darker rose to a sort of deep mauve. We all knew these signs. A storm was on the way. Several parishioners had already left, genuflecting as they slipped out with heads bowed. I had to stay until the final amen, of course. I thanked the girl and folded the music, leaving it on the organ, and bowed to Father, who put up a hand as if to stop me though I hurried on, hoping to make it back to Temps Perdu before the rain started, glad that at least I had remembered the raincoat, for I was so forgetful in those last days of pregnancy. Above all, I did not want to get wet, as it took days for things to dry on the wooden racks on the balcony at Temps Perdu, due to the humidity.

Now the yellow air had turned dark and thick, though wind had begun to whip along the crowded sidewalk; traffic jammed the streets. A palm frond fell with a clatter as I rounded the corner and passed the post office. For a second I debated going in there for shelter, but then decided to make a run for it, taking a shortcut on the towpath by the river, which I usually avoided because of the shanties clustered alongside, inhabited by a changing collection of river people, as they were called — hoboes, grifters, drifters, and runaways. Down I went on the steps beside the bridge, then rushed along the dirt towpath, never looking to my left, where I knew that eyes were peering from the makeshift shacks. Occasionally someone called out to me, words snatched up by the rising wind. Halfway home I was already thinking, Oh why had I come this way? Why had I not stayed in the ancient stone safety of St. Catherine's? Where I never prayed when I was playing, though now I began to pray in earnest as the sky turned pitch-black and the first long roll of thunder came across it and then the lightning struck so close that I could feel it all around us, illuminating each tree and leaf and bit of blowing debris on the towpath. "Hail, Holy Queen, Mother of Mercy, our life, our sweetness and our hope," I said, but it was already too late.

"Honey, honey now, you better get out of dis storm, you better get on in here, cherie." A deep voice, as big hands pulled me into the shack. Then those hands were on me — on *us,* everywhere — until I was down on my back in the mud, down but still twisting and fighting him off and then I was biting, hard, and he was yelling, and then a woman was yelling, too, saying, "You crazy thing, what you do, what you doing to her, oh Mother of God! You damn fool, what you doing here? Oh God, what you done?" and then I was rolling over and out, under the side, and stumbling back up onto the towpath where all was rushing dark and trees were falling everyplace. I knew somebody was coming after me. But then we were hit, hard, from the back, and I fell forward onto my knees in the mud.

I was already in labor when I woke up, I could feel her alive and coming, straight through a wall of pain. But why wasn't I at the charity hospital? Instead, I was surrounded by the beloved and concerned faces of my friends at Temps Perdu — the Hungarian tumblers from upstairs, identical twins; the sword swallower, Jean LeBlon; the jugglers; Madame Romanetsky's son Michael; the old clown Hugo; and the little dwarf lady, Mrs. Franz, who had made me the soft pink blanket. I saw them all in the yellow glow of a hurricane lamp and several big, fat wavy candles that cast a flickering circle of light around all of us. The river people had brought me here, carried me *here,* through the flooded streets. I suppose I had told them to. The storm still roared outside, I could hear it. I knew we were lucky to be alive.

"But where is Madame? Where is Madame?" everyone kept asking and then there she was finally, the fortuneteller, Madame Romanetsky, a huge presence in her familiar scarlet cape, striding into the circle abruptly, shedding water as she came straight over to me and placed both hands on my abdomen. Beneath the dripping black curls, a huge smile appeared on her face. "Aha! Show-time! Yes, my little Evalina?"

"Yes," I said, smiling back, as she touched my forehead gently, the sign of the cross.

"Then let's get to work. Michael, go get

us a basin of water, and another sheet or two, and Sasha, you bring all the towels you can find . . ." Madame Romanetsky barked out directions as people scattered to do her bidding. Meanwhile she shed layer after layer of clothing, from spangled dress to shift to undershirt and knee-length shorts, then tied back her snaky hair, whereupon it became clear that she was actually a man. In fact he was a handsome man. He grinned at me. "Surprised, no?"

"Yes," I managed to say.

"Do not worry, my sweet. I have done this before. Many times before, in a different life. Doctor Roman is here now! And soon" — gently he parted my knees and peered below, holding a candle — "very soon, I'd say — another person will be here with us in the room as well. A miracle! Now, Michael, the basin, please, and that cloth . . ." He washed my face off carefully with the cool water, clucking and dabbing at my injuries. "Never mind, my sweet," he said, "soon you shall be pretty again, and best of all, you will have a baby!" He gave me water to drink, then brandy, making me swallow it straight from the bottle. "Medicine!" he grinned. "And now, my friends, if you will —" Doctor Roman made a sweeping gesture, clearing most from the room, before he washed me carefully all over. By then I was beyond embarrassment, having passed into that realm of gold, of purest pain and joy. I was thinking, *I will remember this moment for the rest of my life.* And now it is true. "Soon," he said. "It will be soon. And when I tell you, push!"

Suddenly it was happening, I was pushing and then she was coming, and then she wasn't, though my blood poured onto the towels. Doctor Roman was reaching inside me. He sat up. "Go — bring Mrs. Franz back, like the wind," he said to Michael, beside him.

"This will be more complicated than we would wish," he told me, "as this baby is choosing to make its entrance feet first! Perhaps it will be a tumbler — a little acrobat, no? Ah, Mrs. Franz!" for she had arrived and stood trembling beside us, her mouselike face terrified. "Can you help us?"

"No . . . no . . ." She spoke faintly.

"Ah, but you *must* help us, dear, for your hands are so much smaller than mine. You see? Look!" Doctor Roman spread his own large hand in the air. "Now, go over there and wash up in the sink, with the soap, and then come back, yes, that's it. Now come here, beside me, where you can see." The Hungarian twins stood holding the hurricane lamp out over us, first one of them and then the other, both still as posts, never wavering. "And I will be right here, darling, just do exactly what I tell you. You are a huge help, darling little Mrs. Franz, you will save the day." Mrs. Franz was crying silently, huge tears rolling down her mousey face, all nose, and then I couldn't see her anymore over the great heaving mound of my belly, and then I couldn't see at all, anything.

When I came to, Doctor Roman was cutting the cord with a sharp silver knife, and I was already holding my baby who was beautiful, just beautiful, as I had known she would be, round blue eyes and all that curly dark hair, and perfect in every way. I touched her fingers and her toes. "All present and accounted for!" said Doctor Roman, beaming. Others were clapping him on the back, but Michael kissed him full on the mouth. *Oh!* I thought. *Not his son* . . . the sword-swallower's girlfriend came in with a big bottle of red wine for everybody to pass around while my baby made snuffly noises as I held her. That was before the storm was over and we went to the hospital, that was before her head began to swell, and swell, and swell. Three days later they took the shunt and the tubes out, and she died in my arms at the charity hospital, where they kept me for a long while afterward.

Pietà. Now I remembered it all — the feel of her, the smell of her, and once I remembered, I had her with me from then on, and I have her still. She will never leave me, nor I her. *Pietà.* I blew out the candles in the drawing room at Highland one by one, put on my coat and gloves and walked out into the beautiful new-fallen snow, still and unbroken all around. I knew I should go back to my room. Instead, looking down toward Asheville, I had a sudden, overwhelming urge to plunge off down that mountainside and find Pan deep in his lair, beneath the smooth white sweep of snow, for he was my kind, and now I knew it. I stood out there until the church bells began to ring out all over Asheville, from mountain to mountain, across the clear cold air. *Midnight, Christmas Eve.* I headed back to Graystone.

CHAPTER 12

Christmas marked the end of something, and the beginning of something else. I could feel it running through my body like my blood. Time itself seemed to change in nature, both speeding up and slowing down simultaneously. The remainder of my life at Highland would be very brief, though the snow made it seem like forever.

And at a mental institution, snow changes everything. Of course, patients are already cut off from the rest of the world, but now they really *felt* like it; now they knew it. Mail didn't come; buses didn't run; frequently, staff members couldn't make it into work. Visitors couldn't get there either. The kitchen ran out of eggs, bread, and once — horrors! — coffee! There was no more required hiking every day in the fresh air. Now everyone must participate in supervised exercise classes in the gymnasium, which didn't go too well, with whistles frequently blown, and patients stalking angrily off the floor. I didn't blame them. The all-important routine was broken, producing anxiety, at the very least, and often more serious disturbances. January and February are the worst months for depression anyway, as everyone knows. All the rooms on the top floor of the Central Building were taken, it was whispered, with extra beds placed up and down the halls.

Yet somehow — perhaps because I was living at Graystone now — I didn't mind the snow. In fact, I liked it. For once, the inexorable kaleidoscope had stopped turning, so that I could catch my breath. Now we all lived inside the snow globe that was wintertime at Highland, 1948. This was our whole world. Yet it was also infinite, the open landscape of our dreams and desires. For the very terrain was changed. Familiar hills and dips and stone benches and even ravines disappeared, to be replaced by the shining topography of the snow. The unbroken surface of a new world stretched out before us, a world where anything was possible.

Soon after Christmas, I was awakened in the middle of the night by an ambulance pulling up in front of Graystone with its red lights blinking in my window; two uniformed crewmen jumped out and opened up the back to haul out a stretcher. They were met on the icy sidewalk by Suzy Caldwell and Dr. Schwartz, suddenly materializing out of nowhere. Beneath the streetlight, Dr. Schwartz's hair surrounded her face like a frizzy dark halo; Suzy's plaid wool pajama pants hung down below her winter coat. I ran down the steps to hold the front door open, while Suzy and Dr. Schwartz followed the men with the stretcher, which contained a prone, tightly-wrapped female figure, hands folded, eyes closed. They set her down in the hall while taking care of the paperwork.

I knelt beside the stretcher. "Amanda?" I asked.

She opened her eyes, then gave me a wink. "Tampa was terrible," she said.

The minute the emergency crew left, Amanda jumped up to hug Dr. Schwartz. "Thank you, thank you, thank you!" she cried. "I can never thank you enough!" Dr. Schwartz put a finger to her lips, and Amanda continued in a whisper. Not only was the Judge a sex fiend, she said; he was also crazy. Amanda understood this now. She had pretended to be catatonic until he finally sent her back to Asheville.

"I swear, it was the only way I could get

out of there alive," she said. "He would have killed me if I tried to leave him."

"I said I'll help you, and I will," Dr. Schwartz promised, "but you've got to be sick for a while, you understand. I could lose my job over this."

Immediately, Amanda's whole pretty face went slack, and her head dropped forward in a parody of depression. "How's this?"

"That's good," Dr. Schwartz said, "but you don't want to overdo it, either. Now Suzy, and Evalina, I don't have to tell you that this is a very sensitive, confidential matter."

"You can count on me, Doc." Suzy sounded exactly like George Fayne in my beloved Nancy Drew books.

"Me, too," I said immediately.

"I know I can, Evalina." She smiled at me. "And you are very, very good at keeping secrets." Thin, small Dr. Schwartz was a moral giant, I realized, a woman of uncommon principle. I respected her immensely.

Amanda was assigned the other corner room upstairs. Her story made me worry about Dixie. Why hadn't I heard from her yet?

A Christmas visit back home with Mama had been entirely too much for Myra, also, who returned to us disheveled and weepy.

And Ruth had been "bored out of her skull" she announced, immediately setting off through the snow on foot to help with inventory at her beloved job in town. Very soon, she'd move into her own apartment and work there full-time, Highland Hospital behind her so long as she took her medications. We were all more or less on our own at Graystone those days, with Suzy Caldwell's visits very infrequent because of the snow.

Jinx certainly made the most of this situation. We all liked her — you couldn't help liking Jinx — that ready grin so full of life, totally undiminished by everything that had happened to her, the bright green eyes darting everywhere, missing nothing. Everyone was drawn to Jinx as if to a flame; when she was present, it was like she was the only person in the room. You couldn't stop looking at her. Yet we were wary of her, too, instinctively I suppose, for we never discussed this among ourselves. It was not so much that Jinx was younger, but that she was so different from the rest of us, different in kind, in a way we soon came to understand. For Jinx had no moral sensibility at all; she believed that the rules didn't apply to her, so they didn't. Boys were often involved, though who knows how or where she met some of them — a grease monkey from town; a Western Union delivery boy in a uniform; another who appeared in a big truck wearing a cowboy hat, grinning from ear to ear. I liked that one.

I knew I should have turned her in the day I came back after work to hear honky-tonk radio music the minute I opened the door and found Jinx and Horace, one of the black boys from the kitchen, drinking from a paper cup and jitterbugging like crazy on the flowered parlor rug. "Hey Evalina! Woo woo!" she called out as Horace swung her around, rolling his eyes at me. The beat was rapid, hard. Horace appeared to be double-jointed as he twisted down to the floor. I took off my coat and sat down to watch, soon joined by Myra who whispered to me in a disconsolate way, "You know, I will never have that much fun in my whole life. Never." A true statement if I ever heard one.

But I never turned Jinx in for anything. I knew that she was only passing through — a phenomenon, like a comet. And only once was I truly upset by her behavior at Graystone.

I had run back in the middle of the day to get something I'd forgotten, and was at first amused to hear the bumping of the bed against her wall, along with masculine laughter and Jinx's own flat little voice. But I soon became uneasy — not only because I feared someone else might come in, too, and then we'd be *compelled* to act — but also because these sounds brought back certain memories. I sank to the steps, clinging to the newel post at the bottom. Then came Jinx's high-pitched animal cry, followed by heavy footsteps on the floor, the slamming door, and suddenly he bolted down the staircase right past me, taking the steps two at a time as he put on his jacket.

But it was a man, not a boy — and I was very surprised to realize that it was Charles Winston, the shell-shocked veteran who had collapsed in Dr. Sledge's therapy group, the one who had shot the little girl during the war. He was almost ready to be released, I knew, back to his family in Winston-Salem and the giant tobacco business that awaited him. Luckily he didn't even notice me, charging right past as he adjusted his cap and pulled on his gloves against the cold. I could hear Jinx running water and singing in the bathroom when I finally crept up to my room and retrieved the music I had come for, then walked swiftly back to the hospital, telling no one.

■ ■ ■ ■

I found myself haunting Hortitherapy whenever I could, especially in the afternoon when my work was finished, always on the lookout for Pan, though he was seldom present, most often out working with the grounds crew as they struggled to keep the roads and walkways cleared. I also looked for him as I walked to and from Graystone, and watched for him from the hospital windows throughout the day, but he was hard to see. He was always hard to see.

Mrs. Morris kept a fire in her woodstove and a pot of spice tea going on top of it, trying to maintain the sense of homeyness she strove for, I believe, trying to create a little oasis of life in all that snow. Actually there was not much real work to be done in the dead of winter, though she was endlessly inventive. Each resident had one or two African violets to take care of, snipping back, watering, and feeding, all of them placed on the long shelf in front of the picture window where they produced a truly breathtaking array of blooms, like a cheerful little crowd with their brightly clustered blossoms. Beyond them, through the picture window, the glistening snow swept up toward the dark tree line.

Jinx refused to grow an African violet. "Oh, I hate these!" she had announced immediately. "They're too weird, like fuzzy little animals." Yet she painstakingly produced a small lopsided basket in Mrs. Morris's basket-weaving workshop, concentrating so hard that she bit her tongue until it bled. Whatever Jinx did, she did *too much,* I had noticed.

I stuck with the plants, as always, which meant, at this time of year, starting seedlings from scratch in the flats. I planted one tray of pansies and later, another of snapdragons, sharing space with Mrs. Fitzgerald, who showed up to work silently and methodically beside me.

She must be getting better, I thought, for she had obviously been issued a day pass from the top floor, though she did not look much better, face flat and pasty, eyes down. She carried her tray over to the light table carefully, positioning it just so beneath the hanging fluorescent tubes, then wiped her dirty hands right down her pale gray skirt — she wore no smock — and left immediately, speaking to no one, though Mrs. Morris paused in another conversation to look up. I watched Mrs. Fitzgerald go, too, remembering how much she had always loved flowers — flowers both in the ground and on the canvas, huge and phantasmagorical — and hoping that this joy might come back to her. She always got better at Highland, didn't she? Miss Malone had said so.

"Gotcha!" a voice behind me, a poke in the back. I whirled around and it was Pan in his usual motley, stamping his boots, red-faced and grinning at me beneath a wool cap, though he wore no overcoat, as usual, never seeming to mind the cold or even to feel it.

"Hello," I said, while from across the room, Mrs. Morris gestured to him. But he shook his head, waving to her with brick-red hands — where were his gloves, in this weather? Then he headed back to the utility room with me following involuntarily. He leapt up to grab a big pair of clippers off the wall, then turned to see me standing there. That rare, wide smile spread all the way across his face; though snaggletoothed, he had the whitest teeth, the biggest grin.

"Come on," he said, or I thought he said. Half the time when I was with him, I wasn't sure what he said, or if I was making up what he said, right out of my own head. He turned to go.

"Wait for me outside then. Down by the well," I had the presence of mind to whisper, for I had to get my coat and I knew I could not be seen leaving with him. He disappeared without my knowing if he had understood me or not. Heart in my throat, I said good-bye to Mrs. Morris, refusing her customary offer of tea, which I usually accepted. I buttoned up my coat and put on my gloves and my hat and wound my matching muffler — all knitted by Mrs. Hodges, of course — around my neck, then paused at the door to look back once again at this place I loved so much — filled with light and green things growing, flowers all in their rows, the scent of cinnamon and cloves, the productive bustle of activity. Warmth.

But I was headed outside, into the heart of winter.

By then, it was close to four o'clock, on one of the coldest days yet. The last of the sun shot over the snow at a brilliant, blinding slant. In fact, I couldn't see Pan at all as I tried to peer down the hillside; but when I reached the old covered well, there he was sitting on top of it, feet dangling, as if he had been there forever. Roy Rogers sat below, immobile and alert.

"Here I am," I said unnecessarily, moving to the side so that I could actually *see* him in the sun's last glare.

" 'Bout time." His whole face was open

and ruddy, that big grin. I started smiling, too, and couldn't stop, though my mouth didn't seem to work right in this extreme cold. He slid off the well and stood very close to me, looking straight into my eyes. His own eyes were tawny, golden, one of them slightly darker than the other. It was a little like being hypnotized.

"Why aren't you working?" I asked. "Don't you have to cut something down?" I pointed to the clippers.

"Naw," he said, or maybe it was "now," for then he whistled sharply to his dog, who leapt up and stood quivering. "Going home." He jerked his head toward the forest below and started off down the cleared pathway with me struggling to keep up behind him, though he didn't actually know I'd be following — how did he *know*? The kids on the crews used to say that Pan had eyes in the back of his head. He never once looked back, nor did I. I couldn't even see them in front of me — Pan and his dog — as we walked straight into the setting sun. Then he plunged abruptly off the cleared walkway into the open snow and then I *could* see them, and I could see each tree's long purple shadow lying out behind it as I followed him into the forest. It was such hard going in the deep snow that finally I began to step into his footsteps, which was easier.

And where was the path? I had thought there would be a path. But no, on we went down the hill past great outcroppings of rock and clumps of rhododendron as big as a house — what Ella Jean used to call a "laurel hell." Once Pan held up his hand and stopped dead in his tracks, so I did, too — and so did Roy Rogers, to my amazement. For five deer were crossing a little clearing ahead of us, picking their delicate way on spindly legs. We didn't move a muscle until they were gone. The deeper we went into the forest, the darker it got, though the snow itself took on a pale blue radiance that seemed to rise up from the ground. I wasn't even cold — or tired — when suddenly we were there, Pan's hut, or cave, or whatever it was — I could never decide what to call it, set right into the side of a cliff covered in rhododendrons. Now I saw why he needed the clippers. Weighed down by snow, a great limb from one of the huge evergreen trees above had fallen across the entrance. Working in that blue half-light, Pan quickly cut and pulled branches and brush back from a simple plank door, then lifted up the latch to let me in.

It was much warmer inside, though the

darkness was total. A match flared, then the yellow light of a lantern. Roy barked once, and was fed. Pan put something from his pack into Roy's waiting bowl; whatever it was, it disappeared in an instant. Then Pan crossed to the small fireplace and lit a fire that caught instantly, too.

I had a moment to look around. It was like being in a fairytale, or a children's book, or an animal's house. A house like a hole in the ground, with no windows, its dirt floor deep in pine straw packed down into a sort of mat. Rudimentary wooden furniture made by Pan himself — for I had often seen him over at Brushwood building things for Mrs. Morris, chests and benches and such, sanding them and rubbing them with linseed oil until the wood gleamed. Pan had a little square table with the lamp on it, one chair, a couple of wooden chests, for clothes and supplies, I guessed, and a shelf that held a number of small wooden animals that he had obviously carved himself. The raised bed tick was covered by old blankets and quilts more of which also hung on the walls, such as they were. The space was so tiny that it seemed entirely natural to me when Pan dusted off his hands and helped me take off my coat, hanging it from a peg before leading me over to the bed, as there was no place else for both of us to sit and be comfortable. He took off his boots and put on some moccasins that he had made from some kind of animal skin. I took off my high-topped shoes and my damp socks. He gave me two of his own socks to put on, one orange, one brown. To be in this strange dwelling was like being in the hold of a boat, I decided, deep inside a sailing ship upon the high seas, crossing the ocean.

Pan grabbed up an old guitar and played me a tune. "Oh Polly, pretty Polly, come go along with me," I sang along with him. "The first time I saw you, it wounded my heart." I had not known he could play guitar. And I was fascinated to realize that he had no hesitation with words when he sang, though his regular speech was sparse and halting at best. I lay back on the blankets to listen, but then he put the guitar aside and began matter-of-factly to unbutton my dress, as if it were a job of work to be done. And indeed, it took him forever, with all those little bone buttons up the front so difficult for his hard, thick fingers, biting his lip and saying "pretty girl, pretty girl" over and over until it was almost a song, too. Then he pulled my dress off and took off his own shirt and undershirt and I could see all the springy brown hair on his muscled chest and his white arms like sculpture in a museum. Pan had a particular smell about him, earthy and somehow familiar. I unbuckled his belt and pulled down his pants and he came to me finally, which was what I wanted, I knew it then, everything I wanted then or ever. The bed tick smelled piney and musty, like nothing else in the world, and the yellow firelight leapt all over the colors and patterns of the quilts on the wall, fans and flowers, diamonds and interlocking rings.

"Ain't you hungry?" Suddenly Pan sat up, his thick hair touseled and sticking out every whichaway, which made me laugh, and I started tickling him which made him roll over on me again.

"Now I am *really* hungry!" I announced after that, and sat wrapped in a blanket to watch him get up and pull his pants on and disappear behind the quilt at the back where the cave grew narrower and deeper, as I would learn. He came back with a big piece of raw meat and some potatoes, which he cut up on a smooth rock by the fire and then fried in a long-handled iron skillet right there, sprinkling the food with salt and pepper, those familiar little paper packets from the dining hall. Had Flossie given these to him? And what about the old guitar? I remembered all the instruments on the porch that night we "sang the moon up" at the Bascomb homestead in Madison County.

Pan brought the whole skillet over to me, right there in the middle of the bed. "Can I have a fork?" I asked, and he brought that, too, and we ate sitting in the bed with the old black skillet on a pallet on our crossed knees, facing each other and sometimes feeding each other, too, Pan eating with his hands, though carefully, with his customary precision, me half naked and not even caring, though I did put my coat and my shoes on eventually to slip outside and pee, amazed at the brightness of the moon and all the sounds of night creatures in the forest. When I opened the plank door to come back in, I heard music again, the most beautiful, plaintive song, which he was playing on his harmonica. There is nothing like a harmonica to express yearning, I think. Pan just shrugged when I asked him what the melody was, then nodded when I asked him if he'd made it up.

He reached into the chest that doubled as a table by the bed, came up with a bottle, then screwed off the top and took a big drink of it before handing it over to me.

"Brandy," I said. I took a long swallow that burned all the way down but went straight to my head as I went on talking and talking, telling all those secrets I'd been so good at keeping. Though his eyes stayed right on me, bright as a bird's, I knew he didn't understand most of what I was talking about, but it didn't matter. It never mattered. I was more myself with Pan in his lair than I had ever been before, or ever have been since. I talked until we finished the brandy and he reached for me, and then I slept like a stone until sometime later in the night when I woke up in a panic and started shaking him.

"Oh Lord," I cried, "I've got to get back. You've got to take me back right now." For with no windows, I couldn't tell what time it was — it could have been noon, for all I knew! And I had morning music groups with Phoebe Dean.

"Okay, it's okay." Pan was dressed instantly, though it took me a few more minutes.

It turned out to be that magical time just before dawn, a time that I had never experienced out in nature before, the pearly sky lightening to the palest pink then deepening to salmon, winter trees like black lace against it, scratchy little tracks everywhere visible now in the snow, a rabbit jumping across our path, a nearby owl still to be heard.

"Looky there." Pan pointed up and there was the owl himself in the crook of a massive tree; his huge head with its unblinking eyes swiveled all the way around to watch us as we left. *"Too — tooo — whooo?"* he called after us. *"Me!"* I felt like screaming out the answer. "Me, Evalina, that's who!" As before, Pan went ahead, with me stepping in his footsteps where it was easier to walk. Now it seemed like no time at all until the forest opened upon the long white slope of the Highland Hospital grounds yet at a different place, I believed, from where we had entered. I could not be sure. Pan came to a stop, me beside him. Looking back at our single track, I wondered, was I even there? Now I could see the gracious buildings clustered on top of the hill, two hawks swooping figure eights against the gorgeous sky. The melody from "Morgen" ran through my mind. *"And all around us will sing the muted silence of happiness."* A gray van drove slowly up the main driveway with its lights on, then the red and white grocery truck. Once again, I was starving. I turned to kiss Pan good-bye, but he was already gone.

■ ■ ■ ■

"Freddy's back!" The girls chorused later that day when I returned to Graystone after work, bone-tired yet still exhilarated. Our sitting room looked fussy and foreign to me now, like a room in an old French novel. Amanda and Myra had made brownies, which smelled wonderful baking.

"He is?" I hung up my coat and sank down upon the couch, scarcely able to comprehend this news.

"Yep," Jinx said matter-of-factly. She stood in the middle of the floor holding the blue mixing bowl and licking chocolate off the spatula. "Freddy's already been here twice. He's *after* you, Evalina. He wants to jump your bones."

Everybody giggled.

"Oh, he does *not*!" I said.

But just at that moment, Freddy himself burst in the door with a whoosh of cold air and his red cheeks redder than ever, wearing that silly hat with the earflaps, crossing over to the sofa to grab me up in the biggest hug. "Here you are! Man, I've been missing you!" he cried.

And Reader, I confess: My heart did not sink but soared to see him again, to hear him say, "my girl," and to watch him fill up our whole parlor with goodness and vigor. I found myself smiling foolishly along with the others when he produced a cloth bag filled with gifts "from home" — which I began opening one by one, as everyone else tactfully disappeared — except for Jinx, of course, who recognized no social cues. Jinx had no more manners than a goat.

One by one, I opened the sweetest gifts:

— A needlepoint purse made by Freddy's sister Elaine, with a repeating pattern of roses and hearts;

— A dainty gold locket which had belonged to some great-aunt or other, long deceased. Her initials were E.M.M.;

— A carefully wrapped package of divinity fudge, which I had never heard of, though apparently it is considered a great treat in Indiana;

— A loaf of his mother's prize Nut Bread ("Very appropriate!" I had to say) — plus the family recipe written out in her spidery hand along with the notation, "How to keep Freddy happy";

— Two mysterious hand-sewn items made of red-and-white-checked gingham cloth gathered up by elastic, with ruffles all around their bottoms.

"What do you think these are?" One in each hand, I held them aloft.

"Damned if I know." Even the gift-giver looked perplexed.

"*I* know," Amanda announced, gliding through. "They're for the kitchen. You put one over your toaster and the other over your Mixmaster."

"But why?" I asked.

"So nobody has to look at them, I guess," Amanda said. "You know, to beautify your kitchen. I used to have some of those myself, back in the Dark Ages."

"Or you could just wear them, I reckon," Jinx suggested, grabbing one to pull it down over my head like a dustcap. Immediately, Freddy put on the other. Then we couldn't even look at each other without going off into fits of laughter, while Jinx got so tickled that she had to lie down and bang her heels on the floor like a little girl. Suddenly Freddy stopped laughing and stared at me, very serious beneath his ruffled hat, until I had to turn away. From that day forward I was his girl for real, and we both knew it.

But this had nothing at all to do with Pan.

January 25, 1948. How well I remember this afternoon! Like one of Mrs. Fitzgerald's arresting paintings hung in permanent exhibi-

413

tion on the wall of my memory . . .

A canceled music group had given me a free hour to duck into the Art Room, where I sat chatting with Miss Malone as I attempted to shape a little clay animal for Pan's collection of "critters," as he called them. This was to be an elephant, for Pan had no African or exotic animals at all, only realistic depictions of the creatures in his own forest. But I was finding this simple project harder going than I had expected, as my elephant kept tipping forward, to Miss Malone's amusement and my annoyance. "His head's too big," she said, which gave me a sharp pang as I thought of Robert.

To change the subject, I pointed at the exhibit wall before us, where several of Mrs. Fitzgerald's latest paintings were on display, all very different from her pastel scenes of travel in Europe, or the amusing, magical renderings of fairy-tales and Alice in Wonderland. The new paintings obviously reflected the more withdrawn, serious Mrs. Fitzgerald who had come back to us now — incomprehensible scenes done in glaring colors — blood red, royal blue. Each was crowded with human figures in attitudes of tragedy, torpor, or even death. Some were clearly women, with round, high breasts exposed; others were probably men, though it was impossible to distinguish the sex of many, much less decipher the meaning of these pictures.

"What's going on?" I asked Miss Malone. "What do these mean?"

"Well, she's very preoccupied with religion," Miss Malone began.

"But wait — Mrs. Hodges told me she was in love with a Russian general," I said.

"Oh, that!" Miss Malone smiled. "That's just an idée fixe, it comes and goes, it's been going on for years now. I guess the religious fixation has, too, but it's gotten more intense recently. Much more intense. Notice the crosses everywhere — and there are Bible verses printed out on the back of all the canvases, too. Each one is a specific scene from the Bible, though I admit, it's sometimes hard to tell —"

"Rowena!" It was Mrs. Fitzgerald herself, rushing across the room. "Rowena, you won't believe it!" she cried, as somewhat taken aback, Miss Malone stood to hug her. "She's here, she's here, she's already here! Oh Rowena — they just called me from the hospital."

"That's wonderful, Zelda." Indeed, Miss Malone looked overjoyed herself, both for her favorite patient and because she and Karen were genuinely fond of children; they adored them, in fact, arranging games and activities for them at every staff picnic and event. I had always thought it a great pity that they would never have one of their own.

"This is a new grandchild?" I ventured.

Mrs. Fitzgerald turned a beaming face upon me, radiant as a spotlight, and suddenly I saw her old self pictured there, and remembered how beautiful she had been when I first saw her. "This is a brand-new little girl who has most recently arrived upon the earth, a very little girl with a very large name." — now Mrs. Fitzgerald was hugging me, too — "Her name is Eleanor Lanahan, isn't it clever of such a little girl to have such an important, serious name as Eleanor? To balance out the Lanahan, don't you see, so now it's a seesaw name, with equal weight, three syllables, on each side. A felicitous name, a noteworthy name. Names are very important, you know. Furthermore, Eleanor Lanahan has beautiful manners as well, having already invited me to pay her a visit in six weeks' time." Mrs. Fitzgerald was practically babbling, her face alive and glowing.

"Congratulations," I said sincerely. "This is wonderful news."

Mrs. Fitzgerald nodded vigorously. "She will be an angel in the world, I am making sure of that. These are for her, and for little Tim, too" — indicating the pictures with a sweeping gesture — "that they may know the teachings of our Lord Jesus Christ, and walk in godliness all the days of their lives, and dwell in His house forever."

"Why, what a lovely thing to do for them, such a thoughtful gift," I heard myself say, while privately I thought that these paintings would terrify a child.

"And they are for you, too, Patricia Pieface!" Mrs. Fitzgerald announced suddenly, "for you were once my little girl, too, weren't you?" She hugged me fiercely, terrifyingly, and then was gone.

"I don't have a clue what that was about," I told Miss Malone honestly, in answer to her inquiring look. "Just nonsense." Yet my voice caught in my throat.

"Ah, nonsense," she mused slowly. "*Non*-sense. *Non*-sense often contains the most sense, and the deepest truths of all. I've been listening very closely to my guests for many years, you know."

"Your guests?"

She smiled. "Well. The patients. It has been a privilege." Miss Malone made a little bow then, to what deity I didn't know. "And none more so than that one —" She indicated the way Mrs. Fitzgerald had gone, then followed slowly after.

I stayed alone to look at the paintings more closely.

"The Deposition" struck me as especially horrible, with the dead Jesus being taken down from the cross, apparently, amid a plethora of unaffected naked ladies stacked about the canvas. Another woman appeared dead or at least unconscious in "Do Not Steal," and an actual fight was featured in the foreground of "The Parable of the Vineyard." Only "Adam and Eve" held any appeal for me, though still I would never let a child see it, for it was disturbing in another way, with both Adam and Eve naked and vulnerable in the spiky, scary garden featuring large cats with hooves and the huge, vertical snake. Somehow — perhaps because they looked like paper dolls — these two young unmarked people seemed like Zelda and Scott to me, back when they were young and alone together with the whole world laid out before them tempting and beautiful, yet dangerous, too, with apples on every tree. I closed my eyes and wished — or prayed, I can never tell the difference — for a better life for those precious little children, Tim and Eleanor Lanahan, and I hope that they have experienced it.

Leaving, I turned off the lights and picked

up a scrap of paper from the floor, which turned out to be part of a letter which Mrs. Fitzgerald must have been composing for Scottie, her daughter.

On Photography

Please send a photograph of little Eleanor Lanahan immediately, without fail, along with another of that handsome big boy Tim. Also it is well to impress him with a sense of responsibility for her even now, you know, for anything can happen to a girl, hence a big brother is a pearl beyond price, an edifice against disaster, which lurks everywhere.

On Baby Food

Do not buy the tinned baby food but boil up your own, whatever fruit or vegetables you have at hand until soft and mushy, then mush them up some more. Eschew salt! For salt is the enemy of the Liver. And children are like little puppies, you know, they will eat anything, so the responsibility is ours.

It was beyond me to imagine Mrs. Fitzgerald ever making any baby food herself; I thought perhaps she had read such advice

in a ladies' magazine, and had appropriated
it.

LACKING THE COOK

On the topic of Many Little Meals: Do not
scorn paper napkins and plates au contraire invest in a goodly score of these and
plastic utensils as well. Lacking that one
necessity, the Cook, the modern household must needs make do. A countertop of
dirty little dishes disheartens all. This
includes the returning husband.

ON BABY TALK

Though baby talk may prove irresistible to
grown-ups, do not indulge yourselves in it
too much, as all children love to learn real
words, actually preferring, for instance, the
word BEAR to "poo-ba," and BELL to "ding
dong," and EATING AT A RESTAURANT
to "gogo yumyum," and GRANDMOTHER
to "Googy" though Googy herself would
never complain, and will happily answer to
anything.

ON YOURSELF

You cannot imagine the beauty of your
own little self as a child, those fat apple
cheeks and round eyes, nor the joy we
took always in your very being which

seems to me a miracle even now. I know there are bad times which you must remember, for bad times stick in the mind while good times pass as a summer day, but our love for you never wavered, like that steady green light at the end of the pier in Daddy's book. For you completed us, you were always the best of us, oh how we loved you with all our hearts.

I smoothed out the sheet of wrinkled paper carefully and gave it back to Mrs. Fitzgerald the following day, though she scarcely glanced at it, sticking it into her notebook without comment.

Remember when I told you that I had gone back to Graystone to pick up some music I had forgotten? The time I encountered Charles Winston pounding down our stairs? There is more — much more — to this part of the story.

For that morning, Phoebe Dean had asked me, right out of the blue, if I knew anything about Mardi Gras, and whether it involved any particular sort of music. "The activities committee is planning a dance," she'd said, "like we used to have, remember? I think it's a great idea — it'll get us all out of the winter doldrums. But the next holiday is

Valentine's Day which just makes a lot of people sad because they don't have any romantic attachments right now, living here — and anyhow, Valentine's Day is too soon. We'd never have time to get ready. So I looked at the calendar and what did I see coming right up? Mardi Gras, that's what!" She slapped the table in her characteristic way. "So the dance is set for March tenth, and that's our theme. If anything can pep us up around here this winter, that'll be it. Now, I am hoping that the jazz group can perform — what do you think?"

"You mean *our* jazz group?" I smiled to think of nervous little Louis Lagrande and red-faced Freddy. "Sure," I said. "Absolutely."

"Oh, good," she said. "The biggest problem we've encountered is Dr. Bennett — you know how he is about money, or maybe you don't, but he won't spend a penny he doesn't have to, and he says we can't hire an orchestra. So *our* job, Evalina, will be to get hold of some typical Mardi Gras recordings to broadcast for the dancing, and perhaps some music for you to play as well —" She fixed me with her typical pop-eyed expectancy. "What do you say?"

"Phoebe, do you have any idea that I am actually *from* New Orleans?"

"Go on!" Now she slapped her big thighs in astonishment.

"Absolutely," I said. "I grew up there." I did not tell her anything else. "So yes, I can definitely help you. The music is wonderful — jazz, blues, Dixieland band, Ella Fitzgerald and Louis Armstrong . . . You can get hold of plenty of recordings from people right around here, I'll bet — for instance, Richard Overholser has got a huge collection of jazz. And I've already got some sheet music —" I had quite a lot of it, actually, which I had purchased at a local estate sale, tipped off by Mrs. Hodges.

"So you could play something suitable then, before the program begins?"

"Oh honey," I said, "I can even play ragtime!" I was surprised by the sudden, deep excitement welling up inside me. "And we can start things off with a Mardi Gras parade. That's the tradition, you know."

Phoebe had clapped her hands, setting off a flurry of activity. As a result, ballroom dancing and parade marching were now being offered for Exercise in the gymnasium, along with the regular calisthenics. Word came that people were really enjoying it. It was funny to hear the strains of "When the Saints Come Marching In" or "Carnival Time" come wafting out from the big old building, over the snow.

Now that I was indispensable — the Mardi Gras expert — I found myself attending my second committee meeting in the Art Room, where soon, Mardi Gras masks would be made. Miss Malone was showing us the big silly feathers and the tubes of glitter that had already come in. The only item that would be entirely "store-bought" would be the strands of Mardi Gras beads, which I had assured them all that we *must* have. No substitutes!

"Evalina, you'll be glad to know that they're already on the way," Miss Malone announced. "And we ordered tons of them because they're so incredibly cheap, too. I'm amazed!" For Dr. Bennett's budget had turned out to be as draconian as feared, with no provision for live music at all except for such talent as we could summon up from our own midst. We were still hoping that Mrs. Carroll would be back in time, but oh, how I longed for Nina Simone, long gone, the toast of Europe. She would have been perfect.

"Anything else we need to take up today?" Phoebe Dean asked. A little late-afternoon silence descended upon our committee, there in the corner of the Art Room: Miss

Malone, myself, Phoebe Dean, Mrs. Morris, and old Mr. Pugh, who had the final word on all such parties, outings, and public events. Beyond the round table where we sat, several of Miss Malone's "guests" continued their work, including a small group who were piecing a quilt together, and Mrs. Fitzgerald at her easel, utterly absorbed, as usual. "All right then, thank you very much!" Phoebe Dean clapped her hands a final time and stood up. Now that I was more staff than patient, I realized that many of the Highland activities were held as much for the staff as for the patients.

I still don't know what made me think of it. But as I put on my coat, I had a sudden inspiration.

"Mrs. Fitzgerald," I called out softly to her. "Mrs. Fitzgerald?"

She looked up, emerging from whatever state or vision produced those paintings. She focused upon me. "Oh, Patricia," she said. She smiled.

"Actually, this is Evalina —" Mr. Pugh began.

"It's all right, Harry." Miss Malone cut him off. "That's just a nickname. They're old friends."

I went over to stand in front of her easel. "We are going to have a dance," I said, "like

425

the dance we had before, with the nursery rhyme theme, don't you remember? When you were Mary, Mary, and choreographed the performance with all the flowers —"

"The Waltz of the Flowers," she said immediately. "From the Nutcracker." She put her brush down.

"Exactly," I said. "You choreographed the whole thing, and you had a garden full of dancing flowers, but you were the prima ballerina. The star."

"That was a long time ago," she murmured, looking down now.

Afraid that I was losing her, I came a bit closer. "Now it's time for another dance," I said. "For a Mardi Gras party. And we need *you* to choreograph it. What do you say?"

She twisted her hands in her lap, still looking down, saying nothing.

"Nobody else can do it," I said.

"Oh no," she murmured, shaking her head. "It's too late, too late, my flowers are dead, and all those lovely boys gone off to war."

"Evalina." Miss Malone put a restraining hand on my arm.

I knew that Mrs. Fitzgerald was remembering the Beauty Ball back in Montgomery when she was sixteen, when she met Mr. Fitzgerald, then a soldier, the beginning of everything. "Please," I said.

"No, no, no, no, no . . ." Mrs. Fitzgerald started saying until it was a chant, swinging her bowed head back and forth like a metronome.

I felt terrible.

Miss Malone was drawing me gently away when Jinx Feeney popped up suddenly out of nowhere, as was her wont.

"Oh, *come on*!" she cried. Her nasal voice sliced into the quiet afternoon and left it in pieces on the floor. "Do it! Do it for me! I want to be in the dance *soooo* much. They told me there would be parties, and dances here — *you* told me!" She pointed at me. "But you just lied — they haven't had a one yet. Please do it! I'm a great dancer, I swear. You want to see the jitterbug? Look at this!" Jinx started throwing her skinny little body into contortions right there in the Art Room. "Oo Poo Pa Doo!" she sang at the top of her lungs.

Mrs. Fitzgerald was looking at her now. We were *all* looking at her.

"Wanna see the Charleston?" she cried, dropping down to do something very fast and complicated with her knees.

"Who *are* you?" Mrs. Fitzgerald asked.

"I'm Jinx, Zelda" — never even slowing down.

"But my name is Zelda, too."

"Well, mine's not. I'm Jinx! What about the Black Bottom?" She broke into a bump and grind that was as funny as it was lewd.

I started laughing and couldn't stop.

"Or the Hootchie Cootchie?" This was even worse.

Now Mrs. Fitzgerald was laughing, too. "Oh, we can't do *that,*" she said. "We'd never get away with it! It will have to be something more dignified — fun, you understand, but more dignified, more appropriate —" She turned to me. "Ponchielli," she said.

"What?" I was taken aback.

"The air from *La Giaconda,* of course!" Mrs. Fitzgerald stood up and put her paint-splattered hands on her hips in a purposeful way. " 'The Dance of the Hours,' it's quite short. I shall begin immediately." She grabbed up the black notebook.

"Oh, goody, I am *soooo* glad, thank you, thank you, thank you!" Jinx combined her little-girl quality with a final bump and grind as she exited the Art Room, soon followed by Mrs. Fitzgerald, her color heightened, mumbling to herself.

"Well, girls, you've certainly gone and done it now," Mr. Pugh said.

" 'The Dance of the Hours' is what Mrs.

Fitzgerald performed on the night she met Mr. Fitzgerald," I told them, "at the Beauty Ball in Montgomery, when they were young."

"Jinx may remind her of the girl she was then, all those years ago. Zelda was pretty wild herself, you know." Mrs. Morris smiled.

"That Jinx is a real force, isn't she?" Mr. Pugh said.

"She's terrifying — and wonderful," said Dr. Schwartz. "I have absolutely no idea how things will turn out for her. She could do anything."

"And she probably will," Miss Malone agreed. "But Jinx is just biding her time with us. My real concern is for Zelda, of course. This supposed Mardi Gras dance will take place only a few days before she is scheduled to go New York to visit her daughter's family and meet that new grandchild. I hope all the excitement won't derail her."

"I believe — I *hope* — it will be therapeutic," Dr. Schwartz said.

"Can you play that music?" Phoebe asked me.

In the back of my mind I heard Mrs. Carroll saying, so long ago, *Evalina can do anything.* "Of course," I said.

Thus it was decided.

Before heading back to Graystone, I ran

up to the practice room for my things and found the bright spray of shiny green leaves and waxy white berries that had been placed across my keyboard. I knew what this meant. Everything else — Mrs. Fitzgerald, Jinx, the Mardi Gras dance — went completely out of my head. Stuffing all the day's papers into the canvas pack I had started carrying, I wound an extra muffler around my neck and went out the side door, which looked down the hill toward the old well where Pan sat whittling, his dog at his feet. He vanished immediately. After a decorous pause, I set off down that walk myself, following him into the trees, where I knew he would be waiting.

CHAPTER 13

Freddy started talking about Valentines's Day at least two weeks before it arrived. "You'll need a new dress," he had announced. "Something special, something fancy."

"Like what?' I was amused.

"Ohhh — silk!" he cried. "Or lace. Or something."

"Can it be black?" I asked, for that one black dress, off the shoulder yet suitable for concerts, still comprised my entire dress-up wardrobe, and I had no money to buy another.

Freddy considered this. "I guess. But we're going to a dinner dance at a really fancy place," he blurted out finally.

"The Grove Park?"

Freddy grinned triumphantly. "*Not* the Grove Park!" he said. "Anybody might see us at the Grove Park! Besides, this is Valentine's Day. I want to take you someplace else, someplace glamorous, someplace you've never been before. We'll need to leave here by three o'clock so we'll have plenty of time to explore before dinner. It's a *four-course dinner,*" he added, "so don't eat any lunch that afternoon. We want to get our money's worth."

I had to smile at this typical remark, so Midwestern, so, well, Freddyish. Still, I couldn't even imagine how much this evening must be costing him. "You're really not going to tell me where we're going, then?"

"Nope." He shook his head.

"Good," I said, for I do love surprises, if they are good ones, and I had had precious few good ones over the years. Also I loved it that Freddy had gone to so much trouble. But what in the world would I wear?

Sworn to secrecy, my chums came to the rescue. Ruth snuck out an armful of cocktail dresses from the exclusive downtown shop where she worked, then tossed them out on the bed, a rainbow of colors, as Amanda and Myra crowded into my room to look, too.

"I like the pink," Amanda said immediately, holding up a ruffly chiffon dress that looked like a valentine itself.

I knew I'd feel silly in it, but I held my tongue.

"No, no, the blue — it looks more like Evalina," pronounced Myra, choosing a three-quarter-length royal blue sheath with a jeweled V neckline and a matching cape. "See, it's sort of demure, but really sophisticated."

But *I'm not,* I was thinking hopelessly, *I'm not sophisticated at all,* when suddenly Jinx blew into the room and grabbed up a silver lame gown with a low, scooped neck and a swirly circular skirt. She held the dress up to herself, posing dramatically before the mirror, then started dancing with it, one arm out-thrust as if she led an imaginary partner up and down the hall. Jinx looked like such a waif — a little outcast, a tramp — yet every move she made had style, you had to hand it to her.

"But what about *this* one?" Ruth held up a dress with a white silk top and a layered black chiffon skirt. "Black and white is *in,* honey. It's the cat's meow."

"Nope." I smiled at everybody. "I'm going to choose —" I paused dramatically, then grabbed the silver dress from Jinx as she glided back into the room. "Ooooh, goody!" she squealed.

"Really?" Myra looked aghast. "You'd

really wear something like that?"

"Absolutely," I announced, as surprised at myself as they were, and wondering whether I'd actually have the nerve to do it.

But Freddy's reaction was worth the risk, seeing his eyes grow round as plates behind his glasses when he came to pick me up that Saturday afternoon. "Say, honey, you look swell! Just gorgeous — like a real movie star." I imagined my chums all laughing behind their closed doors. Of course I had to cover up my fancy dress with the old loden coat when we left, but nothing could spoil that initial effect.

Luckily there'd been a bit of a thaw during the past two days, so the road was clear as we drove down our mountain and headed east, out of town, which surprised me. "How far away is this?" I asked, and he said, "Fifteen miles," so I put my sunglasses on and settled back to enjoy the view of snowy peaks shining in the sun. "Now you really look like a movie star," Freddy said. I felt like one, too.

Big heaps of old snow had been pushed to the edge of the road all along, forming a wall of gray ice that would not melt until spring. But the highway was okay as we drove down past Black Mountain and headed off onto a secondary route. Freddy was holding my hand across the seat. "Now can you guess?" he asked.

I shook my head, still wondering a half hour later as the road began to climb, turning first tortuous and then downright scary. Freddy had to put both hands on the steering wheel. We crept along.

"Chimney Rock." I read the sign aloud. "Is *that* where we're going?"

Freddy shook his head no, still pleased with himself.

At length our road entered a dark forest that opened suddenly upon a large lake glistening in the sunshine. "Oh, my goodness!" I was completely surprised.

"Lake Lure," Freddy announced as if he had invented it. Then I remembered hearing the nurses mention this place where they sometimes came on picnics and dates. Past shuttered lodges and summer houses we drove around the edge of the lake until we came to the big white hotel that we could see shimmering across the water like a mirage, its arched balconies and terraces extending down to the water's edge. LAKE LURE INN 1927, announced the script emblazoned high up on its arched stucco façade — the height of elegance. This time, Freddy relinquished his station wagon to a valet without fear that he'd never see it again, and we had time for a walk along the balustrade at the lake's edge. A cold brisk wind blew off the water and destroyed Brenda Ray's attempt to style my fly-away hair.

"But this is just lovely," I said. "It looks so much like Switzerland."

"Does it now?" Freddy smiled happily as we walked along. He was a big, hard-working, good-hearted boy, really, easy-going and easily pleased. *"A girl could do a lot worse now, mark my words, lassie!"* Mrs. Hodges seemed to be saying in my head. The cold, clean air filled my whole body, swelling my heart. We held hands like children, walking along, though I was glad we did not go too far, as I could not afford to ruin Ruth's sling-back silver slippers. I knew I could never replace them.

We stood on a promontory looking back at the Moroccan-style hotel beginning to bustle with activity now, arriving vehicles and people — Valentine's Day sweethearts like ourselves. The water winked in the sun; the white mountain shone like a silver dome. Maybe I could really do this, really be "Freddy's girl." In a few months' time I would no longer be a part-time patient but an official staff member, Phoebe's assistant,

Dr. Schwartz had confided.

"Okay, let's start back," he said, checking his watch. "We don't want to miss a thing."

Oh, how I loved him for that remark! I squeezed his hand.

We were given pink champagne cocktails in long-stemmed glasses in the elegant lobby, which I found disconcerting due to its mirrored walls: who was that girl in the silver dress? I found myself sneaking glances at her, as if I were spying. We made conversation with a man from Greensboro who said he was "in the tobacco business," and his beautiful wife; I wondered, but did not ask, if they knew Charles Winston. An ancient couple, brittle and frail as insects, told me that they had met on Valentines Day sixty years earlier. "May you be so fortunate," the bent-over wife whispered into my ear.

When the French doors into the dining room were opened all at once, a collective gasp "Aaaah!" went up from the entire company. The semi-circular dining room had been specially decorated with pink linen, candles already glowing, and a long-stemmed rose on every table. We were given a choice location right in front of one of the huge windows facing the water. Though the sun was actually setting behind us, the surface of the entire lake turned red as we ate our lobster bisque and raw oysters, which Freddy politely declined, watching me down mine in amazement. "Chicken duxelles" were followed by "steamship" rounds of roast beef. Freddy ate his and mine, too, for I was overwhelmed by that point, though tickled to note that my date was getting his money's worth. Dancing began as the orchestra played a medley of popular love songs: "I've Got My Love to Keep Me Warm," "People Will Say We're in Love," "Embraceable You."

"It's funny how many songs are love songs." I said.

"I wouldn't know about that," Freddy said, "but I can name every bone in the human body, all two hundred and six of them. Come on, now!" he pulled me awkwardly to my feet, and I realized he must be a little drunk. "Let's get those tibias and fibulas moving!" First came a slow dance, "In the Still of the Night," on which I did fairly well, but became alarmed when it was followed by the livelier tune "I'm Gonna Sit Right Down and Write Myself a Letter." Freddy twirled me around then suddenly relinquished me on this one, apparently expecting me to improvise some steps on my own, which he seemed to be doing. I grabbed his hand, hard, and pulled him back to me. "*Never* do that again," I said.

"Why not?" he was grinning. "Give you a chance to shine."

"No. Please. I love to be led. I'm an accompanist, remember?"

"You are many things, Evalina," Freddy said, suddenly serious, into my ear, into my hair, which was all grown out now. "It may take me a lifetime to find them all out." He led me around the polished floor that was thinning out now as couples sat down to the selection of fancy desserts on each table. More champagne arrived. Freddy really was a bit tipsy, overturning his first glass of it. Our unobtrusive waiter brought him another flute of champagne and another pink linen napkin, intricately folded — as they all were — into the shape of a swan. *Little swan.* Joey Nero rose before my eyes, smiling and swarthy, filled with so much dangerous life.

"To you, Evalina!" Freddy raised his glass.

"No, to you. No one has ever been so nice to me," I said honestly.

He turned redder than ever.

I tipped his glass with mine, the crystal ringing. We drank.

"Let's get a room," I said.

Freddy stood right up and flung his napkin

on the floor. We left our desserts untouched upon the table.

Later I realized that I should not have been surprised to learn that Freddy, at thirty three, was still a virgin. He had worked so hard to put himself through medical school that he'd had no time for girls. And he was so kind by nature; of course he would have wanted to take care of girls, rather than taking advantage of them. He would have thought of his sisters.

But I was not his sister.

"I'm your tour guide, remember?" I announced, surprising myself, and was further surprised by Freddy's quick open ardor and my own rising response, there in a complicated antique four-poster bed in a room that would surely put this debt-ridden young doctor in the poorhouse . . . if it didn't get him fired first. From now on, we would have to be very careful.

But we got our money's worth, at any rate.

At some point during that night, I woke up and went to the window to look out at the moon hanging huge and low now over the water. It made a path straight to me.

"Evalina?" Freddy got up and stumbled toward me.

"Look," I said. "When I move, the moon moves, too. It comes toward you wherever you are, doesn't it? Why is that? Here, Doctor, you try it."

At first Freddy smiled indulgently, but then he tested out my theory, and it was true. "Oh Evalina," he said. "Everything will come to you in time, honey. It will, I promise."

Though life inside the snow globe continued as before, our closed world defined by the wintry landscape and us captive within it, I grew more and more anxious as the February days passed swiftly one after another and March drew nigh. Why, oh why had I ever thought of the Mardi Gras performance? As if it were not enough to help plan the dance itself! Why had I ever brought Mrs. Fitzgerald into it?

For now she seemed more remote than ever, scribbling obsessively in the black notebook though reluctant to schedule any rehearsals. "Not yet, not yet," she said, clutching the notebook to her chest. "There is a moment of completion, of fullest comprehension, which must arrive of its own accord, as if it were a messenger from another land, astride a horse." She swept out the door and down the hall.

"Oh brother," Phoebe Dean said to me. "If they're going to do it, they've got to start practicing, right? Especially since they're all mentals. It'll take a while — remember Miss Mary?"

I certainly did. And I was already prepared, having obtained the sheet music of *La Giaconda* in its entirety through a mail-order company. I remembered now that Joey Nero had once sung the tenor role, Enzo Grimaldo, in Toronto. Yet this did not bother me at all but pleased me somehow, as if I were taking back that part of my life. And it is such fanciful, happy music — a joy to play. I felt that it would be good for the participants to dance to it — therapeutic, as Freddy would say. But who would the participants be? And when would we start?

Just when Phoebe was on the verge of canceling the performance, Mrs. Fitzgerald appeared in our music room dressed in a black, flowing sort of jersey shift, with black tights and the pink ballet slippers. "Now," she said, opening the notebook.

Phoebe and I were speechless as we stared at the diagram before us, which I shall attempt to reproduce here.

GOD IS TIME

a ballet of infinity

tout crépuscule
le bout de la journée
black trees laced onto
   the silver sky
alors il est arrivé!

ARABESQUE
ARABESQUE

trailing home in the rain
we have lost our shoes
and all our money
   torn dress drags
   spangles in the mud

maelstrom of life!
orgiastic pain
   purple
      blue
red

GRAND JETÉ!
GRAND JETÉ!

never-ending

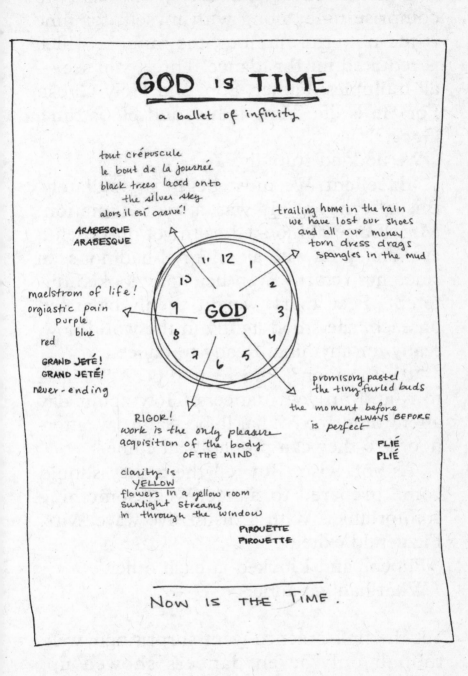

GOD

12 1 2 3 4 5 6 7 8 9 10 11

promisory pastel
the tiny furled buds

the moment before
is perfect   ALWAYS BEFORE

PLIÉ
PLIÉ

RIGOR!
work is the only pleasure
acquisition of the body
         OF THE MIND

clarity is
   YELLOW
flowers in a yellow room
sunlight streams
in through the window

PIROUETTE
PIROUETTE

NOW IS THE TIME.

"I shall need eight dancers," she said, "to comprise nine, along with myself, for nine is the powerful number, the number which is required for this dance. Three, you see — all multiples: Father, Son, and Holy Ghost. For He is life. Time is life, and He is time. Got it?"

We nodded stupidly.

"Excellent. We must begin immediately, this afternoon." It was a transformation. Mrs. Fitzgerald looked calm yet purposeful, eyes snapping with an energy I had not seen since her return. Even her body looked different. Feet apart, weight evenly balanced on each, she stood lightly in the world now, ready for anything. Ready to dance.

"It's too soon," Phoebe told her. "We have to round up your dancers. How about day after tomorrow? That'll be Saturday afternoon, so they can probably all come."

"As you wish. But tell them they should come prepared to dance. Wear something comfortable." With a dismissive wave, Mrs. Fitzgerald exited.

Phoebe and I looked at each other.

What had we done?

Yet the first practice went surprisingly well, though only seven dancers showed up. "Don't worry, we've got another coming next time," promised Dr. Schwartz, who was present, too. I was very glad to have her and Phoebe there, and Karen Quinn as well, who had asked to perform, as she loved modern dance herself. "Though it has been years," she confessed ruefully, large and very strong-looking in her green leotard and tights. Her feet were huge, bare, and very white. The others included my housemates, Myra, Amanda, Ruth, and Jinx, of course, the most enthusiastic of all — plus a shy new girl named Pauletta, and Mrs. Morris's oldest daughter Nancy, a high school girl who had been taking ballet lessons in town for several years.

"First we shall limber up." Mrs. Fitzgerald nodded to me and I began to play some little études as background music. "Just follow me." She led them in a series of stretches, up, down, forward, side to side, in time to the music. It all looked surprisingly professional to me. But why not? Mrs. Fitzgerald had told me herself that she was once asked to join the San Carlo Ballet Company in Naples and offered a solo role in *Aida,* though she had refused, to her eternal regret. Down in the front row, I could see Dr. Schwartz begin to relax as well. Mrs. Fitzgerald sank gracefully to the floor, where the exercises continued, then ended with the girls all sitting cross-legged in a semicircle, Ruth and Myra breathing hard.

"This don't look like any ballet dance *I* ever saw," Jinx announced. "When do we get to jump up and leap through the air?"

Everybody laughed.

Mrs. Fitzgerald rose to stand before us all. "This will not be, strictly speaking, a ballet, my dears." She was still composed. "It is, rather, an interpretive dance, a very famous dance, about the nature of time. You will form a circle, for you shall be Time itself — the minutes, the hours — and the music will tell the passing of the day from morning till night, or of a human lifetime, by extrapolation."

"By *what*?" Jinx asked.

"Extension," Mrs. Fitzgerald said. "Imagination. Use your imagination. I know you've got one. Play it for us, Evalina" — which I did, noting their immediate smiles. I knew it would make them happy.

"So. You will come in first and form a great circle, which will turn and turn . . ."

"Ecclesiastes," Jinx said.

This remark stopped Mrs. Fitzgerald in her tracks. Then she smiled — that lovely and rare occurrence. "Exactly, my dear! Just exactly! Now let's try it. Go offstage there,

446

and come in like this, in a line, but see the step? Watch the step, you over there. Now you're gliding, you're gliding, now form the circle, now let's go around — and around and around" — as I played.

"Now I want you to split up into groups of three. You girls over there — and you three in the center, come forward a bit, please — and the rest come over here, that's right. Now we shall learn a little routine, a sequence of steps and movements. Evalina!" I played. "Again." I played again as she performed the routine three times, then made a turn. But now Mrs. Fitzgerald seemed short of breath, and for the first time, I realized that I could see her age — forty-eight — which she must have been feeling, too, because she stopped suddenly and pointed to Jinx, saying, "Here, dear, why don't you come up and lead, while I help the others individually?

Without a word, Jinx went forward and performed the steps flawlessly, as I played the spritely tune again and again while Mrs. Fitzgerald moved from group to group, instructing — reaching down to point Amanda's toe, pulling Myra's shoulders back so she would stand up straight, telling Ruth to be quiet. Jinx led them as if she'd been doing it for years, again and again, until Mrs. Fitzgerald clapped her hands three times and said, "Enough! Very, very good work, girls. Now you may go. Though I want you to practice, practice, practice on your own, the little routine which you have just learned. Practice before a mirror, if possible." It would not be possible in most of the hospital. "If you get lost, ask that one," pointing to Jinx, who nodded solemnly. "And I shall meet with you again on —" She looked out at her little audience.

"Monday at five o'clock," Phoebe Dean called out. "One hour before supper. Here."

The dancers came down off the stage and milled around, finding their belongings and putting on their coats; their chatter filled the auditorium. They had ceased to be patients; they could have been any young women, anywhere. I closed the piano, gathered up my music, and stepped off the stage to join the rest. Finally the girls began trooping up the aisle, followed by Mrs. Fitzgerald, who paused to address Phoebe and Dr. Schwartz. "So, what did you think of the rehearsal? Some promise here, I'd say, especially the little redhead."

"Oh yes," we all gushed, and that fleeting smile appeared on Mrs. Fitzgerald's face again.

"You, Patricia," she said, pointing at *me*

now, "are *fine.* You are wasted upon us. And now, in the name of the Father and of the Son and of the Holy Ghost . . ." she murmured as she continued up the aisle alone.

"Hey Zelda," Jinx's flat carrying voice came suddenly from the dark at the back of the auditorium, "you wanna smoke?"

And then they both were gone.

Dr. Schwartz and I followed more slowly, Phoebe and Karen staying to straighten up and turn out the lights.

"You know what I wish?" I said, on impulse, turning to Dr. Schwartz. "I would give anything if Dixie could be here, if she could be in this dance, too. She would just love it, wouldn't she?" — as Dixie had such a gift for fun. "I miss her so much. Have you heard from her at all? Because I haven't, not a word. I don't understand it. I keep thinking about her."

Dr. Schwartz hesitated, looking down. Finally she put her hand on my arm. "It's so strange that you would mention Dixie to me right now. You are very, very perceptive, Evalina — maybe you're psychic or something." She smiled to show me that she was just kidding. "Because the fact is that Dixie has been upstairs in the Central Building for some time now, but tomorrow she will be moving down to the second floor, and urged to participate in the life of the hospital again. So she might well be one of the 'hours' in this performance, if she wants to. In fact, we have saved the last spot for her, just in case. This was my own little secret. She can start on Monday. What do you think of that?"

I gave Dr. Schwartz a hug. "Oh, that's wonderful," I said — my first reaction. But of course I knew it wasn't wonderful for Dixie. "What happened, though? She looked so happy when she left for Christmas. So did Frank — remember?"

"The short answer is, we don't know what happened. And we may never know. All we can do is treat the illness, which is depression, as best we know how. And our knowledge is very limited, pitifully limited."

"But you would think," I pursued, "on the face of it, that she's got everything — a husband who loves her, two children who love her — and she's rich, too. She can go back to college like Richard said. She can do anything she wants or have anything she wants — except get that baby back, I guess. Do you think that's the problem?"

"I think it may have been a factor, certainly, but most people get over such loss, or grief, or even traumas we can't imagine.

In fact most people will experience periods of depression in their lifetimes, and then they will get better eventually. There is the question of the body, which insists upon life — the organism itself wants to get better — the body always chooses life."

"So you're saying that Dixie —"

"I'm saying that the problem is that there's no problem. No single cause. That question is not even relevant when we are dealing with clinical depression. This is what people don't understand. Nobody understands it — especially not the relatives, or the people that love them, like Frank Calhoun. Everybody keeps thinking that there's a reason, something that can be changed, something that can be fixed, and then the patient will be fixed, too. I'm saying that Dixie suffers from recurrent bouts of immobilizing clinical depression — a serious illness which we know virtually nothing about, except that there seems to be a genetic component. It does run in families. Someday medical science will learn much, much more about it. But personally I believe that some particular chemical is missing in the brain — rather like diabetes — and that once we figure out what it is, perhaps we can replace it. For now, all we can do is tranquilize them to take the edge off their pain, give them a more orderly routine for a bit, a sympathetic ear and a respite from their own troubling lives, and jumble up their brains in a way we do not really understand, which may be completely irresponsible, for all we know." She sounded grim.

"Shock treatments," I said.

"Yes, and Dixie's got only two weeks to go on them, so there's no reason she can't participate in this dance *if she wants to,*" Dr. Schwartz emphasized. "We'll see. Anyhow, she's better."

So was Mrs. Fitzgerald, clearly, outside sitting on the top step of Homewood's stone portico, smoking a cigarette and laughing like crazy at something Jinx was telling her. What? I felt a bit jealous. I had known Mrs. Fitzgerald for years, and never had such rapport.

We went down the steps past them.

"You'd better get out of this cold," Dr. Schwartz called back. "It's time to go."

"We will when we finish these smokes," Jinx hollered out after us. "Bye now." Though she was the youngest of us all, Jinx treated everybody — even the doctors — as equals.

Then the lights went off abruptly and all we could see of them were the fiery red dots of their cigarettes, glowing in the chilly dark.

For the first time, I thought I could feel spring in the air as I left Homewood at the end of the day. It had not snowed for almost a week, and the sun had shone all day long. Despite the continuing cold temperature, patches of grass were emerging everywhere, as rivulets of melting snow coursed down the slope, along the sidewalk. Rehearsal had gone well again, and I realized how much I enjoyed this kind of accompaniment, especially since Dixie had joined us. She struck me as very much her old self, friendly and laughing, interested in each person. Everyone seemed to light up while she was talking to them. No stranger, watching her in conversation, could ever have guessed that Dixie was a hospital patient in the middle of a course of shock treatments for clinical depression. Anyhow, I was overjoyed to have her back among us, as one of the "hours." If I were not so grown up, I might have skipped down the hill, heading back toward Graystone — while keeping an eye out for Pan, of course, as always, though he was nowhere to be seen.

Instead, I rounded the corner and was surprised by an unfamiliar sight. A big old mud-splattered red truck pulling a silver hump-backed trailer with a long dent in its side, battered but shining in the sun, with yet another, smaller trailer hooked on behind, were parked right in front of our house. These vehicles looked as if they had escaped from the Dust Bowl, or from some Western movie set.

"Evalina?" Suddenly the passenger side door of the truck burst open and here she came running up the sidewalk, Ella Jean in a long leather coat with her black hair swinging below her shoulders, high-heeled cowboy boots slipping on the melting ice. She grabbed me up in a tight fierce hug.

"I can't believe it," I said, when I could speak. "Flossie told me you're a star, and now you even look like one!"

"Flossie — *Lord*!" Ella Jean rolled her eyes and gave me her jack-o'-lantern grin. "Flossie is crazy as a coot, taking after Mama if you ask me. Still yet, she's the one that told us you was back up here again, or I never would of knowed it. Told us where you was living, too. Lord, we've been about to freeze out here, waiting on you to get back from wherever you been keeping yourself all day."

Who was *us*? I looked over her shoulder to see a big, gangly boy wearing a cowboy hat jump out of the driver's seat, stamping out a cigarette and grinning from ear to ear. He came forward to greet me. "Bucky Pardoe," he said, "pleased to meetcha." His name made me laugh because he had the biggest, whitest buck teeth you can possibly imagine, along with straight yellow hair that stuck out from under his cowboy hat like straw. Though Bucky Pardoe was the opposite of handsome, his sky blue eyes were sharp, and I could tell instantly how smart he was. He had a sort of "go get 'em" style.

"I'm Evalina." I stuck out my gloved hand.

"I know it, honey. I know all about you. That's why we're here."

I looked at Ella Jean.

"Come on along with us," she said, "and we'll tell you. Just throw that book bag up on the porch and come on."

"But don't you even want to come in and see where I live?" I asked.

"Hell no, we don't, we want you to come *out.*" She laughed. "We've been driving all night, we're plumb wore out and now we're starving to death. We're going over to Fat Daddy's and eat us some barbecue. I been telling Bucky how good it is. So you come on with us. You know you want some barbecue."

I did not hesitate, sticking my bag inside the door without even telling anybody at

Graystone where I was going. I ran back down the steps to the truck where Ella Jean had already taken her seat.

"Wake up, Jesse," Bucky hollered as he opened the door on the driver's side, and to my immense surprise, yet another man sat up in the smaller backseat and blinked at me through his long black hair.

"This here is Evalina," Bucky said.

"That I was telling you about," Ella Jean added. "The Cajun girl."

"I'm not Cajun." I turned to look at her in surprise.

"Well, I'm not really Cherokee either." Ella Jean was laughing.

"Honey, in this business everybody has got to be somebody." Bucky helped me up into the cab and handed me over to Jesse with gentlemanly finesse.

"How do," Jesse said, taking my hand as if it were something precious. He had fine, thin hands with long fingers, hands that looked as if they had never done one day's manual labor in his life. In fact, Jesse's features were aristocratic, too — prominent nose and chin, long thin nose and heavy dark brows. "You sure do mean a lot to that one," he nodded toward Ella Jean up in the front seat, "and she sure does mean a lot to us. It is a privilege to meet you."

Most people picked up off the street in front of a mental institution do not receive such treatment. I smiled and settled back on the sheep's-wool rug that covered the cracked leather seat as we drove down the mountain into town. The floor of the cab was crammed with boxes, boots, bottles, parcels, and sacks of every sort.

"Are you from the South, too?" I asked him. Somehow I didn't think so.

"Very acute," Jesse said, smiling at me. His eyes were a sort of dark violet color, with shadows around them. "No, I grew up in a number of different places around the world. My father was based in Washington. Then I went to school in Boston."

"Where in Boston?"

"Harvard University," he said. "Believe it or not that's where I got interested in music, this kind of music. I came to the mountains to collect it, and started playing myself, and just never left. Never went back up there."

"What did your family have to say about that?"

"This is my family now," Jesse said, looking out the window.

We were pulling into the parking lot of Fat Daddy's Bar-B-Q, where Ella Jean had taken me years before. Bucky finally found a space along the fence that would accommodate us. The ramshackle restaurant meandered along a hilltop north of town, with a giant wooden pig out front and smoke rising from the long cookers out back. Not a single thing had changed, that I could see — not the heavy wooden booths with the red cushions and red-checked linoleum tablecloths, or the wooden floor with sawdust on it, or the neon beer signs along the mirrored bar. The raised dance floor, empty now, shone behind a brass railing. Autographed pictures of country music stars covered the walls. "See, looky here." Ella Jean pulled Jesse over, pointing at a skinny, grinning Jimmie Rodgers, the "Singing Brakeman." "He used to live right here in Asheville," she said. A photograph of Bill Monroe and his Blue Grass Boys hung next to Uncle Dave Macon, the "Dixie Dewdrop," in his double-breasted waistcoat, high wing collar, black felt hat and bright red tie. I guess it was true what Bucky had said, that everybody had to be somebody in country music.

"Can I start you off with some beer, hon?" The waitress wore a short red dress and a white ruffled apron, her plump breasts peeking over the top. Her ponytail swung side to side as she sashayed off to get the pitcher of beer Bucky ordered, along with a

Coca-Cola for me and a "couple of shots" for Jesse, which turned out to be little glasses filled with — what? "Bourbon," Jesse told me, downing one while sipping his beer more slowly. Ella Jean had ordered pork barbecue plates for everybody, along with slaw and rolls and hushpuppies and five or six vegetables and sides.

A silence descended as they all chowed down. "Appetite must be catching," I remarked, eating ravenously myself. "I told you, didn't I?" Ella Jean said, sitting back. "Lord that corn pudding was good. My Aunt Roe used to make corn pudding." Before I could have imagined it, all the plates were empty. Bucky got up and played the jukebox: Bob Wills's "San Antonio Rose," Ernest Tubb's "Walking the Floor Over You," which even I knew was very popular, and some Roy Acuff. I finished my Coca-Cola and started drinking beer myself. It tasted pretty good, too. Almost empty when we came in, the restaurant was filling up now with big solid mountain families, couples out on the town, groups of both men and women. The waitresses swished back and forth with platters of food. The noise level rose. Bucky ordered another pitcher of beer and a pan of banana pudding which I was sure I could not eat a single bite of. It was gone within minutes.

I felt like I was in another world, a secret world filled with delicious food and wonderful smells and vibrant colors and catchy music that existed deep inside the Asheville I knew. I felt like Alice, fallen down another rabbit hole.

"Thank you so much for bringing me here," I told them.

"Oh, we've got an ulterior motive," Jesse said.

"What does that mean?" asked Ella Jean.

"It means you're up to something." I smiled at her and she smiled back.

This was Bucky's cue. He leaned forward, blue eyes bright as buttons. "You got it, Sugar," he said. "You know Ella Jean and me have been together ever since we met up with each other two years ago on a National Barn dance show out in Tulsa, Oklahoma."

"Love at first sight," Ella Jean said.

"Joined at the hip," Bucky said.

"Where'd you get *him,* then?" I pointed to Jesse, who grinned.

"San Antonio. I'm a yodeling fool," he said. "Just wait till you hear me."

"So now we're the 'Kissin' Cousins,' " Bucky announced, "and we're headed over to Kentucky where we've got a great job waiting on us at John Lair's Renfro Valley Show in Mount Vernon, about sixty miles from Lexington."

"John Lair knows more about folk music than anybody in America," Jesse put in.

" 'Cept maybe you," added Bucky, chewing on a toothpick. I could see why Ella Jean loved him — he exuded good will and confidence. Son of a piano man, he'd grown up in southwest Virginia, playing every instrument there was.

"But we've got one big problem," Bucky went on. "We're doing the show this coming Saturday night and we need us a keyboard player. Bad."

It was already Thursday.

"What happened to the keyboard player you had?" I asked.

"Pregnant. We just got done delivering her back home to Danville, Virginia, where her mama wasn't none too happy to see her."

I looked from Bucky to Jesse, who held up both hands. "Not me," he said. "Act of God."

"I see." Now I looked at Ella Jean. "Whatever makes you think I could actually do that? Play keyboards for a country band, I mean? I went to Peabody," I said to Jesse, who nodded.

But Ella Jean said, "Evalina can play

anything. All she has to do is hear it one time." I knew she was right. I could do it. And then I could sleep in a truck and eat in places like this one, with people like these, and travel all over the country, playing music every night. My palm itched furiously as I thought about it.

"Come on and go," Ella Jean said. "You know you want to."

"I do," I said. "But I can't. I just can't. I've got some things here to take care of. Some things to finish up right now."

"You're going to regret it," Jesse said, looking at me. I thought of Matilda Bloom telling me I'd better grab that brass ring, that it ain't gonna come around again. And I had a feeling this might be my last chance.

But I also knew I had no choice. I couldn't leave them now, my people, my kind.

"Cousins, I thank you," I said, standing up. "Thanks for a wonderful, wonderful evening. But I guess you'd better take me on back now."

Which they did, though I still dream of what might have happened had I gone with them, all the highways we would have traveled, and all the things I would have seen. Jesse became famous, of course, while Bucky and Ella Jean got married and stayed on in Renfro Valley and had five children. I own several of Jesse's albums, and I have saved that copy of *Life* magazine with his picture on the front of it.

"Where you been?" Jinx slit her green eyes at me as I slipped quietly back into Graystone.

"Just out with some old friends." I hoisted my book bag.

"Who?"

I didn't answer, but followed her over to the window as she peered out between the venetian blinds at the messy, empty street.

By rehearsal time the next afternoon, I could hardly believe that Ella Jean's visit had really happened — it seemed like a dream, disappearing more and more throughout the day. I didn't mention it to anyone.

This was an important rehearsal. Satisfied that the hours had finally "got" the first part of the dance, which was quick, fanciful, and even humorous — as keyed by the spritely music — now Mrs. Fitzgerald was leading them into the slower middle section, where the mood turns to doubt. The movements she showed them were somber and slower; I played softly. A beseeching tone crept into the music as each group searched a different section of the stage, peeping and bend-

463

ing, then extending their arms in an attitude of loss.

Ruth stopped right in the middle of it. "So what's going on already?" she said in her most aggravating voice. "I hate this! The first part was fun, but this is making me nervous. We don't *have* to do this. I'm not going to do it if it makes me nervous, if it's not fun."

"Me neither," Amanda said. "This is stupid. It's depressing."

"Y'all need to shut up," Jinx spoke flatly. "You just shut up and do it. Or maybe Dr. Schwartz needs to give everybody another pill." Some of the hours laughed, but Pauletta, the new girl, covered her face with her hands and started to cry. Mrs. Morris's daughter looked confused.

"Now, girls." Mrs. Fitzgerald appeared entirely unperturbed as she turned gracefully to address them. "I am impressed by your sensitivity to the music and your understanding of this dance. Yes, the mood has changed. We are entering the middle phase of life where one often gets lost in a dark wood. We must go through the darkness to find the light. Of course you would understand this, you of all people. For this is art, and you are born artists, ballerinas every one of you! And now you must be-

464

come frantic, running in a circle, just so —"
She nodded to me, and I played spiky
arpeggios while she led them to form the
great circular clock again. Miraculously, not
a one had dropped out. "And now the clock
strikes six." Again she nodded to me as I
struck the slow, sonorous minor chords.
"And now you all must run off the stage —
you four to stage right, you four to stage
left. Yes, run off! Quickly! Run, run, run!
That's it."

The hours stood in the wings, panting
hard, exhausted though proud of themselves.

"We shall leave the stage bare for four full
measures before the grand finale, which will
be fun, I assure you! And you shall have
earned it, you see? For this is art — no light
without the darkness!"

"So what's the grand finale?" Ruth asked,
her trademark sarcasm gone for once.

Mrs. Fitzgerald stood tall and gave them
her most radiant smile. "It is — the *cancan*!" she promised. "Next time! Now once
more, back into those dark woods again,
girls, before we leave . . ."

I began to play the slow middle movement
as they scattered obediently into their tenta-
tive search across the stage with Mrs.
Fitzgerald watching them, nodding, pleased.

"Hellfire! That ain't dancing, that's just running around. Anybody can do that, that's got legs! I can dance better'n that with my eyes closed!" A piercing country voice cut into the ballet.

Mrs. Fitzgerald walked forward to center stage and held up her hand like a traffic cop, stopping the dancers, and I ceased playing, too, which was a good thing as my hand had begun to itch furiously. "Who is that? Who is there?" Shielding her eyes with one hand, Mrs. Fitzgerald pointed imperiously past Dr. Schwartz and Phoebe Dean, sitting in the front row. They turned around in their seats to look up the center aisle, too.

"No spectators, please. This is a closed rehearsal." Mrs. Fitzgerald spoke firmly.

"Well, I can dance, too." The voice rang out in the dark auditorium. "I can dance better'n any of y'all. Ask anybody. And I have been on the stage, too, you might say, over in Knoxville, Tennessee, which none of these others has, I can tell you for a fact. Not a one of them. I'm the best dancer that ever was, and I'd be glad to help y'all out, iffen you was to ask me."

"Oh, thank you so much for volunteering," Dr. Schwartz began quickly, "but actually —"

"I ain't asking you, ma'am. I'm asking *her,*

that one up there on the stage," came the voice.

"Now, Flossie." I stood up at my piano but could see only her yellow hair in the dim recesses of the auditorium. "Of course you're a great dancer, but you must have misunderstood. This program is just for —"

"You shut up! You just shut up, Miss Priss, I know all about you. *All* about you, don't think I don't — haven't even got enough sense to get on the bus!"

"That's enough." Mrs. Fitzgerald had come forward to the footlights now, hands on her hips, wearing her Cherokee face. She sounded very definite and even mean. "You — must — go — now!" She spaced out the words for emphasis. "Auditions are closed."

"They wasn't no auditions. This ain't nothing but a exercise for crazy people —"

Karen Quinn moved forward to stand on one side of Mrs. Fitzgerald, with Jinx already on the other.

But Mrs. Fitzgerald didn't need any help. *"Go now!"* She looked terrifying, like one of her own paintings.

"Bitch!" we heard, followed by the slamming, echoing door. Some of the hours giggled.

"My goodness," Mrs. Fitzgerald said mildly. "Now, girls, one more time —"

I couldn't believe they'd do it, but I started playing, and the hours started dancing again. Suddenly it was all over — both the unsettling incident and Mrs. Fitzgerald's change in mood. She was pleasant and professional as she told them good-bye and let them go, chattering and excited, back into their own afternoons, Flossie's outburst already forgotten.

"This is not the first time I have wondered about that kitchen girl," Dr. Schwartz told the rest of us, "though of course one rarely sees her . . . but there's something, something . . ."

"There's something wrong with her," Phoebe said flatly.

"Perhaps I should speak to Dr. Bennett about her," Dr Schwartz mused, putting on her coat.

"Don't," I said, "She comes from a very poor family. I know she needs the job —"

They both looked at me.

"I knew her sister, Ella Jean, when I was here before."

"You are always surprising me, Evalina," Dr. Schwartz said thoughtfully as we all left together.

Later, as Phoebe Dean and I entered the music room together, she remarked, "You know, I think I do remember the other one, the sister — isn't she that girl who used to come in and play music with you?"

"That's her," I said. "Ella Jean Bascomb. Their mother worked in the kitchen. Mrs. Carroll didn't like for me to be friends with her."

Phoebe snorted. "I can just imagine!"

Then she pointed at my piano, where a handful of purple and blue crocuses lay scattered across the keyboard.

CHAPTER 14

Rehearsals went smoothly after that, with no more interruptions from Flossie. But the kaleidoscope whirled toward Mardi Gras with dizzying speed. Now that I was playing New Orleans music for the gym classes, too, I was so busy that I could scarcely take in anything at the time; though in retrospect I vividly recall the morning I entered the greenhouse looking for Pan and found him working with Mrs. Fitzgerald on one of the long flats of seedlings that were already being prepared for spring.

Together they bent over their task, marking the rows and dropping the tiny seeds, murmuring intently, heads so close that their hair touched, as if they were one. What were they saying? What could they possibly be saying to each other? Especially when Pan scarcely spoke to me. Though I felt that he loved me, in his way, it became clear to me in that moment that he loved these oth-

ers, too — whoever he was with, I sometimes felt, whenever he was with them, with
no more discrimination than one of his
beloved animals — Mrs. Fitzgerald and
Mrs. Morris and Flossie and who else? Who
else? The terms were such that I could never
know.

Yet I didn't care. I was beyond that. For
when I was with Pan, I was happier than I
had ever been in my life; I felt more *myself*
in his lair than anyplace else on earth. I was
at home there. I would take what I could
get.

And then there was the dinner when Ruth
sat down next to me and began to whisper
excitedly in my ear that Freddy had asked
her to go shopping with him to help choose
my engagement ring.

"I don't have an engagement ring," I said
stupidly, staring at Ruth's bright red lipstick.

"Well no, of course you don't, you silly
thing. He's going to *buy* you one, stupid! At
Carpenter-Matthews, I think. So my question for you is, whaddya want? A diamond,
sure, but square-cut, emerald cut, round, or
what?" She took a bite of meatloaf then
waited, chewing industriously.

"I — I don't know." I put my fork down.

"Well, you better be thinking about it,"
Ruth said seriously. "This is your big

chance, honey. It's now or never. You'd better speak up." She took another bite.

I stood abruptly, grabbing my tray of half-
eaten food.

"Look at her, she's in shock," Ruth said
to Dixie.

Dixie jumped up and gave me the biggest
hug. "Get an emerald cut. That's what I've
got." She flashed her beautiful diamond
rings. "And you'd better choose me for your
matron of honor," she whispered. "Frank
and I can drive back up for the wedding.
Oh, Evalina, I just want you to be as happy
as we are." There was not a trace of irony in
Dixie's smiling face. With only a few shock
treatments left to go, she looked so animated
and beautiful again that Jinx had gotten jealous, trying to dance in front of her until
Mrs. Fitzgerald caught on and sent Jinx
back to her place.

We rarely saw Jinx at Graystone during
those days. Ever since Suzy Caldwell had
stopped coming by (due to Dr. Bennett's
ever-tightening purse strings), there was not
much communal activity in parlor or
kitchen. This was fine by me, of course. I
had my own secrets to keep. A long stem of
pussy willow, almost in bloom, had appeared on my piano that week, and then a
single yellow daffodil. And then, with only

one week to go before Mardi Gras, it snowed again, a deep, soft, wet spring snow nipping both forsythia and redbud, canceling all activities, freezing us back in our snow globe where I was actually relieved to be, where I didn't have to deal with anything or anybody because there would never be any consequences outside our own closed world.

During the second night of that last snowfall, I was awakened by police sirens shrieking past Graystone on their way up to the hospital grounds. One, two, three police cars . . . I lost count, running downstairs to join Ruth and Myra who already stood at the parlor windows, clutching their robes around them. I had wrapped myself up in one of Mrs. Hodges's afghans.

"What on earth . . ." Myra trailed off, biting her lip.

"I can't even imagine," Ruth said. "But obviously it's something really awful."

"Don't you think we ought to go up there and find out?" I wanted to.

"No, no, absolutely not!" Ruth was always so bossy. "Whatever it is, we'd just be in the way. Besides, we'll find out soon enough anyway, and frankly, I'm sure it's something we'd rather not know."

"Mama always said, 'Don't borrow trouble,' " quavered Myra, who was much better now but still got easily upset.

"Wait a minute! I thought your damn mother *died,*" Ruth said.

"She did, you mean thing!" Now Myra burst into loud, choking sobs, so I hugged her, as somebody clearly had to. I could feel her fragile shoulder bones like stunted wings beneath her robe. I thought of Mrs. Fitzgerald, who had lived with her mother for so much of her life. And of my own mother, dead so long, too young.

Just then there came a pounding at the door.

"Don't open it." Myra grabbed at Ruth's robe.

"Now honey, don't be silly." Ruth slid the safety latch and threw the door open and there stood Mr. Pugh, incongruous in a red knit cap that could have belonged to some large child, swinging his arms and stamping his feet on the mat. Snow fell off him in clumps. Even his glasses were wet.

"Can I come in, girls?"

We stood back.

"I've come to tell you what's going on. We thought that all this excitement might have awakened you."

"I'll say!" Ruth exclaimed. "So what's

happening, Sir?"

The old teacher took off his knit gloves and held them in his red hands. "It's already happened, apparently. It's all over."

"What?" We breathed as one.

He hesitated for a moment, then said, "It seems that Charles Winston died earlier tonight at a hotel in downtown Asheville, the Haywood Park, where he had rented a room."

"Doesn't he have a room at the hospital?" Ruth asked.

"Of course. But apparently he had gone down there and rented this hotel room under an assumed name, so it took them a little while to find his wallet and figure out who he really was. The police had already notified his family about his death before we even knew, unfortunately." Mr. Pugh shook his head.

"Charles Winston is *dead*?" I heard myself ask. I thought of his nice smile and his worried gray eyes with that vertical line between them, as if he were always squinting into distance.

Mr. Pugh nodded, his glasses glistening in the yellow light from our potbellied Victorian lamp.

"But how?" Ruth asked.

"Gunshot wound to the head," Mr. Pugh

answered, as we all drew closer, "which made it very difficult to identify him. Suicide, obviously, though there was no note. The police are here right now, going through his belongings. That's what all the fuss is about, all these unnecessary sirens alarming everybody. You may not realize it, but this is — was — a young man from a very prominent family, perhaps the most important in North Carolina. He was an only child. So this is a terrible tragedy, girls, of course, but it happens. It happens not infrequently, the lingering trauma of war." Mr. Pugh looked somber. "In any case, there's nothing for you to be scared of here. Nothing at all. Don't wake up the others, and go back to sleep yourselves, if you can. There'll be a convocation at ten o'clock in the morning at Homewood. Any more questions now?"

We all shook our heads, and I stepped over to hug him, the sweetest and best old man.

"You'll be okay, Evalina," he said. "All of you will be just fine. Good night, see you in the morning."

Arm in arm, Ruth and Myra went back upstairs. Their doors shut one by one. I turned off the downstairs lights, then followed them, sitting on the top step until all noise from their rooms had ceased and I could hear Myra's stuffy breathing grow regular.

I had never felt more awake in my life.

First I tiptoed over to open Amanda's door. In the streetlight coming through the window, I could see her long blonde hair spilling across her pillow. She sighed and turned in sleep. I closed the door.

Then I opened the door next to mine. "Jinx?" I whispered urgently, knowing I would wake her immediately as she was such a light sleeper — "Just a cat napper," she always said — a habit formed in those scary places where she had lived.

"Jinx?" again.

Nothing.

"Jinx."

Nothing.

Finally I reached for the switch by the door and snapped on the overhead light.

Her bed was tightly made, with hospital corners and not one wrinkle, the way she had learned to do it at the reformatory. In fact, her room looked so neat that it might easily have been unoccupied. Even the top of the dresser was bare except for a red plastic comb. Had she run away? No, I decided, opening the dresser drawers one by one to find her few clothes, which were pitiful, actually, especially the gray and threadbare underthings. It was hard to imagine the vital, colorful Jinx clad in such as these. She always made such a vivid impression that I guess I'd never noticed what she wore. The bottom drawer contained several old sweaters and a pair of thick wool socks with a man's gold watch stuck in one toe.

What if Jinx came in and found me looking through her things? She'd probably kill me. I didn't care, though. For I was becoming more and more agitated, with a growing sense that I was searching for something, like the "hours" in the dance. I opened the mirrored medicine chest over the sink, which contained a bottle of Jergens lotion, a bottle of aspirin, toothpaste and toothbrush, a fancy enamel pillbox filled with pills (whose?), and some shampoo I'd been missing. I left it there. Quickly, I went through the few clothes hanging in her closet.

Then on impulse I dropped down to my knees to look under the bed, where I found two of Pan's hand-carved animals. The bear stood up on its hind legs, twelve inches tall, so beautifully detailed that you could see its individual teeth and even its hair; it must have taken him days to carve the hair, and I could imagine him doing it, night after night by the oil lamp and the fire. And there was a little fox in an attitude of listening, with lifted head, pointed nose, and a long, bushy tail that curled just so. Remembering the elephant that I had painstakingly crafted for Pan's collection, clumsy and comic with its big head, I was suddenly, deeply furious.

Shakily I got to my feet, replacing everything just so before I went back to my own room and dressed, putting on my warmest socks and my boots, my jacket and gloves and scarf, wrapping it around my head until it half covered my face. When I opened the kitchen door, I was relieved to see that the low gray sky was clearing at last; patchy clouds raced across it so that occasionally the half-moon shone out on the snow. There was a lot of activity at the hospital — red lights, blue lights, car lights, and voices — as I started up the hill, staying off the sidewalk, keeping to the shrubbery and bushes. The heavy, wet snow clung to my boots and slowed me down. I looked both ways and waited carefully before making my way across the road as quickly as I could. Finally I reached the old well, our landmark. I headed downhill straight for the forest just as the clouds cleared and the moon popped out revealing a stretch of snow as shining and open as it had been the very first time I ever went there.

My feet lightened as I ran across it to the trees. But where was the opening, the forest door? I ran down the tree line, then doubled back. Nowhere could I find it, nowhere could I see the entrance, the path. I started crying. Soon I was exhausted, running back and forth along the tree line, at the same time terrified that someone would see me. Finally I just beat my way through the brush and into the deeper woods at random. Surely, I thought, I will find the path now, the path will appear any minute, yet it did not. I recognized nothing. I could not even find that huge outcropping of rock. Instead I tumbled down an embankment and became ensnared in laurel branches like grasping hands. Twice I tripped and fell. The tears froze on my face. The third time I just lay there in the snow for a while to rest, listening to the crackle of ice and the creaking of the trees and the rustling sounds of the night forest all around me and getting very sleepy, though I remembered that this is how people freeze to death. It is easy and lovely and pleasant, like sleep — the most pleasant way to commit suicide. But I was not Charles Winston. I had nearly lost my life already, and now I wanted it. I wanted it all — that brass ring, the whole ball of wax. The world. I struggled desperately to get up on my elbows, then managed to sit further up and hug my knees beneath my wet pants. The sky shone lighter now through the lacy black trees. *Morgen,* I remembered. *Morgen.*

Luckily, getting out of the forest proved easier than getting in. Not a soul was stirring as I entered Graystone in the pale dawn light. I turned Jinx's knob as soon as I got upstairs, and there she was, sleeping soundly and innocently facedown and spread-eagled in her own bed like a child — or like a snow angel, I thought, remembering the game we had all played in the snow at Christmas time, which now seemed like eons ago.

And Jinx was the first person I saw when I came downstairs the next morning ready for work. There she sat in the parlor, dwarfed by a big fat uniformed policeman and another man I had never seen before, an older man wearing a suit and tie. He had a thin, pale, impassive hatchet face, incongruous against our pansy-patterned wallpaper. In fact they both looked ridiculous sitting on our curvy, old-fashioned furniture, as if they had walked into a doll's house. Jinx looked like she had just gotten out of bed, tousle-headed and sleepy-eyed, wearing an old plaid flannel robe that was obviously much too large for her. She could have been about eleven years old, sitting there with her feet tucked under her. Seeing me, she stretched and waved with total self-possession, as if nothing at all were wrong. "Hey, Evalina," she called.

"Now Miss Feeney, I asked you a question," the policeman said sternly. Both men leaned forward on their spindly seats.

"You tell me the answer then." Jinx yawned and pushed the hair back out of her eyes. "I don't even know what y'all are talking about."

"Oh no, what's the matter? What's going on?" Amanda came clattering down the stairs. "Is Jinx all right? Evalina?"

"Hush, honey, I'll fill you in." Ruth was right behind her. "Jinx is fine, everybody's fine. Just keep going."

The men stood up. "Good morning, girls, our apologies for this rude awakening, heh-heh," the big policeman said. He had a wide, fake grin I hated. It was not really an apology, either. He liked to scare people; you could tell. "Yes, you may go on about your business, for the time being. We know who you are, we know where to find you. We just have a few questions to ask your friend here."

"What? Who?" Ruth said.

"Me, I reckon." Jinx looked utterly bored.

The front door flew open and it was Mr. Pugh again, with Mr. and Mrs. Morris right behind him. "Now just a minute here, you can't barge into a hospital residence like this and disturb our clients!" Mr. Pugh looked as if he had not been to bed all night long. Mrs. Morris immediately went over to sit beside Jinx on the loveseat.

"Oh yeah, is that right?" The men stood up and the policeman held out a piece of paper to Mr. Pugh, who barely looked at it before handing it over to Mr. Morris, who was a lawyer.

"We have some questions to ask Miss Feeney concerning her —" the big policeman hesitated — "acquaintance with Charles Winston. Matter of fact, Miss Feeney is going to have to come downtown with us."

The other man looked intently from one person to another but never said a word. He was some kind of detective, I thought.

Mr. Morris whispered something to Mr. Pugh while Mrs. Morris hugged Jinx. Behind us, Myra came out of her room and sank down upon the top step, starting to wail.

"You see?" Mr. Pugh said.

"Evalina, you and Amanda and Ruth go

on now," Mrs. Morris directed from the loveseat in her even voice. "Go ahead, take Myra with you. Everything will be just fine, don't worry. We will take care of this situation, and we will take care of Jinx, too. She will be accompanied at all times. This is obviously a case of mistaken identity or something."

It took some coaxing to get Myra into her coat and lead her out to catch the bus with Ruth. "Jiminy cricket," was the last thing I heard Jinx say as we all exited the door together into the cold bright morning of March 7.

The convocation in the Homewood auditorium was brief, low-key, and factual — exactly what we had come to expect from Dr. Bennett. It was neither a memorial service nor a religious service, but simply an acknowledgement of the previous night's events. Dr. Bennett stood before us in his customary dark blue suit and red tie, flanked by an American flag in a stand, brought in for the occasion. My grand piano was closed.

"Good morning," he said in his no-nonsense way that I always found reassuring though sometimes annoying. "We know that you were all upset and some of you were very alarmed by the disturbances of last night. We apologize for the police sirens and the noise, which was totally unnecessary, in our opinion. Be that as it may. As all of you undoubtedly know by now, these events came about from the unexpected death of our friend and client Charles Winston."

"He was a war hero," a male voice yelled out.

Dr. Bennett hesitated only briefly. "Yes, Captain Charles Gray Winston the Third was indeed a war hero, as he was a son and a family member and a friend to many — many of you here in this room as well as all over this state. Raised in Winston-Salem, he graduated from Virginia Military Institute before entering the United States Army. His untimely death is a great tragedy for his family and certainly for all of us at Highland Hospital who had grown to enjoy and respect and care for him." A military man himself, Dr. Bennett faltered and almost choked up.

"Those who live by the sword will die by the sword!" rang out that same voice, which I now recognized as belonging to another one of the veterans, a large, agitated redhead with an especially fine baritone. There was a pause and then a brief scuffle as he was escorted out.

Dr. Bennett cleared his throat. "Of course this is a very emotional time for many of us. I urge you all to disregard whatever accounts you may read of Charles Winston's death in the newspapers and remember him as he was in life, a valued and almost fully recovered member of our community. I encourage you to concentrate upon your own goals and your own recoveries.

"A routine police investigation is in progress, as required by law for any unattended death. We intend to cooperate fully with this investigation and urge you to do the same, though we ask that you please notify a staff member if you are so approached directly.

"And now let us bow our heads in a moment of silence and thanksgiving for the life of Charles Gray Winston the Third."

Dixie grabbed my hand and squeezed it as the unaccustomed silence stole over us all like a warm blanket, like a blessing. Nobody spoke. Nobody moved.

"Thank you." Dr. Bennett pulled out his familiar little notebook. "As of this moment, all groups, meetings, appointments, classes, and meals at Highland Hospital will proceed as regularly scheduled. Signup sheets have been posted outside the dining hall for the symphony and also for the upcoming trip to the basketball game in Charlotte. We remind you of the podiatrist's visit to our clinic this afternoon; the bridge club meeting tomorrow afternoon at four p.m., refreshments furnished; and of course the ongoing preparations and rehearsals for our Mardi Gras party this coming Friday evening, to which everyone is invited. I'll see you there." His farewell gesture was a cross between a wave and a salute.

Despite Dr. Bennett's attempt at establishing calm, rumors went flying all that long day, whispered in the halls between groups, over sandwiches at lunch, at the big tables in Art where people were putting the final touches on their fantastical Mardi Gras masks, and on the paths and sidewalks between buildings.

Charles Winston was married. No, he was engaged. Charles Winston was engaged to be married. He had shot himself between the eyes with a pistol. No, it must have been a shotgun, they said his brains were all over the wall. No, it was a pistol. They said his blood was all over the room. No, it was a pistol, but there had been two shots fired. What? Two shots. But everybody knows you can't shoot yourself twice, can you, if it's a suicide? Can you? So maybe it wasn't a suicide.

"Maybe it was murder," Karen Quinn

whispered into my ear as I took my seat at the portable keyboard in the gymnasium. Then she jumped out onto the floor and got her straggly "second line" up on their feet to join her. I played the rocking intro to "Go to the Mardi Gras," and they set off grumbling around the floor to the shuffle beat that soon proved irresistible. It *did* sound exactly like a parade coming down the street. After a couple of laps, I switched over to "Jock-A-Mo" while Karen built on the momentum to get them dancing. Harry Bridges, the redheaded veteran who had caused the ruckus in the auditorium earlier, was dancing up a storm now, taking a turn with several of the older ladies, who seemed to be enjoying themselves enormously. *I will never understand anything,* I thought. *"Laissez les bon temps roulez,"* big Karen said, dancing past, winking at me. *Is this crazy?* I wondered. But nothing is crazy in an insane asylum.

March 9. The oblivious sun shone brightly all that long day; by late afternoon, the snow was gone. Tiny blades of bright green grass glistened on the muddy hillsides. Forsythia waved by the dining hall door like the yellow flag of spring. "Look!" Dixie pointed to a clump of purple crocuses as we set off down the hill for rehearsal right after supper. But here came Freddy in his station wagon, slamming on the brakes and jumping out to pull me into the rose arbor.

"Why, what in the world!" I said.

"Bye now!" Dixie and Amanda were giggling.

Freddy was still dressed in his white doctor coat and a nice striped tie. He pulled me to him and gave me a big, minty kiss. "There!" he said as if it were a mission accomplished. Then he held me out at arm's length and gave me a long searching look. "I've been missing you, Evalina, that's all. I haven't even gotten a glimpse of you for two, maybe three days."

Was that true? I hadn't realized it.

"But it'll be all over soon," Freddy said cheerfully, which gave me the most ominous feeling, somehow. My palm began to itch and my heart beat furiously.

"Evalina? Honey? What's the matter. You're white as a sheet. Do you feel okay?"

"I'm just tired," I said. "There's been so much going on."

"That's what I'm talking about. Charles's death, and this performance coming up — I know you're working yourself to death. But all this Mardi Gras stuff will be over with after the party, right? So I've got a big surprise for you, a special date on the next Saturday night afterward, an overnight."

"Oh, I don't know," I said.

"At Lake Lure, Evalina!" he burst out like a child.

"But Freddy, that's way too expensive. That's crazy — you don't have that kind of money. Why don't I just sneak into Mrs. Hodding's house again with a special bottle of wine?" At first Freddy had been too straitlaced to let me come to his boarding-house on nearby Montford Avenue.

"Nope," he said firmly. "This is something special. We've got some decisions to make. I've already booked the room and made our dinner reservations."

We stood inside the white lattice walls of the rose arbor, looking out upon the beautiful hospital grounds in the last of the light as people we knew and loved, patients and staff alike, went back and forth on the sidewalk. The climbing roses were already sending out spikes of new growth all over their trellises; spring was here, but suddenly I felt as if I were in a prison. I didn't know how I was going to get out of it.

"Honey?" Freddy took me in his arms again, as big and solid as a bear. "Kiss me?"

I did.

Anybody could have seen us.

I was late for rehearsal but it didn't matter; it looked like everybody else was late, too, except for Mrs. Fitzgerald, who sat onstage at my piano bench, hunched over, legs crossed, tapping her satin slipper–clad foot on the floor as she eyed the door. "Get up here, Pie-Face," she said to me. Nervously I took my seat next to her on the bench, opening the piano and arranging the sheet music I had brought in my book bag. Mrs. Fitzgerald didn't budge, even as the others began to arrive. I already knew that Myra would not be here because she had "fallen apart" at the library and was now in the hospital "but just overnight," according to Dr. Schwartz.

Jinx was not present.

Neither was Mrs. Morris's daughter Nancy, nor Mrs. Morris herself.

"So where are they all? The rest of them? My *corps de ballet*?" Mrs, Fitzgerald shot a black look down at Phoebe and Dr. Schwartz on the front row.

"Well, it's been such an unusual day, hasn't it?" Dr. Schwartz said calmly. "I imagine you should just go ahead with the ones you've got — there's another rehearsal tomorrow anyway, right?

"Dress rehearsal," Mrs. Fitzgerald said darkly. She switched legs, now banging her other foot on the floor, and I shifted accordingly on the piano bench. "But where is that little redhead, little Orphan Annie I call her? She is the heart and soul of it, my heart and soul."

When no one answered, she finally stood up and walked forward. She clapped her hands and said, "Dancers on stage!"

Up they came, indeed a diminished lot in the unforgiving stage lights. Amanda was pale and silent, Pauletta was red-eyed and twitchy, and even Ruth looked tired and unsure of herself. Only Karen Quinn and Dixie appeared ready to dance, Karen in her usual aura of health and solidity, Dixie radiating charm in every direction. Frank was coming up for the dance, she'd told me excitedly, and they'd be leaving a day or two later. So would Mrs. Fitzgerald, almost done with her course of treatments and headed off to New York City to visit her daughter, Scottie, and her growing family, which now included the much-heralded baby Eleanor. Amanda was leaving, too, but not for Tampa; she would be traveling in Italy with two old friends, her college roommates. She had filed for divorce from the judge.

"Places!" Mrs. Fitzgerald snapped as they tried to find their groups, though Pauletta had started crying in earnest now, rubbing at her face with the tail of her sweater.

I played the jaunty, now-familiar prelude.

But Mrs. Fitzgerald held up her hand. "This is ridiculous. My dear, can you *not* stop weeping? This is very annoying." At which Pauletta cried even harder and Dixie left her own place and ran across the stage to comfort her.

"That's it, then. Enough. *Alors. Arretez!*"

"This is going to be the biggest flop," Ruth complained to Karen Quinn as they escaped offstage. "Nobody knows what they're doing. We've never even gone through the whole thing. It's ridiculous."

Mrs. Fitzgerald whirled to point at her. "Nonsense! You are ballerinas, every one of you. *Artistes.* You shall be present for dress rehearsal tomorrow and you shall dance brilliantly. *Superbe! Magnifique!*" She grabbed her fringed purple shawl off the top of the piano and threw it haphazardly around her shoulders before rushing down the steps and striding up the aisle, still in her ballet shoes, muttering to herself, unlit cigarette already in hand.

"Oh, brother," said Phoebe Dean.
"Oh no," said Dr. Schwartz.

CHAPTER 15

I don't think I have ever been more nervous — Phoebe Dean, either. We arrived very early for dress rehearsal and she paced back and forth in front of the stage while I practiced my Mardi Gras music on the grand piano and Cal Green's crew put the final touches on the stage set which they had constructed in Shop. *"When the saints come marching in, oh when the saints come marching in, well I want to be in that number, when the saints come marching in!"* Phoebe jumped up on stage to sing along with me in her big, churchy voice while Cal grinned at us and his crew of patients snapped their fingers appreciatively. "Yeah!" one large man yelled. It was amazing, really, what they had built — the sturdy wooden facsimile of a clock tower such as you would see in Europe, its plywood façade painted to look like ancient stones, Notre Dame in Paris or the Cathedral St. Louis in New Orleans.

"Oh when the sun begins to shine, oh when the sun begins to shine —" Phoebe and I started in on the second verse.

Cal climbed atop a ladder while his helpers carefully handed up the big clock face we had all seen in the Art Room for weeks now, its black Roman numerals painted in Gothic lettering. Miss Malone herself arrived just in time to stand and watch this procedure, hands on her wide hips. *"Oh Lord I want to be in that number, when the sun begins to shine!"* We finished, and I switched over to "Tipitina," which sounded good, too. Everything always sounded great on that piano. By then I was feeling better; a keyboard can always calm me down.

"That looks perfect, Cal," Phoebe called out as he descended from the ladder.

Cal tipped his hat, that same old khaki hat he had worn for all the years I had known him at Highland. "Come on boys, let's get out of here, we've got work to do." His crew followed him reluctantly, with the big man dancing like crazy all across the stage, surprisingly light on his feet.

Then Miss Malone came up on the stage herself to look at the clock more closely. It seemed to pass her inspection. "Okay, Karen," she yelled out suddenly, surprising me, "where are you?"

"Got it covered, Boss" came Karen's voice from somewhere high overhead. "Here we go!" The first gossamer strip fluttered down from the catwalk far above the stage, waving behind the clock tower, followed by another, then another, then another, in shades of blue and red and yellow, Mrs. Fitzgerald's favorite primary colors, I remembered. She always liked to paint straight from the little pots, never mixing the colors. The banners waved and shimmered nearly to the floor.

"Oh my goodness, how gorgeous, Rowena!" Dr. Schwartz cried out as she arrived, but Miss Malone was still not satisfied, calling up to Karen to move this one or that one in order to achieve just the right fantastical backdrop. Finally Karen was allowed to climb down, receiving a squeeze from Miss Malone for her efforts, and spontaneous applause from the rest of us.

I had just switched over to "Jambalaya," tinkling the treble keys, when the back door opened and Phoebe leaned over the piano to say, "Uh-oh. Here comes trouble." Of course we were all wondering this very same thing. Mrs. Fitzgerald entered, wearing her enormous purple shawl. I took my hand off the keys immediately, but Dr. Schwartz said softly, "No, no, Evalina, just keep playing, please, that's a girl," which I did, while Mrs. Fitzgerald strode purposefully down the aisle without a word and came to a stop before the stage where she stood dead still for a long second before finally clapping her hands together and crying "Bravo, bravo! Bravo, Rowena!" her face transformed, alight.

Miss Malone bowed her head in silent acknowledgment, according Mrs. Fitzgerald that great respect she always gave her. Miss Malone would have done anything — *anything* — for Mrs. Fitzgerald, I believe.

And Mrs. Fitzgerald was glowing as she stood transfixed before her festive tower.

"Oh, look!" "Wow!" "Look!" sang out the "hours" as they came tramping down the aisle, bundled up in their winter coats.

I kept on playing like a person possessed until Mrs. Fitzgerald finally waved her hand at me. "That will certainly *do,* Patricia!" she said, "That's entirely enough out of you!" though with a smile. "It's time to get down to business." She threw her shawl across my piano and stood revealed in her black leotard and tights, with a swirling purple skirt that shone and moved as she moved, like liquid, like her banners.

"Come on, come on now, dears, it's time," she called out to the girls.

But the girls clustered together and hung back, keeping their coats on.

"What is it? Come on now!" Mrs. Fitzgerald moved toward the front of the stage.

"I think perhaps they are embarrassed," Dr. Schwartz said softly. "This is the first time they have worn their costumes."

Several of the "hours" nodded.

"What? Oh, that is ridiculous!" Mrs. Fitzgerald snapped.

But I understood perfectly. I would never have done what they were doing, not in a million years.

Mrs. Fitzgerald got that dangerous, smoldering look. *"Places!"* She clapped her hands.

As suddenly as that, electricity filled the air.

"Oh, okay —" Dixie was the first, laughing as she ran up the steps with her red skirt floating out around her like a full-blown rose; then Amanda in yellow — all yellow, her flying hair, too; then Karen Quinn, large and orange. Ruth surprised me by looking absolutely beautiful in her electric blue skirt, frizzy red hair pulled back into a tight chignon. She waved at me as she ran past my piano. Shy Pauletta was pretty and graceful in her pink skirt — and not crying, for once. But Nancy Morris was the big surprise. In her shiny white skirt she looked lovely and moved slowly, with perfect composure, a *real* dancer, heading into a future that seemed to stretch before her across the stage. Mrs. Fitzgerald smiled at her. "Nice. Very nice, dear."

But then the thundercloud came back, as Mrs. Fitzgerald counted on her fingers: "— five — six — only *six*? *Where are the others*? Where is my Little Orphan Annie?"

"Probably in jail," Ruth said under her breath.

"Perhaps you can improvise a bit," suggested Dr. Schwartz.

"This is totally unprofessional. Where are they? It *will not do*!" Mrs. Fitzgerald seemed to swell before our eyes, dire and regal, a menacing queen.

"Jesus Christ!" from Ruth.

"He ain't in this dance" came Jinx's flat nasal voice as she ran down the aisle. "*I'm* in this dance! And *you* are, too — what the hell are you doing down there?" now grabbing up Myra, who'd been cowering between the seats. "Come on! If I'm coming, you're coming, too —" dragging Myra down the aisle with her.

All the hours were laughing now, and Mrs. Fitzgerald clapped her hands. "Places!"

I switched into the upbeat intro as — at

last — the great clock took form before us on the stage. And now I understood the purpose of the colors, as the girls in the pastel skirts took their positions at the small numbers, the palette darkening as time progressed around the clock toward Mrs. Fitzgerald herself at twelve.

"Come on, now, come on!" Jinx, in green, pushed pale-blue Myra across the stage, pliant as a pipe cleaner.

"Oh buck up, honey!" Ruth snapped, and surprisingly, Myra did, slipping in at five.

Jinx went over to seven and stretched, perfectly at ease, grinning out toward the empty auditorium that suddenly seemed to fill with people, a phantom audience, a full house. And it was again true, as it was always true, that once Jinx was onstage, you had to look at her. You had to. Her flaming red hair moved loosely all over her head as she stretched, limbering up, her green skirt swirled out and then clung to her legs.

Mrs. Fitzgerald took her own place at the top of the clock, then nodded to me. I played louder, moving into the actual music. Each hour turned in place, then twirled, all the skirts swirling about them, the many ruffling layers making them look like so many carnations. And then the great clock turned, the whole clock went round, all those carnations, including Mrs. Fitzgerald, now one of them. The kaleidoscope, I thought. *Of course, the kaleidoscope.*

"Now we're in business!" Phoebe announced.

But no one heard her, or took any notice of her, as round and round they went. It's amazing what a costume can do — the physical transformation that occurs — the liberating effect upon the psyche. Though each girl must have tried on her skirt at least once in the Art Room at some point, presumably — or even several times, for fittings — they had never worn them in public, or all together. Round and round and round they went, then sallied forth in their groups of three to dance charmingly, that first hard sequence now fully natural, like the routine of our lives.

Each hour was distinctive, each different from all the others, each very beautiful in her own way, and I can see them yet in my mind's eye — Dixie the blooming red rose she had been all her life; sweet pink Pauletta, whom I didn't really know; Ruth with all that energy focused for once, a blue bolt of lightning; bright orange Karen Quinn, practical and useful as a marigold; Jinx, a streak of green neon; pale blue Myra, fluid as water; pure white Nancy Morris, all talent and resolve, like a distant star; Amanda come into her own at last, a sunflower of Provence; and Mrs. Fitzgerald herself, regal and secret as an iris, born to dance — oh why hadn't she joined the San Carlo company when they asked her? Why not? Why do we do the things we should not, and not do the things we should? But no matter. For the garden blooms, the seasons pass, the great clock turns.

I strike the time.

And ah, alas, now the hours must scatter, searching, searching, arabesque, arabesque, the plaintive notes, the frantic search until the clock strikes again and all the hours — *all*! — flutter offstage like a cloud of butterflies.

The audience whispers, rustles, and several among them start to applaud, then stop in confusion. A deep hush descends upon us all — the audience, the empty stage. The moment extends . . . and extends . . . until the suspense becomes unbearable.

Then *voila*! I hit the jubilant C chord and here they all come back, leaping and strutting, laughing and smiling, to form a lineup straight across the stage, like the girls in the Moulin Rouge. Even Mrs. Fitzgerald is fully engaged, enjoying herself, face like a flame.

She nods at me, I hit the C again, and suddenly it's the cancan, the *cancan*! As surprising and improbable as anything in life. "*Kick,* one two three! Kick, one two three!" she cries out. "Kick high! Over your head!" The beautiful skirts are petals, they are wings, lifting my chums, the hours, oh *fly*! Fly away, fly away, fly away home.

Our little audience is on their feet now, holding on to each other, laughing and crying, as are we all. *Kick, one two three!*

Together the hours bow, together raise their clasped hands then stand exhausted, amazed by what they have just done. Mrs. Fitzgerald awards them with her rare smile. "Go, go home now," she says to them. "Get some rest. I'll see you tomorrow."

The Mountain Times, *Asheville, N.C., March 11, 1948* — A fire started in the kitchen of the Central Building of Highland Hospital last night and shot up the dumbwaiter shaft, leaping out onto each floor. It was discovered by nurse Jane Anderson who had earlier administered sedatives to all the patients on the 5th floor. At 11:30 she thought she smelled smoke and went downstairs to investigate. She opened the kitchen door to behold a bizarre sight — the big kitchen table burning all around the edges of its galvanized top with the flames rising over a foot high, making it look like "one of those fiery hoops animals jump through in circuses." Confused and terrified, she did not try to extinguish this burning rectangle but ran back upstairs to the nurses' station on the fourth floor and started trying in vain to telephone her supervisor, Willie May Hall, over at Oak Lodge, as she had been told to do in case of a fire or other emergency. But the hospital's telephone exchange was not working properly, so finally she called the Asheville Fire Department.

The first alarm came into their headquarters at 11:44 according to Fire Chief J.C. Fitzgerald — fourteen minutes after Miss Anderson first smelled the smoke. He said that the fire had been burning for 40 to 45 minutes by the time they got there. "If the alarm had been given 30 minutes earlier," he said, "there would have been no need for anyone losing their lives."

But the heat had grown so intense by the time the firemen arrived that their gushing water had absolutely no effect on the leaping flames. For the fire had spread rapidly, racing along the halls and filling the stairways with smoke. There was no sprinkler system and no fire alarm system. The top floor was entirely locked down to insure the safety of all those whose insulin shock treatments were in progress. But most windows and doors on the other floors were locked as well, severely hampering the efforts of the hospital staff, local police and citizens, and firefighters who arrived in force when they finally got there. The fire filled the sky. Orange-tipped flames laced with black and white smoke shot up from the hospital like fireworks, lighting up the whole night . . .

I ran up the hill with Amanda and Ruth but then lost them amid the flood of shouting, converging townspeople. A sobbing black-smudged patient in his pajamas ran into me, going the other way. My eyes stung from the smoke.

The Central Building looked as if a child with a fiery crayon had painstakingly outlined it: the roofline, the walls, each floor, the windows in which black, gesticulating figures stood framed. I could feel the heat long before I neared the building — or got as close as I could get, I should say, for the police had cordoned it off to make way for those who were still going in and out, bringing patients to the waiting stretchers and ambulances. Everyone was screaming, or crying, or yelling — a huge moan went up as one of the burning fire escapes — for they were made of wood, too — broke loose and fell, with people on it.

Here and there I glimpsed familiar faces in the intense red glow, but not many, and not for long, and not Freddy or Phoebe or Dr. Schwartz or the Overholsers or anybody I really knew except for heroic Carl Renz, easily identifiable due to his size, who kept walking in and out of the burning building like a robot calmly carrying people in his arms. Two days later he would die as a result of his own burns. Mr. Pugh would be hospitalized for months.

The police were trying to disperse the crowd, but I could neither leave nor look away from the black figures in silhouette against the orange and red flames until the roof began to collapse and they were gone, my princesses, my chums, and it was over. Dixie died there, and Mrs. Fitzgerald, and Pauletta, and four other women. I remembered what Mrs. Fitzgerald had said in Art so long ago, about the danger of putting princesses in towers. Her body would be identified only by her charred ballet slipper, and Dixie's by her dental work, that perfect smile.

Still I could not leave, for on the balcony still standing at the end of the top floor, several stockings hung out on a clothesline were dancing, dancing, dancing in the rising heat of the fire, and as I watched, I thought of Mrs. Fitzgerald and also of my own mother, and how much I had loved her, beautiful dancer, as I had loved my own big-headed baby girl. *"Places!"* I cried, clapping my hands as they danced on for as long as they could, Mamma and Mrs. Fitzgerald, through their hard, bright lives.

CHAPTER 16

I am in New Orleans now, where I teach
private piano lessons and am proud to be a
staff accompanist at the venerable Petit
Theatre. I live alone — by choice, I might
add — for I have had a few suitors here,
most as odd as myself, yet not unattractive.
After the fire, I found I could not marry
Freddy, somehow, but the Carrolls gave me
the small remainder of my inheritance from
Arthur Graves, which has allowed me to
return to this city.

And as for the fire, I am certain that
Flossie set it, though I never said so, and
other people voiced other opinions. Mrs.
Hodges recalled hearing that Mrs. Fitzgerald herself had started other fires in the
past, one in California and one at "La Paix"
in Baltimore, and mentioned her fondness
for cigarettes, which "that Jinx" was always
slipping her despite the rules. Others believed that Jinx set the fire herself, for she

509

took advantage of the commotion to vanish entirely, escaping both the remainder of her mandated stay at Highland Hospital and any possible prosecution in the death of Charles Winston. She has never been found. Pan disappeared as well, though I am not at all convinced that this had anything to do with Jinx Feeney. It is my personal feeling that he simply went to ground, moving farther back into the wilderness, like an animal fleeing a forest fire.

But I know he will come to me eventually, which is why I settled upon this particular apartment in the Garden District quite near Audubon Park, where he will be able to get a job with the landscaping crew. Oh, but this place was hard to find! Since New Orleans is below sea level, there are no basements anywhere in the entire city. Even the cemeteries are all above ground. Yet I feel strongly that Pan will be more comfortable in some sort of lair, and at last I found this little spot, which is actually a half-basement, seven steps down from street level, the butler's former dwelling beneath the grand historic mansion above. It also has the unexpected advantage of being much cooler in the summer, and warmer in the wintertime.

I have furnished it quite simply with

second-hand things, as you see, the piano being my only extravagance, if you can call it an extravagance. For me it is a necessity. A row of small square windows at the top of my parlor look out upon the street, and I do mean directly upon the street, and I love to sit right here in this soft green velvet armchair and watch the passing feet, the grand parade of humanity that moves along St. Charles Avenue day and night. High heels, sandals, tennis shoes, brown feet, white feet, cowboy boots, shiny pimp shoes, sensible brogans, and little patent leather pumps with white lace socks such as I once wore myself to Sunday mass at St. Louis Cathedral. It is a great variety, especially at Carnival time.

So I like to sit here and drink a bit of sweet wine in the late afternoon and watch the parade until it relaxes me after a long day's work. It is so relaxing that sometimes it puts me right to sleep, and once I awoke with a start to find *his* feet there right above me, those handmade moccasins that I'd know anywhere, stopped on the sidewalk mere inches from my window. I flew for the door but by the time I got up to the sidewalk, he was gone. I do not for one minute believe it was a dream, as my friend Clara has suggested. I believe he will return, and I shall be here. I am not yet too old to bear another child, and I should like to do it, under more auspicious circumstances, of course. Why not? Freddy and Dr. Schwartz are married now, and *they* are expecting one, according to Phoebe Dean. Pan can learn to speak as the baby speaks, and we will all be very comfortable right here. This apartment is larger than it looks. My palm has been itching of late, so I believe he will return soon, possibly in time for Mardi Gras, and I shall be here waiting. Oh hurry, hurry, hurry up, the azaleas and jasmine and bougainvillea are blooming now the parade is almost constant it's time it's time it's almost carnival time when he will appear at my door his face like a flower.

ACKNOWLEDGMENTS

I am grateful to the many people who helped in bringing *Guests on Earth* to publication. Mary Caldwell, medical ethicist and lifelong Asheville resident with early work experience at Highland Hospital, was invaluable in her careful reading and detailed advice; she also consulted with noted Asheville psychiatrist Dr. William Matthews. Linda Wagner-Martin, author of *Zelda Sayre Fitzgerald, An American Woman's Life,* generously shared her research with me, including photocopies of Zelda Fitzgerald's unpublished letters and writings in her own hand, archived material in the Princeton University Library, Manuscripts Division, Department of Rare Books and Special Collections. Opera singer Andrea Edith Moore gave me several crucial, critical readings of the novel and allowed me to trail around observing her in performance and in practice sessions with her accompanist, Deborah Hollis; both agreed to interviews. Frances and Ed Mayes offered their expertise in Italian. I am indebted to Shannon Ravenel, for her brilliant editing of this manuscript; to Jill McCorkle, for her helpful early reading; to Jim Duffy and Susan Raines, for their knowledge of New Orleans; to Diane Plauche, for naming the "Intermezzo" section; to Hillsborough piano teacher and accompanist Grace Jean Roberts, for musical advice and teaching techniques; to Barbara Bennett, for alerting me to the Samarcand Manor mattress-burning case; to Scott Hill of Durham, North Carolina, a piano student of Mrs. Carroll's throughout her youth, for her reminiscences; to ballad singer Sheila Kay Adams, my friend, who kindly took me up to Madison County, North Carolina, many years ago when I was researching Appalachian mountain ballads for my novel *The Devil's Dream;* to Mona Sinquefield, for her help with research and manuscript preparation though draft after draft; to Chris Stamey, for his careful copyediting; to my agent, Liz Darhansoff, for always "being there" in every way; and to my husband Hal Crowther, for weird facts, companionship, risotto, and encouragement during the long years of writing this book.

Much information is available through the University of North Carolina at Asheville's D. Hiden Ramsey Library Special Collections/University Archives as well as the Pack Memorial Library on Haywood Street, part of the Buncombe County Public Library system. Here I learned about early life in Asheville and the Highland Hospital's history, and about the tragic 1948 fire.

Adonna Thompson at the Duke University Medical Center Archives in Durham, North Carolina, was especially helpful when I began this project, guiding me through their Highland Hospital Records 1934–1980. Though actual patient records are not available, letters, clippings, memorabilia, and the many various archived Highland Hospital publications over the years proved invaluable to me in gaining a sense of hospital life during the years covered in my novel, 1936 to 1948. Here I found catalogs, brochures, programs of events such as concerts, dances, and celebrations of all kinds, the *Highland Highlights* magazine, and the wonderful *Highland Fling* newspaper published by the patients.

"Evalina Toussaint," a story excerpted from an early draft of this novel, was published in *Smoky Mountain Living,* vol. 10, no. 1, winter 2010.

I also have my own personal knowledge of the landscape of this novel. My father was a patient there in the fifties. And I am especially grateful to Highland Hospital for the helpful years my son, Josh, spent there in the 1980s, in both inpatient and outpatient situations. Though I had always loved Zelda Fitzgerald, it was then that I became fascinated by her art and her life within that institution, and the mystery of her tragic death. I always knew I would write this book.

A NOTE ON SOURCES

Although Zelda and Scott Fitzgerald, Dr. Robert Carroll and Grace Potter Carroll, and other people who actually lived appear in this book as fictional characters, I wanted to depict them as truly as possible. I have been grateful for a number of sources, starting with the excellent biographies *Zelda,* by Nancy Milford; *Zelda Sayre Fitzgerald: An American Woman's Life,* by Linda Wagner-Martin; and *Zelda Fitzgerald: Her Voice in Paradise,* by Sally Cline. Zelda's own writing is found in her novel *Save Me the Waltz* and in *The Collected Writings of Zelda Fitzgerald,* edited by Matthew J. Bruccoli, with an introduction by Mary Gordon; *Dear Scott, Dearest Zelda: The Love Letters of F. Scott and Zelda Fitzgerald,* edited by Jackson R. Bryer and Cathy W. Barks; as well as unpublished writings in several archived collections. Other helpful books for me were

F. Scott Fitzgerald: A Life in Letters, edited by Matthew J. Bruccoli; Fitzgerald's novels *The Great Gatsby, Tender Is the Night, The Beautiful and the Damned, This Side of Paradise;* the nonfiction pieces in *The Crack-Up,* edited by Edmund Wilson; and *Exiles from Paradise: Zelda and Scott Fitzgerald,* by Sara Mayfield. Dr. Robert S. Carroll's books include *The Soul in Suffering* and *The Mastery of Nervousness.*

My single most illuminating source was *Zelda: An Illustrated Life: The Private World of Zelda Fitzgerald,* edited and introduced by Eleanor Lanahan, the granddaughter of F. Scott and Zelda Fitzgerald, who has also written a book about the life of her mother entitled *Scottie: The Daughter of . . .* An essay by Peter Kurth in *Zelda: An Illustrated Life* details the Jazz Age world that the Fitzgeralds inhabited, and Jane S. Livingston, formerly the chief curator of the Corcoran Gallery of Art in Washington, D.C., offers insights into Zelda's art, which is well represented here with reproductions of eighty of her best paintings from every phase of her life, along with her drawings and constructions, the beautiful and sometimes terrifying paper dolls, plus biographical photographs, artifacts, and other memorabilia. Another big, wonderful book is *The*

Romantic Egoists: A Pictorial Autobiography from the Scrapbooks and Albums of Scott and Zelda Fitzgerald, edited by Matthew J. Bruccoli, Scottie Fitzgerald Smith, and Joan P. Kerr.

Other books include *Sexual Reckonings: Southern Girls in a Troubling Age,* by Susan K. Cahn; *Clothes for a Summer Hotel, A Ghost Play,* by Tennessee Williams; *After the Good Gay Times: Asheville Summer of '35, A Season with F. Scott Fitzgerald,* by Tony Buttitta; *Gone With the Wind, the Three-Day Premiere in Atlanta,* by Herb Bridges; *Asylums,* by Erving Goffman; *Great and Desperate Cures: The Rise and Decline of Psychosurgery and Other Radical Treatments for Mental Illness,* by Elliot S. Valenstein; *My Lobotomy,* by Howard Dully with Charles Fleming; *The Center Cannot Hold,* by Elyn R. Saks; *Surviving Schizophrenia,* by Dr. E. Fuller Torrey; *A Moveable Feast,* by Ernest Hemingway; *The Girls Who Went Away: The Hidden History of Women Who Surrendered Children for Adoption in the Decades Before Roe vs. Wade,* by Ann Fessler; *Beloved Infidel,* by Sheilah Graham and Gerold Frank; *Women and Madness,* by Phyllis Chesler; *The Madwoman in the Attic,* by Sandra M. Gilbert and Susan Gubar;

The Writing on the Wall: Women's Autobiography and the Asylum, by Mary Elene Wood; *The Female Malady: Women, Madness, and English Culture, 1830–1980,* by Elaine Showalter; and *Theaters of Madness: Insane Asylums and Nineteenth-Century American Culture,* by Benjamin Reiss.

Articles: "The Doom of the Mountains," by Ted Mitchell, *Our State* magazine, March 1999; "Zelda Sayre, Belle," by Linda Wagner-Martin, *Southern Cultures,* summer 2004; "Professional Contributions to Invalidism," by Dr. Robert S. Carroll, *The Scientific Monthly,* vol. 2, no.1, Jan. 1916; "Creatures of Fire" by David Allen Joy, *Smoky Mountain Living,* summer 2010; "Hortitherapy: To Teach the Art of Living," by Steve M. Coe, *Highland Highlights,* fall 1973; "Literary Ghosts of Asheville," by Hal Crowther, *American Way,* 1992; and "Sacrificial Couples, the Splendor of Our Failures and Scott and Zelda Fitzgerald," draft of a paper given by Allan Gurganus at the International F. Scott Fitzgerald Society Conference in Asheville, North Carolina, in September 1998, which he generously shared with me.

ABOUT THE AUTHOR

Lee Smith is the author of sixteen previous books of fiction, including the bestselling novels *Fair and Tender Ladies* and *The Last Girls,* winner of the Southern Book Critics Circle Award. Also the recipient of the 1999 Academy Award in Fiction from the American Academy of Arts and Letters, she lives in Hillsborough, North Carolina. Her website is www.leesmith.com.